YOU'VE NEVER READ
A NOVEL LIKE THIS ONE . . .

"When Auntie Edna fell off the bus, she
landed on her pate and remained unconscious
for sixty-three days. At the end of this period, she died, and they had a funeral."

With this disarmingly direct first paragraph,
Peter Tinniswood sets the scene and the tone
of this remarkably funny, remarkably pene-
trating and amazingly original novel.

The editors guarantee that the reader has an
entirely new reading experience ahead of
him . . .

D1108637

A
TOUCH
OF
DANIEL

BY PETER TINNISWOOD

CURTIS
BOOKS

MODERN LITERARY EDITIONS PUBLISHING COMPANY
NEW YORK, N.Y.

CHAPTER ONE

When Auntie Edna fell off the bus, she landed on her pate and remained unconscious for sixty-three days. At the end of this period she died, and they had a funeral.

At the party Uncle Mort, husband of the deceased, said:

"What I can't fathom out is why conductor didn't tell her they was only stopped at a zebra crossing."

"Well, he were one of them Pakistanis, weren't he?" said cousin George, who had brought his blue hankie.

"Aye, you've got something there," said Uncle Mort, and he placed a spoonful of piccalilli on his pressed beef sandwich.

Carter Brandon was most sympathetic to everyone connected with the unfortunate occurrence. He poured out tea for the three great aunts from Glossop, drove his Uncle Mort to the beer-off for a refill and was attentive to every comment.

At six o'clock the minister left, and Uncle Mort ripped his trousers on Cyril's bicycle in the hall.

"Why can't you put the bloody thing in the shed?" he said. "Christ knows how many times I've had to tell you about it."

"Because I'm racing on Saturday, that's why," said Cyril.

"And with his poor dead mam still warm in her grave and all," said one of the great aunts from Glossop, and the other two clicked their thin, yellow tongues.

At seven o'clock Uncle Mort packed them all off, and Carter Brandon drove his mother home.

"Your Uncle Mort took it very well, I thought," she said.

"Mm," said Carter Brandon.

"She had a tragic life did our Edna what wi' losing their Norman in the floods and having her mother all them years. And then, just as she gets shut of the old lady, she has to go and fall off a bus like that."

Carter Brandon swore under his breath at a lorry driver, who was hogging the crown of the road. A stream of oily smoke oozed from under the lorry's tailboard.

"I remember as well as owt the day our Mort brought her home for the first time. Oh, she were small. She were right peteet. A right pretty little thing she were. She'd them big blue eyes of hers, and her feet was so dainty. She looked

5

proper comical stood next to our Mort in the parlour. Me
dad said: 'Well, sit thee down, lass. We'll not bite thee.' He
were like that was me dad. Do you remember your grandad,
Carter?"

"Course I do."

"He stood six feet three in his stocking feet."

"Mm."

"It were the war what killed him off. He never got over
Hitler invading Poland like that."

Carter Brandon stopped the car to buy a packet of cigarettes, and, when he returned, his mother was sobbing softly.

"Don't mind me, I'm just having a little weep to meself,"
she said.

"Come on, cheer up, it may never happen," said Carter
Brandon, patting his mother on the knee.

Ten minutes later they arrived home and had supper.
Carter Brandon's father read the evening paper as he ate his
cream crackers, cheese and pickled onions.

"It were the same minister what were at your Beattie's
funeral," said Mrs. Brandon.

"Oh aye," said Mr. Brandon.

"He gave ever such a nice address, didn't he, Carter?"

"Mm," said Carter Brandon.

"He were awful nice to our Mort at the party. And he
asked about you. I felt so ashamed. He said: 'Has Mr.
Brandon not come then?' And I had to make an excuse.
I felt so ashamed."

"Oh aye," said Mr. Brandon.

Carter Brandon took the dog for a walk at eleven o'clock,
and then he went to bed. Just after midnight the pickled
cucumber he had eaten at the funeral party began to play
him up. So he went downstairs and mixed himself a glass
of bicarbonate of soda.

"Are you all right, Carter?" his mother shouted sleepily.

"As right as rain."

He slept soundly until it was time to get up at half past
six.

On the way to work his father said:

"I'm sick and bloody tired of your mother."

"Are you?" said Carter Brandon.

"I am that. And that yacky sister-in-law of hers, falling
off chuffing bus like that—it's typical of her whole bloody
family."

Carter Brandon wound down the window next to him and
said:

"Is that too draughty for you?"

"She makes me sick, honest to God, she does. Cream crackers, Cheshire cheese and pickled bloody onions—I've had them for supper every night of me married life come hail, rain or shine. It's not right."

Carter Brandon took the roundabout a little too quickly and narrowly avoided a collision with an electric milk float.

"If I had my way, there'd be no more onions in our house. Christ alone knows where she gets them pickled onions from. They're like moth balls. And I'll tell you this—them cream crackers she gets are always stale. You've only to look at the crumbs to see that. And she couldn't tell a good piece of Cheshire cheese from my bloody arsehole."

At the factory gates Carter Brandon drew up and said: "Well, tarra then, see you tonight."

His father nodded and plodded off through the gates, the tip of his *Daily Herald* sticking out of his raincoat pocket.

That night Mr. Brandon did not return home. Nor the next night, nor the next night, nor the next night.

"He's probably walking round losing his memory," said Mrs. Brandon, bursting into tears again.

"Never mind. Don't worry. The police are doing all they can," said Carter Brandon.

Mrs. Warrender, the neighbour from number thirty-six, put her hands on Carter Brandon's shoulders and pushed him out of the room.

"Come on, Carter, you're only upsetting your mam, talking like that," she said. Then she whispered: "Don't worry, luv, I'll stop the night with her. What are neighbours for, I always say."

After six weeks they got a postcard from Mr. Brandon. It was postmarked 'Stevenage,' and it said: "Dear All, Just a line to say I'm all right and don't worry. Your Husband, Les."

They took it to the police station, and the sergeant examined it carefully.

"The seventeenth, eh?" he said. "That means he posted it yesterday from Stee-ver-nage. Aye. Mm. Aye well, I'll get on to them and tell them to keep a look out for him."

"Oh, I wish you would," said Mrs. Brandon.

Carter Brandon took her to supper at the Trocadero Grill, and she had the mixed grill, although she did not touch the sausages.

"Them chipolatas, I never liked them," she said.

A couple of weeks later Mr. Brandon returned home, and his wife said:

"And what time of year do you call this to be coming

back? You've made me look a right one, I'll tell you. There's been your Arnold on the phone every night for eight week, and all the neighbours knew about it. We had an advert in the *News of the World*."

Mr. Brandon smiled and sat down in the rocking chair by the fire to pull off his boots. He was clean and well-groomed. He had bought a new tie, and his trousers were pressed.

"Have you not brought no washing back with you?" said Mrs. Brandon.

"No."

"No, I know you, Leslie Brandon. You wouldn't, would you? I've got to rip clothes off your back before you think of changing them. You've probably not changed your underpants all the time you've been away, have you? I don't know what they'd have thought about me, if you'd had an accident, and they'd taken you to hospital.

"I'll say this about our Edna, she always kept herself spotless underneath. I bet when they examined her after her accident, there wasn't a speck on her underneath."

They had cream crackers, Cheshire cheese and pickled onions for supper.

But Mr. Brandon only smiled.

Next morning was Sunday, and Uncle Mort came round to tea.

"You've got to look at it from her point of view, Les," he said while Mrs. Brandon was washing up. "I mean, you piss off like that without telling a living soul where you was going. Well, she's forced to worry, in't she? It's only human nature, when all's said and done."

"Mm," said Mr. Brandon.

"You know what women are."

"Oh aye, I do that," said Mr. Brandon.

"Are you going to make a four at whist, Carter?" said Mrs. Brandon, when she had finished her duties in the back kitchen.

"All right."

"Well, you can play with your dad then," she said a little snuffily.

They played whist until it was time for Uncle Mort to go home.

"You'd best be going off home now, Mort," said Mrs. Brandon. "You know your Edna never liked you being out after dark. Carter'll run you home, won't you, Carter?"

"Mm."

In the car Uncle Mort said:

"You know, your dad's a funny chap at times, in't he?"

"How do you mean?" said Carter Brandon.

"Now, I'm not saying owt against him, lad. I'm not doing that."

"I know."

"But you know what I mean. Buggering off like that without telling his own kith and kin what he were up to. Well, that's a rum way of carrying on, in't it?"

"I suppose it is."

They drove by the side of the canal. The headlights of the car picked out the heavy frost, coating the telephone wires. There were lights, gleaming in the big mill on the other side of the valley.

"Tarra then, Uncle Mort."

"Tarra, son, and don't tell your mam I've been talking about your dad."

When he got home, Carter Brandon found his mother and father kissing in the back kitchen. His mother broke away quickly and smoothed her pinny.

"Oh, it's you," she said, and Mr. Brandon smiled his long, slow smile.

Nothing much happened during the summer and autumn.

CHAPTER TWO

They had a good time over Christmas. Uncle Mort came to stay for three days, and they had turkey and mince pies. On Christmas Day Uncle Mort said:

"I says to our Cyril, when he tells me: 'Well, you're a bright bugger, aren't you, getting her up the spout like that? I've no bloody sympathy with you.'"

"You shouldn't talk like that, Mort," said Mrs. Brandon.

"Well, he's no more sense than our cat," said Uncle Mort. "I says: 'I thought you'd more sense.'"

"I shouldn't mither too much, Mort," said Mr. Brandon. "It'll all come out in the wash."

"That's you all over," said Mrs. Brandon. "In't that typical? What about her? There's neither of you, thinking about her, is there?"

"She's just a little tart is Rita," said Uncle Mort.

"That's not the point. Your Cyril's old enough to know

better than getting girls into trouble at his age. It's always the girl what suffers in these cases. She's the one what's having the baby, not your Cyril."

"I wouldn't put that past him neither, the young bugger," said Uncle Mort.

"Now then, our Mort, less of that talk," said Mrs. Brandon.

At midnight Carter Brandon brought back Pat for a drink.

"Hello, Pat, luv," said Mrs. Brandon. "What'll you have to drink?"

"What have you got?" said Pat.

"Ee, that'd be telling, lass," said Uncle Mort, and he and Mr. Brandon spluttered with laughter into their beer glasses.

"Take no notice of them, luv," said Mrs. Brandon. "Will you have a sherry or owt like that?"

"Have you got a Babycham?" said Pat.

"Aye, course we have, luv," said Mr. Brandon, and he poured her the drink and smiled at her.

"All the best, Pat, luv," said Mrs. Brandon, raising her glass.

"Cheers," said Pat.

Carter Brandon and Pat sat on the sofa, which was covered with dog hairs. The fire flickered, and Uncle Mort began to nod off.

"Where do you work, luv?" said Mr. Brandon.

"She works as a hairdresser at Maison Enid's in Corporation Street, don't you, luv?" said Mrs. Brandon.

Pat looked at Carter Brandon and then nodded.

"Do you do all that there peroxiding then?" said Uncle Mort.

Pat looked at Carter Brandon again and giggled.

"No, it's all colour rinse now," she said.

"Oh aye," said Mr. Brandon.

The clock struck two, and Mrs. Brandon sided the table and said:

"Well, come on, Pat, luv, it's time you was getting home. I don't want to push you out, but your mam'll be wondering where you've got to, won't she?"

Carter Brandon stopped the car in a side road near Pat's home and switched off the lights.

Immediately she drew up her legs on the seat and turned her face to him. He wrapped his left arm round her back and placed his right hand under her chin. She raised her face, closed her eyes, and he kissed her on the lips.

After a while she stuck her tongue in his mouth and wiggled it round. Her shoes had dropped off, and he could smell her feet.

He undid the buttons on her blouse, and she shifted forward so he could unfasten her brassiere.

"Ooohooohooo, give over, will you," she said. "I love you, Carter."

"Mm," said Carter Brandon.

She looked in the driving mirror, combed her hair, and said:

"Are you coming to our social on Wednesday?"

"I'm playing snooker on Wednesday."

"Charming. Sorry I spoke," said Pat.

Getting out of the car, she smiled and said:

"When am I going to see you again then?"

"I'll give you a buzz at work next week."

"All right, luv," she said, and she blew him a kiss from the gate.

Carter Brandon nodded and drove home.

On Boxing Day afternoon Carter Brandon and his father went to the match. The home team won 13-2, and Mr. Brandon was delighted.

"By God, that were a bloody good try young Leather-barrow scored. By God, it were," he said.

They stopped for a drink at 'The Griffon'. Mr. Brandon had a pint of black and tan, and Carter Brandon had a pint of best bitter. They stood at the bar.

"That hooker of theirs, weren't he a dirty little bastard? By gum, he were," said Mr. Brandon.

"Old Cleggy sorted him out, though, didn't he?"

"He did that. He must have caught him flush on the stones with his knee cap."

"You could see he felt it."

"What? Felt it? He'll not be on nest for a couple of weeks, I'll tell you that for nowt."

They finished their drinks, and Mr. Brandon bought another round.

"Will you have a chaser with that?" he said.

"Aye, go on then."

So Mr. Brandon bought two double whiskies, and they sat down in the corner by the old upright piano.

"Did I ever tell you what I did, when I left home that time?" said Mr. Brandon.

"No."

"Aye, I thought I didn't."

He lit his pipe, tamping down the loose tobacco with a box of Swan Vestas. Then he puffed sharply several times, and, when the pipe was lit, he placed it on the rim of the large ashtray on the table before them. Then he said:

"It were rum really. I just took a notion to go, when I were waiting at bus stop. I just missed one bus, and I thought: 'Chuff me, I'm not waiting for another.' So I stuck me thumb up and got a lift on a bread van as far as Wolverhampton. I stayed there a couple of days, and then I went to London. Well, I'd got no cards or owt, you see, so I couldn't get a decent job."

"What did you do then?"

"Oh, this and that. And then I got a bit brassed off, so I thought I'd come home."

"What was that postcard from Stevenage?"

"Oh that?" said Mr. Brandon.

They drank their beer, went home and had cold turkey and chips and sherry trifle for tea.

"I don't know how you can watch that bloody rugby," said Uncle Mort. "It's not a patch on a good game of football. It bloody isn't."

In the evening Cyril came round, and they drank a few bottles of beer and watched television.

On New Year's Eve there was much merriment in the district, and several people were fined on the following day for drunken behaviour in the streets.

CHAPTER THREE

On the first day of spring cousin Cyril was decapitated. It was most unfortunate for everyone concerned.

The young man, engaged in the first race of the season, had ridden his bicycle with such vigour that it had seemed likely that he would win the event and the first prize of half a canteen of cutlery. Then, as fate would have it, he had collided with an excursion motor coach.

The damage to the coach was slight. The damage to Cyril was considerable. The driver lost his twenty-four years' no-accident record, and Cyril lost his life.

So Uncle Mort moved into the Brandon household.

"I kept telling him he were asking for trouble, riding with his head down," said Uncle Mort.

"He couldn't see where he was going, could he?" said Mr. Brandon.

"That's just it," said Uncle Mort. "You've hit the nail right on the head there."

They had tripe and onions and rhubarb tart for tea, and Carter Brandon took Pat to the dance.

"Linda Preston's getting engaged on her birthday," she said, as they drove to the dance.

"Oh aye," said Carter Brandon.

"Him who's got the ginger hair."

"What about him?"

"That's who she's getting engaged to—Ken Balmer."

"I don't know him."

"Oh, you don't know owt, do you," said Pat primly.

Next day Uncle Mort said to Carter Brandon:

"You're about the same build as our Cyril, aren't you?"

"Now then, Mort, don't go on about it," said Mrs. Brandon. "You'll only make yourself badly, living in your memories like that."

"Nay, I'm just saying he might as well have our Cyril's clobber, if it'll fit him. I mean, I'd rather him have it than moths."

"That's very nice of your Uncle Mort, isn't it, Carter?" said Mrs. Brandon. "Aren't you going to say Thank You?"

"Thank you," said Carter Brandon.

"I'm not certain what he's got. I do know he bought a new suit from Weaver to Wearer just before he got hisself bloody killed."

They went into the box room, which had been turned into Uncle Mort's bedroom. There was a smell of wintergreen ointment. On the dressing table was a picture of Auntie Edna. She was looking straight at the camera with her hands folded on her lap, and her hair a little awry from the wind.

Uncle Mort opened the wardrobe.

"I've got all his stuff in here. You might as well have it all, it's no use to me," he said.

There were three suits, a suedette jacket with knitted sleeves and a casual jacket with plum and navy blue stripes.

"Hey up, look at these ties," said Uncle Mort. "Have you ever seen such a collection? It's a good job he's not wearing none of these wherever he is, otherwise they'd throw him out and tell him to come back properly dressed."

There were five sweaters and seven pairs of shoes, three suede, three black and one pair of ice calf sandals. There were also two pairs of pyjamas.

"I'll tell you what, though," said Uncle Mort. "I'll have these singlets for summer. Mine have all rotted on me. It's because I sweat so much, do you see? I'm like a lump of lard in summer me. When it's hot, I sweat me chuffing heart out."

They had boiled ham salad for tea, and Mr. Brandon, Uncle Mort and Carter Brandon went to the local for a game of dominoes.

They played four hands of fives and threes, and then they got into an argument with Teddy Ward, who drove a lorry for the council.

"Jimmy Delaney never played centre forrard for Scotland," said Teddy Ward. "Outside right, yes. Centre forrard, no."

"You don't know what you're talking about," said Uncle Mort.

"Here's a bloody quid says he didn't," said Teddy Ward, digging his hand into his hip pocket.

"And here's a quid says he bloody did," said Uncle Mort. "What do you say, Les?"

"Ee, I don't know. He could have played for Timbuktu for all I know," said Mr. Brandon.

They walked home in the dark. Uncle Mort led the way with his hands behind his back. Mr. Brandon and his son followed a few yards behind him, their shoulders touching from time to time.

"Hey up then," said Uncle Mort. "Hurry up, I can't wait to get me chops round them cheese and onions."

"Oh aye," said Mr. Brandon quietly.

CHAPTER FOUR

In September Uncle Bob was fatally injured in a piano accident at Egremont. So his widow, Auntie Lil, came to live in the Brandon household.

"Come and sit down, luv, and have a nice cup of tea and some digestive biscuits," said Mrs. Brandon, when Auntie Lil arrived on Saturday morning.

"Thank you, Annie," said Auntie Lil in a weak little voice, and she began to dab at the corners of her eyes with a purple handkerchief embroidered in the corners with blood red forget-me-nots.

"Did you have a good journey, Lil?" said Uncle Mort.

"As good as could be expected under the circumstances," said Auntie Lil.

"Come on, our Mort, don't stand there like a spare part," said Mrs. Brandon. "Go outside and see if you can help our Carter bring Lil's luggage out of the car."

In the street Carter Brandon was trying to drag a large electric sewing machine out of the back of the car.

"What's she got there for Christ's sake?" said Uncle Mort, pointing to the mound of luggage assembled on the pavement.

"You name it, she's got it," said Carter Brandon.

They carried into the house one sewing machine, one knitting machine, a rucksack, a plastic knitting bag, a wicker hamper, a cello case, three bulky brown paper parcels and a large metal trunk.

"Put them in Carter's room for the time being," said Mrs. Brandon.

When Mr. Brandon returned from work at half past one, he said:

"How do, Lil," and then he had a good wash in the back kitchen.

In the afternoon he and Carter Brandon went to the match, which the home team lost 0-2.

"A bloody penalty. Fancy losing by a penalty to that lot," said Mr. Brandon.

"Rum, isn't it?"

"Rum? It's bloody diabolical. I tell you, I wouldn't pay our second row in washers, I would not."

They sat to the leeward of the piano in 'The Griffon,' and watched the people coming and going.

"How long's me Auntie Lil going to be sleeping in my room then?" said Carter Brandon.

"Now, listen to me, son. I'm just as much against having your Auntie Lil staying with us as you are. But in times of trouble family's just got to rally round and help out. And that's all there is to it."

"But it's my bloody room she's sleeping in."

"It's only temporary."

In November Auntie Lil said:

"Now I hope you'll not think I'm complaining, but there's an awful draught comes under the door of my bedroom."

"That's all right, Lil. Les'll see to it," said Mrs. Brandon.

"I don't want to be a nuisance."

"Now then, Lil, you're not to say things like that."

When Carter Brandon brought Pat home for supper, he found his mother and father, Uncle Mort and Auntie Lil, sitting in the back room, staring at Auntie Lil's large metal trunk.

"You've just come in time, Carter," said Mrs. Brandon. "She wouldn't open it till you come back. Hello, Pat, luv, do you know Carter's Auntie Lil?"

"Pleased to meet you," said Pat.

"Well, come on, let's get Long John Silver's bloody chest open," said Uncle Mort.

"You want to have a bit of respect, our Mort, that's what you want," said Mrs. Brandon, as Auntie Lil began to sob softly to herself.

"Give us the key, Lil, and I'll open it for you," said Mr. Brandon.

He got down on his hands and knees in front of the trunk and, after much twiddling with the key, unlocked the trunk and stood back.

"There you are, Lil, you can open it now," he said.

Auntie Lil patted the crown of her head gently and said to the company:

"All my memories are in this trunk. In here is my past. It's my treasure chest of memories, and I want you all to see it, being as how I'm living in your home. It's only right and proper."

Then she wiped her hands on the front of her pinny and opened the lid of the trunk.

Pat leaned forward, but there was nothing to be seen except pink tissue paper. Auntie Lil removed the paper layer by layer, folding each sheet carefully into its well-established creases. When she had finished, there was revealed a large sheet of brown oilskin. She took this in the middle between her thumbs and forefingers, lifted it at arm's length to shoulder height, swivelled it to her right and laid it neatly on the floor beside her.

"Now then," she said and bent over the trunk.

Uncle Mort winked at Carter Brandon, and Mr. Brandon smiled slowly at Pat.

"Now this here," said Auntie Lil, producing a piece of lino six inches square, "this here is a piece of the lino out of the bedroom, where me mother was born."

"It's very nice, I must say," said Mrs. Brandon. "In't it lovely, Les?"

"Oh aye," said Mr. Brandon.

They passed the lino from hand to hand. It was yellow with a faded pattern of pink flowers.

"Well, it's in good nick considering how old it is, I'll say that for it," said Uncle Mort.

"I polish it every morning," said Auntie Lil quietly but firmly.

Next she produced a larger square of lino, which was fraying slightly at the edges.

"Now this here," she said, "this here is a piece of lino from the front parlour of the house, which me mother and dad had, when they was first married."

"Where was that, Lil?" said Mrs. Brandon.

"Leek in Staffordshire," said Auntie Lil quietly but firmly.

They all examined the square of lino appreciatively. There were twelve more pieces to be admired, each one highly polished, each one taken from a room in a house, where Auntie Lil had spent her childhood.

Mr. Brandon lit his pipe, and Auntie Lil produced her next item. It was a thin, droopy brown object, which she balanced tenderly on the up-turned palms of her hands.

"Now this here," she said, "this here is the tail of our Daniel. He were run over by a dray in Birkenhead. Me dad kept his tail as a souvenir."

"What sort of a dog were he, Lil?" said Uncle Mort.

"Oh, he were a lovable animal were our Daniel. He could carry eggs round in his mouth without breaking them," said Auntie Lil.

"I'm not saying he couldn't," said Uncle Mort. "But what breed were he?"

"He was a cross. I think he'd a bit of bulldog in him somewhere."

"Ah, you can't beat a bloody mongrel," said Uncle Mort. "We had one when we was first married, a right Heinz 57 he were. Trouble with him were he chased bloody motor bikes. Well, we had to get him put down, you see."

"I don't think that's fair to the dog meself," said Mrs. Brandon. "It was up to you to train him proper. I mean, it's only human nature for dogs to chase motor bikes."

They broke off for supper, which consisted of tea, pickled onions, cream crackers and Cheshire cheese. Then Auntie Lil resumed her revelations.

"Now this here," she said, "this here is the first bedsock I ever knitted."

"Oh, isn't it lovely, Lil?" said Mrs. Brandon. "What a lovely shade of khaki."

"I knitted it in 1940 for our boys in the trenches."

"What a nice thought, Lil," said Mrs. Brandon.

"Well, why didn't you send it then?" said Uncle Mort, and Auntie Lil began to sob again.

"I'm surprised at you, Mort, saying things like that," said Mrs. Brandon. "You know all about that bedsock. You must have heard the story umpteen times be now. You know very well how it upsets our Lil."

Auntie Lil, shaking her head, took off her spectacles and wiped them on the front of her pinny.

"Come on, Lil, don't upset yourself no more. You put them away for the time being and get yourself off to bed," said Mrs. Brandon. "We'll finish them off another day. We'd love to see what else you've got, wouldn't we, Les?"

"Oh aye."

"Wouldn't we, Mort?"

"Oh aye."

"Wouldn't we, Carter?"

"Mm."

"Wouldn't we, Pat?"

"Yes."

In the car outside Pat's home Carter Brandon said:

"Your breath smells of onions."

"So does yours," said Pat. "It pongs."

They kissed tenderly, and Carter Brandon caused Pat considerable excitement when he unzipped her dress and kissed the small of her back.

"Bloody Fair Isle," said Uncle Mort in the pub one Sunday morning. "She's knitted me another Fair Isle jumper on that bloody machine of hers."

"It gives her summat to do, though, doesn't it?" said Mr. Brandon.

"Aye, I know that, but why does she have to take it out on me? Christ knows how much stuff she's knitted me in Fair Isle," said Uncle Mort. "I've got five pairs of mittens and a couple of balaclavas already."

"She still thinks she's knitting for the troops," said Mr. Brandon.

"Aye, and by the way they fit me she thinks she's knitting for a regiment of bloody midgets. Look at this one, it's too tight. I can't stand up straight in it. It's giving me duck's disease—here's me front me arse is coming later."

"Same again?" said Carter Brandon.

"No, I'll have a bottle of Guinness in mine, Carter," said Uncle Mort. "I'd better start building me strength up in case she knits me a bloody overcoat."

In the afternoon Carter Brandon drove his parents to the

home of Pat and her mother to take afternoon tea in the afternoon and high tea in the evening.

Mrs. Brandon made Mr. Brandon wear his new Harris Tweed jacket and the grey flannel trousers she had bought at C&A's.

"And don't keep fiddling with your tie while you're there neither," she said. "And, if she offers you cream, be firm. Say No."

Pat's mother opened the door and said:

"Come on in, Mr. and Mrs. Brandon. I've been looking forward to meeting you for I don't know how long. Pat's told me such a lot about you. I hope you'll not notice the wallpaper in the hall, but you know what it's like when you've no man about the house, Mrs. Brandon. Carter, take your mam and dad into the front room while I put the kettle on."

Carter Brandon showed his parents to the front room.

It was a small room. In one corner was a display cabinet with a gap in the middle shelf, where Pat's mother had removed the best Crown Derby tea service.

"I'll say this, considering everything, she's got it looking lovely. I mean to say . . ."

Pat's mother entered the room, pushing the tea things on a trolley.

"I was just saying, Mrs. Partington," said Mrs. Brandon. "I was just saying that you've got this room looking lovely, wasn't I, Les?"

"Aye."

"Well, you know, Mrs. Brandon, there's not a lot of money coming into this house since Mr. Partington died, but, as I say to our Pat, that's no reason to let our standards drop, is it? I mean, I've always been used to the very best —we always had tangerines for Christmas—and I don't see why I should change now at my time of life.

"Now you'll have one of these scones, won't you, Mr. Brandon? They're home-made. They're not bought. I do all my own baking, you know, Mrs. Brandon. Well, you've got to, haven't you, with present-day prices? I were looking in Pickup's yesterday at their fancies. They'd got them little individual swiss rolls—pass your mam the sugar, Carter— Sevenpence each! Well, I mean to say, it's outrageous, isn't it? There's neither rhyme nor reason in paying sevenpence for an individual swiss roll.

"I'm sorry, Mr. Brandon, aren't we looking after you? Pass your dad the greengage jam, Carter, there's a good boy. Pat! Pat! What are you doing upstairs? Come on, luv, I've got your tea poured out. It's going stone cold. You know what these young girls are like, Mrs. Brandon. They spend half their lives in front of their mirrors. I often say to our Pat, I say: 'When I were your age, young lady, I were up at half past five each morning, helping me mam get me brothers and sisters off to school!' I come from a big family, you know, Mrs. Brandon. Six brothers and three sisters—and all living."

Interesting anecdotes were told about the courtship and early married life of Mrs. Partington during the afternoon. The price of cauliflower was another subject that absorbed them until it was time for high tea.

They sat down to their meal in the back room. The tea pot rested on a chrome stand, the luncheon meat took its place on each of their plates with attendant lettuce leaves, sliced tomatoes, sliced cucumber and hard-boiled egg. In the centre of the table was a large plate of bread and butter.

"Take two slices while you're at it, Mr. Brandon," said Pat's mother.

A cut glass bowl contained canned peaches, and a similar cut glass jug contained evaporated milk.

"Say 'when,' Mrs. Brandon," said Pat's mother, pouring the evaporated milk on top of the peaches, which were lying in a small cut glass dish on the table cloth in front of Mr. Brandon.

"When," said Mrs. Brandon.

A home-made slab cake and a pot of tea rounded off the feast.

"Carter, are you going to help Pat do the washing up?" said Pat's mother.

"Yes," said Carter Brandon.

"There's a good boy," said Pat's mother.

In the kitchen Carter Brandon put his hands on Pat's hips, and she leaned back and rubbed her forehead on his cheek.

They washed the dishes, and when they had placed them in neat stacks on the draining board, Carter Brandon said:

"Are we going for a walk?"

"All right," said Pat.

She put her head round the door of the front room and said:

"We're just going out for a walk, mam. We'll not be long."

"That's right, luv," said Pat's mother.

The television set was switched on, and Pat's mother said:

"Pat's very fond of your Carter, you know. She thinks the sun shines out of him. She doesn't say much. But I mean,

I can tell. I was only just—I'll switch the telly down a bit. You don't mind, do you, Mr. Brandon? But we can't hear ourselves speak, can we, Mrs. Brandon?—I was only just thinking to meself what a grand couple they look, our Pat and your Carter."

"Well, we're very fond of Pat, aren't we, Les?"

"Mm."

Carter Brandon and Pat walked slowly hand in hand up the street. They turned into the path, which led over the allotments and under the railway bridge. Presently they came to a cinder road, which they followed for some yards until they came to a low stone wall.

They sat on the wall and turned to look back over the city. The street lamps of the housing estates in the suburbs climbed sluggishly up the sides of the valley, and in the distance there was the dull, unyielding glow of the furnaces.

"Oh, Carter," said Pat.

"What's up?"

"I'm just thinking."

"What about?"

"I'm just thinking, wouldn't it be nice to have a home of our own and invite people round to tea on Sunday afternoons?"

"Aye."

"Linda Preston's got her name down for a council house."

"Oh aye?"

The Brandons left for home at ten-thirty p.m. Carter Brandon drove quickly, his hand resting lightly on the gear lever by his side.

"Well, I think she's a very nice person is Mrs. Partington," said Mrs. Brandon. "She put a lovely tea on for us. I mean, she couldn't have been nicer, if she'd known us for donkey's years, could she, Les?"

"She can't half talk, though," said Mr. Brandon.

Carter Brandon stopped his car at a zebra crossing to let two elderly Pakistani workmen cross the road.

"I think we should ask her round to our place one Sunday. What do you think, Les?"

"Do what you like. It's nowt to do wi' me."

When they got home, Uncle Mort and Auntie Lil were drinking hot chocolate in the back room.

"Did you have a nice time?" said Auntie Lil.

"It were lovely, Lil. I did enjoy it," said Mrs. Brandon.

"You look as if you've been bloody shell-shocked, Les," said Uncle Mort.

Mr. Brandon shook his head and smiled slowly.

For Christmas Pat bought Carter Brandon a Ronson gas lighter. Inscribed on it were the initials, 'C.B.', and she wrapped Christmas paper round the box and tied on a label decorated with a robin, holly and sleighbells.

Carter Brandon gave Pat two one pound notes to buy some new clothes.

Pat's mother came to the Brandons on Christmas Day, and they had a very jolly party. They all pulled crackers and wore funny hats.

Auntie Lil went to bed early, and Uncle Mort drank too much port and got indigestion.

Carter Brandon drove Pat and her mother home.

"Are you coming in for a drink, Carter?" said Pat's mother.

They drank a glass of medium sherry, and then Pat's mother said:

"Well, I'm going to bed now. Good night, Carter. You won't forget to lock up behind you, will you, Pat? And don't stay here too long, Carter, there's a good boy. I did have a nice time today. Tell your mam I told you, won't you, Carter?"

On his way home Carter Brandon caught a puncture in his car. It took him thirty-five minutes to change the wheel. And that with the aid of a passing police constable!

CHAPTER FIVE

On the third week of January Uncle Mort moved into Auntie Lil's bedroom.

"It's not as if they're children," said Mrs. Brandon. "They know what they're doing."

"They'll not be doing much, I'll tell thee," said Mr. Brandon.

"Now then, Les," said Mrs. Brandon. "Less of that talk, if you don't mind."

It was a winter's afternoon, and Mr. Brandon was on holiday. The snow had cleared, but there were still hard scabs of ice on the allotments.

"It's only sensible really," said Mrs. Brandon. "Our Mort'll be good company for our Lil, won't he?"

"Oh aye, they'll make a perfect couple in bed," said Mr.

Brandon. "Her in her curlers and him in his Fair Isle bed-socks."

"Les, you are awful," said Mrs. Brandon, but she allowed herself to smile.

In the pub in the evening Uncle Mort said:

"It's the best road as far as I'm concerned. I mean, it's not right your Carter being turfed out of his bedroom for all this time, is it?"

"You're right there, Mort," said Mr. Brandon.

"I mean, I might as well kip down with Lil, mightn't I? It'll save your hot water bottles any road."

"That's right."

"What are you looking like that for?"

"Like what?"

"You've got a grin like a Cheshire cat all over your face."

"Have I, Mort?"

"You bloody have an' all," said Uncle Mort. "I know what you're thinking. Well, you can put them thoughts out of your head, Pronto."

On the evening in which the new sleeping arrangements were to be put into operation Uncle Mort, Auntie Lil and Mr. and Mrs. Brandon went out to the local.

They did not drink much. The men had four pints of mixed, Mrs. Brandon had two sweet sherries, and Auntie Lil had one port and tonic water.

When they returned home, Auntie Lil and Mrs. Brandon went into the kitchen to prepare supper.

In the living room Mr. Brandon lit his pipe slowly and peered at Uncle Mort from above the box of Swan Vestas resting on the bowl of his pipe.

"It'll be like a second honeymoon then, won't it, Mort?" he said.

"Now shut your hole," said Uncle Mort, and Mr. Brandon chuckled softly. "It's only people wi' mucky minds will think there's owt wrong with me and Lil sharing a bedroom. It's just an arrangement of convenience, that's all it is."

"That's right Mort," said Mr. Brandon.

In the kitchen Mrs. Brandon said to Auntie Lil, as she poured the boiling water into the brown two pint tea pot:

"Now you're sure you're not just doing it to please us, aren't you, Lil?"

"I'm fully aware of what I'm doing," said Auntie Lil.

"We'd have got you twin beds, you know, if you'd said. You'd only to have said the word, and we should have been only too delighted to have got you twin beds. There was some lovely ones advertised in the Littlewoods catalogue."

"I don't want to be no trouble to no one," said Auntie Lil in that quiet little voice she had made all her own.

"Well, you know best, Lil," said Mrs. Brandon.

"That's right."

They ate their supper quietly. Mrs. Brandon poured out the tea twice, and Uncle Mort ate only one pickled onion.

"Is Carter out with that Pat?" said Uncle Mort.

"I believe so, Mort," said Mrs. Brandon.

"Where've they gone to?" said Uncle Mort.

"I don't know. I heard them saying something about going dancing at Mecca," said Mrs. Brandon.

"You want to take our Lil there, Mort," said Mr. Brandon. "You can wear one of your Cyril's zoot suits."

"Now then, Les," said Mrs. Brandon angrily.

"I used to be very fond of dancing, when I were younger than I am now," said Auntie Lil.

"That's right, Lil," said Mrs. Brandon.

Uncle Mort yawned, stretched his legs and slapped his stomach. Then he looked at the clock, wound his watch and began to rub his eyes.

"He were very good at the Slow Fox Trot was my Bob. It was his specialty. He were so light on his feet, and he'd a lovely sense of rhythm. He used to wear them patent leather dancing pumps. He always carried them to the dance in his dad's attache case. Everyone said, if he'd gone in for it, he'd have won medals for his dancing. We liked the Old Tyme Dancing, too."

"Les did, too, didn't you, Les?"

"It weren't bad."

"There were some lovely dances in them days. We used to have some fun in the progressive barn dances. The MC and his wife were really good. Archie and Madelaine, they called them. I never found out what their surnames was, though I know for a fact her dad used to be verger at St. Cuthbert's. Archie had a little toothbrush moustache and twine toes. He was a real comedian. He used to have us in tucks especially when he sang 'Excelsior' at the annual hot-pot supper. I always liked the Military Two-Step, because the tunes was so nice. But my Bob said the Boston Two-Step was a better dance really. I don't think there's much to choose between the two meself."

Uncle Mort yawned again and got slowly to his feet. He walked to the window, drew back the curtains and looked out. Then he said:

"By, I pity them buggers who's got to be out working on a night like this. Give me a nice warm bed any time."

Mr. Brandon stood up and said:

"Well, I'll be getting off then. Good night all. Good night Lil. Sleep tight, mind the bugs don't bite."

"Good night, Leslie," said Auntie Lil.

Mrs. Brandon began to tidy up the supper pots. She took them into the kitchen, and when she had washed them, she put the milk, butter, cream crackers and pickled onions into the larder. They had eaten all the Cheshire cheese. Then she returned to the living room.

"Course we used to like dancing in the Tower Ballroom at Blackpool in the old days," said Auntie Lil. "It was a lovely floor. You just felt you was gliding in mid-air, when you were on it. Especially in the Valeta."

"That's right, Lil," said Mrs. Brandon, punching the cushions into shape.

"We went to the Tower at New Brighton once, but we didn't reckon much to that. My Bob said the clientele was too common."

"Mm," said Mrs. Brandon, blowing the dust off a small bakelite white elephant on the mantelpiece.

"Well, good night then," said Auntie Lil suddenly. She smiled at Mrs. Brandon, but she didn't look at Uncle Mort.

"Good night, Lil," said Mrs. Brandon from the foot of the stairs. Then she said: "Good night, Mort," and patted him on the shoulder as he made his way upstairs.

When Carter Brandon returned home, he said to his mother:

"Are the two love birds safely tucked up?"

"Now you're not to say things like that, Carter," said Mrs. Brandon. Then she kissed him on the cheek and said:

"Did you have a nice time tonight?"

"Not bad."

"Good night then."

"Good night."

"Which side do you want to sleep on then, Lil?" said Uncle Mort.

"I always used to sleep on the right hand side with my Bob," said Auntie Lil.

"That's all right wi' me," said Uncle Mort.

"But that's right beside the door, isn't it? I might get a draught in me ears. I suffer with me ears, you know."

"All right then, sleep on t' other side. I'm not mithered."

"Yes, but that's in a direct line with the window, in't it?"

"Well, you'll have to sleep on one side or t' other, won't you, Lil? It stands to reason does that."

Auntie Lil drew back the bedclothes and sat down on the side of the bed. She arranged her hair net carefully, brought her ankles together, drew up her knees and slipped daintily into bed.

Uncle Mort climbed in after her and switched off the light. After a while he said:

"By, tha's got cold feet, Lil. They're like a fishmonger's slab. By, they're cold."

Then Auntie Lil said:

"Do you always wear your vest in bed, Mort?"

"Aye."

"It's unhealthy to wear your vest in bed. It blocks up your pores."

"Does it?"

"And you feel no benefit, when you get up in the morning, if you wear your vest all through the night."

"Oh, I didn't know that," said Uncle Mort. Then he said:

"Why don't you budge up, Lil? There's plenty of room, tha' knows. There's no need to sleep stuck on the edge like that."

"I'm quite all right where I am, thank you, Mort," said Auntie Lil.

Then she turned on her side and looked at Uncle Mort, lying beside her with the tufts of his white hair sticking above his ears.

"It's rum, in't it, Mort?" she said.

"It bloody is an' all, Lil," said Uncle Mort.

Everyone in the district was shocked to hear of the death of Linda Preston's fiance, Ken Balmer. He was taken ill on the first Saturday in February, and a week later he was dead and buried.

Some people said he died of an enlarged heart. Others said he had a rare blood disease. Mrs. Warrender, the neighbour from number thirty-six, said he died of too much manking about. But everyone was most upset.

"I just didn't know where to put meself, when Linda Preston told me," said Pat.

"I'm sure you didn't, luv," said Mrs. Brandon.

"I says to her: 'I was only talking to him on Friday night at Mecca. He looked as right as rain, then,' I says."

"It makes you wonder whether there's a God after all,

when things like that happen, I always say," said Mrs. Brandon.

Later, when they were sitting at a corner table in 'The Packet,' Pat said to Carter Brandon:

"I just don't know what I'd do, if you was to die all of a sudden like that, Carter."

"Oh, you'd find another bloke all right. I mean, you're not bad-looking, are you?"

"Thanks very much. That's a right compliment, I must say."

"What's up? What have you got a mug on for? What have I said now?"

"That's just it. What have you said?" said Pat, swishing the cherry stick in the bottom of her glass of Babycham.

They had two more drinks and then they went out to catch the bus. It was raining hard, and after a few minutes Pat allowed Carter Brandon to shelter under her umbrella.

"I'll be glad, when my car's back on the road again," said Carter Brandon.

"Never mind, luv," said Pat, squeezing his arm just above the elbow.

They sat on the front seat of the top deck and smoked two cigarettes each before reaching the terminus. Then they had a ten minutes' walk through the rain until they reached Pat's house.

"Carter, lad, you're wet through," said Pat's mother. "You look like a drowned rat. Now come on in front of the fire and dry off before you catch your death of cold. Look at your trousers, lad, they're wringing wet. Come on, you'd best take them off and I'll dry them out for you."

"No, that's . . ."

"Now then, no arguing. Do as you're told. Take them trousers off before you come to some harm. Pat, go upstairs in my wardrobe and bring down them trousers of your dad's what he did the gardening in. Now then, Carter, off with them trousers. I'll go out of the room while you change. And take the things out of your pockets and put them on that table. If there's anything that'll scratch it, put it on the mat. Now hurry up before you catch your death of pneumonia."

Carter Brandon undid his shoes and took off his trousers. They were sodden to the knees.

"Are you done, Carter?" said Pat's mother.

"Yes, thank you, Mrs. Partington."

"Here you are then, I'll throw you Mr. Partington's trousers through the door."

"Thank you very much, Mrs. Partington."

They were grey flannel trousers with a broad chalk stripe. They fitted him well.

"Are you decent now, Carter? Can we come in?" said Pat's mother.

"Yes, thank you, Mrs. Partington."

"Oh, they fit him very well. Don't they fit him well, Pat?"

They drank cocoa out of blue and white striped mugs. Carter Brandon's trousers steamed in front of the fire and made a most unpleasant smell.

"Well, I'll be off to bed now, Pat, luv. I'll put your trousers in the airing cupboard just to make sure, Carter. Now give them half an hour—a good half hour—and they'll be all right for you to go home in. Good night, Pat. Good night, Carter."

"Good night, mum."

"Good night, Mrs. Partington."

"Now you'll not forget to lock up behind you before you go to bed, will you, Pat?"

"Good night, mum."

"Good night, Mrs. Partington."

When she had gone, Pat switched off the light and sat beside Carter Brandon on the sofa. He put his arm under her armpit and began to stroke her right breast.

Pat wriggled and rolled her head from side to side. Suddenly she clasped him tightly and began to kiss him rapidly on his lips, his cheek, his neck and his shoulders. Then she undid the front of his shirt and kissed his nipples. It tickled.

"Oh, Carter, I love you. I do love you, honest."

Carter Brandon slipped his hand under her skirt and placed it on her thigh just above her stocking tops. She shuddered and dug her fingernails into his back.

"How about getting sort of married then?" said Carter Brandon.

She stiffened. Then she drew back her head slowly and stared into his eyes.

"Pardon?" she said.

"You know, sort of get married like."

"Oh, luv, I thought you was never going to ask me," she said. "I thought you was only going out with me to muck around."

Carter Brandon nuzzled into her neck with his nose. They kissed again and again.

When Pat switched on the light, she said:

"When are we going to get the ring?"

"We'll go on Saturday morning, if you like."

"I can't make up me mind whether to have a solitaire or a cluster."

She kissed him again, and this time she was relaxed in his arms.

At the door she said:

"Good night, luv."

"Good night."

"I love you," she whispered.

Carter Brandon nodded, and then Pat said:

"Fancy you proposing to me wearing me dad's trousers."

CHAPTER SIX

Everyone admired the engagement ring, and Mrs. Brandon had a little weep to herself in the back kitchen after she had seen it.

Mr. Brandon and Uncle Mort took Carter Brandon to the local, and over several pints of best bitter beer gave him much good advice concerning love and marriage.

Mrs. Partington held a tea party in honour of the newly-engaged couple, and anyone who was anyone in the Brandon and Partington family was invited.

Auntie Lil knitted Pat a green cardigan and a pair of matching mittens, and everyone was captivated by the thought behind the gift.

The swallows came to the outskirts of the city in the spring to be followed a few weeks later by the swifts.

Carter Brandon and Pat lay side by side on their backs in a meadow, watching the swifts, screeching and swooping in the blue sky. In the distance was a long line of Lombardy poplars.

"I don't think we should rush into buying a house," said Pat. "We should wait while we've saved up enough to get it just right when we move in."

"Mm."

"I says to me mother, I says: 'I think it's stupid me, moving into a house, when you can't get it furnished proper.' When I get a house, I want it furnished right from top to bottom. Don't you, though, Carter?"

"What?"

"Don't you want the house furnished from top to bottom before we move in?"

"Oh aye."

On the way home Carter Brandon said:

"I should know one way or the other tomorrow."

"Know about what?" said Pat.

"About my job."

Pat's startled face was suddenly lit up by the neon lights of a synagogue.

"Your job?" she said.

"Aye, there's going to be redundancy at our place. There's about ten in our department will have to go. Didn't I tell you?"

"You most certainly did not."

"I must have forgotten then."

Carter Brandon drove carefully round the roundabout and accelerated up the hill. The exhaust roared as they passed under a railway bridge.

"I suppose you don't think it concerns me at all, do you?" said Pat, when they came to the outskirts of the housing estate, where she lived.

"Course I do."

"You've got a funny way of showing it, haven't you? Who's going to lose their jobs any road?"

"We'll find that out tomorrow."

"Will you get the push?"

"Ee, I haven't a clue."

On Monday morning Mr. Walsh called Carter Brandon into his office. He was wearing his long white overalls with the singe marks on the elbows.

"Now I'm sure you realise my position, Carter," he said. "You've worked well since you've been with the firm, and I'm most satisfied with your work for my department."

He walked round behind Carter Brandon and put his hand on his shoulder.

"If it were left to me, lad, I'd keep you on like a shot. But it's your own union what's decided on this here last in, first out principle. It weren't me what decided that, was it, Carter?"

"That's right, Mr. Walsh."

The district organiser of the union held an emergency meeting in the canteen and handed out his filter-tip Park Drives to his redundant colleagues without prejudice.

"Now, then, you all have your full entitlement of £3 10s union assistance for the first twelve week of unemployment. And after that for the period of eighteen week you have an entitlement of forty-seven shillings and sixpence. Right?"

He took off his spectacles, blew on the lenses and wiped them with his handkerchief. He had leather binding on the cuffs of his jacket.

"In addition to these sums, of course, you'll get your full state entitlements—iyee, unemployment benefit, national assistance etsetterer etsetterer."

He lit a cigarette from the dimp he held concealed in the palm of his hand and blew a fussy stream of smoke out of his nostrils.

"Now, of course, head office here is in close and constant contact with all our branches in Number Four district, and I can say with some confidence that you will all be found employment in the very near future."

"Aye, it's all very well for you to say that," said Sid Skelhorn, who had ginger hair and five children, "but what sort of work are we going to get?"

There was a soft mutter of approval and much shuffling of feet from among the audience.

"That's a perfectly reasonable question, and I'm going to give you the answer."

"That's what we pay us bloody subs for," said Sid Skelhorn.

"I can guarantee that as far as is humanly possible each and every one of you what has been declared redundant will be offered employment in full parity with the job you have just vacated."

"I didn't vacate my job. I was bloody fired," said Sid Skelhorn.

"Correct, Brother Skelhorn," said the district organiser.

They filed out of the canteen, and Sid Skelhorn said:

"Bloody big pillock. He don't gi'e a monkey's bollock for us. And that's the truth is that."

Mrs. Brandon said, as she was mixing the cake in front of the living room fire:

"I think it's disgusting treating you like that. I mean, how do they expect young folk to get on in the world, make a decent living for themselves and bring a family up, when they can just turn round and throw you out of a job like that?"

"You want to get a job on a Esso tanker. See a bit of the world," said Uncle Mort.

"Now then, Mort, that's enough of that talk," said Auntie Lil.

"Bloody hell, she's started on at me now," said Uncle Mort, and he went out into the back garden to join Mr. Brandon, who was oiling his wheelbarrow.

"I shouldn't worry," said Carter Brandon, dipping his finger into the cake mixture, "there's plenty of work kicking around."

There was an evening match, the last of the season, and the home side won 25-3, even though the outside half was carried off with a fractured cheek bone just before half time.

In 'The Griffon' Mr. Brandon was delighted, and in honour of the victory he bought beer and whiskies all round for his son and himself.

"It's a bit of hard luck about your job, in't it?" he said.

"Ah, I'm not mithered."

"No. Young Leatherbarrow'll not play again this year. Not with a fractured cheek bone."

"No chance."

In the Piccola coffee bar that night Pat said:

"You'll just have to sell your car, that's all."

"Sell me car? What are you talking about?"

"We're supposed to be saving for wedding, aren't we? Well, we can't do much saving, if you're on dole, can we?"

"I'll not be on it for long."

"That's what you say."

"I'm not selling me car any road."

When they drew up outside Pat's home, she opened the door and said:

"No one seems to be thinking of me, do they? I'm the one what's got all the worry of saving for wedding. All you do is go boozing with your dad. It's not fair."

She slammed the door and ran up the path. Carter Brandon started to open the door, but, when he saw it was raining, he started the engine and drove home.

April gave way to May, and on a cool Sunday morning in that month of spring flowers and clean cricket flannels Uncle Mort made a momentous announcement.

"Our Lil's going to have a baby," he said.

Mrs. Brandon dropped a piece of fried egg off her fork, and she turned quite pale.

"At her time of life?" she said.

"You old ram," said Mr. Brandon.

"She went to the doctor's yesterday, and he told her," said Uncle Mort.

"She told me she was going to see about her bunions," said Mrs. Brandon.

"That's what she told me," said Uncle Mort gloomily.

"You bloody old ram," said Mr. Brandon.

"Stop talking like that, Les," said Mrs. Brandon. Then she got up from the table and walked up and down the room.

"Well, there's only one thing to be done," she said at length. "You'll have to get married."

"Ay, you've got to do right by her," said Mr. Brandon.

"Oh dear," said Uncle Mort.

"This is a right carry on, I must say," said Mrs. Brandon. "You ought to be ashamed of yourself, our Mort, getting Lil into trouble at your age. You're old enough to be the baby's father."

"I didn't mean it," said Uncle Mort.

"Yes, and I've heard that before," said Mrs. Brandon. "You just didn't stop and think, did you? That's the whole trouble with these unmarried mothers. It's people like you, what didn't mean it."

"Oh, don't go on like that, Annie," said Uncle Mort.

"I suppose I'd better go upstairs and see our Lil," said Mrs. Brandon. "What I'll say to her I do not know."

When she had left the room, Mr. Brandon began to chuckle.

"Well, you old ram," he said. "I didn't think you'd got it in you."

"Neither did I," said Uncle Mort, scratching his chest.

"You must be the oldest bloody juvenile delinquent in town."

"I were only trying to keep warm," said Uncle Mort. "It were our Lil what kept egging me on."

"A shot gun wedding at your age," said Mr. Brandon. "You're not setting our Carter a good example, are you?"

Then he and Carter Brandon began to laugh, and Uncle Mort sat hunched up in the rocker in front of the fire.

"It's true enough," said Mrs. Brandon, standing at the door. "She's two months gone."

"Who'd have believed it?" said Mr. Brandon.

"I'm right ashamed of you, our Mort," said Mrs. Brandon. "What your poor mam would have said if she'd known, I do not know. It's a good job for you she's dead and buried, poor soul, or she'd have given you the thrashing of your life. She were right strict about this sort of thing were me mam."

"I know," said Uncle Mort.

"You'll not be having a white wedding then?" said Mr. Brandon.

"I should think they won't," said Mrs. Brandon. "What the neighbours are going to say, I do not know."

"I wish I hadn't done it," said Uncle Mort.

Auntie Lil got up in the afternoon and sat on the sofa with her eyes lowered. She wore her blue housecoat with the pattern of maroon flowers.

"It's what I've always wanted," she said.

"Well, if it makes you happy, Lil," said Mrs. Brandon.

"My Bob and I always wanted a baby. It were his one big regret that we didn't have issue."

"He'll probably give all the angels a bit of a tune on his harp then, won't he, Lil?" said Mr. Brandon.

"I remember our honeymoon night so well," said Auntie Lil.

"Oh, give over, Lil," said Uncle Mort.

"We caught the seven-fifteen to Skegness, and they all came to the station to see us off. Me mam says to my Bob: 'Tek care of her, son, she's precious to me, you know.' And me Uncle Hector says to me mam: 'You've got to look at it this road—you're not losing a daughter, you're gaining a son.' It were such a consolation to her.

"And when we got to Skeggy we had a cup of tea and a bun, and then we went to the boarding house, where we was staying. Oh, they did make us feel at home. Nothing was too much trouble. They treated us like one of their own. We used to sit in their parlour after tea and have a hand of cards. She'd one of them collapsible card tables she'd won in a whist drive."

"But what happened on your honeymoon night, Lil?" said Mr. Brandon.

"Not in front of Carter," said Uncle Mort.

"My Bob was wearing them green striped pyjamas his mam had bought him special from Bon Marche. Oh, he did cut a dash, when he come in from cleaning his teeth. He says: 'Shall I switch out the light then?' And I says: 'Yes.' I were all of a flutter and tremble."

"Now come on, Lil, come on," said Uncle Mort, squirming in his seat.

"I shall always think of that baby as belonging to my Bob," said Auntie Lil.

"Where do I come into it then?" said Uncle Mort.

"I knew he were there in spirit, when the baby was conceived."

"I wondered what that bloody draught was down the back of me neck," said Uncle Mort.

"Yes, well, I'm very glad for both of you, I must say,"

said Mrs. Brandon. "But now we've got to get down to brass tacks, haven't we?"

"We can't have you turning into one of them unmarried mothers, Lil," said Mr. Brandon.

So it was decided that Uncle Mort should propose to Auntie Lil, and that Auntie Lil should accept.

"Will you marry me?" said Uncle Mort.

"Yes," said Auntie Lil.

As a result Sunday dinner was eaten in a festive spirit by all the participants.

Carter Brandon got a job on the next day.

He telephoned Pat at work and told her the good news. He could hear the driers in the background.

"Where is it then, luv?" said Pat.

"At Wagstaffe and Broome's."

"That's where Linda Preston works."

"Well, it'll be good company for me, won't it?"

He went for a walk in the Memorial Gardens, and at lunchtime he met Uncle Mort in 'The Griffon.' The saloon bar was crowded with commercial travellers and clerks from the council offices, so they sat in a corner of the public bar next to a group of old men, playing dominoes.

"I never thought it would happen to me," said Uncle Mort. "Older you get, bloody dafter you get. Do you know how old I am, Carter?"

"Not really."

"I'm sixty bloody six."

"Go on?"

"I am that."

"You don't look it."

"Don't I?"

"You don't. You look about ten years younger. Anyone looking at you would say you was ten years younger than you are. That's a fact."

"Go on?"

"I'm not kidding."

"Aye well, I'm sixty bloody six."

They played bowls in the afternoon, and it came on to rain in the middle of tea.

"It'll not do the shallots no harm any road," said Mr. Brandon.

In the evening the vicar said:

"I can't say how pleased I am to see a couple like you, settling down together in the twilight of your lives."

"I'm only sixty-six," said Uncle Mort.

Auntie Lil was wearing her mauve hat with the lime green veil. Uncle Mort was wearing the double-breasted navy blue suit he had bought from Burton's for his wife's funeral. The vicar was wearing his plus-fours.

"You know, many people of your age shy away from the thought of matrimony," said the vicar, crossing his legs and clasping his hands on his right knee. "They seem to have got hold of the idea that marriage is only for young people, for people on the threshold of life, as it were."

"That's right, vicar," said Auntie Lil.

"Well, I always say it's never too late for God. Would you like a cup of cocoa?"

"That would be very nice, vicar," said Auntie Lil.

"I suppose our dashing groom would like something a little stronger, perhaps?"

"Nay, I'm not mithered. Cocoa's all right wi' me," said Uncle Mort.

"Splendid. Though, I must confess I do like the odd pint of wallop myself."

The vicar's housekeeper brought in three mugs of cocoa on a round biscuit tin lid. She cleared a space on the study table and took the mugs off the tray. Then she removed the saucer of water in front of the gas fire and returned a few minutes later with a fresh saucer of water.

"Thank you so much, Mrs. Paulden," said the vicar. "Do you smoke?"

"No thank you," said Uncle Mort.

The vicar lit his pipe. It had a bent stem with a silver band.

"Now I'm going to be quite frank with you here," said the vicar. "I may shock you, but I always say this to the young people, who come here for a chinwag before their marriage. And this is what I'm going to tell you—you can keep each other happy in bed for ten years, but you've got to keep Him happy in bed for a lifetime.

"Now I'm not saying that the physical side of marriage isn't important. It is, but it's not everything. Not by a long chalk. There has to be something much deeper, much firmer, much more—how shall I say?—much more fundamental. And that's what I mean by 'the true union of two souls in the eyes of our Lord'."

The vicar began to roll a spill out of a strip of paper torn from the *Manchester Guardian*. Uncle Mort scratched his ear, and Auntie Lil inclined her head a little more to the left and smiled.

"I want you to think very carefully about the responsibilities of marriage. What do I mean by 'responsibilities'? Well, in a word, I mean that mutual trust and understanding and respect, which two soulmates cherish for the rest of their lives on earth. I mean that rock upon which the waves of frustration and discord ceaselessly beat. But, if that rock be strong, if its foundations are solid, the citadel of Holy Matrimony will survive all the onslaughts—and, let's face it, shall we, marriage isn't all a bed of roses. And those pesky thorns can be pretty painful at times, you know. That's what I mean by 'responsibilities', isn't it?"

The housekeeper put her head round the door of the study and said:

"I'll be going now then. I've put your milk in a saucepan on the stove, and there's some egg sandwiches under a saucer in the larder. Now don't forget to let the cat out, will you? You know what happens, if you leave him in all night."

"Thank you, Mrs. Paulden."

"Good night."

"Good night and my good wishes to hubby," said the vicar, and he stood up and drew the curtains of his study. He switched on the lights, but after a few seconds there was a deep click from outside in the hall, and the lights went out.

"I wonder if I could trouble you for a shilling for the meter?" he said.

They walked home arm in arm in the twilight. There were laburnums in bloom in the Memorial Gardens, and in the middle of the Halifax Road roundabout there was a large and colourful display of daffodils.

"I thought the vicar was a very nice man," said Auntie Lil.

"Aye, but he were an old wind bag, weren't he?" said Uncle Mort, and Auntie Lil squeezed his arm and smiled tolerantly.

"Well, it's his job, when all's said and done, isn't it?" she said.

During supper Mrs. Brandon said:

"Now you're not to bother yourselves about wedding arrangements. You just leave everything to Les and me. We'll see to it all, won't we, Les?"

"Aye."

"I'll go down to 'The Whippet' and see Bert and Enid about hiring that big room of theirs. They do lovely catering do Bert and Enid, don't they, Les?"

"Aye."

"She puts on a lovely spread and very reasonable, too, doesn't she, Les?"

"Aye."

"I don't want to be no trouble," said Auntie Lil.

"Now you're not to talk like that, Lil," said Mrs. Brandon. "It's going to be your big day, and you're the only one what matters. If the bride can't have everything how she likes it on her wedding day, it's a poor look out. That's what I always say."

On his first day at work Carter Brandon met Linda Preston in the canteen. She was wearing a bottle green overall, white flat-heeled shoes, and she had her hair in light blue plastic curlers.

"Do you like it 'ere, kid?" she said.

"It's all right, in't it?" said Carter Brandon.

"Oh, it's beltin' 'ere, if you know how to skive. We've got a smashin' Welfare Club."

"Have we?"

"We 'ave these socials first Thursday in every month."

"Do you?"

"And then we 'ave firm's Christmas Social every Christmas. That's a right smashin' do. All the lads are a right yell, when they get tanked up. We don't half have a laugh."

Carter Brandon ate his two slices of cold roast beef, Yorkshire pudding, mashed potatoes and carrots. Linda Preston ate her beefburger, baked beans and chips.

"The food's beltin' 'ere, in't it?" she said.

"Aye."

"Are you coming on Welfare Summer outing?"

"I don't mind."

"Oh, we 'ave a beltin' time on outing. We've got six charas this year. We're going to New Brighton this year. It'll be a right yell, honest."

"Sounds all right."

"You want to see Eric Black, kid. He's your Welfare Committee man. Get him to put your name on the list."

"I'll do that."

They had tinned apricots and custard and a cup of coffee.

When they came out of the pictures, Pat said:

"Did you see Linda Preston today?"

"I just caught a glimpse of her in the canteen. It's a big place, you know."

"I don't know how she can work in a factory like that. It's not very lady-like, is it?"

The drive home did not take them long. The car had new

sparking plugs, and it was running well. Outside her home Pat said:

"In't it a right yell about your Uncle Mort and Auntie Lil getting married?"

"What's funny about it?"

"Nothing. But getting married at their age, it makes you think, doesn't it?"

"I suppose so."

"Do you think they love each other as much as us?"

"I don't know."

"We do love each other, though, don't we, Carter?"

"Oh aye," said Carter Brandon.

He kissed her, and she said:

"I saw some smashin' curtains in Barnett's on Saturday. They were like your mum's got in her front room only they'd got these blue patterns on them."

"Had they?"

He kissed her again, and she said:

"I just can't wait till we get married, Carter."

"Can't you?" said Carter Brandon.

He hit a cat on the way home. When he put the car inside the garage, he noticed blood and fur on the front fender. So he wiped it off with an oily rag.

He did not tell his mother, because things like that upset her.

CHAPTER SEVEN

The room at 'The Whippet' had been booked for three-thirty p.m., and an extension had been sought and gained at the Magistrates' Court.

The wedding invitations had been dispatched and many replies received.

The three great aunts from Glossop were to be brides-maids, Mr. Brandon's eldest brother, Stavely, was to be best man, and Auntie Lil was to be given away by Mr. Brandon.

As the wedding day approached life in the Brandon household became more hectic.

"Now we'll want some bottles for the toast, won't we, Les?" said Mrs. Brandon.

"Aye," said Mr. Brandon.

"If I remember rightly, your Beattie had two bottles of sherry and two bottles of port put aside special, didn't she?"

"Mm."

"But, half a mo, didn't she have a bottle of champagne for close relatives of bride and groom?"

"Eee, I don't know."

"No, that's your whole trouble, in't it? You don't know nothing, if you don't want to, do you?" said Mrs. Brandon, and she stamped into the back kitchen and ran the cold water tap fiercely for a few minutes.

"Now our Stavely understands about getting down here in plenty of time, doesn't he?" said Mrs. Brandon.

"I told him in t' letter," said Uncle Mort.

"I know. But you know what he's like. They don't look after them proper in that Old Folks' Home. They'll let him come out looking any old how. Look when he come to your Edna's funeral. He looked a sight. Fancy wearing wellington boots at a funeral."

"Well, it were raining, when he set off."

"I think our Stavely's going a bit feeble, you know. Are you sure he understands you're getting married?"

"I told him plain enough in bloody letter."

"I know. But look what happened when he come to your Edna's funeral. He didn't really understand what were going on. He didn't know why we were there. When we come out of crematorium he says: 'Where's our Edna then, is she took bad or summat?'"

"Daft old bugger."

"I'll send Carter down in t' car to fetch him. He can come down and stay with us a few days before wedding, so we're sure he knows what he's doing."

"Just look at this," said Mrs. Brandon, reading the letter from the three great aunts from Glossop. "They're never going to be bridesmaids in that rig-out?"

"You can't boss them about at their age," said Auntie Lil. "I told them what I wanted, but they insisted on wearing their confirmation frocks."

"They'll turn up looking like bloody Marx Brothers," said Uncle Mort.

"I'll send Carter up to Glossop to fetch them. They can stay with us a few days before wedding, so we're sure they know what they're doing."

"Now I've asked you to come here for what I like to call my 'wedding interview.' I want to make sure that you're fully and totally conversant with what I like to call 'the service of Holy Matrimony'," said the vicar.

"After all, this is going to be the greatest day in your lives, and we want to make sure it's not spoiled by any silly hitches, don't we?"

He went through the service with them step by step, and then he said:

"And now we come to the question of music, don't we? My organist, Mr. Pope, will attend to the anthems, of course, and I imagine you'll want the choir."

"That'll be nice," said Auntie Lil.

"But we want to know what hymns we're going to sing, don't we? Now have we any special favorites?"

"What's that hymn they sing at Cup Final?" said Uncle Mort.

After much discussion they chose some lovely hymns.

On Wednesday evening Pat said to Carter Brandon:

"What's your mam wearing?"

"Mm?"

"What's your mam wearing for the wedding?"

"I don't know."

"I just don't want to clash, that's all."

They walked along the canal towpath and then climbed over a stile into a field.

A bay pony in the far corner watched them. The field was scarred by ditches and long lines of newly-turned soil. At the side of the ditches were the pipes for the drains.

"I'm coming round to your house Friday night," said Pat.

"Are you?"

"You don't sound very interested."

"I am. What are you coming round for?"

"To do your mam and your Auntie Lil's hair."

"Oh."

Carter Brandon helped Pat pick her way across the field, where the new houses were being built. She was wearing navy blue shoes with scarlet high heels.

There were mortar mixing machines here and there, and holes for the foundations. Piles of bricks and tin huts for the workmen completed the picture.

"They're spoiling the countryside with building all these houses, aren't they?" said Carter Brandon.

"Well, people have got to live somewhere, haven't they?"

said Pat. "I mean, there must be hundreds of young couples glad to live here. I mean to say, by rights we should be looking for somewhere like this."

They walked along the old country lane with its crumbling stone walls and dark green clumps of rhododendrons. The hawthorn hedges were laden with blossom, and there were clumps of cowslips trodden underfoot by the workmen.

"I used to build dens here, when I were a little lad," said Carter Brandon.

"Dens!" said Pat scornfully, and in the distance the pony whinnied.

When they were inside the car, Pat smoothed down her skirt and said:

"Do you see much of Linda Preston at work?"

"Not a deal."

"She told me she sees you quite a bit."

"Oh."

"She told me she often has dinner with you in the canteen."

"Did she?"

The sun was shining, when Carter Brandon drove across the moors to collect his Uncle Stavely. He was accompanied by Pat.

The sun glinted on a reservoir. Sheep grazed on the gritty grass at the side of the road. When the car approached, the lambs thrust their heads into their mothers' soot-matted fleeces and wagged their tails.

Carter Brandon stopped the car and opened the windows. He could hear a diesel train, rattling behind a spur of grit-stone rock. Sheep were bleating on the high fells, and curlew trilled.

"It's nice here, in't it, Carter?" said Pat. "It's dead peaceful."

In the distance to their right the moors lurched down to the plain. In the foreground a pair of housemartins hunted above a crumbling shepherd's cottage. Its windows were boarded up, and a rusty bucket lay on its side by the front door. A thin tornado of gnats spiralled above a rowan tree. The wind blew gently.

They smoked a cigarette, and then Carter Brandon drove to the town, which contained the Old Folks' Home, which, in its turn, contained Uncle Stavely.

"Now think on, won't you?" said the matron. "He's not to have too much excitement."

"No," said Carter Brandon.

"And keep him off the rich foods. You see, his tummy, well, his tummy isn't used to rich foods. It's all right for you. Your tummy's used to rich foods. But he's an old man, and he's not got the tummy no more for those sort of foods."

"Yes."

"Now remember what I told you," said the matron to Uncle Stavely. "No rich foods. We don't want you constipated again."

"Pardon?" said Uncle Stavely.

"And don't sit in no draughts and remember to take your pills."

The matron leaned through the car window and said to Pat:

"Now think on, won't you? He's his little red pills and his big green pills. Now he's to take two red pills after every meal, and a green one every three hours crushed up in an eggcupful of warm water."

Then she raised her voice and shouted at Uncle Stavely:

"I'm just telling the young lady about your pills."

"Oh."

"I shall know, if you've not been taking them. And so will doctor."

"Aye well, he'll be all right with us," said Carter Brandon, starting the car engine.

"Now think on, won't you? If his feet start swelling, he's his little blue pills to take. And don't let him crunch them. He's to keep them on his tongue and let them dissolve."

"Aye."

"If your feet start swelling, no crunching your pills. You're to let them dissolve on your tongue," she shouted at Uncle Stavely.

"On his tongue, yes," said Carter Brandon.

The matron stood on the steps of the house and waved her handkerchief as they drove away down the drive.

"Do you fancy a vessel or owt, Uncle Stavely?" said Carter Brandon.

"She'll not have packed me best braces. She never packs me best braces. Pardon?" said Uncle Stavely.

Carter Brandon drove swiftly across the moorland roads. From time to time Pat placed her hand on his thigh. Flies were flattened and shredded on the windscreen.

"You didn't meet Corporal Parkinson then?" said Uncle Stavely.

Carter Brandon and Pat shook their heads. Pat turned round to Uncle Stavely and smiled.

"We share a room together in the home," said Uncle Stavely. "He's my oppo."

"Is he?" said Pat.

"Pardon?"

"Is he?" said Pat.

"He's a veteran is Corporal Parkinson. He fought in the Boer War with the colours. He's got a lump of shrapnel the size of my fist in his hip. He didn't get that in the Boer War, though. He got that when he were in the Andrew. Pardon?"

After three or four miles the road dropped down off the tops into a small village hunched into the side of the valley.

"Do you fancy a vessel, Uncle Stavely?" said Carter Brandon.

"Aye, I do that."

The public house was cool, and on the tables were bottles and glasses left from the previous evening. Uncle Stavely had a bottle of Guinness, and Carter Brandon had a pint of bitter.

"They tell me our Mort's getting married again," said Uncle Stavely.

"That's right, Uncle Stavely."

"Your mam wrote me a letter telling me."

"Did she?"

"It were wrote on blue paper. I don't often get letters wrote on blue paper. White—yes. Blue—no."

A man with thick leather gaiters round his calves came in and nodded to them.

"Grand day," he said.

"It is that," said Carter Brandon.

"What's our Edna got to say about it then?" said Uncle Stavely.

"Well, she's dead, you see, Uncle Stavely. That's why Uncle Mort's getting married again."

"Dead is she?"

"That's right. That's why you came to her funeral. Do you remember?"

"Now you know what you've got to do as best man, don't you, Stavely?" said Mrs. Brandon that evening.

"Best man?" said Uncle Stavely.

"Bloody hell," said Uncle Mort.

"You're going to be best man at our Mort's wedding. That's why you've come here," said Mrs. Brandon. Then she added for the benefit of the rest of the assembly: "You know, they don't treat them right and proper in these old folks' homes, do they?"

"You're going to be best man at my wedding, Stavely," said Auntie Lil.

Mr. Brandon coughed, scratched his armpit, stood up and said:

"Do you fancy a beer, Stavely, lad?"

"Pardon? That'd be nice."

After the men had left for the public house Mrs. Brandon said to Auntie Lil:

"They do not, they don't treat them right and proper."

"He hasn't had his ears washed for days," said Auntie Lil.

"And did you see the state of his knees?"

"I'll swear he doesn't know why he's here," said Auntie Lil.

"Well, don't worry, Lil luv. If we keep telling him often enough, he's forced to cotton on by the time wedding comes round."

On Sunday Carter Brandon and Pat drove to Glossop to collect the three great aunts.

"Linda Preston says you're going on works outing to New Brighton," said Pat.

"Aye."

"You didn't think of telling me, did you? After all, we're only engaged, aren't we? I mean, I don't really matter, do I?"

"Oh, give over."

"Yes, it's all very well for you to say that, but it's a bit of a carry on, when one of me best friends had to tell me what me fiance's up to."

Carter Brandon gritted his teeth and clenched the steering wheel.

"Linda Preston seems to know more about you these days than what I do. You can imagine what I felt like, when she told me you was going on works outing. I had to pretend I knew. And that's a right carry on, in't it?"

Carter Brandon overtook a tractor pulling a trailer. A border collie standing on the trailer wagged its tail and barked as they passed.

He looked in his driving mirror and then drew into the side of the road. He switched off the engine and turned to Pat.

"Are you going to give over mithering?" he said.

"What do you mean?" said Pat sharply.

"If you don't give over mithering, I shall open that door and tip you out arse over bloody tit."

When the three great aunts from Glossop arrived at the

Brandon household later that evening, they were given a most cordial welcome by Mrs. Brandon.

"Now then, Auntie Maud, come on, luv, be careful of the step. Hello, Auntie Mona, how are you, luv? Careful, Auntie Mary, don't trip over the dog. How are you, luv?"

The three great aunts from Glossop sat side by side on the sofa. They smelled of bandages, and they sucked mint imperials.

Mrs. Brandon passed round the plate of scones and filled the cups of tea balanced on the respective aged knees of the three great aunts from Glossop.

"Did you have a good journey?" said Auntie Lil.

"Our Carter's a very careful driver, isn't he?" said Mrs. Brandon.

"He doesn't drive too quick, does he?" said Auntie Lil.

"What I say is, it's good to see our Mort and Lil settling down together at their time of life. They'll be right good company for each other," said Mrs. Brandon.

"We've got some lovely frocks for you to wear at the wedding," said Auntie Lil.

"You'll have to go down to Mrs. Pearson's for a fitting tomorrow," said Mrs. Brandon. "We got them in the spring sale at Thompkinsons's, and Mrs. Pearson's going to alter them special for you."

"You'll each have a bouquet of tea roses and lily of the valley," said Auntie Lil.

"Is our Edna going to be at wedding?" said Uncle Stavely.

The three great aunts from Glossop looked at each other and then retired to the bedroom of Mr. and Mrs. Brandon.

"We'll have to do something about our Stavely," said Mrs. Brandon over breakfast next morning. "He can't be best man at wedding, looking like I don't know what."

"He'll be all right, if he gives his boots a good polish," said Mr. Brandon, who was reading the Daily Herald.

"Now just see here, Les," said Mrs. Brandon. "I'm not having Stavely going to wedding, looking as though he's just dropped off rag and bone man's cart. We've got to keep up appearances. It's me the neighbours'll be talking about, if Stavely doesn't go dressed proper."

"Eee, what a fuss. What a bloody fuss," said Mr. Brandon and he stood up and walked to the window. He pulled back the lace curtains and looked into the garden.

"I'll tell you what," he said at length, "he can have that brown suit I wore at our Beattie's funeral if you like. It's no good to me now. It's too tight."

"I was going to suggest that," said Mrs. Brandon, clearing up the table.

When Uncle Stavely rose from his bed, a fitting took place in the front room. The trousers were hoisted over his ankles and held in place by a pair of Mickey Mouse braces, and the jacket was draped over his upper portions. An inspection followed supervised by Mrs. Brandon and Auntie Lil.

"Well, the trousers need taking up, don't they?" said Mrs. Brandon. "You see, we can't put his braces any higher or we'll cut his crutch in two."

"I'll be able to take up two or three inches on the turn-ups," said Auntie Lil.

Mrs. Brandon and Auntie Lil walked slowly round the perimeter of the room, staring at Uncle Stavely. Then Mrs. Brandon pounced and shook his shoulders.

"Now come on, Stavely, luv, straighten your shoulders a minute then we can see what we're doing," she said. Then she said to Auntie Lil, "He's all skin and bone. There's nowt to him."

"What's all this in aid of?" said Uncle Stavely, as he was being redressed by Mrs. Brandon.

"It's to make sure you look nice and decent for the wedding."

"Oh, there's going to be a wedding, is there?" said Uncle Stavely. "I've not been to a wedding for donkey's years."

CHAPTER EIGHT

Carter Brandon and Linda Preston walked in the sunlight to the canal and sat together on a brick wall.

They had taken lunch in the canteen, and there was still ten minutes before the afternoon hooter blew. The sun shone on the water, and a narrow boat loaded with coke for the gas works lay moored alongside a wharf. A mute swan drifted along the canal with its left leg stretched out stiffly across its back. A rim of black scum arched across its breast above the water line.

"Do you want a fag, kid?" said Linda Preston.

"Aye, I don't mind," said Carter Brandon.

She took out a packet of Park Drive from her overalls.

"Oh Christ, I've only one left," she said.

"That's all right," said Carter Brandon.

"No, I'll cut it in half, kid."

"No, you have it."

She dug two long, pointed fingernails into the cigarette and pulled the two ends apart.

"Have you got a light?"

"No."

"You're a right useless chuff, aren't you?" said Linda Preston.

They sat smokeless and silent, staring into the canal, and, when the hooter blew, they walked back through the maintenance yard and the unloading bays.

"Pat's a bit snotty-nosed these days, in't she?" said Linda Preston.

"Is she?"

"I seen her yesterday, and she pretended she hadn't seen us."

"Did she?"

"She bloody well did, the cheeky cow."

"I shouldn't worry."

"Eee, I'm not worrying, kid. I couldn't give a bugger what she does."

She hooked her thumb in his pocket, as they walked down the yellow-distempered corridors. They stopped outside the machine shop, and Linda Preston ran the fingers of her right hand down his shirt front.

"See you at dinner tomorrow then?"

"All right."

"Tarra."

"Ta ta."

The fittings of the three great aunts from Glossop had been successfully executed, and the suit for Uncle Stavely satisfactorily altered. Catering arrangements for the reception at 'The Whippet' were in an advanced stage.

"I says to Enid: 'You'd best order fourteen dozen bridge rolls, luv. If you don't, these hungry arabs'll start eating your curtains,' I says," said Mrs. Brandon.

"Fourteen dozen bridge rolls?" said Mr. Brandon. "What are you doing—stocking up for a bloody famine?"

Uncle Mort, whose brooding silence had become more intense since his successful proposal of marriage, nodded.

"Fourteen dozen bridge rolls," he said glumly.

"You men! You've no idea about catering, have you?" said Auntie Lil, who was knitting a pair of bottle green socks for Uncle Mort.

Carter Brandon left to meet Pat outside the Town Hall.

He pulled up and pipped his horn sharply three times. Pat ran across to the car.

"Hello," said Carter Brandon.

"You're ten minutes late."

Carter Brandon started the car and drew out from the pavement.

"Where are we going then?"

"Please yourself," said Pat, looking fixedly out of the side window.

"I thought we might go to 'The Pack Horse'."

"Please yourself, I said."

They drove to 'The Pack Horse.' It was a stone-built inn with an inner courtyard of buckled flagstones and chestnut trees. It lay at the head of a shallow valley, which had once been one of the main routes for the pack horse caravans, bringing salt from Cheshire. A trout stream ran at the foot of the walled gardens. There were stepping stones and an old mill, in which a pair of grey wagtails was nesting. Higher upstream there were dippers.

Carter Brandon ordered a pint of black and tan, and for Pat he bought a Babycham. The cherry was gratis.

"Look, we might as well get things straight," said Pat.

"What do you mean?"

"I mean, are you serious about us getting married?"

"Course I am."

Pat pursed her lips and wound her watch rapidly.

"Well, you've got a funny way of showing it, that's all I can say. The way you spoke to me on the road to Glossop, I've never been spoken to like that before. Never," she said.

"I said I was sorry."

"Yes."

"I couldn't say more than that."

The music stopped, and a wasp flew in through the window and bumbled blindly above their drinks.

"Oooh a wasp," cried Pat, taking hold of Carter Brandon's hand.

The wasp settled on a beer mat and Carter Brandon hit it hard with the side of his hand. He picked up the pieces and dropped them in the ashtray. Then he screwed up the beer mat and let it fall on the floor.

"You see, Carter, luv, I mean, we haven't done a thing about a house or owt like that, have we?"

"No."

"Me mam says it's about time we got all that sorted out. She says time's running short, and I agree."

"Yes," said Carter Brandon.

"I mean, we haven't arranged dates. We haven't seen the vicar or owt."

"No."

"You see, there's the question of finances, in't there? Can we afford a house, or should we go into furnished rooms, or should we wait till we can afford our own house? There's all those sort of considerations to consider."

"Aye."

"Or we could go and live with me mother. I mean, there's a spare bedroom there, and it's all very well-furnished. It's not a year since she got that new fitted carpet for the back room, and she's got a right good electric cooker with barbecue attachment."

"I don't reckon much to living with your mother," said Carter Brandon, putting his arm round Pat.

She snuggled into his shoulder and then turned and kissed him under the chin.

"I love you," she said. "Do you love me, Carter?"

"Yes."

"Honest?"

"Yes."

"How much?"

"What?"

"How much do you love me?"

"Hey up, give over, that bloke with the greyhound's looking at us."

They sat there happily, watching the arrivals and departures of the public house's patrons. Then Linda Preston walked into the private bar. She was escorted by a young gentleman with long sideboards and bitten fingernails.

"Hey up, look what the wind's blown up," she said. Then she turned to her escort and said: "Get us a rum and pep and a packet of smoky bacon crisps, kid."

Pat stiffened and drew away from Carter Brandon.

"Budge up, kid," said Linda Preston, sliding on the bench next to Carter Brandon. "God, you've got right bony hips, haven't you? Hasn't he got bony hips, though, Pat?"

Carter Brandon coughed and hunched his shoulders. Pat sniffed sharply.

"What brings you here, any road?" said Linda Preston.

"It wasn't my idea," said Pat.

"Hey, you want to go into the concert room. It's beltin' music there, kid."

"We've got more important things to do," said Pat.

Linda Preston arched her eyebrows and wriggled her bottom on the bench.

"Have you really?" she said.

Her escort returned with the two drinks. One he gave to Linda Preston. The other he retained for his own pleasure. Then he turned his back on them and scratched his bottom slowly.

Linda Preston threw a packet of cigarettes on to the table.

"Help yourselves," she said.

"Ta," said Carter Brandon. He took one from the pack and offered it to Pat. She shook her head violently.

"I hope you've got a light this time," said Linda Preston.

"What do you mean—'this time'?" said Pat.

"Hey up then, kid, don't talk to me in that tone of voice. Don't try and get stroppy with me or owt," said Linda Preston.

"What's she mean—'this time'?" said Pat to Carter Brandon.

The escort turned and moved towards them, sucking his teeth and hooking his thumbs into his belt. He was wearing lime green luminous socks, and he had a wad of cotton wool in his right ear.

"There's no need to drag Carter into it, kid," said Linda Preston. "Honest to God, some folk. Honest to God."

She stood up, clicking her tongue. She gave her skirt three sharp tugs and turned to Pat.

"Pure as the bloody driven snow, aren't you?" she said. "Little Miss Virtuous. Little Miss Never-Had-It. Honest to God, some folk. Honest to God."

Then she pushed her way through the crowd, and, followed by her escort, disappeared into the concert room.

Dusk was dribbling down over the moors as they drove home. The gorse flared yellow across the valley. There was the smell of new-mown grass.

"You knew she'd be there," said Pat, when Carter Brandon stopped the car outside his fiancée's home.

"No I didn't," he said.

"Yes, you did."

"No, I didn't."

"Yes, you did."

"Mm."

Carter Brandon adjusted the driving mirror and yawned.

"Did I tell you I'm thinking of getting a radio for the car?" he said.

"A radio? A radio at this time?"

"What's up?"

Pat began to weep. It started softly, and then it developed into a thin, monotonous wail.

"A radio for the car when we're supposed to be saving to get married," she spluttered between the gasps and shudders.

Carter Brandon put his arm round her shoulders, and she turned and thrust her head into his chest. He could feel the tears on her cheek through his shirt. He ran his hand through her hair and lightly followed the line of her ears with his fingers. She had no lobes.

"I do love you," she said. "I do."

When Carter Brandon returned home, he found consternation reigned in the household.

Mr. Brandon had a gazeteer on his knees, and Auntie Lil and Mrs. Brandon were bending over an atlas spread out on the large drop-leaf table. Uncle Stavely was sitting on the sofa.

"We've just remembered," said Mrs. Brandon to Carter Brandon, as he stood in the doorway, "they haven't fixed up their honeymoon or owt."

"We've been so rushed," said Auntie Lil.

"What about this here?" said Mr. Brandon.

"What?" said Mrs. Brandon.

"The Bahamas."

"The Bahamas? I'll give you the Bahamas," said Mrs. Brandon. "Now come on, Les, get your thinking cap on and try to be a bit of use for a change. Come on, Carter, give your dad a hand. And you, our Mort, shift yourself, don't just sit there like a wet lettuce."

"Bloody hell," said Uncle Mort.

"How do you fancy the North Wales coast, Lil?" said Mrs. Brandon.

"I'm telling you, they'll not get in at this short notice," said Mr. Brandon. "I'm telling you that for nowt."

"Course they will," said Mrs. Brandon.

"Why can't we stay at home and go out on day trips?" said Uncle Mort.

"Because, Mort, this is supposed to be a honeymoon," said Auntie Lil. "It's supposed to be a week of blissful enchantment we shall cherish and remember all our lives."

"Oh, I didn't know that," said Uncle Mort.

"What about Colwyn Bay, Lil?" said Mrs. Brandon. "Arthur and Nellie from the Christmas Club have got a smashin' address there. Course, they always go late, but they have wonderful food, don't they, Les? Arthur says he's never seen such food. Second helpings and all."

"Aye, he's a right gannet is Arthur," said Mr. Brandon.

"Corporal Parkinson had nine honeymoons. Pardon?" said Uncle Stavely.

"I thought you was asleep, Stavely," said Mrs. Brandon. "Eee, just look at him. Just look at you, Stavely, your flies are undone."

Carter Brandon fastened Uncle Stavely's flies and wiped his nose.

"Who's Corporal Parkinson when he's at home any road?" said Mr. Brandon.

"He's my oppo," said Uncle Stavely. "He had fifteen honeymoons."

"Did he, be God?" said Mr. Brandon.

"He had a honeymoon in Ty-eeti. The girls don't wear no knickers in Ty-eeti."

"Now then, Stavely, that's enough of that sort of talk," said Mrs. Brandon.

"How do you mean, they don't wear no knickers?" said Uncle Mort.

"Mort!" said Auntie Lil.

"What's up?"

Auntie Lil dabbed the corners of her eyes with a small lace hankie. It had purple flowers embroidered in the corners.

"Now look what you've done," said Mrs. Brandon.

"I were only trying to improve me general knowledge," said Uncle Mort.

"He married a darkie from Madagascar," said Uncle Stavely.

"Yes, I'm sure he did, Stavley," said Mrs. Brandon. "How do you fancy Bridlington, Lil?"

"She were eaten by man-eating sharks."

"It's a bit cold this time of year, but it's very bracing, in't it, Les?"

"Mm."

Carter Brandon coughed, and the clock next door struck eleven.

"He's my oppo is Corporal Parkinson. Pardon?"

"Course, there's always Blackpool, Lil. There's always Blackpool."

"Aye, there's always Blackpool, Lil," said Mr. Brandon, yawning and stretching his arms.

"I think I'll take the dog a walk," said Carter Brandon.

"Bless him," said Auntie Lil.

The dog ran in front of him, snuffling in the gutter. A few large drops of rain began to fall. He turned up his coat collar and stood under one of the lime trees that lined the main road. Then he went home.

"It's all fixed up," said Mrs. Brandon. "Your Uncle Mort's

going to write to that address your dad and me had in Morecambe two years ago."

"Corporal Parkinson married a Chink woman with a
wooden leg," said Uncle Stavely. "Of course, that were in
Liverpool."

"In Liverpool, were it?" said Uncle Mort.

Carter Brandon went to bed and dreamed about blue-
birds and girls with no knickers, making day trips to New
Brighton.

CHAPTER NINE

On the day of the wedding Mr. Brandon's alarm clock
went off at six thirty-two a.m. precisely. It was a mariner's
brass-cased alarm clock that had served Mr. Brandon's father loyally and faithfully on numerous voyages to Ecuador
and the like.

As the bell rang the clock did a ratchety hornpipe on the
glass-topped linen basket. Mr. Brandon switched it off and
yawned.

"What's the weather like, Les?" said Mrs. Brandon, who
was wearing a pink nightgown and a green plastic nightcap.

"Eh?"

"Is the sun shining or what?"

Mr. Brandon peered out of the curtains, yawning and
scratching his navel. The crutch of his pyjamas was ripped
along the seams and a button had come off his jacket during
the night.

"It's a clear blue sky," he said.

"Good," said Mrs. Brandon. "I wonder how our Mort
slept at Mrs. Partington's?"

"All that nonsense about groom not seeing bride," said
Mr. Brandon, scratching his chest.

"That's you all over, in't it? No sense of the romantic,"
said Mrs. Brandon, and then she got up and went to the
bathroom.

Carter Brandon rose shortly after his parents. The dog,
which was lying at the foot of the bed, thumped its tail and
looked at him over the top of its eyes.

In the valley a slow, low sliver of mist followed the course
of the river and made feathery doilies round the mill chimneys. A cloud of black smoke hung over the marshalling

yards. A trio of mute swans wheeled over the mill lodge near the central abattoir and then dropped out of sight among the cooling towers and gasometers.

"Are you coming, Carter? Your breakfast's getting cold on the table," shouted Mrs. Brandon.

Mr. and Mrs. Brandon and their son, Carter, aged twenty-two years seven months, breakfasted on shredded wheat, bacon, eggs and fried bread, toast and lime marmalade and cups of tea.

"I see Freddie Trueman's in trouble again," said Mr. Brandon, taking out his pipe and pouch and rustling his *Daily Herald*.

"Now come on, Les, shift yourself. There's no time for smoking," said Mrs. Brandon. "Help me side the table, and I'll get breakfast ready for Lil and the others."

Carter Brandon picked up his father's *Daily Herald* and began to read. His mother came out of the kitchen and snatched the paper out of his hands.

"Now come on, Carter, shift yourself. There's no time for reading," she said. "Get yourself washed and shaved and changed. You've a lot to do before the wedding, you know."

Carter Brandon washed, shaved and changed himself and when he came downstairs, his mother was reading a letter.

"It's from Morecambe," she said. "She can do with them. She's expecting them tonight."

"Grand," said Carter Brandon.

"I told you it'd be all right," said Mrs. Brandon to her son. Then she shouted to her husband in the kitchen: "I told you it'd be all right."

Carter Brandon, dressed in his new lightweight Hardie Amies grey suit and his new plum and purple socks bought from Timpsons, sat on the sofa and picked up the *Daily Herald*.

"Now don't start reading again, Carter. Get yourself off to Pat's and bring her back here. She's not going to have all that time to see to our hair before wedding," said Mrs. Brandon, punching a cushion.

"Right," said Carter Brandon, and he drove to the home of his fiancee.

Mrs. Partington met him at the door and said:

"Hello, Carter, luv, come on in. Wipe your feet, there's a good lad. Oh, she does look lovely. I say it myself, and I'm her mam, but she looks smashing. Pat, luv, come on, hurry up, Carter's here. She looks a picture, Carter, she really does. Your Uncle Mort's not slept a wink all night, you know. I asked him if he liked a flock pillow or a feather pillow, and he said he weren't mithered either road. Well, I says to him: 'It's all very well saying that, but if you're used to a feather pillow, you'll not sleep on a flock pillow.' Pat, luv, what are you doing up there? Carter's here. So I give him two, Carter. I give him a choice, do you see? But he didn't sleep. He said he did. He says: 'I slept like a log, thank you, Mrs. Partington.' But I heard him up in the night at least three times. At the very least, three. And it might have been five. I'm a very light sleeper since Mr. Partington was took from me. I expect it's his nerves, you see. That's what it is, the groom's always nervous night before his wedding. I mean, there's nothing wrong with the bed. It's spring interior, you know. Pat, luv, shift yourself. Carter's bursting his boilers down here."

"Is that you, Carter?" shouted Uncle Mort from upstairs.

"Yes, Uncle Mort."

"I've lost me back collar stud."

"Have you?"

"Never mind, luv," shouted Mrs. Partington. "You can borrow one of Mr. Partington's. I'll come up and get it out of the dressing table for you."

Pat appeared at the top of the stairs. She ceased her downward trek momentarily, when she saw Carter Brandon, and then quickly recovered her composure and completed the descent without further incident.

Mrs. Partington said:

"Oh, she looks a treat. You look smashin', luv. Give us a kiss. Wait a minute. Turn round. Are you seams straight? Come here. No, turn round again. That's it. You'd got a hair on your collar, you see. You do, you look smashin' although I say it myself. Don't she, Carter, don't she look a picture?"

"Yes."

Carter Brandon turned to Pat, as they waited at the traffic lights at the junction of London Road.

"You look very nice," he said. And then he coughed and hunched his shoulders. "Aye, you look all right."

"Thank you," said Pat. She was wearing a light blue linen suit and navy blue shoes with matching gloves and handbag. She had pink petal earrings and a pink coral necklace. Her charm bracelet jangled as she rubbed face powder off her sleeves.

They were held up again at the roundabout near the Memorial Gardens. A man with a hose was watering the tulips. When he scratched the back of his neck, the stream of water wobbled.

"Hello, Pat," said Mrs. Brandon. "Will you have a cup of

. . . oh, you do look nice. Doesn't she look lovely, Les?"

"A little bobby dazzler she is," said Mr. Brandon.

"Oh, doesn't she look lovely, Carter? Aren't you proud of her?"

"Mm," said Carter Brandon.

Auntie Lil, dressed in housecoat and blue plastic curlers, was sitting at the table, eating her breakfast.

When she saw Carter Brandon and his fiancee, she put down her fork and began to sob softly.

"Now then, Lil, buck up, luv. Don't take on like that," said Mrs. Brandon.

"I was just thinking back to the morning of the day I married my Bob," said Auntie Lil. "I ate a very hearty breakfast, consisting mainly of toast and home-made lemon curd."

"Home-made lemon curd, eh? Les loves that," said Mrs. Brandon. "He always makes a right glutton of himself on home-made lemon curd."

"I don't know who was more nervous, me or me dad. Me dad was a conductor, you know. He had thirty-three years' service on the trains and he only retired on account of his varicose veins. He was the conductor of the Jubilee Year tram, you know."

"Was he?" said Mrs. Brandon, wriggling her fist inside the tea cosy.

"They made a special uniform for him out of navy blue barathea with red piping on his cuffs and trousers. The Lord Mayor shook his hand and complimented him on the way he held himself. I've got a photo of him in me trunk. Course, public transport runs in the family. Me granddad was a driver in the days when they had horse-drawn trams. He was killed under very tragic circumstances was me granddad. The horses bolted, and me granddad was thrown off, and the back wheels ran over his head. They said the horses took fright, when they saw the Zeppelin."

"Did they? Poor things," said Mrs. Brandon. "Come on, Lil, eat up. Your bacon's going cold."

Carter Brandon took the dog for a walk. They went to the park. One of the keepers was cutting the bowling green with a hand-mower.

"Haven't seen your Uncle Mort lately," he said.

"He's getting married today," said Carter Brandon.

"Poor sod."

The dog chased a tennis ball thrown for it by Carter Brandon. Then, when Carter Brandon's back was turned, it commenced digging a small crater in the football pitch.

"Hey up," shouted the keeper. "Your bloody tripe hound's digging up the football pitch."

"Come here! Heel! Heel!" shouted Carter Brandon. The dog slunk up to him and cringed at his heels. There was still soil on its nose.

Their arrival home coincided with a fresh outburst of ire on the part of Mrs. Brandon. The objects of her rage were the three great aunts from Glossop.

"But you can't wear your confirmation frocks," she was shouting. "We bought you new frocks special at Thompkinson's spring sale. Mrs. Pearson's altered them special for you. You didn't say nothing about wearing your confirmation frocks, when you had the fitting."

"We always wear our confirmation frocks at weddings involving members of the family," said one of the great aunts.

"That's right," said another.

The third remained silent, but nodded her head firmly in support.

"They can't wear their confirmation frocks, can they, Les?" said Mrs. Brandon.

"Eee, don't drag me into it," said Mr. Brandon, who was lathering his face in the kitchen. His braces were looped round his waist, and he was wearing odd slippers.

The three great aunts from Glossop sat in battle order on the sofa. Their confirmation frocks were made of satin and lace with puffed sleeves and tassels on the hems. The bosoms were smocked in red and green, and they wore white straw hats with white silk ribbons hanging from the brim. Their stockings were white, and their shoes were black patent leather with large silver buckles.

"I'm not saying you don't look very nice. You do, you do," said Mrs. Brandon. "But these frocks we've got you are more . . . well, they're more up-to-date."

"We always wear our confirmation frocks at weddings involving members of the family," said one of the great aunts.

"That's right," said another.

The third stood up, and her two sisters followed her out of the room and upstairs to the back bedroom.

"They look like the bloody Brothers Rotten," said Mr. Brandon.

"You're no help to me," said Mrs. Brandon. "You should have told them. You should have put your foot down."

"Aye well."

Mrs. Brandon began to vacuum clean the room. A shaft of sunlight that stretched from the window to the rocking chair was suddenly filled with slowly-revolving motes of dust.

"This dog, it's always moulting," said Mrs. Brandon. "Now then, Les, listen to me. Are you sure we've got enough drink in for those we invite back after the wedding?"

"I've told you umpteen times, yes."

"Yes, but you know what your Arnold's like. He'll go through a crate of Guinness on his own. And your cousin Danny's not behind the door, when it comes to supping."

"There's enough. Don't mither."

Mrs. Brandon turned her attentions to her son.

"Carter, come on, don't sit there, picking your nose," she said. "Get yourself off to the florist's and pick up the bouquets."

"Right."

"And don't forget the buttonholes," she shouted, as he was leaving the front door. "I don't trust that feller. He's boss-eyed."

Carter Brandon whistled to the dog, and it sat beside him in the front seat on his journey to the florist's. Its nose made tiny sticky patches of moisture on the side window.

Mr. Costain, greengrocer and florist, nothing but the best, quality his middle name, said:

"Here you are, four bouquets. Four bouquets. Right?"

"Right."

"Go on. Count them."

"Four."

"Right."

"What about buttonholes?"

"Now then, see here. I couldn't do you no carnations. No. You see, what it is, I wouldn't want to give you them. I wouldn't want to let them out of the shop. Do you see what I mean?"

Carter Brandon nodded. Mr. Costain was wearing a white jacket. In the lapel was the badge of the Territorial Army. A blue ballpoint pen was stuck behind his left ear. There were ink marks on his temples.

"See here, them carnations, them carnations is part of a duff assignment from the market gardens. Look at them. See that. All the petals is dropping off, do you see?"

"Mm," said Carter Brandon.

"Now listen to me. I can do you roses. White roses. Very nice, too. And very reasonable. Two and six a throw. Very reasonable is that for white roses at this time of year."

"Aye well, righto."

"Right. Well, you stay stood standing there, and I'll fix you up."

The shop smelled of oranges. In the window were three

pyramids of South African apples. A large strip of flypaper hung from the light fitting in the centre of the shop.

Mr. Costain returned with the buttonholes. He wore light yellow sandals. The big toe of his right foot was sticking out through a hole in his maroon socks.

"See, there's a dozen buttonholes. White roses. Right?"

"Thank you," said Carter Brandon.

Arrangements were well under way, when Carter Brandon returned with the dozen white rose buttonholes.

Auntie Lil's hair had been combed out from the curlers and established in its rightful position by Pat. Mr. Brandon was cleaning his shoes, the three great aunts from Glossop were sitting on the sofa, chewing Pontefract cakes. Mrs. Brandon was cleaning the front room windows with a yellow chamois leather cloth and Mrs. Warrender, the neighbour from number thirty-six, was giving a helping hand.

Mr. Brandon put on his shoes, stretched out his arms and said:

"Where's my *Daily Herald?*"

"I haven't moved it," said Mrs. Brandon. "It's probably where you left it."

"It is not."

"Well, I haven't moved it, Les."

"Bloody hell, I haven't even read it yet. I've not even started to read it."

"Have you looked under the sofa cushions?" said Mrs. Brandon.

Mr. Brandon disturbed the three great aunts from Glossop one by one and looked under the cushions still warm from their bottoms.

"It's not here," he said. "I bet you've thrown it out. I know you. Any paper lying round, and out it goes willy bloody nilly. You gave me call-up papers to the dustbin man."

"Now don't start that. I've enough on my plate without you mithering me about your *Daily Herald,*" said Mrs. Brandon.

"It's a lovely day for a wedding, in't it?" said Pat.

"It is that," said Carter Brandon.

They went out into the garden. Roses were blooming on the trellis. Two young starlings flew up from the bird table. A black cat with a white tip to its tail stared down at them from the fence. Carter Brandon tickled it under the chin, and it purred.

"I hope the weather's like this when we get married," said Pat.

The sun smacked on the greenhouse windows and stiffened

the shirts hanging on the washing line next door. There was not a cloud in the sky.

Pat took hold of Carter Brandon's hands. She stood on tiptoe and kissed him under the chin.

They went in, and Pat began work on Mrs. Brandon's hair.

Presently Auntie Lil came downstairs and stood shyly in the doorway. Everyone turned to her.

"Very nice, Lil," said Mrs. Brandon. "Very nice indeed. You look radiant. Right radiant."

Auntie Lil, about to be given in marriage by Mr. Leslie Brandon, was wearing a full-length empire-line dress of white embossed brocade with a matching train. She wore a head-dress with a three-tiered, shoulder-length bouffant veil secured at the front by a single rose.

"Serene, that's what you look. Serene," said Mrs. Brandon. "Now careful where you sit, Lil, you don't want to get dog hairs on your frock. Les, put a bit of newspaper on the Lloyd Loom chair, will you? That's right. Now sit yourself there, Lil."

Auntie Lil smiled meekly at the three great aunts from Glossop.

"I was going to wear the dress I wore at my wedding to my Bob," she said. "But I had to cut it up for curtains during the war. I've still got a piece, though, in my trunk. I'll show it you some time."

"You're putting on weight, Lily," said one of the three great aunts from Glossop.

Auntie Lil blushed, and Mrs. Brandon said hurriedly:

"Hey up, has anyone seen our Stavely?"

"When I finished dressing him, he said he were going to the lavatory," said Mr. Brandon.

"Nip upstairs, Carter, and see what he's doing," said Mr. Brandon.

Carter Brandon went upstairs and looked in the spare bedroom which was the temporary pied-a-terre of his Uncle Stavely. The bed was unmade. A pair of false teeth stood in a glass of water on the bedside table. The room smelled of hollow chests. There was no sign of Uncle Stavely.

He looked in the front bedroom, the back bedroom, the attic and the bathroom, but there was no sign of Uncle Stavely.

"Uncle Stavely? Uncle Stavely, are you there?" he whispered.

There was no reply, so he rattled the door handle and knocked more loudly.

"Uncle Stavely?" he shouted. "Uncle Stavely, are you in there?"

"What's to do?" his father shouted from downstairs.

"I think he's locked himself in the lavatory."

"Bloody hell," said his father, running up the stairs three at a time. He beat the door rapidly with his fists.

"Stavely, what are you doing? Stavely! Come on, open the door."

They were joined by Mrs. Brandon. Half her hair was in curlers.

"Stavely, Stavely!" she shouted. "Well, don't just stand there, Les. Do something."

Mr. Brandon kicked the door. Then he hit it hard three times with his bottom.

"He could be dead. He could be dying. He could have had one of his attacks. I know him, he's had one of his attacks. Where's his pills? Stavely, what's up with you, luv?" cried Mrs. Brandon.

"We'll have to force the door, that's all," said Mr. Brandon.

"Stavely, are you all right? Are your feet swelling?" shouted Mrs. Brandon. "Quick, Carter, get his pills. We'll shove them under the door to him."

"What's the matter?" shouted Auntie Lil.

"It's all right, Lil," said Mr. Brandon. "Our Stavely's playing silly buggers in the lavatory."

"Stavely," shouted Mrs. Brandon, hammering on the door.

"Don't panic, woman," said Mr. Brandon. "I tell you what, Carter, nip next door and get their ladders. You can climb up and get in through the window."

"He's not climbing no ladders in his new suit," said Mrs. Brandon.

"Go on, get off and fetch them ladders," said Mr. Brandon. Then he bent down and shouted through the keyhole: "It's all right Stavely. Hold on, lad. Our Carter's coming in to get you out."

"Can you see owt through the keyhole?" said Mrs. Brandon, banging on the door with her elbows. "Stavely, Stavely, have your fingers turned blue?"

Carter Brandon put the ladders against the side of the wall and began to climb. When he reached the lavatory window, he squeezed his hand along the frame until he found the catch. Then slowly and with difficulty he released it and opened the window.

Uncle Stavely was sitting on the lavatory. He was smoking a cigarette and reading a newspaper.

"Are you all right, Uncle Stavely?" said Carter Brandon.
Uncle Stavely turned and smiled.

"Oh," he said. "I'm sorry, I didn't know you wanted to use the lavvy. Have I kept you waiting long?"

"Is he all right?" cried Mrs. Brandon.

"Yes," shouted Carter Brandon.

"What's he doing?" shouted Mr. Brandon.

"Reading a paper."

Uncle Stavely pulled the chain and opened the door. He nodded to Mr. and Mrs. Brandon.

"I see Freddie Trueman's in trouble again," he said.

"Bloody hell, so that's where my *Daily Herald* went to," said Mr. Brandon.

Half an hour later the living room of the Brandon household was expectant. Mrs. Brandon had sponged down Carter Brandon's new trousers and sewn a button back on his new jacket. Mr. Brandon had made a pot of tea, and the assembly was enjoying the fruits of his labours.

Auntie Lil, sitting on the very edge of the Lloyd Loom chair, said:

"My Bob wore spats at our wedding. Dove grey spats. I thought he'd hired them, but it transpired later that they was given to him by his second cousin, who at that time lived in Port Sunlight and was later trampled to death in Uganda."

Mr. Brandon said:

"I like drinking tea out of a mug me. I can't stand drinking tea out of these fiddling little china cups."

Pat said:

"It's a lovely day for a wedding, in't it?"

One of the three great aunts from Glossop said:

"I'll swear our Lily's putting on weight."

The other two great aunts from Glossop said nothing.

Uncle Stavely said:

"After his wedding Corporal Parkinson discovered that this Chink woman's wooden leg was hollow. She kept porridge in it. Pardon?"

Mrs. Brandon said:

"Right, Carter, it's time for you to pick your Uncle Mort up. Now you know what you've to do?"

Carter Brandon said:

"Yes."

"You've to take your Uncle Stavely with you, pick up your Uncle Mort and drive straight to the church."

"Yes."

"Now there's to be no stopping off in pubs on the way, do you understand?"

"Yes."

"Now when you get to the church, sit at the front alongside your Uncle Stavely, because you'll most likely have to hold him up during the ceremony."

"Yes."

"Now you know what you've got to do, don't you, Stavely?"

"Pardon?" said Uncle Stavely.

"You know, they really neglect them at these old folks' homes. I don't think he's cottoned on yet, if truth be known," said Mrs. Brandon.

"I'm being best man at our Mort's wedding," said Uncle Stavely. "I've got to give Vicar ring and then I've to make a speech at the reception. Pardon?"

"Well, I don't know about speeches, Stavely, but you've got everything else right," said Mrs. Brandon.

"I'm making a speech," said Uncle Stavely.

"Yes, well, off you go with our Carter, and we'll see about that, when time comes."

Mrs. Brandon escorted Uncle Stavely and Carter Brandon to the front door. Then she said to Carter Brandon:

"And, whatever you do, make sure he's done himself up before you go into church."

"Mm."

Then she called to them, as they were getting into the car:

"You've plenty of time, you've a good hour. And remember what I told you about . . ."

She looked up and down the street, and then she mouthed in capital letters the word, *pubs*.

Carter Brandon drove by side roads to Pat's house in order to avoid the Saturday morning shopping crowds.

They drove through the quarter where the Pakistanis lived. The houses were drab, and there were many brown-skinned men in the streets, carrying string shopping bags.

Just past the Coronation Park main entrance near the pitch and putt course they were stopped by a policeman.

"Draw into t' side, will you, luv?" he said.

"What's up?" said Carter Brandon, seeing a fire engine turning into the road a few yards ahead.

"A bloody monkey's escaped," said the policeman. "It's bit a little lad, and it's up a tree now."

Carter Brandon opened the side windows and watched the firemen unfurl the ladder. One of the firemen adjusted the strap under his helmet and began to climb. An RSPCA inspector stood in the middle of the road, shielding his eyes from the sun as he peered up into the trees.

"Why have we stopped?" said Uncle Stavely.

"There's a monkey up a tree," said Carter Brandon.

The fireman reached the top of the ladder. He unbuttoned the top of his tunic, took a banana from his pocket and held out his hand. He signalled with his other hand, and the ladder was extended further into the tree. He caught his helmet on a branch and it was pushed to the back of his head.

"Corporal Parkinson once had a pet gorilla," said Uncle Stavely. "He taught it how to stand to attention and play the piano. Pardon?"

The fireman adjusted his helmet, and, stretching forward, pushed the banana into the foliage. Carter Brandon screwed up his eyes and saw the monkey, sitting on a bough close to the trunk of the tree. Its nose was twitching, its head was hunched and its eyes were flashing from side to side. It was hollow-chested and sharp-elbowed.

Gradually it shifted along the branch towards the banana held by the fireman, glancing over its shoulder every inch it moved. The fireman made 'tseeping' noises. The monkey paused, leaned forward and bit the fireman's thumb.

"Jee-sus," cried the fireman, thrusting his hand under his armpit. The monkey scampered back into the depths of his foliage. A few drops of blood spattered on to the pavement.

The policeman put his head by the window.

"Right, luv, single line. Drive slow, eh?"

Carter Brandon edged his car past the fire engine, changed gear and then swung up the hill towards Mrs. Partington's.

She said:

"Hello, Carter, luv, come on in. Wipe your feet. He's all ready for you. He's wearing one of Mr. Partington's back collar studs. He couldn't find his own. I says to him, I says: 'Are you sure you brought it?' And he says: 'Yes, I am, Mrs. Partington.' And I says: 'Well, it's a mystery to me because there's nowhere it could have gone to.' "

"Is that you, Carter?" said Uncle Mort from inside the front room.

"Yes," said Carter Brandon.

Uncle Mort appeared at the door. He smiled weakly and said:

"Now look at your tie, luv. Look at that knot," said Mrs. Partington. "Come here, let me do it for you. Stand straight. Lift your chin up. There. That's better. That's better, in't it, Carter?"

Carter Brandon nodded.

"Well, I wish you all the luck in the world. I'm sure you'll be very happy. If you're only half as happy as me and Mr. Partington was, you'll be very lucky. Very lucky indeed. Wait a minute. Look, you've still got the maker's tag hanging to the back of your jacket. There, that's better."

"Can I give you a lift to the church, Mrs. Partington?" said Carter Brandon.

"No thanks, Carter luv. I'm coming down be bus. I'm not quite ready yet, you see. Thanks all the same, though. Hey, I'll not know which side of church to sit on, will I? Bride or groom's, eh? I'll sit on the groom's side since I had the pleasure of him sleeping with me last night. Still, you don't want to be stood here gossiping. Off you go."

"Thank you very much for everything," said Uncle Mort.

"It's been a pleasure. Now off you go. And good luck to you, luv. Hey, and make sure best man's got ring."

As soon as they got into the car Uncle Mort said:

"Right, where's the nearest boozer?"

"Me mother said . . ."

"Give over. I'm not going into no church without some strong liquor inside me."

They stopped at a newly-built public house, called 'The Green Man'. They went into the saloon. It had green carpets and red, low-slung chairs. Above the bar there was a lobster pot and two brass navigation lights.

"Three whiskies," said Uncle Mort.

He downed his glass in one gulp and patted his stomach.

"Three more," he said.

They took the drinks to a table and sat down. Uncle Stavely spilled little driblets of whisky down his shirt front and upset the ashtray over his trousers.

"By gum, I'm nervous," said Uncle Mort. "There's all hell going on down there in me stomach. Me legs are like two sticks of jelly."

"Here's your buttonhole," said Carter Brandon.

"I've not been so nervous since Manchester United played Blackpool in the '48 Final. I were nervous that day. I trod on the dog's tail umpteen times—a thing I never do."

"If you get hiccups during the service, hold your breath and count up to ninety-nine," said Uncle Stavely.

"All this bloody nonsense about groom not seeing bride," said Uncle Mort. "I didn't sleep a wink last night what with sleeping in a strange bed."

"Corporal Parkinson always sleeps in a hammock. He swears by it. Pardon?" said Uncle Stavely.

"She's a funny woman is Mrs. Partington," said Uncle Mort. "She came and tucked me up in bed. I thought she was going to make me say me bloody prayers."

"And she can talk, too, can't she?" said Carter Brandon.

"Talk? She could talk the hind leg off a bloody donkey could that one. Yak, yak, yak all evening. By gum, you're taking something on, Carter, getting that one as your mother-in-law. What?"

"Aye."

"By, I'm right nervous."

They had three more whiskies and arrived at the church with a quarter of an hour to spare. Uncle Stavely handed round mint imperials.

"I thought they might come in handy," he said. "So I took a handful from the handbag of one of them old boilers from Glossop. Pardon?"

Carter Brandon sat next to Uncle Stavely. The sun glowed ruby and emerald through the stained glass windows. The vicar shook their hands. The verger sat in a corner by the organ, reading the morning paper.

The guests arrived and settled themselves in their places. The organ struck up the Wedding March, and everyone stood.

"Let this be a warning to you, Carter," Uncle Mort whispered out of the side of his mouth.

CHAPTER TEN

Everyone agreed that the wedding ceremony was most appropriate for what it set out to do, i.e. join Auntie Lil and Uncle Mort in holy wedlock.

The vicar conducted the service admirably and appealed most eloquently to the guests not to throw confetti in the road outside the church.

"Our good friends from the council do tend to look with disfavour on the extra burden of work given to our good friends from the cleansing department, don't they?" he said.

Uncle Stavely performed his duties satisfactorily, and Uncle Mort said "I will" in a clear, loud voice.

The guests were ferried by car to 'The Whippet,' where popular mine host, Bert Coleridge, and his popular better half, Enid, ushered them into the large party room upstairs.

Among those present were Uncle Arnold and Auntie Norma from Sheffield, cousin Danny, his wife, Dorothy, and children, Kirk, Grant and Karen from Doncaster, cousin Celia and that Mr. Coppersedge from Derby, Mrs. Partington, Frank Ashcroft (representing the Lacey Street Bowls Club) and Mrs. Frank Ashcroft, cousin George, who had brought his blue hankie, cousin Elsie from Bournemouth, Hants, Mr. Ivan Kiddling (ex-neighbour) from Egremont, and Mr. Cyril Stokesby (former colleague of groom). Teddy Ward could not attend owing to a prior umpiring engagement.

They were welcomed by Auntie Lil and Uncle Mort as they entered the large party room.

"Pleased you could come," said Auntie Lil to Mr. Ivan Kiddling, who, as usual, was wearing a pink silk bow tie with floral pattern. He had left his Anthony Eden hat on the back seat of his car.

"Aye well, ta," said Uncle Mort to cousin Elsie from Bournemouth, Hants, who congratulated him by affixing two large rubbery lips to his cheek and sucking violently.

On the walls of the large party room were photographs of darts teams and outings to the seaside. A large shield at the head of the room was inscribed with the letters, RAOB. On the opposite wall was a calendar with a picture of the Queen, under which was written, "Oughthwaites Ales Do You Good—By Gum They Do'.

The meal was most palatable. There was brown bread and butter and white bread and butter with the crusts cut off, salad, consisting of two slices of ham, one slice of brawn, three lettuce leaves, half a radish, and a whole tomato. Pickle and chutney were provided for those who favoured an element of piquancy.

"Eating all them pickles, you'll be burping all the way home," said Auntie Norma to Uncle Arnold.

After the salad came fruit salad and cream. The constituents of the fruit salad were most varied. Fancy cakes followed.

The waitresses, dressed in black frocks and white pinnies, were Mrs. Toothill and Miss Spinthett. They poured tea from a large, two-handled aluminum tea pot.

Pat smiled at Carter Brandon several times during the course of the meal, and Uncle Stavely upset his fruit salad over Mr. Brandon's lap.

Enid, wife of popular inn-keeper and ex-Green Howard, Bert Coleridge, whispered into Mrs. Brandon's ear:

"Is everything all right, Mrs. Brandon?"

"Lovely, Enid. Lovely."

"Are you sure?"

"That boiled ham, you must tell me where you got it from, luv. It were delicious. It just melted in your mouth."

The two waitresses cleared the tables with speed, decorum and courtesy. Cousin Danny lit a Panatella, and that Mr. Coppersedge from Derby put his hand on the knee of cousin Celia, also from Derby, when no one was looking.

"You'd better read telegrams and all that, Les," said Mrs. Brandon.

"I'm reading telegrams," said Uncle Stavely. "And I'm making a speech. Pardon?"

"Now, Stavely, you know . . ."

"Don't you 'now Stavely' me, Annie. I knew you when you was running round Dickinson Street with your drawers hung down round your ankles."

"Hey, hey, Stavely," said Mr. Brandon. "Less of that."

"I'm best man."

"Go on then," said Mr. Brandon. "You read the telegrams, you make your speech, and God help us."

Uncle Stavely banged on the table with a spoon and said:

"Silence! Now I'm going to read telegrams. Pardon? There aren't many, and I'm not surprised what with what they charge you these days. Any road, I think it's a waste of time meself. Pardon?"

Carter Brandon handed Uncle Stavely the telegrams.

"This one says, 'Many Congratulations On Your Union —Mr. and Mrs. Copson and Ida'."

Everyone applauded.

"This next one's got flowers all over it. It says, 'If You Can't Beat 'Em Join 'Em Stop If You Can't Join 'Em Beat 'Em—All The Best Tulip Street Old Comrades Association'."

Everyone applauded, and the laughter was led by Uncle Arnold, cousin Danny, Cyril Stokesby and Miss Spinthett, who blushed.

Three more telegrams were read, and Mr. Leslie Brandon made a short speech, proposing the toast of the bride and groom. Uncle Mort replied with two well-chosen words, and the clock struck four. A canary sang in a downstairs room.

Then Uncle Stavely rose to make his speech.

"There was an Englishman, a Scotsman and a Irishman. Pardon," he said. "And they was sat in this 'ere pub on the night before they was to get wed. Pardon? Any road, the Englishman says, he says: 'First thing I'm going to do on my honeymoon night is get a stiff brandy and soda.' And Scotsman says—I can't do Scottish accent very good—he says:

'Furrest thing A'hm a going to do on ma honeymoon neet is get a stiff double whisky, ochay.' Any road, this Paddy gets on his hind legs, and he says, he says: 'Sure and be Jaysys,' he says. 'Begorrah and Beyjaypers, first ting oim going to do on moi honeymoon noit is to get a stiff orange squash.' Well, the Englishman were right flabbergasted, when he heard this, and he says—no, hold on, it were the Scotsman what . . . aye, that's it, the Scotsman, and he says . . . no, it were the Englishman. I were right in the first place. Aye, the Englishman says: 'What's tha' want to have an orange squash for?' you see. And this Paddy . . . no, I've got it wrong. Corporal Parkinson knows the full story. Any road, the point of the story is when the Scotsman says something or other about his sporran coming in handy. Pardon?"

Uncle Stavely blew his nose and sat down for a few seconds to rest his feet.

"Very nice speech, Stavely," said Mrs. Brandon. "Very nice indeed."

"I've not finished yet. Pardon?" said Uncle Stavely, rising to his feet with a speed that astounded cousin Celia and that Mr. Coppersedge from Derby.

"I've known our Mort who's groom for donkey's years being as how he's Annie's brother," said Uncle Stavely. "In fact, I knew his dad first, when they lived in Gladys Terrace. His dad were a right villain, but I'm glad to say that Mort has not took after him. As far as I know, he's lead a clean and upright life apart from that time one Christmas Eve, when we found him pickled with his trousers seat ripped out in Abe Fairclough's allotment. And Lil, I've not known her for long, but I do know that when she wed that feller wi' big ears, she made him a good wife, so there's no reason to suppose she'll not do the same for our Mort, provided she don't let him sup too much. Pardon?

"Now then it's my task to propose a toast to the bridesmaids. Now I know some folk say they're a bit funny at times and hard to get on with, but they've always been all right with me. Any road, spinsters always do get a bit queer at their time of life, don't they? So raise your glasses and 'ave a drink to Mona, Mary and . . . what's her name?"

"Maud," whispered Mrs. Brandon.

"Mona, Mary and . . . I've forgotten her bloody name again. Any road, I give you 'the bridesmaids'."

The guests stood and raised their glasses, took a sip from the selfsame glasses and said, some softly, some loudly:

"The bridesmaids."

They had games and dancing. Uncle Arnold organised the

games, which, in the main, consisted of activities involving ping pong balls, balloons and dessert spoons fastened to pieces of thread. Cousin Danny operated the record-player, and Auntie Lil was driven back to the Brandons' by Carter Brandon to change into her going-away outfit.

While Auntie Lil was changing upstairs, Carter Brandon went outside and leaned on the front gate.

There was a heat haze. Children were playing in the streets with skipping ropes and whipping tops. The milkman was collecting empty milk bottles. His horse was troubled by the flies. It was a brown and white mare, called Dolly.

"How did it go?" said Mrs. Warrender, the neighbour from number thirty-six.

"All right," said Carter Brandon.

He set out with Auntie Lil back to the reception. She held her handbag very tightly.

"When I married your Uncle Bob, you was only a little boy, Carter," she said. "You was wearing a satin blouse, and you handed us a horseshoe on the steps outside the church and saluted. You was ever so shy, and your Uncle Bob gave you a silver threepenny piece."

"Did he?" said Carter Brandon, overtaking the lorry that sold mineral waters in their district on Saturday afternoons.

The lorry was stacked with stone flagons of ginger beer and sarsaparilla.

"I'd love a drink of sarsaparilla," said Auntie Lil.

"All right then, we'll have one," said Carter Brandon, turning left at the traffic lights into Derbyshire Road. He stopped outside the temperance bar, and helped his Auntie Lil out of the car. She took his arm, and they crossed the pavement.

The ball jangled, when they opened the door of the temperance bar and jangled again, when Carter Brandon closed the door.

"Will you have a pint?" said Carter Brandon.

"That would be nice."

"Two pints of sassy," said Carter Brandon.

It was cool and dark inside the temperance bar. The counter and fittings were made of varnished teak, the bare floorboards were springy and covered with a thin layer of sweet-smelling pine sawdust. There were herbs hanging from the ceiling. Rows of cordial bottles gleamed dully from the shelves. In the display cabinet on the counter were chunks of Spanish, boxes of liquorice root and corn plasters, packets of asthma cigarettes and sachets of sherbet. It was good to be out of the heat.

Auntie Lil sat on a high stool and took a sip from the sarsaparilla.

"Lovely," she said. "Lovely."

The sarsaparilla had a sharp liquorice taste and held deep inside it the chill from the stone cellars, where the barrels were covered in cobwebs, and mice played at night.

"We once went out on a hike your Uncle Bob and me," said Auntie Lil, taking another sip of sarsaparilla. It left a crescent of froth on her upper lip. "We took the train to Hayfield, and we walked as far as Jacob's Ladder and back. It was a lovely summer's day, and you could see for miles and miles. We didn't meet a soul, and we stopped by a stream to eat our sandwiches. Your Uncle Bob had brought a pitcher of homemade dandelion and burdock, and he put it in the stream to cool. We had cheese and cress sandwiches and slab cake. Your Uncle Bob always put mustard on his cheese, but I hadn't packed none as we weren't married yet, and I didn't know his personal preferences.

"When he took the pitcher out of the stream, it was so cold you could scarcely bear to touch it with your hands. We hadn't brought no cups, so we had to drink straight from the pitcher. It was so heavy your Uncle Bob had to hold it to my lips. He said: 'Aren't you going to wipe top after I've been drinking from it?' And I said: 'No.' I can taste the first sip I took from that pitcher to this very day."

When they returned to 'The Whippet', Auntie Lil said to Carter Brandon:

"Thank you very much, Carter. I did enjoy that. You're a good lad. Yes, you're a good lad to your mother and me."

They all gathered at the door to wave good-bye to Uncle Mort and Auntie Lil.

"Have a lovely time, Lil," said Mrs. Brandon, sniffing hard two or three times.

"Aye, that's right," said Mr. Brandon.

"I hope you'll not forget to return Mr. Partington's collar stud," said Mrs. Partington. "I'm not saying you won't, but, you never know, you might forget it in the excitement of your honeymoon."

Uncle Arnold lurched to the car door and said:

"Hey up, don't . . . don't do owt that I wouldn't do, Mort. Eh? What? Eh?"

Carter Brandon could hear Uncle Arnold's signet ring scraping on the car roof, so he released the handbrake and drove his aunt and uncle to the bus station.

CHAPTER ELEVEN

The days lengthened. Then little by little the days shortened.

The swallows began their second brood. A sudden thunder storm struck on the first day of July, and, when it passed, the streets were full of dead nestlings, mostly house sparrows and starlings.

Uncle Mort and Auntie Lil returned from their honeymoon. It had been most enjoyable, they said, and they had sent eight postcards.

Carter Brandon found an owlet one morning on his way to work. He kept it in a cardboard box in the garage and called it Bentley.

His mother said next morning over breakfast:

"I can't help worrying about your Stavely, Les."

"What's wrong?"

"I keep thinking of him in that Old Folks' Home. I'm sure they don't look after him proper. They're probably very kind to him and all that, but it stands to reason they won't look after him like his own would."

"Aye."

Mrs. Brandon buttered another slice of toast and spread it with some of the home-made lemon curd Auntie Lil had made during pauses in her post-honeymoon knitting.

"You see," she said, "be rights, he's head of the family now your dad's dead, and it doesn't seem right him being cut off from us like this in a strange house."

"Aye."

"I think he should come and live with us here. I've been giving the matter a lot of thought. We can easy do that attic up for him. It'll be very nice for him. He'll be good company for our Mort, and, if he gives me his old age pension each week, we won't notice no difference in the house-keeping."

"Well, you please yourself," said Mr. Brandon.

So it was decided there and then on a Saturday morning in July that Uncle Stavely should join the Brandon household.

During the lunch interval at the county cricket match on the same day Uncle Mort said:

"It's going to make the house right crowded, in't it?"

"It is that," said Mr. Brandon, finishing off his pork pie.

"Same again?" said Carter Brandon.

"Aye, go on," said Uncle Mort.

Carter Brandon brought three more bottles of Blue Bass, and they moved back to their places on the bench to applaud the players coming out after lunch.

"I'm not saying owt against Stavely, but he is a bit of a rum bugger, in't he?" said Uncle Mort.

"He always has been a strange 'un," said Mr. Brandon, pouring the beer carefully into the plastic beaker. "He never really got over Elsie whatshername back-heeling him like that."

The weather was overcast, and the ball was moving through the air. Occasionally it rose sharply off a length. Four wickets had fallen, and the visitors were still struggling in the middle seventies.

"I reckon that's why he went to sea," said Mr. Brandon. "He just upped and off one day, and first thing we heard of him was when we got a card from Goole three years later."

"Course, your old feller were like that, weren't he?" said Uncle Mort.

Carter Brandon bought three more bottles of Blue Bass, and they applauded several fine pieces of fielding by the home side.

"They want to bring the spinners on," said Carter Brandon.

"Spinners? Spinners?" said Uncle Mort. "You don't know what spinners are, lad. Hedley Verity, Cec Parkin, Tich Freeman—now they was real spinners. By God, they was. This lot aren't fit to lick their boots. They are not."

"Same again?" said Mr. Brandon.

"Hey up, you'll be having us on me ear," said Uncle Mort. "Aye, go on, give us another."

Carter Brandon drove them home at the end of the day's play and went straightaway upstairs for a bath.

Auntie Lil said:

"Mort, you've been drinking."

"I only had a couple."

"It's not right. Not with me in my condition," said Auntie Lil.

Carter Brandon met Pat outside the Town Hall, and together with Derrick Warrender and his girl friend, Jessie Lewis, and Tommy Coghill and his fiancee, Joyce Robertshaw, they went to a dance at the RAF club.

Music was provided by Wally, piano, Dave, drums, Lew, guitar, Ernie, sax-clarinet, and vocals were the responsibility of Beryl, companion of Wally.

Carter Brandon asked for the pleasure of Jessie Lewis's company in a waltz.

"Thank you," she said.

Tommy Coghill danced with his fiancee, and Derrick Warrender danced with a girl who worked in the poodle parlour in Back Hassall Street.

The music stopped, and Jessie Lewis held on to Carter Brandon's left hand, as they stood in the centre of the room. She had long legs and full thighs. Her front teeth protruded slightly, and her hair was blonde with tints of ash grey at the tips.

Carter Brandon slightly increased the pressure of his right hand on her back, and she pressed her thighs into him. He looked down at her, and she smiled and touched his chest with her breasts. They were well-formed breasts, tanned from the sun and firm from the tennis and swimming.

"Thank you," she said at the end of the dance and walked back quickly to her place. Carter Brandon followed and handed round his cigarettes.

"I like to see you dancing with other girls," said Pat, when they were sitting on high stools at the cocktail bar a few minutes later. The barmen wore white bum-starver jackets with Air Force blue epaulets.

"Do you?"

"Yes. I think it's only right that a feller should dance with other girls. I mean, it makes him appreciate his own more, don't it?"

"Oh aye."

"I mean to say, I know some girls what won't let their fellers out of their sight for a minute. And they're not even engaged like us."

"That's right."

In Pat's front room after the dance and after Mrs. Partington had retired for the night, Pat said:

"Take your work's outing to New Brighton just as an example. Well, I trust you on that. And I hope you'd trust me, if positions was reversed."

"Certainly," said Carter Brandon, removing her jumper and brassiere and pulling her down on the sofa beside him. She slid her hand inside his shirt, and they rolled from side to side as they kissed.

"You're still going on it, aren't you?" said Pat. "You haven't changed your mind or owt?"

"Course I'm still going. I've paid me money haven't I?"

He put his hand up her skirt and wriggled his fingers into the waistband of her panties.

Mrs. Brandon wrote to the matron of the Old Folks' Home and received a reply which indicated that the restoration of Uncle Stavely to the bosom of the family would afford her some pleasure.

Accordingly she set out by bus to make the necessary arrangements for the transfer of domicile of her brother-in-law.

Over a lunch of cold lamb and fried potatoes Auntie Lil said to Uncle Mort:

"Well, I've held my peace till now, Mort, but I think something ought to be said."

"So do I," said Uncle Mort.

"When my baby comes, I just won't be able to do with an old man round the house, coughing and not wiping his nose."

"Aye, he's always got a dewdrop on the end of his beak, I'll give you that."

"You see, Mort, facilities here aren't adequate."

"There's only one lavvy for a kick-off."

"But it's not just the hot water and washing and ironing I'm thinking of. It's the privacy," said Auntie Lil, popping an iron tablet into her mouth.

Uncle Mort fetched a tray from the kitchen and began to stack it with the dirty lunch plates.

"I think you ought to say something to Les before this goes any further," said Auntie Lil.

Uncle Mort met Mr. Brandon outside the factory gates and took him for a pint at 'The Griffon'. They sat by the old upright piano shortly to be replaced by 'Maurice at the Hammond Organ'. It was part of the brewery's modernisation plans.

"What's all this in aid of then?" said Mr. Brandon.

"I'll tell you what it is," said Uncle Mort. "It's Lil."

"She's not been took badly, has she?" said Mr. Brandon, filling his pipe.

"No. What it is she's kicking up a bit about your Stavely coming to live at our place."

" 'Our' place?"

"Your place."

"Oh aye?"

Uncle Mort undid three shirt buttons and refastened two of them.

"Aye well," he said. "I told her it's none of her business."

"You did right, too, Mort."

"Oh, I told her straight. I told her how we was only staying at your house by virtue of your good offices. I did that. Have another pint."

"Ta."

When Uncle Mort brought back the two pints of bitter, he found Mr. Brandon, leaning back in his chair and frowning.

"See here, Mort," he said. "You'd best tell Lil that I don't want no trouble in my house. I've had my bloody share what with your father living with us till he died and then her Auntie Madge all through the war and then cheese and pickled bloody onions."

"Aye, I'm with you there, Les."

"Mm. Well."

"I'll tell her. You leave it to me, Les. I'll tell her that. Aye."

Harsh words were exchanged when the men were met by Mrs. Brandon at the front doorstep and Auntie Lil in the front room.

However, a tasty meal of fried liver and onions followed by rhubarb and custard soon restored the good spirits of the company.

"Well, it's all fixed up," said Mrs. Brandon. "I saw matron and it's arranged that Stavely can leave next Saturday. So you can go over, Carter, and collect him in the car."

"I can't," said Carter Brandon. "I'm going on works outing that day."

"How are we going to bring him over then?" said Mrs. Brandon. "It's going to cause a right upheaval, if our Carter can't collect him."

"It'll cause a right upheaval any way, won't it?" said Auntie Lil, popping a vitamin pill into her mouth.

"I'll collect him," said Mr. Brandon.

"I thought you told me you was helping Teddy Ward put his greenhouse up?" said Mrs. Brandon.

"I'll collect him, I said. Now be told and give over bloody mithering," said Mr. Brandon. "Are you coming for a quick one then, Carter?"

"Right."

"I think I could manage another one, too," said Uncle Mort.

"That's all right, Mort. We'll have one tomorrow. I've something personal I want to talk about with our Carter."

"He's not going anyway," said Auntie Lil. "Not with me in my condition."

Mr. Brandon and Carter Brandon sat in a corner of the vaults away from the darts and dominoes players.

"Did I ever tell you what happened that time I left home?" said Mr. Brandon after they had sat in silence for half an hour.

"You told me a bit about it."

"Aye well, I stayed in lodgings at Kentish Town in London. I did odd jobs for the council, and I were unfaithful to your mother."

"Were you?"

"That's why I went to Stevenage. I met this lady in a pub in Willesden, and I yielded to temptation in Kensal Green."

"Oh."

"That's why I went to Stevenage."

"Who was the woman?"

Mr. Brandon knocked his pipe out in the ashtray and stood up.

"Well, I don't know about you, but I could do with me bed," he said.

They walked back in the dusk. As they turned the corner into the road where they lived, the dog came bounding out of a garden and jumped at them, wagging its tail. It sped off in front of them down the pavement with its tail between its legs. Then it skidded to a stop, raced back and jumped at their chests.

"Give over, get down. Get down, you mad bugger," said Mr. Brandon.

When Carter Brandon went into the kitchen to fetch a glass of water before going to bed, it got out of its box, stretched, yawned and wagged its tail limply.

Carter Brandon gave it half a digestive biscuit and scratched it under the chin.

That night in bed Auntie Lil nudged Uncle Mort and said:

"Well, did you tell him?"

"What?"

"Did you tell him about the upset Stavely's going to cause? Did you convey my feelings on the subject to him?"

"I did."

"What did he say?"

"I put my foot down in no uncertain manner and I told him good and proper. I give him a good piece of my mind."

"What's he going to do about it?"

"Go to sleep, Lil. You need all the rest you can get in your condition."

"Did you tell him about the hot water and the airing cupboard and the privacy and the . . ."

"Sssh. Sssh. You'll have the whole bloody house awake."

Linda Preston and Carter Brandon sat on the bank of the canal, feeding potato crisps to two cygnets.

It was lunchbreak, and the weather was still overcast. Great banks of purple-centred clouds were building up behind the distant hills, and the smoke from the mill chimneys hung low over the roofs of the city.

"I've got an owlet in our garage," said Carter Brandon.

"A what?"

"A baby owl. I found it on my way to work. It's a tawny owl."

"I didn't know there was no difference between one owl and the next me," said Linda Preston.

"Oh aye, there's tawny owls and barn owls and little owls and short-eared owls. Aye. You can tell a tawny owl because it's got black eyes, and it goes ke-wick, ke-wick, ke-wick."

"How does it go?"

"Ke-wick, ke-wick, ke-wick."

Linda Preston laughed. Then she crooked her arm round his neck and rubbed her nose against him.

They stopped outside the machine shop as they had done every day that week, and Linda Preston said:

"I've just realised, kid. A week this Saturday, and it's the works outing."

"Aye."

"Are you looking forward to it?"

"Not half."

She laughed again and kissed him on the neck. It was the first time she had kissed him. It made him perspire.

At the end of the corridor she turned, blew him a kiss and shouted:

"Ke-wick, ke-wick, ke-wick."

CHAPTER TWELVE

"You never told me you had a baby owl," said Pat.

"Didn't I?" said Carter Brandon.

"No, you didn't. I heard it from Jessie Lewis. She told me. She knew about it."

"How?"

"That's what I say. You tell me."

"Well, I never told her."

"No, and you never told me neither. It's a bit of a devil, when your fiancee's the last one to hear about you having a baby owl."

They were driving home on the Sunday of the week which was to contain the Wagstaffe and Broome Welfare Club outing to New Brighton.

They had taken tea with Pat's colleague at Maison Enid's hairdressing salon, Mrs. Vickers, who lived in a self-contained flat in another part of the city.

It began to rain, and Carter Brandon switched on the windscreen wipers.

"She's a funny one that Mrs. Vickers, in't she?" said Pat. "She's all sort of bitter and twisted, in't she?"

"Aye."

"The things she was saying about us getting married. Well, it's all very well, but I don't think it's right for a woman to talk about intimate things like that, especially in front of a feller who's not married."

"Mm."

The rain was drumming on the roof of the car and streaming down the windows. There was a steady dribble of water, running through a gap in the off-side rear door.

"I'll have to seal that up with Bostik," said Carter Brandon.

"I can't help liking her, though, can you?" said Pat.

"No, she's not bad. She's got a sense of humour."

"What did you think to them curtains of hers in the dining room?"

"I didn't notice them."

"They must have cost the earth. And you should have seen all the dresses and blouses and skirts she'd got hung up in her wardrobe. If you ask me, it's no wonder her husband ran off with a bus conductress. Poor devil probably didn't get enough to eat."

The rain stopped and they drove back to Pat's home along the steaming roads. They passed the Salvation Army band, marching to the Central Hall. A girl with rimless spectacles dropped her tambourine.

After they had kissed on the sofa, Pat said:

"You've not changed your mind about going on the outing?"

"No."

"Well, I can trust you, even though you never told me about the baby owl."

Mrs. Brandon took her son's brown mohair sports jacket and slim-line worsted trousers on Monday morning to the dry cleaner. And in the afternoon she went to the market and bought four rolls of wallpaper.

These she presented to Mr. Brandon on his return from work in the evening with the comment:

"When you've had your dinner, you can just get cracking on knocking that attic into shape for our Stavely."

Mr. Brandon and his son stripped the attic walls and then applied the new paper. Mr. Brandon did the measuring and cutting, Carter Brandon did the papering and Uncle Mort mixed the paste.

In the local that evening Uncle Mort said:

"By, it gives you a right thirst this work, don't it?"

"Work?" said Mr. Brandon. "You've hardly done owt bar dropping tacks all over the landing."

"Aye, I know. But that paste, it gets on me chest, you see," said Uncle Mort, emptying his pint glass and stubbing out his cigarette.

Teddy Ward came in and said:

"Hey up then, Les, I hear your Stavely's coming to live at your place."

"Aye," said Mr. Brandon. "Our Carter and me have done up the attic for him."

"What about me? Don't I get no credit for it?" said Uncle Mort.

"You? You've got two bloody left legs, you," said Mr. Brandon. "Honest to God, Teddy, he mixed some paste for me. Well, it were the consistency of molasses. You could have done a bloody tap dance on it, if you'd a mind."

"Well, if that's your attitude," said Uncle Mort, standing up and putting on his cap.

"Nay, sit down, I'm only joking."

"No, if that's your attitude, I'm off," said Uncle Mort, and, without so much as a backward glance, he made for the door. And, without so much as a forward glance, he tripped over the umbrella belonging to Mrs. Warrender, the neighbour from number thirty-six, and upset two pints of mild, a port and lemon and a glass of cloves cordial.

On Thursday evening Auntie Lil said to Carter Brandon:

"Your dad upset your Uncle Mort something grievous last night."

"He was only joking, Auntie Lil."

"Your Uncle Mort doesn't think so, and neither do I."

They were sitting in the temperance bar, drinking sarsaparilla.

Earlier in the evening Auntie Lil had said quietly:

"Do you know what I fancy? I could just fancy a drink of sarsaparilla at that temperance bar. Would it be too much of a trouble, Carter, for me to prevail upon you to take me? I don't want to impose on no one."

"Course, it's not too much trouble, Lil. Carter'll be only too pleased to take you, won't you, love?" Mrs. Brandon had said, and Carter Brandon had gathered up the pieces of the model Sopwith Camel aeroplane he was making and returned them to the old Welsh dresser in the garage.

A small boy came into the bar and bought two liquorice bootlaces and a blackcurrant ice lolly.

"Bless him," said Auntie Lil. Then she put her hand on Carter Brandon's sleeve and said softly: "Now I know you're a bit upset about your Uncle Stavely coming to live with us, Carter."

"How do you mean?"

"Far be it from me to interfere, but I understand exactly how you feel. It's only natural that a young man like you should resent the upheaval caused by an old man, who with the best will in the world can't be described as anything but cantankerous."

"I hadn't thought about it."

"I know it's going to be very difficult for you. He takes a lot of looking after does your Uncle Stavely, particularly in the sphere of ablutions. And he's very selfish with some very strange habits. A lot of the burden's going to fall on you, you know."

"Oh aye?"

"When things get very bad, just make allowances for him. He's an old man. He's set in his ways, and he'll probably feel completely at sea being on dry land after all those years he spent at sea."

"All right, Auntie Lil."

"I don't suppose wiping your nose was one of the things they taught them in the Merchant Navy."

They crossed the pavement to the car, and Carter Brandon saw Jessie Lewis on the other side of the road. Auntie Lil said:

"Who was that young lady, Carter?"

"Jessie Lewis."

"Is she a friend of yours?"

"Not really."

"She's a very attractive young lady, isn't she?"

"She's all right."

"She certainly seemed pleased to see you."

On Friday morning over breakfast there was a knock at the front door. Mrs. Brandon answered it and brought Derrick Warrender into the front room.

"It's Derrick," she said.

"Hey up, Dekker," said Carter Brandon.

"Shall you have a cup of tea, Derrick?" said Mrs. Brandon.

"No ta, Mrs. Brandon, I'm late already. I just called to ask your Carter what he was doing tonight."

"Nothing much."

"Aye well, Jessie was on the phone last night. She was wondering if you and Pat would like to make a foursome tonight."

"I don't mind. Aye."

"Right then. Shall we meet at 'The Whipping Top' about eight?"

"Fine."

Carter Brandon drove his father to work. It was raining, and people jumped back from the bus queues as they drove past.

They had the road up in Derbyshire Road, so Carter Brandon took the lower road, which followed the line of the river past the Moffat Street Parcels Depot and the old tram sheds. The water oozed brown and scummy over a rubble weir. A log had wedged itself against the lip, and entangled in its branches was a drowned lamb with sodden fleece and bloated belly.

"Your Auntie Lil's been complaining to your mother about your owl, you know," said Mr. Brandon.

"What about?"

"She says its hooting is keeping her awake at night."

"It isn't old enough to hoot."

"That's what I said. I told her it's its mates what's doing the hooting."

"You're right."

"Any road, it's none of her business. I told your mother that. It could hoot bloody Halleluja chorus all night, and it's still nowt to do wi' your Auntie Lil."

It was still raining at lunchtime, so Carter Brandon and Linda Preston lingered in the canteen after their lunch of Lancashire hot-pot and jelly and custard.

"It's going to be a devil, if this weather doesn't clear up, kid."

"It'll be all right."

Sid Skelhorn of the ginger hair and five children came to sit at their table. He had joined the firm two weeks after Carter Brandon.

"I'm going to have all me bottom teeth out this afternoon," he said.

"Aren't you coming on outing then?" said Linda Preston.

"Course I am. It'll be ideal for a liquid diet, won't it?"

They stood outside the machine shop, and Linda Preston said:

"Bright and early tomorrow, kid."

"Aye."

"And don't forget to wear your best mankin' clobber."

She skipped off and blew him a kiss from the end of the corridor.

"Where are we going, luv?" said Pat.

"I thought we'd go to 'The Whipping Top'," said Carter Brandon.

"Beltin'. We haven't been there for ages, have we?"

"No. Derrick Warrender said he'd be there with . . ."

"Jessie Lewis?"

"Aye. I sort of arranged to meet him there."

"I see."

They crossed the city boundary and dropped down into the undulating hills that held the pit villages. In the villages there were rows of colliers' cottages with the front doors opening straight on to the streets. The slag heaps were old and weary, and many of them had coarse shrubs and grass on their lower slopes.

"She's a funny sort is Jessie Lewis, in't she?" said Pat.

"I don't know owt about her."

Carter Brandon stopped the car by a hedge, and they got out to feed a couple of pit ponies, which were grazing in a scrubby meadow. One of the ponies was piebald, the other was chestnut. They smelled strongly, and the hairs on their muzzles were short and spiky.

"Well, she lives in a flat on her own," said Pat.

"What's funny about that?"

"I don't know. I'm just saying she lives in a flat on her own. Any road, let's change the subject, shall we?"

They arrived at 'The Whipping Top' at half past eight and found Derrick Warrender and Jessie Lewis waiting for them in the saloon bar.

"Shall we go on the dance then?" said Derrick Warrender. He worked in the Penny Savings Bank and had prospects of promotion.

"Aye," said Carter Brandon.

They found a table near the bar, and, after ordering drinks, settled down to enjoy the music of Ged Strong and the Diabolos, assisted in the intervals by the Les Botham Duo.

"Are you coming for a bit of a twist then?" said Pat to Derrick Warrender.

"Great," said Derrick Warrender, and they walked on to the dance floor hand in hand.

"Do you want a dance?" said Carter Brandon to Jessie Lewis.

"No thanks. I'll have a cigarette instead."

Carter Brandon gave her a cigarette, and she said:

"Thanks. Was that your Auntie Lil I saw you with on Thursday night outside the temperance bar?"

"Yes."

"I believe she's pregnant."

"You what?"

"Well, that's that Derrick's mother says."

Carter Brandon coughed and said:

"Well, it's news to me."

"She probably made it up. Gossip's a bit on the scarce side at the moment."

Jessie Lewis had long, slim fingers with clear half moons on the unvarnished nails. There were faint nicotine stains on her right index finger.

"How's your owl?" she said, smiling faintly at Carter Brandon, who was rummaging in the ashtray with a spent match.

"He's doing champion, thank you. He's beginning to lose his down now."

"Is it a tawny owl? I suppose it is."

"Aye."

"There used to be barn owls, where I lived. We used to see them hunting at dusk."

"Did you?"

"I suppose he eats quite a lot, does he?"

"Oh aye, he's a right gannet when it comes to his grub. He goes through a box of mealworms in a week, and he's very partial to dog meat."

"I'd love to see him."

"Aye well," said Carter Brandon, coughing and raising his right shoulder. "Aye well, you'll have to get Derrick to bring you round some time."

"Thank you. I will."

Pat and Derrick Warrender returned to the table. Carter

Brandon danced with Pat two or three times, but Jessie Lewis excused herself for the rest of the evening. She said she had a headache.

"You know how it is with us girls, Carter," she said.

She was wearing a pale blue sheath dress, and, when she bent forward to flick her ash into the ashtray, Carter Brandon could see her breasts moving firmly.

They drove home behind Derrick Warrender in his old open MG sports car. Jessie Lewis was wearing a headscarf.

The sky glowed red above the high moorland hills, and Pat said:

"It looks as though you're going to have a fine day for your precious outing."

"Why?"

"Red sky at night, sailor's delight."

"Me granddad was a sailor," said Carter Brandon.

CHAPTER THIRTEEN

The red sky at night brought a clear sky at morning. The day of the outing had dawned bright and clear.

Mrs. Brandon said to Carter Brandon:

"Are you sure you don't want no sandwiches?"

"No ta, I'll be all right," said Carter Brandon.

"I mean to say, if all the others are taking sandwiches, you don't want to be left out in the cold, do you?"

"I'll be all right."

"It'll be no trouble."

"The lad's told you. He doesn't want none," said Mr. Brandon, whose alarm clock had once more proved to be a model of punctuality and clarity.

"Are you sure you've got train times right?" said Mrs. Brandon to her husband.

"Yes," said Mr. Brandon.

"Now make sure our Stavely doesn't sit in no draughts, and don't forget to ask matron what his proper bed time is and what sort of underpants he's used to wearing."

"No."

"And, Les, make sure you get a corridor compartment."

"Yes."

"And make sure he's brought his pills."

"Right."

They were just about to leave, when Auntie Lil came downstairs, wearing a maroon quilted dressing gown over her nightie.

"I don't want to be no trouble, but I was wondering if your Carter wouldn't mind doing me a small favour," she said.

"Course he won't. What is it, Lil?" said Mrs. Brandon.

Auntie Lil was holding a small box camera. She had a brown canvas case slung over her shoulder.

"This camera was given to me by the girls from the Ointment Department to mark the occasion of my marriage to my Bob," she said.

"What a nice thought," said Mrs. Brandon.

"I'd like your Carter, if he would be so kind and if it isn't too much trouble for him, to take some snaps for me."

"Aye," said Carter Brandon.

"My Bob and I went to New Brighton several times, and I've nothing but happy memories of the place. We went with Edwin and Fanny Spencer one year, and my Bob took a snap of me, looking at the one-legged diver, who in days gone by used to dive from the pier. He also took one of me and Fanny sat on a pair of donkeys. At that time Fanny was rather on the portly side, and I chastised her for putting so much weight on such a small donkey."

"Quite right, Lil," said Mrs. Brandon. "You did right."

"I'd like our Carter to take some snaps of the sands and the prom. I don't want to impose."

"Righto, Lil," said Mr. Brandon, pushing Carter Brandon to the front door. "Leave it to him. He's a dab hand with a camera."

"Have a nice time then," said Mrs. Brandon. "And, Les, if you can't manage all the luggage, get yourself a taxi."

"Aye, and I'll ring you for advice, if me nose needs blowing," said Mr. Brandon.

The streets were empty. Speckles of sunlight glinted in the mortar of the soot-grimed buildings. A bag of chips had burst its seams in the gutter. Tiny, iridescent, self-contained flies sizzled among the cold grease. Pigeons puffed out their mantles, gurgled into their chests, goose-stepped and bowed. The station clock was three minutes fast.

"Enjoy yourself, lad," said Mr. Brandon.

"Right. Have a nice trip."

They parted, and Carter Brandon walked up the hill past the Postmen's Club and the Essoldo picture house to the bus station.

Herbert Lowfield from Dispatch was organising the departure. He wore a ginger Harris Tweed sports jacket, black Homberg hat and green corduroy trousers, and held a large gold pocket watch in his hand at arm's length. He had a black policeman's whistle on the fob chain.

"Brandon C?" he said, consulting his list.

"That's right. Aye."

"Coach Number four. Report to Albert Hollins."

"C Brandon?" said Albert Hollins.

"Aye. That's right."

"Seat number sixteen."

"Ta."

He climbed into the coach and found his seat. In the seat next to him by the window sat Linda Preston.

"Hiya, kid. I wangled it so's you and me could sit together," she said. She was wearing a black and white hooped cotton sweater and black volages. She had her hair dyed orange.

"Hey up," said Sid Skelhorn now minus bottom teeth. "Talk about belisha beacons."

"Hark at him," said Linda Perston. "You'd wonder where the bloody yellow went."

"Now then, me gums is giving me gip," said Sid Skelhorn.

The crates of beer were loaded into the boot of the coach. Herbert Lowfield blew his policeman's whistle. Connie Watkinson from Packing came running across the forecourt, holding her headscarf in place with her right hand. She clambered breathlessly aboard the coach, and Sid Skelhorn shouted:

"Come and sit on me knee, Connie."

And she replied:

"Me curlers'd all stick up your snitch, chuck."

And at that the six coach procession set off for New Brighton in the fair county of Cheshire, England, United Kingdom, Europe, Western Hemisphere, World, Universe.

"Do you want one of me sandwiches, kid?" said Linda Preston, resting her head on Carter Brandon's shoulder.

"I've just had breakfast," said Carter Brandon.

"Do you want another treacle toffee?"

"I'm still sucking the one you gave me."

"Do you want a Park Drive?"

"I've just put one out."

"Do you want a kick up the backside?" she said, and, laughing, linked arms with Carter Brandon.

They reached New Brighton just before eleven and climbed down stiffly from the coaches.

Herbert Lowfield blew his whistle and shouted:

"Let's be having you in a group. Come on, form your-selves in a group and have your picture took."

Ray Finnigan from Front Office took the photographs.

"Say 'Cheese,'" he said.

"Cheddar," shouted Linda Preston, and everyone laughed.

"Now then, listen this way," said Herbert Lowfield. "Coaches leave from here at ten-twenty prompt. Right! I'll repeat that. Coaches depart from here at ten-twenty p.m. dead on the dot. Right? Right, now we don't want no hang-ing round for laggards so we'll synchronise our watches. It is ten fifty-nine precisely three seconds from one, two, three, now. Right?"

"Daft pillock," said Sid Skelhorn.

"Now then, if anyone cares to join me, I'm going to Hoy-lake to visit me cousin," said Herbert Lowfield.

He blew his whistle, and the group broke up. Linda Pres-ton took hold of Carter Brandon's hand and they walked along the sands and over the causeway to the fort at Perch Rock.

There were herring gulls, circling and gliding on the warm currents of air. A flock of pigeons flew low across the river towards Waterloo and the sands. A lone carrion crow pecked among the sea-wrack on the water's edge. A little boy was sitting on the causeway, fishing for crabs with a length of string.

"In't it a beltin' day for an outing, kid?" said Linda Preston.

They went into the pub, where they had arranged to meet Sid Skelhorn for drinks and conversation. Eric Black, one of the Welfare Committee men, was playing the piano. He had removed his jacket, and Connie Watkinson was sitting on his knee, singing.

A party of ladies from Matlock was sitting at a long table, drinking bottles of Guinness and pale ale. A sailor was leaning against the bar, talking to the barman. Eric Black struck up 'All The Nice Girls Love A Sailor', and the sailor downed his beer in one gulp and left, muttering under his breath.

Sid Skelhorn bought more drinks and said:

"I had gas, you see. When I come too, dentist showed me this wisdom tooth. Well, the bloody roots was still twitching. They was all . . ."

"We know, we know. There's no need to set it to music," said Linda Preston. "Ooh he's dead crude him, in't he?"

Connie Watkinson slipped off Eric Black's knee and lay on her back on the floor, kicking and giggling.

"Hey up, she's wearing red 'uns," shouted Sid Skelhorn.

"Cheeky monkey," she said, as she climbed back on to Eric Black's knee.

"Do you know 'Bless This House', luv?" said one of the ladies from Matlock.

Eric Black ran his thumb from right to left across the keyboard, and Sid Skelhorn stood up and sang:

"Herbless herthis house ho herLord herwe herpray,

"Hermake hit hersafe herby hernight and herday."

Someone threw a beermat, and the landlord said:

"Hey, buggerlugs, you can dut dat out for a start off."

"It was only fun," said Sid Skelhorn.

"Dat's what I say, you can currit out," said the landlord.

Linda Preston bought Carter Brandon a red cardboard fez, when they left the pub.

"It suits you, kid," she said. "Honest, it does."

"He looks . . . he looks like bloody King Farouk," said Sid Skelhorn, and then he began to sing:

"King Farouk, King Farouk,

"We'll hang his . . ."

"Thank you, thank you, Mario Lanza," said Linda Preston. "A little of that goes a bloody long way."

They dodged into a shop doorway and watched Sid Skelhorn reeling away down the prom. He had half a bottle of whisky sticking out from his hip pocket.

"Let's go for a trip on ferry boat," said Linda Preston. She put her arm round Carter Brandon's waist and steered him to the landing stage.

They boarded the ferry boat, which moved away past a dredger and turned for Liverpool. The New Brighton lifeboat, moored near the landing stage, pitched and tossed in its wake.

They went to the top deck, and the river breeze ruffled their hair and made their eyes water. Behind them on the horizon were the big ships, coming in with the tide across the Mersey Bar.

"I love a boat trip me," said Linda Preston.

They leaned over the rails and watched the docks slip past. Through the cranes and derricks they could see the red and black smoke stacks of the Cunarders, the blue and black stacks of the Alfred Holt ships, which sailed to the Philippines and the Far East, and the yellow stacks of the Elder Dempster line, whose ships sailed to the ports of West Africa.

They moved into the bows. The sun beat down on them and made rainbows in the spray. An Isle of Man steamer was tied up at the Pier Head. As they passed, a sailor hauled down the Blue Peter.

"Shall we have a look at Liverpool then, kid?" said Linda Preston.

They spent a pleasant afternoon wandering round the city. There were fine Georgian houses round the Anglican cathedral and railway lines along the Goree, where the Overhead Railway once ran.

"They used to call it 'The Dockers' Umbrella'," said Carter Brandon.

"Eh?"

"They called the Overhead Railway 'The Dockers' Umbrella', because the dockers could walk underneath it when it rained and not get wet."

"Get out."

"Aye, me granddad told me that."

They had a cup of tea and a bun and sat on a bench at the Pier Head. A small Dutch coaster passed in front of them, making its way upstream to the Manchester Ship Canal. It was followed shortly after by a boat, bringing Guinness from Dublin.

"How's the love life, kid?" said Linda Preston.

"What do you mean?"

"Is our Pat still keeping you short?"

"Pardon?"

"You're not getting your ration, are you, kid?"

Moored in mid-stream was a tanker in ballast. A man in blue dungarees emptied a gash bucket into the water, and three young herring gulls and a lesser black-backed gull squabbled among the litter.

"Tell me something, kid," said Linda Preston.

"What?"

"Have you ever had it?"

"Aye well."

"You haven't, have you? I can see it in your face. You haven't."

Carter Brandon coughed and hunched his shoulders.

"You haven't had it, have you? You poor sod."

They watched a Canadian Pacific liner manoeuvre alongside the landing stage. Three tugs nudged and pulled. Two men in a rowing boat sculled rapidly into the gap between the liner and the dummy barges. Ropes were thrown to them, and they passed them to the men on the stage. Then, as the liner edged slowly into the barges, the men sculled away into open water.

"They want danger money for that, kid," said Linda Preston.

They had fish and chips for supper. The chips, made in a coke-fired frier, were crisp and golden.

"Bloody yum yum," said Linda Preston, and they travelled back to New Brighton by the Underground Railway.

They walked back hand in hand to the coaches. They could smell the salt from the river, and the evening breeze off the Irish Sea chilled them. Carter Brandon put his arm round Linda Preston.

"Hey up. Pat'd burst fifty bloody blood vessels, if she could see us now," said Linda Preston.

"Aye, she would that."

"She's a good kid really, you know, when she's not playing her Lady Bountiful act. You want to hang on to her."

The crates of beer were stacked on the back seat, and no one stinted himself or herself in using their contents. Just outside Warrington the men stopped the coach in a lay-by, and all the girls turned their heads away except Connie Watkinson, who said:

"I think Bernard Garside's got the biggest."

Linda Preston curled herself up on the seat beside Carter Brandon and pressed her body into him. He blew softly into her ear, and she shuddered.

Connie Watkinson threw one of her curlers at Albert Hollins. It caught the rim of his right ear and made it bleed.

"Hey up, you bloody near took me ear off. Give over frigging about," said Albert Hollins.

"Ah, bless his little cotton socks," said Sheila Warburton.

"Ah, bless his little cotton socks," said all the other girls.

"Aye, it's all very well to take the piss like that," said Albert Hollins, "but I had an operation on that ear, when I were twelve."

Linda Preston put her arms round Carter Brandon's neck and pulled him down beside her. She kissed him fiercely and ran her hands up and down his thighs. She had a strong, wiry grip, and her teeth were small and sharp. She nipped Carter Brandon's tongue hard, and he broke free from her arms and said:

"Loody Lell."

They drew into the bus station at one o'clock in the morning. It was raining. Two policemen in capes stood in the shadows, watching them descend from the coaches.

"Well, tarra then," said Carter Brandon.

"No, you don't, kid," said Linda Preston. "You can bloody well tek us home be taxi."

Linda Preston lived in a row of hunch-backed terraced houses near the old Midland Railway warehouse. The street lamps were out, and it was pitch dark. There was a faint smell of gas. The moon shone briefly through the rain clouds, and Carter Brandon saw a motor cycle and sidecar with broken axle squatting on the cobbles outside her house.

"That's our Eddie's," she said.

She put her key in the front door, and Carter Brandon said:

"Well, tarra then."

"No, you don't, kid," said Linda Preston.

She held him firmly by the arm and dragged him into the house. She opened the door of the back room and pushed him inside. The table had not been cleared, and there were cigarette stubs on the stained rug in front of the black-leaded range.

"What about your mum and dad?" said Carter Brandon.

"Me mam's dead drunk, and the old feller's in the sanatorium," she said.

She drew the curtains and kicked a pile of dirty washing into the corner.

"Well, then," she said, placing her hands on her hips.

"Aye well," said Carter Brandon.

"You haven't, have you?"

"Mm."

"All right, kid," she said, taking off her clothes rapidly. "Now's your chance to break your duck."

Then she undressed Carter Brandon and seduced him among the stains and cigarette stubs on the threadbare rug.

When Carter Brandon got home, he realised he had lost his Auntie Lil's camera.

Next morning Uncle Stavely, who had been conducted to the house by Mr. Brandon without incident, burned a hole in his eiderdown with a cigarette.

"And that's only a start," said Auntie Lil to Mrs. Brandon.

Mr. Brandon watered his tomatoes, Uncle Mort read the *Sunday Pictorial*, the *News of the World*, *The People* and *Reynolds News*.

Mrs. Brandon peeled potatoes and mixed the batter for the Yorkshire pudding, and Auntie Lil stayed in bed until it was time for lunch.

In the evening Jessie Lewis came to see Carter Brandon's owlet.

CHAPTER FOURTEEN

"That's it then. It's all over," said Pat.

They were standing outside the Town Hall on the Monday evening after the outing to New Brighton. Carter Brandon took her arm and pushed her into his car. As soon as they were inside the car Pat said:

"Here's your ring back. As far as I'm concerned the engagement's off. Finished. Finito."

"What are you talking about?"

"You know perfectly well what I'm talking about."

"No, I don't."

"You're not fit to be engaged you. Mankin' round with another woman, when you're supposed to be engaged to me."

"If you're talking about the outing, nothing happened. Nothing," he said.

"I know. I'm not talking about that. I'm talking about Jessie Lewis."

"What?"

"You might well look like that. You must think I'm simple or summat. You must think I'm blind. I've seen the way you've been chasing her. I've seen the way you was dancing with her at the RAF club. I've seen the way you was talking to her at 'The Whipping Top'. Don't tell me that little meeting were an accident."

"Derrick Warrender fixed it up."

"Pull the other one, kid, it's got bells on. And what about yesterday? I suppose Jessie Lewis didn't come round to see your owl, did she? I suppose you'll be saying that's another figment of my imagination."

"How did you know about that?"

"And I suppose you didn't meet her outside the temperance bar the other night, did you?"

"I only waved to her."

"I've talked it over with me mam, and we've decided. It's no use carrying on no longer. You can have your ring back, and we'll finish here and now."

She placed the engagement ring in the glove compartment and turned her face away from Carter Brandon. Her stockings rasped as she crossed her legs.

Carter Brandon leaned across her and opened the door.

"Tarra," he said.

"Is that all . . ."

"Tarra."

She slammed the door behind her, and the car rocked slowly on its springs. Carter Brandon watched her through his driving mirror. When she reached the High Street, she stopped and glanced over her shoulder at his car.

He made a swift three-point turn and drove slowly towards her. She turned away, but he knew she was watching his reflection in a shop window. He turned left into the High Street and drove off.

When he told his mother the news later that evening, she said "Oh dear" and went into the kitchen for a quiet weep.

"Corporal Parkinson's a expert on engagements," said Uncle Stavely. "He were engaged to five women at the same time. He'd one in Leith, one in Bicester, one in Newton Abbot, one in Mesopotamia and one in Darlington. Then the Boer War broke out in South Africa, and he married a Hottentot instead. Pardon?"

Carter Brandon went into the garage and gave his owlet a dead mouse he had found lying on its side by his father's compost heap. The owlet stared at the mouse and clicked its beak.

"Come on, Bentley, it's a nice mouse," said Carter Brandon.

The owlet fluffed out its feathers and shook itself.

"Don't you want it?"

The owlet hopped off Carter Brandon's wrist and fluttered unsteadily to one of the beams in the garage. It hunched its shoulders and closed its eyes.

A light was burning in Auntie Lil's bedroom. She had made only one sortie from it since the arrival of Uncle Stavely and the report of the loss of her camera.

July came and Auntie Lil's stomach began to show signs of the developing foetus contained therein. Uncle Mort sat in the front room most of the day, cleaning shoes. Mr. Brandon won a silver goblet in a handicap bowls tournament.

One day the doctor came to visit Auntie Lil.

"Good morning," he said. "How are you feeling today?"

"Not too good," said Auntie Lil weakly. A half empty glass of barley water stood beside her on the bedside table.

"She'll not leave the room, doctor. I keep telling her it's unhealthy. She wants to exercise her tummy muscles," said Mrs. Brandon. "She wants to get some fresh air into her lungs."

The doctor examined Auntie Lil carefully and said:

"What seems to be the trouble?"

"Nothing much," said Auntie Lil. "I can't put a name to it."

"She wants to get some colour in her cheeks," said Mrs. Brandon.

"I wonder if you'd mind leaving the room for a moment, Annie, while I discuss something personal with doctor," said Auntie Lil.

"Not at all, Lil. Not at all," said Mrs. Brandon. "If you want anything, doctor, just give us a shout. I'll only be in the kitchen."

"Now then," said the doctor, when Mrs. Brandon had left the room.

"It's Stavely," said Auntie Lil. "Stavely is Mr. Brandon's eldest brother."

"I see."

"Well, he's putting the evil fluence on my unborn child."

"Pardon?"

"I can feel it as I lie in bed at nights. Inside me. Waves of evil fluence passing into me from Stavely's bedroom. They come through the ceiling, down the light fitting, straight through the coverlet and then into my womb."

"I see."

"I know about these things, you know. I'm in constant touch with the supernatural. At certain times there's not a thing you can tell me about what's going on in The Other Side. I warned my Bob not to go to the whippet meeting on the day he died. But he ignored me, and fate, not to be denied, took him from me through the agency of a runaway grand piano."

The doctor said to Mrs. Brandon, as they were drinking tea in the front room:

"They all go through this stage, and at her age we must be very careful and very understanding."

"Yes, doctor."

"Her heart's A1, and the rest of her's bang on, too."

"Yes, doctor."

"I've persuaded her to get out of bed."

"Yes, doctor."

"You see, it's her mental state that's a trifle dicey, so it's up to you to keep her mind occupied."

"Yes, doctor."

"Does she do the pools?"

"No, doctor."

"That's worth a thought then. Get her cracking on the

Australian football pools. One of my expectant mums got a third divvy last week, you know. Twenty-five smacker."

"I'll get the coupons straight away," said Mrs. Brandon.

In the evening, as they were sitting in the local playing dominoes, Uncle Stavely said to Uncle Mort:

"Your Lil's putting the evil fluence on me."

"You what?" said Uncle Mort, dropping two dominoes on the floor and knocking the peg board with his elbow.

Uncle Stavely laid the six-three domino on the opposite end to the double six and said:

"That's right, Mort. Come on, mark up eight on the peg board."

Carter Brandon moved the peg eight places on the board, and then he tapped the side of his hand on the table.

"Knocking," he said.

"What are you insinuating about Lil?" said Uncle Mort.

"She's putting the evil fluences on me," said Uncle Stavely. "They're coming from her unborn child. Pardon?"

"He's pots for rags. He's going off his bloody beanpole," said Uncle Mort.

"I can feel it at dead of night," said Uncle Stavely. "It comes from her womb. Then it comes up through the coverlets, works its way up the light fitting, seeps through the floorboards and attacks me as I lay in bed. Pardon?"

Mr. Brandon wiped his nose with his hand, and Carter Brandon knocked on the table and said:

"Knocking."

Uncle Mort threw his dominoes on the table, put on his cap and left, uttering these words:

"Right off his bloody beanpole, he's going."

"It always comes does this evil fluence, when the owl starts hooting," said Uncle Stavely. "Right, shall we have a game of three-handed? Pardon?"

It was the evening of Auntie Lil's first day out of bed since the visit of the doctor. The Brandon household was sitting in the front parlour.

"I don't blame you about the loss of the camera, Carter," said Auntie Lil. "It was fate intervening once more."

"That's right, Lil," said Mrs. Brandon.

"I'm sure it's found its way to a good home. It's probably being looked after with almost as much care and devotion as I lavished on it for all them years."

"I'm sure it is, Lil," said Mrs. Brandon.

"Corporal Parkinson's got a picture of the last Tsar of all Russia riding a camel in state," said Uncle Stavely.

Uncle Mort sat silently in a corner, polishing Mr. Brandon's best brogues. At his feet he had a box full of old, uncleaned shoes and boots.

"My Bob said that when we had issue, he was going to buy one of them plate cameras with flash attachment. He'd got it all planned out. If the light were good, he weren't going to use no artificial lighting. He'd just sit our child naked on the rug and take a photo of him, so we could stick it in our album and cherish it and look at it, when our child left home to make his own way in the world. Only if the lighting weren't good, was he going to use the flash attachment. That's why he was going to buy it, just to be on the safe side."

That night in bed Auntie Lil turned to Uncle Mort and said:

"It's starting, Mort. The evil fluence is starting. Can't you feel it? Can't you hear it dripping from the ceiling and seeping through the coverlet?"

Uncle Mort switched on the light and put his arm round Auntie Lil's shoulder.

"No, don't touch me. Don't touch me. You'll catch it yourself, and then you'll be done for."

Upstairs in the attic Uncle Stavely tossed and turned in his bed. Then he pulled back the sheets, put on his old dressing gown and hammered on the floor with the heel of his boot.

"What's that?" said Uncle Mort.

"Ke-wick, ke-wick, ke-wick," went a tawny owl from somewhere in the back garden.

Carter Brandon drove Uncle Mort to the Lacey Street Bowls Club and watched him play a doubles match in partnership with Frank Ashcroft.

Afterwards they drove to 'The Griffon', where they had arranged to meet Mr. Brandon, who was working overtime.

They drank pints of black and tan and sat in silence until Uncle Mort said:

"I wonder what's happened to that lass our Cyril put in the family way?"

"She's married. She married this Indian what runs a restaurant. She's expecting another nipper."

Uncle Mort rubbed his chin with his right hand and nodded.

"I wonder if she's suffering from the evil fluence?" he said.

At half past nine Mr. Brandon came into 'The Griffon'. He was accompanied by Jessie Lewis.

"I hope you don't mind, but I just met Mr. Brandon outside, and I'm gasping for a drink," she said.

"Sit yourself down, luv. What'll you have?" said Uncle Mort.

Jessie Lewis drank a half pint of shandy, and, when she had finished, she said:

"Hello, Carter."

"Hello."

She had a canvas bag with the handle of a tennis racket, sticking out from the end. There was a faint patch in the sun tan round her ankles, where she had been wearing ankle socks.

"I haven't seen you for ages, Carter," she said.

"Mm."

"Are you still going round with Derrick Warrender?" said Mr. Brandon.

"Off and on."

"Time, you lads. Time, please. Time, you lads," shouted a barman, ringing a brass handbell as he made his way through the various rooms of the pub. "Time, you lads, please. Haven't you no bloody homes to go to?"

They stood on the pavement outside 'The Griffon'. A fire engine bell clanged in the distance. A pigeon flew above their heads and landed on a ledge behind a neon sign. Its feet scuttered on the stonework in the shadows, and it lost its hold and flew off, banking steeply to avoid the trolley bus wires.

"Aye well," said Carter Brandon, coughing and hunching his shoulders. "Can we give you a lift home then?"

"No thanks," said Jessie Lewis. "I live miles out of your way."

July gave way to August, and the weather broke.

CHAPTER FIFTEEN

One rainy evening in early August Uncle Stavely said: "I shall want four brass hooks for a hammock, a spirit stove and a chemical lavatory."

"What for, Stavely?" said Mrs. Brandon.

"For Corporal Parkinson."

"For Corporal Parkinson?" said Mr. Brandon.

"He's coming to live with me," said Uncle Stavely. "He's my oppo. Pardon?"

Auntie Lil put down her knitting, packed it carefully in her raffia bag and left the room. Shortly afterwards Uncle Stavely retired to bed, and Mrs. Brandon said to her husband:

"Well, what do you make of that?"

"A chemical lavatory!" said Mr. Brandon. "He'll blow the whole bloody house up."

Next morning Mrs. Brandon said as she was packing her husband's sandwiches:

"Well, I can't see no harm in it really. It'll be company for our Stavely, and if this here Corporal Parkinson gives me his old-age pension, it won't make no difference to the house-keeping."

"Please yourself," said Mr. Brandon.

The sun made a watery appearance in the afternoon as Uncle Mort, Auntie Lil and Uncle Stavely were sitting in the front room.

Auntie Lil was knitting a pink hot water bottle cover, Uncle Mort was cleaning Carter Brandon's tennis pumps and Uncle Stavely was sucking a domino.

Uncle Mort went into the hall and tapped the barometer. When he came back, he said:

"Changeable."

Mrs. Brandon brought them tea and arrowroot biscuits on a tray.

"Does anyone mind if I dunk me biscuits?" said Uncle Mort.

Auntie Lil switched off the knitting machine and turned to Mrs. Brandon.

"Well, what's the decision?" she said.

"If he wants, he can have Corporal Parkinson to stay with him," said Mrs. Brandon.

Auntie Lil took out a lime green silk handkerchief from her handbag and began to sob softly.

"If my Bob were here, he wouldn't stand for it," she said. "He'd have put his foot down long ago."

"Now then, Lil, don't take on," said Mrs. Brandon.

"You're just trying to destroy our child," said Auntie Lil. "There's none of you really want it. You're all jealous because me and my Bob are having a baby at our age."

And she stood up and left the room, bound for the stairs, and ultimately her bedroom.

Uncle Stavely said:

"It'll have to have strong hooks, because he's a very restless sleeper is Corporal Parkinson."

Auntie Lil was still sobbing when she was joined in the marital bed by Uncle Mort.

"What do you mean—you and your Bob's baby?" he said.

Auntie Lil moved to her side of the bed and said:

"I shall always think of it as my Bob's child. You were just the agency that united me with my Bob on The Other Side."

"That's the first time I've been called an agency, Lil," said Uncle Mort, and after a few minutes he left the bedroom to commence cleaning Mr. Brandon's wellington boots in the front room.

Carter Brandon came in a few minutes after midnight and made two cups of cocoa, one for himself and one for Uncle Mort.

On account of the unseasonable inclemency of the weather Mr. Brandon had lit a fire, and they sat staring into the embers.

"Have you noticed any evil fluences in the house, Carter?" said Uncle Mort.

"No."

"Neither have I."

Uncle Mort began polishing the wellington boots. He spat on them and rubbed them furiously with a duster torn from a shirt tail. Then he blew sharply to remove the spots of dust.

"It's a rum do," he said.

Carter Brandon went into the garage with the box of mealworms. The owlet fluttered down from a beam and landed on his shoulder. It began to nibble the rim of his right ear, and he held up a mealworm, which wriggled damply between his fingers.

The owlet waddled sideways down his arm and put its foot on one end of the mealworm. It took the other end in its beak and tugged sharply. The worm stretched and snapped. The owlet swallowed the piece in its beak, gulped and blinked. Then it flew up to the rafter and clicked its beak.

Carter Brandon dropped the half mealworm into the box and locked the garage. As he was getting into bed he could hear Uncle Stavely, hammering on the floor with the heel of his boot.

Mrs. Partington came round later in the week and was offered crumpets and dividend tea by her hostess, Mrs. Brandon.

"I hope you don't mind me coming round like this, Mrs. Brandon. But under the circumstances, I think it's only right and proper that we should talk things over," she said.

"Have another crumpet," said Mrs. Brandon.

"Thank you, they're very nice. They're lovely, aren't they? Do they come from Pickup's? Well, I've come about our Pat. She's took it very badly. Very badly indeed. I can't get a word of sense out of her. She just sits up there in her room all night long, moping. 'Pat,' I say. 'Pat, luv, why don't you tell your mammy what's to do?' I say. 'Get it off your chest. You'll feel a thousand times better.' But no. Not a word, Mrs. Brandon. Just a long, brooding silence."

"Our Carter's not said nothing to me about it neither," said Mrs. Brandon.

Uncle Mort glanced into the front room, but withdrew his head rapidly, when he saw the identity of Mrs. Brandon's guest. He went into the kitchen and began cleaning Mr. Brandon's bowling shoes.

"I do know this, though," said Mrs. Partington. "Our Pat's heartbroke. It's broke is her heart. Her heart's broke. It's rent. It is. She's took it right badly. Thank you, I will have another crumpet."

Mrs. Brandon worked the fingers of her right hand into the wave at the front of her hair and said:

"It's upset our Carter, too."

"Now I'm not saying owt against your Carter, Mrs. Brandon. He's a nice lad. A very nice lad. I'm very fond of him. Very fond of him indeed. But I do think honestly he could have come round to explain things to me personal like. Especially after I'd lent his Uncle Mort Mr. Partington's back collar stud. I says to our Pat, I says: 'I do think he might have had the decency to come round to see me and give me his side of the story.'"

"Well, of course, Mrs. Partington, it might not be Carter's fault, might it?" said Mrs. Brandon. "I mean to say, there's two sides to every story, isn't there? I mean to say, there's neither of us knows the full story, is there? I mean to say, I haven't had your Pat's version of it, have I?"

Uncle Stavely came into the room, stared hard at Mrs. Partington, sat on the sofa and said to her:

"I'm Uncle Stavely. I was best man at Mort's wedding. I made a speech, and the wedding cake gave me constipation. Pardon?"

"How do you do, pleased to meet you," said Mrs. Partington. "In't he like Mr. Brandon, though? You can see the family likeness, can't you? He reminds me of a feller who used to serve in the greengrocer's twenty years ago."

Uncle Stavely stared at her unblinkingly for several seconds. Then he snorted, folded his arms across his chest, closed his eyes and fell asleep.

"I think it's up to us to do all we can to bring them together again," said Mrs. Partington. "It's having a very bad effect on our Pat, that I do know. She'll hardly eat any toast at breakfast, and she's gone right off potatoes."

"Yes well, they'll sort themselves out in their own good time, I've no doubt," said Mrs. Brandon.

"But will they, Mrs. Brandon? I'm not so sure. These youngsters can be very stubborn when they set their minds to it. Very stubborn indeed."

"I'm sure everything will turn out for the best," said Mrs. Brandon. "Have another crumpet."

Shortly after Mrs. Partington parted company from Mrs. Brandon, Carter Brandon found himself engaged in supervising the installation of a new jig in the machine shop.

"Up to your right a bit, Ernie," he said.

The four men from maintenance had wheeled the jig into the machine shop on a wooden flat, and Albert Hollins had signed their chitty.

"Have you got any leverage there, Terence?" said Carter Brandon.

The machines were throbbing, and a spoon vibrated in a mug on the window ledge.

Albert Hollins touched Carter Brandon on the shoulder and shouted in his ear:

"Your old feller's been on the phone. He says, can he see you urgent outside where he works."

"Urgent?"

"Go on then. I'll finish this lot off."

Carter Brandon met his father in a cafe a short way from the main factory gates and ordered two mugs of tea with condensed milk. Mr. Brandon passed an envelope across the table.

"Read that," he said. "It come to the works this morning."

Carter Brandon took out the letter and read the following type-written message:

"Dear Mr. Brandon,
     I love you,
          Yours faithfully,
               Mrs. Otter (Celia) XXXXXXXXXX."

"Oh aye," said Carter Brandon.

"That's the lady I was telling you about," said Mr. Brandon. "She's the one I yielded to temptation with in Kensal Green."

"How did she get your address?"

"I wrote to her shortly after I come home. I'd mislaid me shoehorn, and I thought I might have left it at her house."

"Had you?"

"No."

"Has she been writing regular?" said Carter Brandon.

"Apart from the letter giving me the bad news about me shoehorn, no."

"What are you going to do then?"

"I don't know. That's why I've shown it to you."

Mr. Brandon scratched his knee and took out the *Daily Herald* from his hip pocket. He folded it double, spread it on the table and began to read.

"You'd best keep it out of the way of me mother."

"Pardon?"

"The letter."

"Oh aye."

"What do you feel about this Mrs. Otter then?" said Carter Brandon.

"Oh her?" said Mr. Brandon, standing up from the table. "I must be off now. Thanks for your advice."

Carter Brandon parked his car in the cul-de-sac next to the Co-op printing works. He cut through Water Alley and met Sid Skelhorn and Eric Black in the public bar of 'The Griffon'.

"What's tha' having?" said Sid Skelhorn, who had now lost his toothlessness.

"Pint of bitter."

"Same again, luv, and one for me mate here," said Sid Skelhorn to the barman. "These bloody false teeth. I feel as though I've got keel of bloody Queen Mary in me mouth."

They drank their pints quickly. Eric Black had been to the barber's earlier in the evening, and a little greasy tuft of hair stood up from the back of his head and waggled every time he spoke.

"We thought we'd go down to Luxor Club," he said.

"Les Girls, eh?" said Sid Skelhorn. "They've four strippers and they each do two turns. Sixteen lovely wobbly titties for two bob. You can't gripe at that."

"I wonder where our Carter is?" said Mrs. Brandon. "It's

most unlike him to go out without telling us where he's going."

"I shouldn't wonder if he's not got an assignation with that young lady he met outside the temperance bar," said Auntie Lil.

They were sitting in the dusty twilight of the front room, eating cashew nuts.

"It needn't be an up-to-date chemical lavatory," said Uncle Stavely. "In fact, he's probably got his own."

"That's right, Stavely," said Mrs. Brandon, and Auntie Lil bean to sob softly.

"What's to do, Lil?" said Mr. Brandon.

"Everything's going against me and my Bob having our child," she said.

"Now then, Lil," said Mrs. Brandon.

"It's bad enough your Stavely putting evil fluences on our unborn child."

"Pardon?" said Uncle Stavely.

"It's bad enough having an owl in the garage, hooting all night long."

"It's not old enough to hoot, Lil," said Mr. Brandon.

"But to bring a stranger into your home, who sleeps in a hammock and uses a chemical lavatory, well, it's too much. If you wanted to kill our unborn child, you couldn't be going about it better."

The first stripper was a negress. She waggled her hips, and the drummer caught her brassiere on the end of his stick. Everyone applauded, and one or two thumped on the tables with their pint mugs.

A bouncer walked round the room with a leather thong held taut between his hands. Two long-haired Alsatians cringed at his heel.

The negress ran a banana between her naked breasts, and the waiter said:

"Same again, squire?"

"Aye," said Carter Brandon. "Ta, and one for yourself."

The negress turned her back to the audience, and, facing the band, removed her G string. The drummer licked his lips, rolled his eyes and winked at the audience.

The negress had thin legs and a yellow-capped pimple on her left buttock.

"What's he want a chemical lavatory for, any road?" said Mr. Brandon to Uncle Stavely as they were eating supper.

"Field hygiene," said Uncle Stavely. "Pardon?"

"Oh aye," said Mr. Brandon. Then he said to his wife: "Are you sure you're doing right, bringing this Corporal Parkinson to stay here?"

"He'll be good company for our Stavely," said Mrs. Brandon.

"He'll bring his own hammock, so you've no need to start buying him one," said Uncle Stavely. "His hammock was the only living thing to be saved when his ship was sunk by pirates in the South China Sea."

"I'll write to matron first thing and get it all fixed up," said Mrs. Brandon.

A comedian came on stage and said:

"It's a weird life, though, in't it? In't it a weird life? I've just come back from London me. London. Marvellous. Swinging, ring-a-ding-ding eh? It's a big place, though, in't it? In't London a big place? My word. They give me this little booklet. A little booklet full of handy tips about London. You know the sort of thing—what to do if accosted by a prostitute in Piccadilly . . . and how to get there. No, no, come here. Listen. A mate of mine, a mate of mine bought this ticket for a Policeman's Ball. 'Is it for a dance?' I says. 'No,' he says. 'It's for a raffle.' For a raffle? Got it? No, never mind, lad. He's miles away him . . . not far enough for me. No, no. Listen."

Uncle Mort sat in the bedroom, polishing a pair of leather gaiters that had belonged to Carter Brandon in the days of his childhood.

Auntie Lil switched off the wireless and said:

"We always booked in for a show for every night of our holidays in advance, my Bob and me. Oh, we did have some laughs. We saw Flotsam and Jetsam. He had a lovely voice. I can't recall which one it was, but he had such a lovely deep bass voice.

"And there was this magician on the Central Pier at Blackpool and he said: 'I'd like a gentleman to volunteer and come up from the audience to help me with this trick.' And my Bob went up there. I didn't know where to hide meself. He were very fond of the stage was my Bob. 'The Boards,' he called it. He used to play the musical saw at Scout gang shows. Any road, this magician—I forget his name—well, he undid my Bob's braces so's his trousers fell down, and after the show he gave him an autographed photo, inscribed 'To A Good Sport'. I've still got it in my trunk somewhere. My Bob said he wasn't even aware that his braces was being detached from his trousers. And there wasn't even a trouser button missing, when I looked next day. That proves what a good magician he was, doesn't it?"

The comedian said:
"And now I have a request from the management, a request from the management. Will all you gentlemen, all you gentlemen using the lavatory after seeing these gorgeous strip-tease young ladies kindly take care not to make a mess on the ceiling. Hello, that's the first one he's got all night. What have you been putting in his ale, purple bloody hearts?"

"Clarkson Rose was always very good," said Auntie Lil as Uncle Mort climbed into bed alongside her.
He switched off the lights, and Auntie Lil began to sob.
"What's the matter now, Lil?"
"I'm just weeping for happiness, Mort. I can just see my Bob's face when I present him my new baby. He'll be as proud as punch. Oh, he will be proud, bless him."

Mr. and Mrs. Brandon had retired to bed, when Carter Brandon returned home. His mother had left him a plate of cheese sandwiches and a slice of Battenburg cake.
He gave the cheese sandwiches to the dog and put the piece of cake into his pocket to give to the cygnets the following day.

CHAPTER SIXTEEN

Mrs. Brandon was as good as her word, no better, no worse. She wrote to the matron of the Old Folks' Home and received a reply on Saturday morning.
She went into the garden to communicate its contents to her husband, who was sterilising plant pots in a zinc bath full of disinfectant.
"Well, it's all right, Les," she said. "Under certain conditions."
"What conditions?"
"Well, it appears that as we're not Corporal Parkinson's own kith and kin, we've to sign some forms."
"What forms?"
"Sort of foster parent forms."

"Oh aye," said Mr. Brandon, scraping the rim of a plant pot with his son's jack knife.

"Yes, we're to be legally responsible for him," said Mrs. Brandon. "I suppose it's if he should get into HP debt on a washing machine or something."

Mrs. Brandon left her husband to his plant pots and looked in at the garage, where her son was recharging the battery of his car.

"It's all right for Corporal Parkinson to stay with us," she said.

"Mm," said Carter Brandon, who was dressed in a brown boiler suit and rubber overshoes recently polished by Uncle Mort.

"I thought owls slept all through the day," she said, as she caught sight of the owlet, cleaning its beak on a piece of dowel rod at the end of the garage.

"No, they often hunt during the day," said Carter Brandon.

Mrs. Brandon left her son to his battery and his owlet and went upstairs to the attic.

"Well, it's all fixed up, Stavely," she said. "Your Corporal Parkinson can come to live here as soon as we're ready for him."

Uncle Stavely was on his knees, rummaging in a leather suitcase at the foot of the bed.

"I'm looking for the old Red Duster," he said.

"What do you want that for?"

"For Corporal Parkinson. He can't sleep at nights unless he has the old Red Duster flying above his head. He's very patriotic."

The afternoon was overcast and drizzly. Mr. Brandon and Uncle Mort took the bus to the Lacey Street Bowls club to compete in *The Evening Telegraph* silver vase tournament.

Carter Brandon took Derrick Warrender to the Coronation Park, and they played pitch and putt.

"How's Jessie?" said Carter Brandon, when they reached the third green.

"All right," said Derrick Warrender, two-putting for five.

In a bunker at the fifth hole Carter Brandon said:

"Are you still seeing much of her?"

"On and off," said Derrick Warrender. "Bloody hell, sliced again."

A golden retriever ran off with Derrick Warrender's ball as it rolled towards the hole on the eighth green. They chased it, and when they returned, Carter Brandon said:

"What does she work at?"

"What? Oh, she's a char or something at one of the big houses up Mosscroft Edge."

At the ninth and final hole Carter Brandon was one stroke up. His drive landed ten yards from the pin, but Derrick Warrender sliced his into a clump of gorse.

They swished their clubs through the spiky branches, looking for the ball, and Carter Brandon said:

"That's a funny job, in't it, a char?"

"Aye."

They found the ball, and it took Derrick Warrender two more shots to reach the green. He three-putted, so Carter Brandon was the victor by four strokes.

"How long's she been a char then?"

"It's no wonder you've won," said Derrick Warrender. "How could I concentrate with you talking all the fucking time?"

The doctor visited Auntie Lil in the afternoon, and when he came downstairs, he said to Mrs. Brandon:

"Who's Bob?"

"It's her first husband," she said. "He's the one who preceded her present husband, Mort, who is, in fact, my brother, so Lil and me are sisters-in-law as well as being related by her previous marriage, because Bob, her first husband, was my mother's nephew."

"Was she fond of her first husband?" said the doctor.

"She worshipped him. Idolised the ground he trod on, doctor."

"Jolly good."

"She's never really been the same since he was took from her. He was run over by a grand piano, you know."

"A grand piano, eh?"

"Very tragic, it were. Would you like another cup of tea before you examine Uncle Stavely, doctor?"

"No thanks all the same," said the doctor. "Jolly good."

Uncle Stavely was examined by the doctor in the front room.

"Well, everything's A1, young man," he said.

"Corporal Parkinson says all doctors are charlatans. And I agree. Pardon?" said Uncle Stavely.

"Stavely!" said Mrs. Brandon. "What will doctor think of you?"

"There's only one thing they're good at—amputations and warts."

"Yok, yok, yok," said the doctor. Then at the front door he said to Mrs. Brandon: "Try to impress upon your sister-in-law that Bob is not the father of her child."

"I will, doctor. I will."

"It often helps in this sort of case," he said. "Jolly good then."

Corporal Parkinson arrived midway through the next week.

Carter Brandon drove to the station with his mother and Uncle Stavely to collect him. Uncle Stavely was wearing his medals.

"Why he had to come be train I'll never know," said Mrs. Brandon. "Our Carter could have brought him easy be car."

"Corporal Parkinson always travels by the permanent way," said Uncle Stavely. "He was once married to a sleeping car attendant on the Trans-Siberian Railway."

They had a cup of tea in the station buffet, and, when the arrival of the train was announced, they went out on to the platform.

"He'll be in the guard's van. Pardon?" said Uncle Stavely.

The guard was handing a brindle greyhound to a porter. It was wearing a muzzle, and a dribble of saliva hung to its tongue.

"Have you got a Corporal Parkinson in there?" said Carter Brandon.

"Aye," said the guard.

He opened the double doors of the van, and they stepped inside.

In the corner was a large wicker bath chair. In the bath chair was a minute emaciated figure. It had several layers of army blankets wrapped round its knees and shoulders. Out of its right ear stuck a large black bakelite hearing aid. Its eyes were masked by dark glasses. Round its neck was a large red luggage label.

"Hello, Corporal Parkinson," said Uncle Stavely.

The label round the figure's neck said: "Corporal Parkinson Retd. Fragile. To Be Called For."

"This must be him then," said Mrs. Brandon. "How do you do, Corporal Parkinson? I'm Mrs. Brandon. Did you have a good journey?"

"You'll have to speak up. He doesn't hear very well at this time of day," said Uncle Stavely.

Mrs. Brandon prodded the figure with the tip of her umbrella and shouted into the hearing aid:

"How do you do, Corporal Parkinson? I'm Mrs. Brandon. Did you have a good journey?"

The figure stirred itself feebly under the blankets and emitted a tinny, monosyllabic rasp.

"He says he had a very pleasant journey, thank you, apart from the greyhound, which spent all the time flecking itself. Pardon?" said Uncle Stavely.

Carter Brandon wheeled the bath chair down the ramp on to the platform and then returned to the guard's van to collect the sea chest and navy blue kit bag, which made up Corporal Parkinson's luggage.

On the sea chest was painted in large white latters: 'Van Spronk J.K.T.—SS City of Paris, Inman and International Line.'

As they wheeled the bath chair to the car Mrs. Brandon said to Uncle Stavely:

"You never told me he was infirm."

"He isn't," said Uncle Stavely. "He's just got a spot of tummy trouble."

"Careful how you lift him out of the bath chair, Carter," said Mrs. Brandon.

When Carter Brandon lifted the figure out of the bath chair, he discovered that it had no legs.

CHAPTER SEVENTEEN

After his arrival in the Brandon household, nothing was seen of Corporal Parkinson for four days.

During the whole of that period there was torrential rain, and at nights the thunder rolled into the city down the valleys from the bleak moorlands, and lightning flickered noiselessly.

Strange cooking smells seeped down from the attic, and every time the dog passed the foot of the stairs the hairs on its spine stood bolt upright, and it made half-stifled whimpering noises.

The owlet turned into an owl and began to make nocturnal flights from the garage. During the day it slept on a rafter in a dark corner and hissed, if anyone disturbed it.

"Well, how's he settling in, Stavely?" said Mrs. Brandon one morning, when she spotted Uncle Stavely, burying a brown paper parcel in the garden by the rhubarb patch.

"He says everything's champion apart from the evil fluences. Pardon?" said Uncle Stavely.

In the local Mr. Brandon and Uncle Mort stared gloomily into their pint pots.

"Do you know what he had yesterday?" said Uncle Mort.

"No," said Mr. Brandon.

"Half a pound of pickled sprats, a two pound tin of corned jock and a chocolate sponge cake."

During the lunch break in the canteen Carter Brandon said to Linda Preston:

"And before he goes to bed at night they play 'The Last Post' on a bugle."

"Bloody hell," said Linda Preston. "Do you want your carrots?"

They finished lunch and lit cigarettes.

"I'll see you then, kid. I've got to fix up with Connie Watkinson about getting our hair done on Friday night."

"What are you doing tonight?"

"I don't know."

"Do you fancy going out or something?"

Linda Preston looked down at the table and scratched the back of her left calf with her right foot.

"All right then," she said.

A rendezvous was established, and Carter Brandon spent the remainder of the lunch break playing draughts with Eric Black.

The evening meal was eaten in silence. Mr. Brandon pushed back his chair and went out into the garden. Uncle Mort followed him, and Auntie Lil started up her knitting machine. Mrs. Brandon went to the foot of the stairs and shouted:

"Are you all right up there, Stavely?"

A door opened, and acrid fumes of burning olive oil plunged down the staircase.

"Pardon?" said Uncle Stavely.

"I'm asking if you're all right."

"Mind your own business. Pardon?"

The door shut, and after a while a kettle drum struck up, and the attic shook to the rhythm of marching feet.

"I've got something to tell you, Annie," said Auntie Lil, switching off her knitting machine. "It's about the evil fluence."

"Oh, yes, Lil," said Mrs. Brandon.

"It's stopped."

The dog pushed open the door with its nose, wagged its tail, sat down on the brown rug in front of the fire and began to lick its testicles. Mrs. Brandon poked it with her foot, and it looked up and wagged its tail.

"I won't tell you about that again," she said.

"It stopped the moment that Corporal Parkinson set foot in the house. I think he's having a good effect on Stavely," said Auntie Lil.

The kettle drum stopped beating, and a bugle began to play 'The Last Post' in thin, wavery, short gasps.

"Well, I'll say this for him," said Mrs. Brandon. "He does seem to be getting him to bed early."

Carter Brandon had arranged to meet Linda Preston outside the Town Hall at eight o'clock. He left home an hour earlier, intending to call at 'The Griffon' for a quick pint.

As he turned into Derbyshire Lane, he saw Jessie Lewis, standing at the bus stop. He pulled up, tapped his horn and unwound the side window.

"Hello," said Jessie Lewis, opening the door and climbing into the car beside him.

She was wearing a light blue denim skirt and a sleeveless navy blue roll-collar pullover. Her hair was swept back into a pony tail secured by an elastic band.

"I'm going swimming at Endcar, are you coming?" she said.

"I haven't got a cossy."

"You can hire one there."

"Aye, all right then," said Carter Brandon.

He hunched his shoulders and slid down in the seat as they passed the Town Hall. There was no sign of Linda Preston. After a while they reached the narrow country lane, which led to the Endcar open-air swimming pool, and Carter Brandon pressed hard on the accelerator.

Earlier in the summer there had been a mild moorland fire, and through the gaps in the dry stone walls they could see the charred heather, which sent up puffs of ash when the sheep plodded across to reach the sweet grass in the hollows untouched by fire.

Carter Brandon hired a pair of swimming trunks and stood on the edge of the pool, slapping his arms across his chest. There was only one person in the water, a bald, stout, middle-aged man, who was swimming slowly up and down the pool with a ponderous side stroke.

The metal locker tag, fastened to a piece of string round Carter Brandon's neck, touched his chest and set off a ripple of stinging goose pimples.

Jessie Lewis appeared from the women's changing room. She was not wearing a bathing cap, and he could see the outline of her nipples through the navy blue cotton of her bathing suit.

"Okay?" she said and plunged into the pool and swam underwater to the other side.

Carter Brandon kneeled down and placed the tip of his elbow into the water.

"Brrh," he said. "Brrrrh."

"It's not cold once you're in," said Jessie Lewis. "Let's dive for pennies."

Carter Brandon closed his eyes and dived into the water. There was a pounding and drumming in his ears, and, when he surfaced, little red lights danced before his eyes.

"Christ, it's cold," he said.

They dived for the penny Jessie Lewis had brought from the changing rooms. In the shifting planes of underwater blue Carter Brandon saw strings of tiny bubbles, streaming out from Jessie Lewis's hair. Once she put her foot on the back of his neck, as he was groping for the penny, and he surfaced, spluttering and coughing.

After ten minutes Carter Brandon said:

"It's too cold for me."

He made three dives from the springboard and one from the top of the eighteen foot board. Then he retired to the changing room, where he rubbed himself vigorously and ricked his toe in the duck boards. He bought himself a six-penny bar of milk chocolate from the automatic dispenser.

Then he sat in the grass at the edge of the pool, smoking and watching Jessie Lewis swimming.

She swam with a weak buoyant breast stroke, her head held high out of the water and her legs kicking twice to every stroke of her arm.

When they left the baths, the middle-aged man in the bottle green woollen bathing suit was still ploughing slowly up and down the pool.

They had fish and chips in the chip shop next to the End-car sub post office, and then they drove to 'The Pack Horse'. The wind had dropped, the clouds had lifted and the last few rays of the setting sun warmed the inner courtyard, where they sat on a bench under the chestnut tree.

"I enjoyed that swim," said Carter Brandon.

"It was fun, wasn't it?" said Jessie Lewis.

A jackdaw stalked up and down the stable roof, crying: "Chacka, chacka, chack. Chacka chacka chack" at a boxer dog tied by a length of rope to a fall pipe below.

On the drive back to the city Jessie Lewis said:

"Did you see Pat?"

"Eh?"

"She was sitting in the private bar. She was with some chap in a uniform. He looked like a merchant navy officer or something."

"Oh aye."

"She saw us, but she didn't let on."

"Mm."

When they reached the city centre, Jessie Lewis said:

"If you drop me off at the bus station, I'll just be in time to catch the bus back."

"No, I'll run you home."

"I'd rather go by bus."

He pulled up outside the bus station and switched off the engine.

"It was a lovely evening. Thanks for the lift. Thanks for the chips. Thanks for the drinks," said Jessie Lewis. And she opened the door and ran across the pavement into the bus station.

Carter Brandon got out of the car, leaned against the bonnet and lit a cigarette. The bus passed, and he saw Jessie Lewis, sitting on the back seat upstairs. She waved, and he finished his cigarette and drove home.

Uncle Mort, who was cleaning Mr. Brandon's old Home Guard boots, which had now been relegated to gardening fatigues, said:

"I've just been out in the garden for a smoke."

"Have you?"

"Aye, and I saw your Uncle Stavely stood at the open window."

"Did you?"

"Aye, and he was semaphoring with a pillow case in one hand and his pyjama jacket in the other."

"Was he?"

"Bloody semaphoring at his time of life, I ask you."

Carter Brandon met Linda Preston in the corridor outside the canteen the following day. He shuffled his feet, hunched his shoulders, coughed and said:

"Aye well."

Linda Preston clutched his arm and said:

"Honest, kid, I'm sorry about last night."

"What?"

"I don't like back-heelin' fellers, but I got sat in front of the telly after me tea and I went flat out. By the time I come round, it were too late to meet you."

"Oh."

"You wasn't hangin' round for long, was you?"

"No."

"I'm dead sorry, kid, honest, I am. Dead sorry."

That afternoon Auntie Lil said:

"I've been thinking, Annie. I've been thinking that we ought to make our guest welcome by giving a small tea party in his honour."

"What a nice thought, Lil," said Mrs. Brandon.

So forthwith Uncle Mort was dispatched to the attic to invite Uncle Stavely and his companion to afternoon tea in the front parlour. He returned with the news that the two old gentlemen were pleased to accept the invitation and could be expected to arrive at fifteen-thirty hours prompt.

Auntie Lil went upstairs to change, and Uncle Mort was sent to the baker's to purchase half a dozen balm cakes, a dozen assorted fancies and a large jar of salmon and anchovey paste.

At fifteen-thirty hours prompt the door of the front room opened to reveal Uncle Stavely, holding in his arms Corporal Parkinson.

"Stavely, you've never struggled downstairs, carrying him like that?" said Mrs. Brandon. "You'll rupture yourself, lad."

"Pardon?" said Uncle Stavely, placing Corporal Parkinson on the sofa and propping him upright with three cushions.

Auntie Lil wheeled in the tea trolley and poured out tea for the small intimate gathering.

"We've heard such a lot about you, Corporal Parkinson," she said. "It's a real pleasure to meet you in the flesh at last."

"He says, thank you very much and do you mind if he drinks his tea out of the saucer?" said Uncle Stavely, tying a small flannel bib round Corporal Parkinson's neck.

"Not at all. Not at all," said Mrs. Brandon.

Uncle Mort blew his nose and said:

"It'll be a nice day, if it doesn't rain."

Mrs. Brandon said:

"Have another fish paste sandwich, Corporal Parkinson. Them balm cakes is fresh from the baker's."

"He says, he can't eat fresh bread on account of his dandruff," said Uncle Stavely. "That dandruff is a legacy of his service in the Camel Corps. Pardon?"

"Well, I never," said Auntie Lil.

"Fancy," said Mrs. Brandon.

"The Camel Corps, eh?" said Uncle Mort.

Corporal Parkinson lifted his right hand very slowly to his chest and began to direct it unsteadily towards his nose. Halfway to its destination the hand wavered, stopped, drooped and fell to his lap.

"The Camel Corps, eh?" said Uncle Mort.

"The camel is a beast of burden, whose temper is uncertain," said Uncle Stavely. "It has a reputation for ferocity and cunning malevolence unmatched among domestic animals. Though a cud-chewer, it has not the four-fold stomach of the cow. Pardon?"

The balm cake sandwiches were finished, and the plate of assorted fancies passed round. Corporal Parkinson inclined his head towards Uncle Stavely and clicked his tongue against his thin, dry lips.

"He says sheep's eyeballs are considered a great delicacy in the Middle East," said Uncle Stavely.

"I can understand that," said Uncle Mort. "I mean, I think personally there's nothing tastier than a good pig's trotter."

"The pig is a most useful animal," said Uncle Stavely. "You can eat any part of it, bar its grunt."

"Bar its grunt?" said Auntie Lil. "That's a good one, Stavely."

The clock struck four, and Corporal Parkinson turned his head to Uncle Stavely once more and allowed his lips to part. Three tinny rasps followed.

"He says, thank you very much for the tea party, he enjoyed it very much, but he's got to get back to his devotions," said Uncle Stavely, and with that he scooped up Corporal Parkinson in his arms and made for the door.

"Well, he does very well for his age, Stavely," said Auntie Lil. "How old is he?"

"A hundred and two," said Uncle Stavely, closing the door with his foot.

CHAPTER EIGHTEEN

The vicar rode down the street on his autocycle. In his right hand he held a bunch of pink roses, and in his teeth he held a curved cherry wood pipe. The sun was shining.

He propped his autocycle against Mr. Brandon's gate post, knocked on the front door of Mr. Brandon's house and was admitted to Mrs. Brandon's front room.

"Many congratulations," he said to Auntie Lil. "I'm delighted to hear you're starting a family. So many of my mums seem to think it's more important to have a new washing machine."

"What lovely roses, vicar," said Auntie Lil.

"It was Edward Carpenter (1844 to 1929) wasn't it, who said so aptly: 'Motherhood is, after all, woman's great and incomparable work'?"

"That's right, vicar," said Mrs. Brandon.

"Can I smell burning?" said the vicar, wrinkling his nose.

"That's all right, vicar," said Mrs. Brandon. "It's just Corporal Parkinson making bun loaf toast."

"I must say the bloom of prospective motherhood looks most becoming on you."

"Thank you, vicar," said Auntie Lil.

"And how's hubby reacting to the great event? Over the moon, I dare say."

"Oh, my Bob's taken it in his stride, vicar. He doesn't show it much, but, if you know him, you can see he's delighted underneath. He's as proud as a peacock."

Mrs. Brandon escorted the vicar to the front gate and watched him tuck his trousers into his socks, and put on his leather gauntlets.

"By the way," he said. "Correct me if I'm wrong, but I was under the impression that your sister-in-law's husband was called Mortimer James Alfred."

"So he is, vicar," said Mrs. Brandon. "Bob is the name of her first husband, who met his end at the hands of a grand piano."

"Yes," said the vicar. "Yes. Well, I think a word in her ear wouldn't come amiss, Mrs. Brandon."

"Certainly, vicar. Certainly."

The vicar's autocycle backfired three times as he rode off down the street, and a small wing nut fell off his luggage carrier and rolled down a grid.

Very little happened in the rest of August. Two men died in a roof fall in a nearby colliery and the weather picked up as September took its rightful place as the ninth month of the year.

Carter Brandon and his father went to see the first trial match of the season. At half time they stood by the tea stall on top of the cinder embankment. In the distance they could see the slag heaps of the coalfield. Two house sparrows pecked at the crumbs of their pork pies.

"What do you think to that Welsh bugger on the right wing?" said Mr. Brandon.

"He can shift," said Carter Brandon.

"I don't like his hands. He's not safe. And he's got a streak of yellow in him, too."

Maurice and his Hammond Organ had been installed in the smoke room of 'The Griffon', so they took their beers to a table in the public room and bought a bag of cockles each from a man in a white coat.

"I got another letter last week," said Mr. Brandon.

"Oh aye?"

Mr. Brandon took out a wad of papers from his inside jacket pocket and placed it on the table.

"There you are," he said, detaching a letter from the bundle, and showing it to his son. It said:

"Flower,
   I wait in vain for a reply to mine of 13th ult.
      Yours affectionately,
         Mrs. Otter (Celia) XXXXXXXX

P.S. I have found your shoehorn."

"Mm," said Carter Brandon.

"She's cunning, though," said Mr. Brandon. "You see what she's doing?"

"No."

"She's trying to tempt me with me shoehorn. She bloody is. She's being right crafty. Knowing how attached I am to that shoehorn, she's using it as a bait to tempt me to write. Cunning old faggot."

"Will you write?"

"Do you want another drink?"

The waiter brought two more pints of beer, and Mr. Brandon paid him with a ten shilling note he took from his breast pocket.

"I had a letter from Pat this morning," said Carter Brandon.

"Trouble?"

"She says she wants to see me."

Mr. Brandon tapped out his pipe on his heel and then began to scrape the inside of the bowl with his penknife.

"There'll be no harm done, I suppose."

Later that evening Carter Brandon met Pat outside the Town Hall.

"Hello, Carter," she said.

"How do," said Carter Brandon.

"Shall we go to the Piccolo for a coffee?"

"If you like."

They found a seat in the basement, which was decorated in the style of an Italian taverna. There were travel posters of Amalfi and Ischia on the walls, and the waiter wore bell-bottomed trousers and a blue and white hooped cotton shirt. A gondolier's straw hat was pinned to the ceiling above the espresso machine. Danish pastries cost one and ninepence each.

"I hope you don't mind me asking you to see me," said Pat.

"No."

"Only I thought you might have got the wrong impression the other night."

"The other night?"

"In 'The Pack Horse'. That feller I was with, he wasn't a boy friend or owt like that. He's me cousin Neville. He's just finished as a trainee radio officer with Marconi. He sailed from Liverpool yesterday."

"Did he?"

"How are you keeping anyway?" said Pat, offering Carter Brandon a cigarette.

"Very well, ta. How's yourself?"

"Oh, very well, considering."

Pat was wearing the suit she had bought for Uncle Mort's wedding and a Wedgwood ring she had bought out of money given to her by Carter Brandon on her last birthday.

She began to make a little pyramid of lump sugar in the earthenware bowl. There were flecks of white on her finger-nails.

"How's Jessie Lewis?" she said quietly.

"Shall I run you home?" said Carter Brandon.

He drove Pat to the end of her road, and, with the engine still running, leaned across and opened the door.

"Tarra then," he said.

Pat closed the door firmly and turned to him.

"You might as well know," she said.

"Eh?"

"I'm sorry."

"Sorry?"

"I'm sorry for having been so hasty. I just flew off the handle. I didn't know what I was saying. What with all the worry of saving up and trying to get you to take an interest in arrangements and then you going off on that works outing and not telling me you had an owl and then that Jessie Lewis and . . ."

Pat began to weep. Her whole body shook. She made no effort to wipe away the tears. She sat and stared at Carter Brandon with her cheeks glistening, and a tiny blue vein twitched in her temple.

When she had finished weeping, she hiccuped, fumbled in her handbag, blew her nose on a paper tissue and hiccuped again.

Carter Brandon hunched his shoulders and coughed.

"Aye. Well," he said.

"Oh, Carter, is that all you've got to say? Is that all you can find to say? I've poured my heart out to you. I've humbled myself in front of you, and all you can say is 'Aye. Well.' "

"Aye. Well," said Carter Brandon.

"Oh, Carter. Oh, Carter," sobbed Pat, and she opened the car door and ran off down the street with her heels click-clacking on the pavement, and paper tissues streaming from her open handbag.

CHAPTER NINETEEN

On the evening of Carter Brandon's meeting with Pat the family was once again awaiting the arrival of Uncle Stavely et oppo in the front room.

"He's a marvellous conversationalist is Corporal Parkinson," said Auntie Lil. "He's got a wonderful fund of anecdotes."

"Aye," said Mr. Brandon.

"He's got a vivid imagination, though," said Uncle Mort. "I take three quarters of his bloody stories with a pinch of salt me."

"That's very ungracious of you, Mort," said Mrs. Brandon.

"Pay no heed to him," said Auntie Lil. "He's just envious. He's consumed with envy. He's been that way ever since I broke the good news of me and my Bob having a baby."

"Oh, hell," said Uncle Mort, who had now developed a craving for sharpening pencils.

On the dot of nine Uncle Stavely appeared with Corporal

Parkinson in his arms. As usual he propped him up on the sofa with three cushions. As usual he tied a bib round his neck with a large reef knot.

On this occasion, however, he varied the routine by detaching the bakelite hearing aid from his comrade's ear, polishing it on his shirt cuff and saying:

"This hearing aid was originally designed by Thomas Edison Bell for the use of General Lechitsky, who commanded the Siberian Rifles in the Russo-Japanese War. In the present war he led the victorious Russian campaign in the Bukovina."

"See what I mean?" said Uncle Mort.

"What?" said Auntie Lil.

"Wait here. Nobody move," said Uncle Mort, jumping out of his chair and dashing to the door. He returned breathless a few minutes later, carrying a frayed cardboard cigarette card album, which he opened with a flourish.

"There you are, you see," he said and began to read from the back of a cigarette card. " 'Allied Army Leaders. Wills Cigarettes. A series of fifty, number forty-six. General Lechitsky."

He handed the card to Auntie Lil.

"I can't read such small print without my glasses," she said.

"Here you are, I'll read it," said Mr. Brandon, taking the card from Auntie Lil's lap. " 'General Lechitsky, born 1856, was the son of a Greek Orthodox priest. Originally destined for the church, he decided . . .' Aye, he's right. It's all here about him leading the victorious offensive in the Bukovina."

"See what I mean?" said Uncle Mort.

"Pardon?" said Uncle Stavely. "That in no way invalidates the fact that Corporal Parkinson's hearing aid was originally designed by Thomas Edison Bell."

"You're quite right, Stavely," said Auntie Lil.

"You'll not find that information on no cigarette card," said Uncle Stavely.

"So be told, you Mort," said Auntie Lil.

Uncle Mort muttered softly to himself and sloped off to the door.

"I'm taking the dog for a walk," he said.

The atmosphere of mutual distrust and suspicion was not eased when Mrs. Brandon said over breakfast the following morning:

"I think it's time you and me had a few words, Carter."

"What about?"

"I've held me peace till now, but it's time you had a good talking to, young man. Do you realise what you've done to Pat?"

"What are you talking about?" said Mr. Brandon. "It wasn't him what broke the engagement off."

"Now that's enough from you, Les," said Mrs. Brandon.

"Here we go, here we go," said Mr. Brandon, pushing aside a plate of half-eaten fried luncheon meat and tomatoes, and leaving the room.

"You've behaved in a most irresponsible fashion. That poor girl, she's pining her heart away. And what do you do? Nothing. Nothing at all. You've made not the slightest effort to patch things up. In fact, you seem to have done everything possible to make things worse. Inviting that girl back home to see your owl—we didn't do things like that, when I was your age. We weren't even allowed to keep owls, let alone bring strange girls back home to see them."

"I'm going to be late for work."

"You just sit yourself down and hear me out. It's high time you was settling down to your responsibilities. You can't go gadding round foot-loose and fancy free for the rest of your life, you know."

"Have I got a clean pair of underpants then?" shouted Mr. Brandon from upstairs.

"In the airing cupboard. Next to Corporal Parkinson's trench comforter," shouted Mrs. Brandon. "There's hundreds of young fellers much younger than you married with a wife and family be now. Mrs. Aitchison's a grandmother twice over, and her Wally's only had his twenty-first last week. You've got a lovely girl, who thinks the world of you. She adores you. She does. She'd make a lovely home for you. She's got lovely taste in soft furnishings and . . ."

"Tarra then," said Carter Brandon, putting on his donkey jacket and picking up his box of sandwiches from the sideboard.

"It's not sunk in, has it? It's not sunk in."

"I'll be back late tonight, so can you put me dinner between two plates?"

Further tension was caused when Auntie Lil announced over lunch:

"I don't think it's right and proper for our Mort to be sharing the same bed as me."

Uncle Mort dropped his fork, and Mrs. Brandon began

to tear up a piece of sliced loaf into very small pieces.

"With me and my Bob about to have a baby, I think Mort's presence in my bed is improper. He's done his stuff, and we're very grateful. But I think he should have the good grace and common decency to relinquish his position in the conjugal bed."

"Well, Lil," said Mrs. Brandon. "It's a question of accommodation."

"There's no need to go to no trouble, Annie. In my possessions I've a camp bed that once belonged to my cousin, Greta, who was a missionary in the Ivory Coast before she eloped with the secretary of the local branch of the Magic Circle. Mort can sleep in it at the foot of my bed."

"Aye, and I'll bark if anyone tries the door handle during the night," said Uncle Mort. "Bloody hell."

However, Auntie Lil's firmness prevented any further discussion on the matter, and the new sleeping arrangements were put into operation that night.

Next day Uncle Stavely appeared at breakfast and, nodding to Mr. and Mrs. Brandon and their son, Carter, placed a manilla envelope beside each of their plates. Then he nodded again and left the room.

They heard him pause outside Auntie Lil's bedroom and heard the rustle of two manilla envelopes being pushed under a door.

Mrs. Brandon opened her envelope and pulled out a card. On top of the card carefully painted in water colours were two crossed flags. One was the Red Duster. The other was a blue St. Andrew's cross on a white background, the international maritime signal for 'Stop carrying out your intentions and watch for my signals'.

Underneath was printed in neat Gothic capitals: 'Corporal Parkinson Retd. and Stavely Brandon, Esq., request the pleasure of your company at an informal gathering in the attic tonight. RSVP.'

"Well, isn't that nice?" said Mrs. Brandon. "Isn't that considerate of them? Well, I never. RSVP, too."

Carter Brandon was playing draughts with Eric Black at lunchtime in the canteen, when Linda Preston came across and said:

"Are you coming for a walk, kid?"

"All right."

"Do you concede then?" said Eric Black.

"Aye."

They walked along the canal towpath and sat on an up-turned bath under the railway arches.

Linda Preston took a cigarette from the packet and handed it to Carter Brandon.

"I saw Pat yesterday," she said. "She come round to our house. She were dead upset. She'd have bloody slit her throat, if I hadn't took her out for a drink."

"Oh."

"She wants to make things up with you."

"I thought she did."

A diesel train passed over them and dislodged soft flakes of soot from the arches. The signal wires twanged and taut-ened, as the signalman replaced the signal at caution.

"She wants you to go round to her house for tea tonight."

"I can't."

"Why not?"

"I'm going to a party in our attic."

"Who's giving it, your bloody owl?"

"Now then."

Linda Preston stood up and walked away quickly down the towpath. Twenty yards away she turned and shouted: "You big bloody ta-ta."

It was to be the first time any of the Brandon household had visited the attic since the arrival of Corporal Parkinson, and the hearts of Mrs. Brandon and Auntie Lil fluttered as they stood outside the door.

Mr. Brandon knocked on the door, which was opened immediately by Uncle Stavely. In the lapel of his jacket he wore a card, on which was printed, 'Stavely Brandon'.

"Cloaks to the right," he said. "Drinks to the left. Buffet straight ahead, and can you bring some chairs up, Les?"

Mr. Brandon and Carter Brandon went downstairs to fetch chairs, and Uncle Mort gave his jacket to Uncle Stavely, who handed him a pink raffle ticket and stuck the stub to the collar with a pin. He gave each one of them a card, on which was written the name of the recipient.

"You do know everyone, don't you?" he said to Mr. Brandon and his son, when they returned with the chairs.

A hammock was slung across a corner of the attic. In it sat Corporal Parkinson, wearing a khaki forage cap. On the wall opposite the window was pinned a cardboard plaque, on which was written in large Gothic letters, 'Welcome To Our Guests'. The other walls were plastered with all manner of newspaper cuttings, pictures torn from magazines, wall maps and charts.

Above Auntie Lil's head was a large wall chart, headed: 'Higgs and Waterglow's Instructional Wall Charts—No. 15, Artificial Respiration'.

Behind Mr. and Mrs. Brandon was a poster. In the foreground of the poster was a soldier in flat cap and knee-length puttees, holding a rifle with fixed bayonet. In the background was a woman in long brown dress, clutching the hand of a curly-haired child and staring back at a blazing farm house. In large blood red capitals was written, 'Remember Belgium', and underneath in white was written, 'Enlist Today'.

To the left of Carter Brandon was an autographed picture of Mr. Rutland Barrington as Pooh Bah in *The Mikado*.

Corporal Parkinson raised his hand and grunted feebly.

"He says, would the ladies care for sherry and would the gentlemen help themselves to ale. Pardon?" said Uncle Stavely.

"My word, Corporal Parkinson, you have done us proud," said Auntie Lil. "Haven't they got the place looking lovely, Annie?"

"It looks a picture, doesn't it, Les?" said Mrs. Brandon.

Corporal Parkinson waved his hand weakly, and Uncle Stavely said:

"He says, victuals is now available at the buffet."

The common factor of the buffet was water biscuits. On them was placed a variety of tempting morsels, including curried kipper, pickled sprats, corned beef and trifle.

The buffet was enjoyed by one and all, and when the drinks ran out, Carter Brandon drove to the beer-off for replenishments.

"It's ages since I went to a good party, Corporal Parkinson," said Auntie Lil. "The last one I went to was in 1948. It was a party given by the District Commissioner and his lady wife for all the scouters and cub leaders, who came under his auspices. My Bob was invited in token of all the good work he had put in with his knots."

"Was he really, Lil?" said Mrs. Brandon.

"Cissie Granger, who'd been Akela of the twenty-third for many years, played the piano and we all sat round cross-legged on the carpet and sang camp fire songs. On the way home my Bob said: 'It's nice to go into other people's homes and have a good sing-song, isn't it?' And I said: 'Yes.' We didn't have no supper when we got in. We'd eaten so much at the party, you see."

"Well, bung ho," said Uncle Stavely, raising his glass.

"Stavely, are you sure you should be drinking so much?" said Mrs. Brandon. "You know what matron said about indulging yourself."

"Corporal Parkinson says matron's got secret vices," said Uncle Stavely. "Don't you, Corporal Parkinson? Pardon?"

Corporal Parkinson did not stir.

"You'll have to speak louder," said Uncle Stavely. "He's a bit hard of hearing at this time of night."

The subsequent polite conversation, animated at times when a subject close to Corporal Parkinson's heart cropped up, was interrupted by a tapping at the window.

"Tap, tap, tap, tap, tap," went the tapping.

Auntie Lil began to shiver, and Mrs. Brandon said: "Whatever's that?"

Carter Brandon opened the window, and immediately his owl hopped on to his wrist, climbed sideways up his arm and stood on his shoulder, blinking.

"It's his bloody owl," said Uncle Mort.

"Where have you been, Bentley?" said Carter Brandon.

The owl revolved its head from left to right, until it reached a position where its head was facing backwards and its body forwards.

"They're clever, you know," said Uncle Mort. "They're bloody clever. There's not many humans could do that, is there?"

Suddenly the owl, which had been staring pointedly at Corporal Parkinson, fluffed out the feathers on its nape and began clicking its beak rapidly.

Then it let out a low moan and with powerful, noiseless wingbeat launched itself from Carter Brandon's wrist and landed on Corporal Parkinson's shoulder.

The old soldier did not move. Neither did his guests. Neither did his co-host, Uncle Stavely, who was asleep.

The owl shook itself, cleaned its bill on one of the hammock strings and very slowly made its way towards Corporal Parkinson's stomach, pausing once or twice to scratch its ear with its right foot.

Once there it stared round the room and, after a moment's silent contemplation, began to click its beak. Then suddenly without warning, without so much as a by-your-leave, it began to peck vigorously at Corporal Parkinson's stomach.

The old warrior waved his arms limply, and the owl pecked more vigorously.

"Quick, Carter, get it off, get it off," cried Mrs. Brandon.

"Do something, Mort," cried Auntie Lil.

Carter Brandon sprang across the room and gripped the owl by its shoulders. He pulled, and the owl's talons scrabbled for a firmer grip in Corporal Parkinson's jacket.

"Get it off, get it off," cried Mrs. Brandon.

Carter Brandon braced himself and gave a short, sharp tug. There was a ripping noise as the owl's talons were detached from Corporal Parkinson's jacket.

"Send for the ambulance," cried Mrs. Brandon.

"Send for the RSPCA," cried Auntie Lil.

Carter Brandon scratched the owl under its chin. Then he placed it on the window ledge and closed the window.

"What's up?" said Uncle Stavely, opening his eyes and yawning.

"Carter's owl has been attacking Corporal Parkinson," said Auntie Lil.

"Pecking his tummy something chronic," said Mrs. Brandon.

"Has it? Pardon?" said Uncle Stavely, closing his eyes and falling back to sleep immediately.

Mrs. Brandon undressed Uncle Stavely and put him to bed, and Mr. Brandon wrote on the bottom of the cardboard plaque of welcome: "Thank you. Ta very much. We enjoyed your party."

Later that night Uncle Mort raised himself on one arm in his camp bed at the foot of Auntie Lil's bed and said:

"Lil? Lil, are you awake?"

"Yes. What do you want?"

"I've got something to tell you."

"What is it?"

"Corporal Parkinson was making eyes at you tonight."

"Don't be silly. Go back to sleep."

"He was making eyes at you, I tell you. He was making advances. I could see him. He's trying to get off with you."

"You're just envious, because he was able to stop the evil fluences, and you weren't. Your efforts in that sphere were completely fruitless."

"He was eyeing you up all night."

"Go back to sleep. You're an envious old man."

Uncle Mort pulled the bedclothes over his head and turned his back on Auntie Lil. He muttered softly to himself:

"I'll punch his bloody teeth in."

"Hoo, hoo, hooooo," went the owl.

CHAPTER TWENTY

"He's trying to make a cuckold out of me," said Uncle Mort in the local.

The three men had been banished from the house for the evening owing to the unfortunate fact that illness had struck the more senior members of the Brandon household, following the party in the attic.

"You're just imagining things, Mort," said Mr. Brandon.

"He's waiting. He's waiting while me back's turned, and then he'll pounce."

"Nonsense."

"These old soldiers are all the bloody same. Look what Lord Nelson got up to."

The doctor said to Mrs. Brandon after he had examined Auntie Lil:

"There's nothing to get alarmed about, Mrs. Brandon. Everything's jogging along splendidly."

After he had examined Uncle Stavely the doctor said:

"There's nothing to worry about, Mrs. Brandon. Just give him these tablets I've prescribed. Three times daily after meals. We'll soon have him on his pins again."

"Yes, doctor, thank you."

"Jolly good."

After he had examined Corporal Parkinson the doctor said:

"Most extraordinary. His stomach is covered with a series of the most curiously-shaped contusions."

"That'll be where the owl attacked him, doctor."

"The owl, eh?"

"It was attempting to eat him."

"Well, try not to let it happen again," said the doctor. "That sort of thing can be quite tricky in a man of his age, you know."

"Yes, doctor."

"Jolly good."

* * *

The hours of the following days were not long enough for

Mrs. Brandon. Up and down the stairs she trod, ministering to the needs of her ailing charges.

Backwards and forwards to the shops she plodded in pursuit of tablets, bottles of medicine, bottles of barley water, packets of junket, packets of sticking plaster, pipe tobacco, cigarettes, aniseed balls and Turkey rhubarb root.

All day long she toiled in the kitchen, washing blankets, ironing sheets, cooking meals and drying dishes. She was only aware of the passing of the days by the steady swelling of Auntie Lil's stomach.

"You really should be doing some exercises, Lil," she said one afternoon as she was changing Auntie Lil's bed. "I read all about it in a women's magazine once."

The shadow of a tree danced in a patch of sunshine on the bedroom wall.

"All in God's good time," said Auntie Lil, clambering heavily into bed. "All in God's good time."

Uncle Stavely was the first of the invalids to recover. He made his first appearance in the dining room on the evening the vicar was knocked off his autocycle by an ice cream van outside the old Moffat Street tram sheds.

"How's Lil?" said Uncle Stavely.

"Very well, thank you, Stavely," said Mrs. Brandon. "She's coming along nicely."

"Corporal Parkinson says he'd like to call on her socially so he can pay his respects. Pardon?"

"What a nice thought," said Mrs. Brandon.

"See what I mean?" whispered Uncle Mort to the dog.

Because of Uncle Stavely's post-illness unsteadiness, it was Mrs. Brandon who carried Corporal Parkinson in her arms to the bedroom of Auntie Lil.

"He says he hopes you're feeling better, and it won't be long before you're restored to full health and happiness," said Uncle Stavely.

"Thank you very much, Corporal Parkinson. It's very nice of you to come and see me. I do appreciate it very much."

Corporal Parkinson grunted.

"Not at all, it's a great pleasure," said Uncle Stavely.

"It's very rare for me to be confined to bed as a result of illness," said Auntie Lil. "Last time that happened was in 1947, when an epidemic of influenza laid me low."

"Did it, Lil?" said Mrs. Brandon.

"My Bob were so solicitous. He were such a solace to me in my hour of need. He took his winter holidays so's he could tend for me. He did all the housework and all the cooking. I made him wear a pinny, so's he wouldn't get grease spots on the front of his trousers. We often used to laugh about that in later years. 'Do you remember that time when you wore my floral pinny?' I would say. And my Bob would chuckle. He had a right infectious chuckle did my Bob. When we went to the pictures, he used to set everyone off with his chuckling. He'd only see the titles of an Abbott and Costello film, and he'd start chuckling."

"Would he, Lil?" said Mrs. Brandon.

"He managed wonderfully well during my illness. He was very good with the ration books. He didn't make a single mistake with the points. He even remembered to buy a new toilet roll."

"Corporal Parkinson is a martyr to flatulence," said Uncle Stavely.

"Is he, Stavely?" said Auntie Lil. "Can't he take nothing for it?"

"And he's had cholera, typhoid, malaria and been bitten by a rattlesnake in his time. Pardon?"

"He's done very well then, considering," said Auntie Lil.

Tea and scones were provided by Mrs. Brandon by way of sustenance, and Auntie Lil said:

"I feel much better. I think I'll get up tomorrow."

That evening Carter Brandon kissed Jessie Lewis for the first time.

She had telephoned him at work and suggested they spend the evening swimming at Endcar.

Carter Brandon had agreed, picked her up at the bus station, driven to Endcar and plunged headlong into the sparkling waters of the swimming pool.

They had dived for pennies, and it was during one of these brief periods of submersion that Carter Brandon had kissed Jessie Lewis on the lips.

They surfaced, and Jessie Lewis said:

"That was rather nice, wasn't it?"

The evening sun was strong, and they lay on their backs in the grass. Swallows skimmed over the hawthorn hedges flanking the lawns round the pool. A blackbird, head on one side, waited for worms to move beneath the glass. The plumage on its head was mottled with white, and several feathers were missing from its tail.

Carter Brandon drove Jessie Lewis to the bus station. Before she got out of the car she kissed him lightly on the cheek and said:

"I suppose your owl is quite grown up by now?"

"Yes," said Carter Brandon, but before he could put his

arm round her shoulder, she stepped out of the car and went into the bus station.

He called in at 'The Myerscough Arms' for half a pint of draught Guinness and a packet of cigarettes. All the way home he could smell the scent of Jessie Lewis's hair.

"Pat's been round to see you," said his mother, who had come to the doorstep to greet him.

"Oh aye?"

"I told her you wouldn't be back till late, but she insisted on staying. She's only just gone. She had to catch her bus."

"Mm," said Carter Brandon, and he began to eat the plate of cheese and pickles his mother had set out on the living room table.

"Why didn't you tell me you'd seen her since you broke off the engagement?" said Mrs. Brandon. "You let me go on and on to you, and you never said owt about having seen her."

"You didn't give him a bloody chance, did you? Yak, yak, yak, yak. The lad couldnt' get a word in edgeways," said Mr. Brandon.

"She looked very nice. She looked lovely," said Auntie Lil. "Tragedy suits her very well."

"Tragedy? What are you on about?" said Mr. Brandon.

"A young lady slighted in love is a very tragic figure, Leslie," said Auntie Lil.

"What about an old man slighted out of his bloody bed?" said Uncle Mort.

"You could see the tragedy in those great doleful eyes of hers," said Auntie Lil. "You could see it in the way she held her head, and in the way her skin was stretched finely and pallid over her cheek bones."

"You're quite right, Lil," said Mrs. Brandon.

"Young ladies in her frame of mind have a certain way of moving, slow and languid, as though they're moving under water."

"Underwater?" said Carter Brandon sharply.

"That's right, Carter—underwater," said Auntie Lil. "There's a great well of tragedy deep inside every woman, you know. It takes very little to tap its waters, which quickly flood the thin carpet of happiness, which it is every woman's lot to bear."

And she began to sob softly, dabbing the corners of her eyes with a linen handkerchief embroidered with purple roses.

"What did Pat want any road?" said Carter Brandon.

"She wanted to see you," said Mrs. Brandon.

"What for?"

"I would have thought that's obvious, isn't it?" said Mrs. Brandon. "It doesn't need a mind-reader to know what she was thinking, does it?"

"We couldn't get a bloody dicky bird out of her all night," said Uncle Mort.

"She just sat there and nodded her head, when she was spoken to," said Mrs. Brandon. "You could see she wasn't far from tears."

The table was sided, and Uncle Mort helped Auntie Lil to her feet.

"Good night, Carter," she said. "Take care of her. She's a lovely girl, and it won't take much for you to remove the mask of tragedy from her. Just a word of kindness, a gesture of understanding, and her whole life will be transformed to sunshine and happiness."

Then she left the room and was helped up the stairs by Uncle Mort and Mrs. Brandon.

Mr. Brandon filled his pipe, lit it and rested it in the ashtray after taking three short puffs.

"You'd best wipe them blonde hairs from your collar before your mother sees them," he said.

Carter Brandon took three hairs from his collar and threw them into the fire place just before his mother came bursting into the room.

"Oh, I see you've got rid of them hairs then," she said. "I didn't say nothing in front of your Auntie Lil, but don't think I didn't notice. It's disgusting. Disgraceful. Going out with other women while your fiancee's at your parent's home all miserable and looking like death warmed up."

"She's not my fiancee," said Carter Brandon. "She's my ex-fiancee."

"That's just splitting hairs. You know perfectly well that you're still engaged. It's just a silly little lovers' tiff you've had, that's all."

"Is it?"

"Any road, I've invited Pat and her mother round to tea next Sunday, so you can just shift yourself and make things up like a gentleman, when they come."

"Christ all bloody mighty," said Carter Brandon, standing up and striding out of the room.

"Well!" said Mrs. Brandon.

"Mm," said Mr. Brandon.

"Well! I've never heard our Carter swear like that before."

CHAPTER TWENTY-ONE

Mrs. Brandon decided that it would be an excellent plan for the male members of the household to take a trip out in the car on the Saturday preceding the tea party.

On the grounds of convenience and convalescence it would prove of great benefit to everyone concerned, she decided. A good time would be had by all.

Sandwiches were packed in a blue soft-topped suit case, Thermos flasks were filled with tea, rugs and ground sheets were stowed in the boot of the car, and the happy band was given fond farewells by Mrs. Brandon and Auntie Lil, standing on the front doorstep, waving their handkerchiefs.

"Where are we going then?" said Carter Brandon, as they turned into Derbyshire Road.

"Well, we can start at 'The Green Man' and work our way up slowly to 'The Singing Throstle'," said Uncle Mort. "Then we can drive out to Endcar, have a kip in the car and come back via that pub Jimmy Ackroyd took over last year."

"We'd better not," said Mr. Brandon. "There'd be skin and hair flying if they found out we'd been supping all day."

"Corporal Parkinson says, why can't we inspect some of the famous battlefields of the Civil War. Pardon?" said Uncle Stavely.

"I'll ram his bloody teeth down his throat, if he doesn't give over mithering," said Uncle Mort.

"Now then, Mort," said Mr. Brandon.

"Well," said Uncle Mort.

"Pardon?" said Uncle Stavely.

Carter Brandon drove out of the city centre, following the river valley through the foothills with the great moorland crags towering in the distance on either side. The heather was in bloom.

He stopped the car on a grassy bank, which formed a promontory in the river. The water was running swiftly. It had been raining in the hills that night, and the trout, noses pointing upstream, lingered long and safe in their deep green pools.

A grey wagtail flicked its tail as it stood on a stone at the water's edge. In the distance a party of meadow pipits mobbed a kestrel sitting motionless in a rowan tree.

The petrol pump broke down shortly afterwards, and

Carter Brandon walked half a mile to a farmhouse to telephone for help.

The breakdown van towed them to the village, and they ate their lunch, sitting on oil drums in the garage yard.

"Shall we go for a vessel?" said Uncle Mort.

"We'd better not. We don't want to give them an excuse for starting a row," said Mr. Brandon.

There were three granite quarries on the edge of the village, and by the time the car had been repaired they were all covered in a thin layer of white dust.

"Shall we go home then?" said Uncle Mort. "I'm fed up. There's too much bloody grass in the countryside for me."

"No. We'd best stay out here a bit longer. She'll go bloody mad if we get back too soon. She'll say we've not enjoyed ourselves."

Carter Brandon drove along the main road for two miles and then pulled into a layby. Uncle Mort and Mr. Brandon joined Uncle Stavely and Corporal Parkinson in the Lady of Nod forthwith, and Carter Brandon got out of the car and sat on the dry stone wall, smoking.

The traffic was heavy, and the air was filled with diesel fumes and dust from the road. He jumped from the wall and walked back down the road to a telephone box he had seen next to an ivy-covered inn with mullioned bay windows and an old stone hitching post outside the low-beamed front door.

He drank a quick pint in the cool, red-tiled vault and then telephoned Derrick Warrender.

"Have you got Jessie Lewis's phone number, Dekker?" he said.

"Aye," said Derrick Warrender. "What's up, are you trying to do a turn with her?"

Derrick Warrender gave him the phone number. Carter Brandon thanked him, replaced the receiver, dialled and, when the phone was answered, said:

"Can I speak to Miss Jessie Lewis please?"

"Wait there," said the voice. It was Irish. A baby cried, and there were footsteps on a staircase.

"Hello," said Jessie Lewis.

"It's Carter Brandon."

"Hello, Carter."

"Aye. Well. What are you doing tomorrow? I thought we could go out in the car like. You know, have a day out in the car sort of thing."

"I'm afraid I'm working tomorrow, Carter."

"On a Sunday?"

"Yes, I'm afraid so."

"What are you doing in the evening?"

"Still working."

"Oh."

"I'll give you a ring at work some time and perhaps we can arrange another day. How about that?" she said.

"When will you ring?"

"Well, I'm pretty busy at the moment. I'll give you a ring, though."

"Mm."

"Thanks for ringing anyway, Carter. I'll have to dash now. Bye."

"Aye. Tarra."

When he got back to the car, he found his father sitting askew in the front seat, grappling with Uncle Mort, who was hanging over the seat, pummelling Uncle Stavely furiously.

"Quick. Grab his bloody trousers and yoik him off," said Mr. Brandon.

Carter Brandon grabbed Uncle Mort by his jacket collar and wrenched him back into the front seat.

"What's all that about?" he said.

Uncle Mort sat in the front seat, panting. His hair was standing up in tufts above his ears, and his shirt collar was flapping loose. His eyes were bulging in their sockets, and he had a small cut on the bridge of his nose.

"I told you I'd punch his bloody head in," he panted.

Uncle Stavely sat in the back, rubbing his ribs and croaking breathlessly.

"I was fighting to keep Corporal Parkinson off him. He'd have murdered him, if he'd got hold of him. Pardon?" he said.

The car was full of the heavy breathing of Uncle Mort and Uncle Stavely. Occasionally the rhythm was broken by a harsh rattle as air was sucked into pinched lungs. Once Uncle Stavely blew his nose.

"Talk about grown bloody men," said Mr. Brandon.

"He wants to keep his eyes off our Lil," said Uncle Mort, turning round and raising his arm.

"Hey, hey, hey," said Mr. Brandon, taking hold of his lapels. "Now come on, calm yourself down."

Uncle Mort and Uncle Stavely tidied themselves up, and Carter Brandon turned the car to commence the journey home.

It began to rain heavily, and Mr. Brandon had to work the windscreen wipers with his fingers.

"Now you say a word of this to Annie, Stavely, and I'll punch your bloody head in for you," said Mr. Brandon.

"And so will I," said Uncle Mort. "I'll give you such a dig in the chops, you'll wonder what bloody hit you."

Mrs. Brandon fussed round them, when they returned home and said:

"Well, did you boys have a good time?"

"Aye," said Mr. Brandon. "Not bad."

"Did you enjoy yourself, Corporal Parkinson?" said Auntie Lil.

Uncle Mort stared at her silently for a few seconds and then, before leaving the room, he said to the dog in a loud voice:

"See what I mean?"

Those who attended the tea party included Mrs. Partington and her daughter Pat, Mr. and Mrs. Brandon and their son Carter, Auntie Lil and her husband, Uncle Mort.

Those who did not attend included Uncle Stavely and his companion, Corporal Parkinson.

Food eaten included crab salad, bread and butter, peaches and tinned cream, Dundee cake and chocolate log.

Food not eaten included curried kipper and pickled sprats.

Topics discussed included the weather, Mrs. Partington's recent and first visit to the launderette, Auntie Lil's recollections of the launching of the Hoylake lifeboat, the increase in the rates, the decline of radio as a popular form of home entertainment, and marmalade.

Topics not discussed included Pat's engagement to Carter Brandon.

After a leisurely evening of nostalgia and sandwiches Carter Brandon drove Mrs. Partington and Pat home.

"Now you'll come in for a cup of tea, won't you, Carter, luv? Yes, you will. You can have cocoa, if you like and if we haven't run out otherwise it will have to be tea unless you like Instant Possum. Now come on, Carter, I'll have the kettle on in next to no time."

After she had drunk one cup of tea at rapid pace Mrs. Partington said:

"Well, I'll leave you two young people to it. You must have a lot to talk about, seeing as how you haven't seen each other for such a long time. I says to your mother, Carter, I says: 'I bet they'll have such a lot to talk about,

when they get together on their own two selves.' Well, I'm
off to bed. You'll not forget to lock up, will you, Pat, luv?
Good night, Carter, tell your mam I did enjoy the evening.
It was lovely. Did she get the crab from Maypole's? Now
think on, Pat, luv, don't forget to lock the front door, you
don't know who might come in at night. You can come
into me bedroom and give us a kiss before you go to bed."

Dusk was replaced by darkness. Pat came and sat by
Carter Brandon on the sofa.

"Do you remember when we used to sit here in the old
days?" she said.

"Aye," said Carter Brandon, shifting slightly millimetre
by millimetre to the other side of the sofa.

"You proposed to me in this room, wearing me dad's
trousers, do you remember?" said Pat.

"Did I?" said Carter Brandon.

"Course you did, you soft thing," said Pat, edging two
millimetres by two millimetres towards Carter Brandon.

The cuckoo clock in the kitchen said 'Cuckoo' eleven
times, and Pat placed her hand on Carter Brandon's thigh.

"You soft thing. You big soft thing," she whispered.

"Aye. Well," said Carter Brandon, opening the zip on her
skirt.

As Carter Brandon was garaging the car Derrick Warrender passed the front gate.

"You got in touch with Jessie then?" he shouted.

"Yes."

"Ay. She told me this afternoon."

"This afternoon? I thought she was supposed to be working."

"Was she hell as like. We've been swimming at Endcar
all day. You should have come with us. It was smashing."

Carter Brandon went into the house and, as he passed the
dog thumping its tail in its box and yawning, he said:

"See what I mean?"

CHAPTER TWENTY-TWO

"Trial period?" said Mrs. Partington. "Well, what's happening, Pat, luv? Is he keeping the ring, or what? I've never

heard of such a thing. Honestly, I haven't. It doesn't make sense. There's neither rhyme nor reason in it. You young people, I can't fathom you out. You've got me completely stumped."

"We're just going to see how things work out before getting engaged again," said Pat.

"What am I going to say to the neighbours when they ask me? What am I going to say, if Mrs. Shanklin says: 'Hello, Mrs. Partington, luv, how's your Pat's engagement going on?' It's going to put me in a right pickle, isn't it? Honestly, Pat, I don't understand Carter at times. I do not."

"Neither do I," said Pat. "Not properly."

Much to everyone's surprise there was a swift and heavy snowfall in the last week of September.

It lasted only twenty minutes, yet when it was finished, the snow lay thick and crisp in the streets, and the blackbirds and song thrushes shivered in the snow-laden shrubs and hedges.

Then the sun came out and within an hour the snow had melted, and the water raced down the gutters and dripped noisily off the trees.

Uncle Mort said, when the table had been cleared after the evening meal:

"I went out in the garden, and do you know what I saw?"

"No, Mort," said Mrs. Brandon. "Les, do you know you've got a hole in your sock?"

"I saw Stavely stood at the open window with nothing on."

"Nothing on?" said Mrs. Brandon.

"He was stood there as naked as the day he was born," said Uncle Mort. "He was feeding Carter's owl."

Mr. Brandon went upstairs and knocked on the door of the attic. It was opened by Uncle Stavely, who was naked except for the hand towel he was holding round his midriff.

"What do you want?" he said.

"Can I have a word with you, Stavely?" said Mr. Brandon.

"Aye, all right. Come in."

As soon as the door was closed, Uncle Stavely let the towel drop. Then he padded across the room and sat cross-legged on the table.

"What do you want?" he said.

"Aye. Well," said Mr. Brandon. "It's about you standing with nowt on at the open window."

"Pardon?" said Uncle Stavely.

Corporal Parkinson was lying fast asleep in his hammock,

which Uncle Stavely pushed with his foot from time to time to maintain the steady swinging motion.

"What are you bloody playing at?" said Mr. Brandon.

"The body needs the beneficial, health-giving rays of the sun. It doesn't get enough, so I'm giving it a treat. Corporal Parkinson says in Finland they run round naked in the snows, men and women together, and beat themselves with birch twigs. Pardon?" said Uncle Stavely.

"I'm not disputing that, Stavely. But this isn't Finland, is it?" said Mr. Brandon. "Let's face facts, lad, this isn't Finland whatever road you look at it."

The alarm clock went off on the mantelpiece. Uncle Stavely switched it off, put on his clothes and woke Corporal Parkinson.

"Thank you for calling," said Uncle Stavely, showing Mr. Brandon to the door. "Would you ask Annie to fetch a box of mealworms next time she goes to the shops?"

"Mealworms? What do yu want mealsworms for?"

"Pardon?" said Uncle Stavely, closing the door in Mr. Brandon's face.

"Well, it's only two months to go before the big day," said Mrs. Brandon. "Are you getting excited?"

Auntie Lil and Mrs. Brandon were sitting in the front room one sunny afternoon in late September. Auntie Lil was knitting a pram cover, and Mrs. Brandon was sitting on the sofa with her shoes off, reading a copy of *Pins and Needles*.

"No," said Auntie Lil. "But my Bob is really on tenderhooks. He's as nervous as a kitten."

"Yes, but . . ."

"And the evil fluences have started again," said Auntie Lil.

"Oh dear," said Mrs. Brandon.

"They started last night. I heard the owl hooting in the back garden and shortly afterwards the fluences began."

"Are you sure they're the same ones, Lil?"

"Positive," said Auntie Lil. "I don't want to be no trouble, Annie, but I wonder if I could bother you to fetch me a glass of warm water. Not too warm. Just tepid. Thank you."

"Certainly," said Mrs. Brandon, moving across the room in her stocking feet.

In the kitchen she pressed a handkerchief soaked in cold water to her brow and took two aspirins in a glass of milk before returning with the tepid water for Auntie Lil.

"You see, what it is, Les, is your Stavely's not in his right mind," said Uncle Mort in the local that night. "If you ask me, he's pots for bloody rags."

"How do you mean?" said Mr. Brandon, packing the dominoes carefully into the wooden box with the sliding top.

"Well, just look at it," said Uncle Mort, settling himself comfortably in his chair. "One, he hardly knew what we were doing at Lil's wedding. Two, he locks himself up all day long in the attic with Corporal thingy. Three, he starts playing the kettle drum and semaphoring. Four, he walks round bollock-naked and starts feeding Carter's owl. And bloody five, he's putting the evil fluences on Lil again."

"Oh, he's doing that again, is he?" said Mr. Brandon.

"It started last night. Lil didn't get a wink of sleep with it," said Uncle Mort. "And neither did I."

They walked home in silence. Uncle Stavely and Corporal Parkinson were in the front room with Mrs. Brandon and Auntie Lil, drinking tea and eating digestive biscuits.

"Don't we get no cheese and pickled onions for us suppers?" said Uncle Mort.

"We're having digestive biscuits for a change," said Auntie Lil.

"Cheese and onions upset Corporal Parkinson last thing at night," said Uncle Stavely. "They make his knees throb."

"Oh aye, oh aye?" said Uncle Mort, pointing his right forefinger at Uncle Stavely. "I might have known you'd stick your beak in."

Then he turned to Mrs. Brandon and said:

"Can I have cheese and pickled onions, Annie?"

"Help yourself," said Mrs. Brandon, pointing vaguely at the kitchen.

A little later as Uncle Mort was wiping up the cracker crumbs from the plate with moistened fingers Uncle Stavely said:

"Corporal Parkinson says that one half of your bad temper is caused by gutsing. Pardon?"

"So help me, I'll, I'll . . ." said Uncle Mort, rising to his feet, fists raised and eyes bulging.

"Mort! Mort!" cried Auntie Lil, as Mr. Brandon caught hold of him by the hem of his jacket and pulled him back into his chair.

"He thumped me, when we was out in the car. Pardon?" said Uncle Stavely.

Silence. Auntie Lil stiffened. Mrs. Brandon slowly raised herself from the depths of the armchair. They both turned to look at Uncle Mort. Mr. Brandon coughed and shuffled his feet.

"Pardon?" said Auntie Lil.

"Corporal Parkinson says he thumped me when we was out in the car. Pardon?" said Uncle Stavely.

"Is this true, Mort?" said Auntie Lil.

"Yes," said Uncle Mort. "And I done it because he were making eyes at you. And I'll do it again, if he doesn't pack up putting the evil fluence on."

And then he stood up and strode purposefully to the door. Once there he stopped and said:

"So be warned."

No one spoke for several minutes. They could hear the dog's lead jingling as Uncle Mort took it down from the shelf in the kitchen. Then they heard the back door slam and the latch rattle on the front gate.

Then Auntie Lil said very quietly:

"You know, I'm sure Mort's going a little simple. He just doesn't seem to be in his right mind these past few weeks."

Uncle Stavely and Corporal Parkinson made their way to bed a few minutes after ten. Auntie Lil followed them shortly after Uncle Mort returned with the dog.

"Now don't start on me," said Mr. Brandon. "It weren't my fault."

"That's right, Les," said Mrs. Brandon.

"What do you mean—'that's right, Les?'"

"What I say. I believe you. You wasn't responsible. Is there any more tea in the pot?"

Mr. Brandon raised his eyebrows. Then he lifted the tea pot lid, looked inside and said:

"Aye, I can squeeze another cup out."

"You've been very quiet tonight," said Pat.

"Have I?" said Carter Brandon.

A street lamp shone on the top of the car bonnet. He could smell the earthy, rooty smell of the bunch of moorland heather which Pat held on her lap.

"You hardly said a word in the pub, and you've not spoken all the way home."

"Oh," said Carter Brandon. "Well, I'm getting a radio for the car tomorrow."

Pat sniffed sharply. A cat dropped noiselessly from a laburnum tree to their right and dashed sideways across the road with its tail held erect and its ears flat over its head.

"Aren't you going to kiss me good night?" said Pat.

Carter Brandon kissed her lightly on the cheek.

"When am I going to see you again?" said Pat.

"I'll give you a buzz in the week. Tarra."

Next morning there was no sign of the owl in the garage.

CHAPTER TWENTY-THREE

Mrs. Brandon fell ill quite suddenly. The alarm clock went off in the morning, and she said:

"I've got a funny taste in me mouth, Les."

And when she lifted her head from the pillow, she came over faint and keeled over onto Mr. Brandon.

The doctor was summoned and, after making his examination, he told Mr. Brandon:

"Nothing to worry about, Mr. Brandon. Just a simple case of exhaustion. Keep her in bed for a fortnight, plenty of rest, no worries and she'll soon be as right as rain."

All that day Mrs. Brandon lay in deep, troubled sleep. Her breathing was heavy, and sometimes her feet twitched, and she made panicky, whimpering noises.

Mr. Brandon, who had taken the day off work, sat by her bed and mopped the perspiration off her brow with a face cloth.

Uncle Mort poked his head round the door and whispered: "How is she?"

Mr. Brandon turned, put his fingers to his lips and shook his head.

A sour smell of overcooked vegetables greeted Carter Brandon on his return from work.

"How long does it take a panful of spuds to boil?" said Uncle Mort. "We're having stewed mutton."

Carter Brandon went upstairs and said to his father:

"How is she?"

His father nodded, and Carter Brandon tip-toed to his mother's bedside.

Her breathing was calm and regular, and there was the faintest touch of a smile on her lips. Her cheeks were sallow, and her forehead was dry and hot to the touch.

"She's a bit better," said Mr. Brandon.

"How's Auntie Lil?" said Carter Brandon to Uncle Mort after he had washed and shaved.

"Very tired," said Uncle Mort. "Exhausted in fact. She hasn't the strength to get out of her bed."

They ate their evening meal in the kitchen and gave the remains to the dog. It ate the mutton rapidly, but backed away from the potatoes and peas, growling. Then it retired to a corner and gulped violently several times before being sick.

"We're in a hell of a mess at home," said Carter Brandon to Sid Skelhorn.

They were in 'The Myerscough Arms', playing snooker.

"You want to get a nurse," said Sid Skelhorn after he had heard Carter Brandon's tale of woe.

"A nurse?"

"Aye. You can get one on the bloody National Health, can't you? Course you can. My missus had one for four week before our Raymond were born."

He potted the black into the bottom left-hand pocket and then missed an easy red lying over the right-hand middle pocket.

"It's these bloody things," he said, taking out his bottom dentures and resting them on the table next to his drink.

"Have you thought of getting a nurse in?" said Carter Brandon, when he was alone with his father later that evening.

"No," said Mr. Brandon.

"I should ask the doctor about it, when he comes round in the morning," said Carter Brandon.

Mr. Brandon followed his son's advice, and the doctor nodded his head rapidly and bounced up and down on his heels.

"Splendid. Splendid," he said. "You've got a watertight case there. Leave it to me, we'll have a nurse round literally before you can say Jack Robinson."

Truth to tell, the doctor was not quite accurate in his assessment of the time needed to acquire a nurse.

He came round in the evening and told Mr. Brandon, who had telephoned his works to say he would be off work all week, that the nurse would be round later in the week.

"Unexpected snag," he said. "Still, fingers crossed. Good show."

"I don't know why you bothered, Carter, luv, I do not," said Mrs. Partington. "I mean to say, I'd have come round to do for you willingly. I mean to say, I'm stuck here on me own all day. I'd have been only too willing and ready to rally round the flag, wouldn't I, Pat? Can't you cancel it,

Carter? Can't you say to the doctor: 'Thank you for all the trouble you've gone to, doctor, but the mother of my fiancee has kindly volunteered to come round and take over the running of the house?' I mean to say, it'll be no trouble, will it, Pat?"

"Well, ta all the same," said Carter Brandon. "I'd better be going now."

He spent the rest of the evening washing dishes and helping Uncle Mort peel potatoes for the following day's meals.

"I haven't seen your owl lately," said Uncle Mort.

"No, he must have flown off," said Carter Brandon.

"Aye, he's probably gone to join his mates. That's what I'd do, if I was in his shoes," said Uncle Mort. "What should I do with the peelings?"

"Stick them in the bin, I suppose."

"What a waste," said Uncle Mort. "There must be hundreds of pigs round here who'd give their bloody hind legs for a good munch at them peelings."

Carter Brandon went upstairs and sat next to his father at his mother's bedside.

"You're a good lad, Carter," she said.

"Mm," said Carter Brandon. "How are you feeling?"

"Much better, thank you," she said. "The trouble is at night."

"At night?" said Mr. Brandon.

"That's when the evil fluences start."

In the morning the doctor said to Mr. Brandon:

"Well, it's all fixed up, Mr. Brandon. Nurse is coming round this afternoon, and she'll be here for as long as you need her."

"Grand," said Mr. Brandon.

"Now what about accommodation?"

"Eh?"

"Well, she'll have to live in, you know. Oh yes, she'll have to live in. Definitely."

Mr. Brandon scratched his chin thoughtfully. Carter Brandon coughed and said:

"She can have my room. I'll sleep down here on the sofa."

"Splendid. All hands to the pump, eh?" said the doctor. Then as he was putting on his hat at the front door he said: "She's one of the most capable nurses in the district. Only young, but don't let that put you off."

"What do they call her?" said Mr. Brandon.

"Nurse Lewis."

"Lewis?" said Carter Brandon.

"That's right," said the doctor. "Jessie Lewis, I believe. Perhaps you know her?"

"Jessie Lewis?" said Carter Brandon.

"That's bloody torn it," said Mr. Brandon.

CHAPTER TWENTY-FOUR

"Derrick Warrender said you worked as a char up Moss-croft Edge," said Carter Brandon to Jessie Lewis.

She laughed and replied:

"Oh, that's just Derrick. If you want to know, I was looking after an old lady. She had a tumour on the brain. She died last Tuesday."

"Oh."

"She left me a pearl necklace in her will."

It was the second day of her service in the Brandon household, and the first time Carter Brandon had been with her alone.

They were standing in the kitchen, washing pots.

She was wearing a mauve dress with puffed sleeves. Over her dress she wore a white apron. The light glimmered in the strands of blonde hair on the nape of her neck. She handed Carter Brandon a brown casserole dish.

"You went swimming that Sunday I asked you out, didn't you?" said Carter Brandon.

"That's right, sweetie," said Jessie Lewis, pulling out the plug from the sink and wiping down the draining board with a dish cloth.

Upstairs in the front bedroom Mr. and Mrs. Brandon were talking earnestly.

"You should have told him, Les. You should have told him she weren't suitable," said Mrs. Brandon.

"Now don't get all aerated, Annie," said Mr. Brandon. "She's just here as a nurse, that's all. And a damn good nurse she is, too."

"I'm not saying she isn't, Les. But what will Pat say, if she finds out?"

"It's got bugger all to do with Pat. If she doesn't like Jessie, she can lump it."

" 'Jessie'?" said Mrs. Brandon. "How long have you been calling her Jessie then?"

"Ee, give over, give over," said Mr. Brandon.

Uncle Mort said, as they were sitting in the front room:

"I wonder, Jessie. I wonder if you could take a look at me back when you've a minute to spare. I'm getting these bloody awful pains where me kidneys should be. Right severe twinges, they are."

"I'll have a look, when I come back," said Jessie Lewis. "Carter's just going to run me to my digs to pick up a few things."

"That's the first thing I knew about it," said Carter Brandon.

Jessie Lewis had a one-room flat in one of the old sandstone Victorian mansions in the northern suburbs of the city.

The roads were lined with great horse chestnut trees, copper beech, lime and sycamore. Here and there monkey puzzle trees appeared over the thick high hedges of privet and hawthorn.

Through the back window of Jessie Lewis's room Carter Brandon could see a man exercising two Afghan hounds on a cricket pitch. The square was fenced off for the winter.

Jessie Lewis closed the door and began searching through her dressing table, throwing her clothes on to the floor as she plundered the drawers.

"Sit down," she said.

Jessie Lewis rammed the clothes back into the dressing table and went to a chest under the windows.

"Here we are," she said, bringing out two books, which she placed in a canvas hold-all.

Carter Brandon kneeled down on the floor beside her and kissed her neck.

She sighed and after a while said:

"Close your eyes."

He closed his eyes, still kneeling on the floor.

"Are they closed good and tight?" she said.

"Yes."

She smacked him hard on the ear and sent him reeling backwards into the chest. His head crashed against a brass knob, and a plant pot toppled slowly on to his stomach, spilling sandy soil down his trousers.

"You can open them now," said Jessie Lewis.

His ear tingled all the way home, and his father said:

"Where's Jessie? Didn't she come back with you?"

Carter Brandon did not reply. He whistled to the dog and

took it for a long walk, calling in at the local for a bottle of
Guinness just before closing time.

"You two-faced bloody A-rab," said Linda Preston to
Carter Brandon in 'The Singing Throstle'.

"What do you mean?" said Carter Brandon.

"Letting me go on apologising for not turning up outside
the Town Hall, and you hadn't even turned up your chuffin'
self. You was off mankin' round with Jessie Lewis."

"Aye, well, I tried to tell you."

"Ah, piss off," said Linda Preston. Then she turned to Sid
Skelhorn and said: "Give us a kiss, Sidney. Let's see what
it's like wi'out teeth."

It was the night of the farewell party sponsored by Terence Lewis of Maintenance, who was leaving the employ of
Wagstaffe and Broome's to emigrate to Southern Rhodesia.

"All them little nig-nog birds, eh, Terence?" said Sid Skelhorn. "That old black magic, eh?"

Carter Brandon drank constantly until closing time and
was quite unsteady of his feet as he sought his car in the
car park.

Linda Preston had her arms round Ferenc Nemec, foreman of the Paint Shop.

"Hey up, he says he's going to show me his Hungarian
goulash," she shouted across the car park. Then Ferenc
Nemec bundled her into his Ford Zephyr.

Carter Brandon had difficulty in finding the headlights and
even more difficulty in switching them on. He peered intently
through the windscreen and drove slowly in second gear
down the hill past 'The Green Man'.

Then he stopped the car on a dark clinker-surfaced road
by the Crompton Street wash houses and was violently sick.

He felt much better by the time he reached home. He
stood in the middle of the garden and called softly:

"Bentley. Bentley. Ke-wick, ke-wick, ke-wick."

But there was no reply.

He sat on the edge of the wheelbarrow, lit a cigarette
and watched clouds scudding across the moon.

A light shone behind the curtains of the attic, and he
could just make out the flicker and flutter of the night light
in the back bedroom.

The landing light went out, and he threw away his half-
smoked cigarette and entered the house yawning and undoing the top button of his shirt.

His bed was already made up on the sofa, and Jessie

Lewis was sitting on the rug in front of the fire, reading a book.

She closed the book and smiled.

"Have a nice time?" she said.

"Mm."

"I've made your bed for you."

"So I see."

Carter Brandon sat in the rocking chair and began to untie his laces.

A few minutes later Jessie Lewis said:

"Don't, Carter, don't."

She was lying beside him on the sofa. Her dress was open to the waist and her breasts were firm and smooth under his touch.

She stiffened momentarily as he ran his lips over her navel.

"No," she said.

She pulled open his trousers and took hold of his testicles.

"No. Please, please. No," she said.

She stood up and stepped out of her dress. She turned her back to him and removed the rest of her clothing. He could see the shadow of her full, up-turned breasts thrown by the faint firelight on the wall.

She crouched down on the floor beside the sofa, and he rolled down beside her.

As he ran his hands over her thighs, and as her breasts sucked and chucked beneath his chest, her whole body became rigid.

"No," she said, tugging his hair and digging her fingernails into his back. "No, no, no."

She lay face down on the floor and crumpled up the rug about her body.

"That always happens, when I get too excited," said Carter Brandon glumly.

The Brandons, relations and friends were delighted with the efficiency, courtesy and pleasant disposition of their nurse.

Uncle Mort was particularly impressed and stood up every time she entered the room.

Mrs. Brandon, grudgingly at first and later enthusiastically admitted that she could find no grounds for complaint, and Mr. Brandon, restored to his rightful position at his lathe between the hours of nine and six, was unsparing in his praise.

"Corporal Parkinson says you've brought a ray of sunshine into our lives. Pardon?" said Uncle Stavely to Jessie

Lewis one evening as they sat in the front room, playing 'Battleships'.

And that night both Mrs. Brandon and Auntie Lil told their respective husbands that the evil fluences had stopped.

Next day Uncle Mort startled Auntie Lil by saying:

"I think I'll take Corporal Parkinson out in his bath chair."

"Now, Mort," said Auntie Lil, who had taken to leaving her bed in the afternoons. "Now don't start that all over again."

"What are you going on about, woman? He's not been out for weeks. It'll do him good to get a breath of fresh air into his lungs—if he's got any," said Uncle Mort.

"Corporal Parkinson says he doesn't want to go out, as the wind's in the north-east quarter and it plays havoc with the wounds in his elbow. Pardon?" said Uncle Stavely.

Uncle Mort ignored the protests and, after wrapping Corporal Parkinson in three Fair Isle mufflers and several layers of rug and blanket, wheeled him through the streets with the dog trotting beside the squeaking wheels of the wicker bath chair.

But when tea time came, they had not returned.

"Shall I go out and see if I can spot them?" said Jessie Lewis.

"I don't want to be no trouble, Nurse Lewis, but it would put my mind very much at ease, if you would," said Auntie Lil.

Jessie Lewis was about to set off in search of the missing couple, when Carter Brandon returned from work in his car with Pat, whom he had met outside the Town Hall.

"Hop in with us, Jessie, and we'll have a look," said Pat.

They drove slowly along the streets, which were gathering a shroud of smoky dust. The weather was fair, and the smoke from the chimney rose straight.

"How are you liking your new job then?" said Pat.

"Very nice, thank you, Pat," said Jessie Lewis.

"Why don't you come out with me and Carter one evening?" said Pat.

"Super," said Jessie Lewis.

"They can't have gone this far," said Carter Brandon. "I'm turning back."

He took a different route home, passing the vicarage, which since the death of the vicar had been unoccupied. Someone had broken an upstairs window, and there were pigeon droppings on the step beneath the porch.

"Are you still going out with Derrick Warrender?" said Pat.

"Off and on."

'We'll have to make up a foursome. That'd be smashing, wouldn't it, Carter?"

There was still no sign of Uncle Mort and Corporal Parkinson, when they got back, and Uncle Stavely was showing signs of considerable distress.

"He's been kidnapped, that's what's happened," he said. "We'll have to pay a ransom to get him back, and I can't afford no ransoms at my time of life."

Carter Brandon took Pat to 'The Whipping Top' after tea, and she had a good time.

"Me mam played all hell up, when she heard about Jessie Lewis staying at your place," she said.

"Did she?"

"But I said there was nothing wrong in that."

"Did you?"

"I did. I says: 'I can trust, Carter,' I says. And that seemed to pacify her."

"Did it?"

"I can trust you, Carter, can't I? Tell me I can trust you."

"Mm."

"Say it proper."

"Yes."

They kissed good night in the car outside Pat's home, and she said with her mouth pressed close to his right ear:

"Have you still got the ring, Carter?"

"Oh aye, I've still got it."

"Where?"

"Good night," said Carter Brandon.

He had only been in the house for five minutes when Uncle Mort returned with Corporal Parkinson.

"Where the bloody hell have you been?" said Mr. Brandon.

"We've been worrying ourselves sick about you," said Auntie Lil.

"It's a good job Mrs. Brandon hasn't heard about it," said Jessie Lewis.

"Did you have to pay a ransom?" said Uncle Stavely.

"Ransom? What are you mithering about?" said Uncle Mort.

"Think yourself lucky you didn't have to pay no ransom," said Uncle Stavely. "He's worth a penny or two on the quiet is Corporal Parkinson. Pardon?"

"Where have you been, that's what I want to know?" said Auntie Lil.

"We sat in the launderette, watching the washing for a couple of hours. Then we went and played crib at the bowls

club. Then we went and had fish and chips with Frank Ash-
croft, Ernie Taggett and that feller with the cleft palate.
And then I lost me way, so I had to get a taxi," said Uncle
Mort. "What's all the fuss about?"

"Corporal Parkinson says he loathed every minute of it.
He couldn't get back quick enough. He refuses point black
to go out with him again ever. Pardon?" said Uncle Stavely.

Corporal Parkinson let out a thin, rasping squeak, and
Uncle Mort said:

"He says, don't listen to what our Stavely says. He enjoyed
hisself very much, and he's disgusted at Stavely making eyes
at our Lil. Pardon?"

CHAPTER TWENTY-FIVE

Mrs. Brandon, restored to health and happiness, placed a
startling proposition to her husband one morning.

It was the occasion of the first Sunday in the month of
October, and there were black-headed gulls scavenging in
the streets by the wool warehouses.

The time was ten-thirty a.m. The setting was the breakfast
table. Also present was Mr. Carter Brandon. His mother
said:

"I think we should move to a larger house."

"Mm," said Mr. Brandon.

"Les! Les, put that paper down and listen to what I'm
saying," said Mrs. Brandon, tapping the pot of marmalade
with her tea spoon.

"I am listening," said Mr. Brandon.

"I said, I think we should move to a larger house."

"A what?"

"You see. You see. I knew you wasn't listening."

"What do we want to move to a larger house for?" said
Mr. Brandon. "I've just ordered nineteen and six worth of
cuttings for me greenhouse."

"I'm not arguing with you," said Mrs. Brandon. "I've
been looking at the house ads while I've been badly, and
I'm going to see estate agent first thing tomorrow morning."

In the evening after tea Mr. Brandon said to Carter Brandon as they stood by the pear tree in the dusk.

"What do you think of that then?"

"What?"

"Moving bloody house."

"Aye."

Mr. Brandon took out his penknife and began to scrape at the bark of the tree.

"It's getting some sort of growth on it. Do you see them little red spots?"

They stood in silence. A light glowed in the attic.

"I wonder what's happened to Bentley," said Carter Brandon.

"Probably looking for a bigger bloody nest for hisself," said Mr. Brandon. And he dug the blade of his knife deep into the bark.

On the following morning Uncle Stavely came down to breakfast and said:

"Corporal Parkinson's at death door."

"He isn't," said Uncle Mort.

"Pardon?" said Uncle Stavely.

"You heard," said Uncle Mort.

Mr. Brandon spread dripping slowly on his toast and said:

"What seems to be the trouble then, Stavely?"

"Nurse Lewis says he's suffering from exposure, and he never ought to have been took out like that at his age. He's moaning something chronic upstairs. Pardon?"

"He were all right when I saw him," said Uncle Mort.

"Has anyone ever told you you've got a big Adam's Apple?" said Uncle Stavely to Uncle Mort. "Corporal Parkinson once knew a bloke, whose Adam's Apple was so big, he strangled hisself on his tunic top during the black-out."

"He said nothing of the sort," said Uncle Mort. "You're making it all up."

Further discussion on the subject of the old soldier's health was prevented by the entry of Mrs. Brandon.

She wore her simulated squirrel coat and the calf-length fur boots bought for her by Pat the previous Saturday.

"What are you all dolled up for?" said Mr. Brandon.

"To see the estate agent," said Mrs. Brandon. "It's important to show a good front on these occasions."

When Carter Brandon arrived home in the evening, his mother and father were arguing in the living room.

"I'm not surprised Lil's been took badly again," said Mr. Brandon. "It's enough to make anyone badly, moving house, particularly if you're pregnant as well."

"I wish you wouldn't use words like that, Les," said Mrs. Brandon.

"It's a wonder I'm not confined to me bed with all this bloody commotion going on."

"I'm only trying to do the best for everyone concerned. I thought our Lil would like to move into a new house with her baby. I thought your Stavely and Corporal Parkinson would have more room for their semaphoring. I thought our Carter would be able to entertain his friends in a separate room."

"But I don't want to entertain my friends," said Carter Brandon.

Mr. Brandon took out his pipe, unscrewed the stem and blew into the mouthpiece.

"You come home, walk straight upstairs and tell her we're moving house without so much as a word of warning, and then you're surprised when she has a relapse," he said. "I almost had a relapse meself, when you told me the price."

"It's a snip. You don't come by houses like that every day of the week for five thousand pound."

"Five thousand quid," said Mr. Brandon. "I'm surprised you haven't fixed us to move into the royal bloody yacht."

Then he went into the kitchen and blew down his pipe again.

Carter Brandon hung up his donkey jacket and went into the kitchen to wash his hands. His father was washing the pots.

"The doctor's up with her now," he said.

"Oh," said Carter Brandon.

Mr. Brandon tip-toed to the door, looked into the living room and then closed the door. He spoke in a whisper.

"It's got six rooms on the ground floor alone," he said. "And apart from that it's got four storeys. It'll be like living in a bloody light house."

After a while Mrs. Brandon came into the kitchen.

"Doctor's just gone," she said. "Les, he says she's not at all herself. He says she might have to go into the nursing home."

"I'm not surprised," said Mr. Brandon. "Where do these plates go?"

"Les, don't you know where things go yet?" said Mrs. Brandon, snatching the dinner plates from her husband's hand and placing them in the bottom drawer of the cooker. Then she turned to her son and said: "Your Auntie Lil wants to see you. Just pop up before you have your dinner, will you?"

"All right," said Carter Brandon, and he returned his dinner to the cooker.

The door of Auntie Lil's bedroom was closed. Carter Brandon knocked, and Jessie Lewis answered:

"Come in."

He went in, and Jessie Lewis put her finger to her lips, took him by the arm and led him to the window. Auntie Lil lay in bed asleep. She was propped up by a bolster, two pillows and the candy striped cushion Mr. Brandon used on his deck chair during the months of summer.

"Have you been avoiding me?" whispered Jessie Lewis.

"No," whispered Carter Brandon.

"Then why haven't you offered to take me out?"

"Because I'm supposed to be engaged to Pat."

"Shush. Not so loud. You'll wake your auntie," said Jessie Lewis, and then she kissed him lightly on the cheeks.

Carter Brandon tried to push her away, but she pressed herself into him and said very softly:

"We must try again some time, mustn't we?"

Then she left the room, and he could hear her singing to herself as she went downstairs.

Auntie Lil opened her eyes slowly. Then she closed them quickly and let out a deep sigh.

"Hello, Carter," she said.

"Hello, Auntie Lil."

"Come and sit here alongside me, Carter. I've something I want to tell you," she said and patted the side of the bed.

Carter Brandon sat on the foot of the bed.

"Do you remember the good times we used to have in the temperance bar, Carter?" said Auntie Lil.

"Aye. Yes, I do," said Carter Brandon. "I do, yes."

"We did have fun in them days. All that sarsaparilla and stuff, we made regular gluttons of ourselves, didn't we, Carter?"

"We did that, Auntie Lil," said Carter Brandon, running his finger round the top of his collar. He had had a shaving rash for four days.

"Your Uncle Bob enjoyed himself, too. You could see that, though, couldn't you? I want you to know that we're both most appreciative of the way you so selflessly gave up your spare time to provide entertainment in that way. Your actions haven't gone unnoticed."

Auntie Lil stared at him silently. She showed no signs of the swellings of pregnancy, and there were red marks from her spectacles on the bridge of her nose.

She wriggled her shoulders and settled herself into the pillows.

"What I'm about to say to you must go no further than these four walls, do you understand that, Carter?"

"Yes."

"Good. Well. I want you to make me a promise."

"Mm."

"I want you to promise me that if anything should happen to me, you'll take sole responsibility for the upbringing of my baby."

Carter Brandon coughed, looked at his thumb nails and said:

"Now come on, Auntie Lil, you're not to say things like that."

"Do you promise me that faithfully?" she said.

"Well, I mean."

"Do you?" said Auntie Lil firmly, trying to rise from the pillows.

"Yes."

A slow smile spread over her face. She sighed deeply and blew him a kiss.

"You're a good lad, Carter," she said. "Now run along and get your dinner. You must be famished, poor lad."

Carter Brandon was just about to open the door, when Auntie Lil said:

"I don't trust no one else, Carter. They're trying to kill me and my unborn child. They're just envious. They're full of evil."

CHAPTER TWENTY-SIX

It was later in the week. Mrs. Brandon had temporarily abandoned her house-moving plans, Uncle Mort had taken Corporal Parkinson for several walks in the park and Auntie Lil was still confined to her bed.

It was the interval at the pictures, too, and Pat was sucking a creamy mint.

"You've been very quiet all evening, Carter," she said. "What's ailing you?"

"Nothing much," said Carter Brandon. Pat linked his arm and snuggled her head into his shoulder. And he put his arm round her and said: "I'm just feeling browned off, that's all."

"Charming," said Pat. "That's a great compliment to me, I must say."

Carter Brandon squeezed her hand and gave her a sharp kiss on the soft skin behind her ear.

"Not with you, love," he said. "It's all the others."

They went back to Pat's home, and they heard Mrs. Partington in the bedroom upstairs. There was a slight thud as she kicked off her slippers, and then she began to wind the alarm clock.

Carter Brandon switched off the light and placed his hand inside Pat's jumper.

"Guess what I've got inside my hand," he said.

"I don't know, luv," said Pat.

"Open it then."

"What are you on about, Carter?" said Pat, wriggling so that she could get hold of Carter Brandon's hand. "Come on, you've got it stuck in me bra."

Carter Brandon took out his hand from under her jumper and held it under her nose.

"Open it," he said.

Pat opened his hand, and there on his palm was the engagement ring.

"Oh, Carter," she said. "Oh. Oh."

"Aren't you going to put it on?"

"Course I am, luv. Are we engaged again then, official?"

"Aye. I suppose we are," said Carter Brandon.

A few days later Auntie Lil said she felt much better and invited all the household to join her in her room.

They assembled in Auntie Lil's bedroom. Mrs. Brandon sat on one side of the bed, Jessie Lewis sat on the other. Carter Brandon brought up the Lloyd Loom chair for Corporal Parkinson, and Uncle Stavely sat on one arm and Uncle Mort sat on the other. Mr. Brandon sat on the linen basket, and Carter Brandon stood next to Jessie Lewis.

Auntie Lil leaned over to the bedside table and picked up eight pencils and eight pieces of paper.

"Now this here is pencil and paper," she said. "I've got them out, because I've got a little task for you."

"Are we going to play consequences?" said Uncle Stavely. "Corporal Parkinson loves consequences. Pardon?"

"No, he doesn't," said Uncle Mort. "He hates them. Pardon?"

"Boys, boys, boys. Please, no squabbling and pay attention to what I'm about to say."

"I should think so, too," said Mrs. Brandon. "Is that door open, Carter? There's a terrible draught whistling down the back of me neck."

"Being as how I'm about to give birth. And being as how the end result of my labours will become a member of the household, I think it's only right and proper that you should all have a hand in deciding on the name," said Auntie Lil.

"No, Lil," said Mrs. Brandon. "That's your's and Mort's responsibility."

"Aye, don't bring us into it, Lil," said Mr. Brandon. "You call it what you want, it'll be all right by us."

"And so I'm giving you all pencil and paper, so's you can write down your choice," said Auntie Lil. "I'm doing that, so there can be no accusations that collusion has took place."

"When we've finished the consequences, can we play charades? Pardon?" said Uncle Stavely.

"It's not sunk in, you know," said Mrs. Brandon. "Tell him, Les. Tell him."

"We're not playing bloody consequences," said Mr. Brandon in a loud voice. "We're playing choosing a name for our Lil's nipper."

"Oh that sounds a good game. I've never played that before," said Uncle Stavely.

"Now, Carter, be a good boy and pass round the pencils and papers," said Auntie Lil.

Carter Brandon followed these instructions to the letter, and, when he had completed them, Auntie Lil said:

"Now then nature being what it is, my unborn baby has a choice of being one of two genders."

"A boy or a girl, Lil," said Mrs. Brandon.

"That's right, Annie," said Auntie Lil. "Well, to prepare ourselves for all eventualities I want you to write down the name of a boy and the name of a girl on your slips of paper. That way we can cover ourselves according to the relevant gender."

"What a bloody palaver," said Uncle Mort. "We never had all this trouble when our Cyril were born."

"No?" said Mr. Brandon.

"Course we didn't. Our Edna says to me: 'If it's a girl, I'll choose it. If it's a boy, you can bloody choose it.' "

"Why the hell did you call him Cyril then?" said Mr. Brandon.

"It was the first name what come into me head."

"That seem to be a most frivolous reason, Mort," said Auntie Lil.

"It wasn't that at all, Mort. Don't tell such fibs," said Mrs. Brandon. "You chose the name after that pet rabbit we had when we lived in Cosgrove Street."

"Did I?"

"You know perfectly well you did. You was very attached to that rabbit, and I don't know how you've got the nerve to dishonour its poor little memory in that way."

Corporal Parkinson was snoring steadily and loudly, and there were dribbles of saliva on his chin. Uncle Mort leaned over him and wiped them off with his handkerchief, and the old soldier stirred in his sleep and groaned.

"He says will you stop touching him like that. He can't stand the feel of linen on his chin. Pardon?" said Uncle Stavely.

"You'll get the feel of my knuckles on your chin, if you don't give over," said Uncle Mort.

"Boys, boys," said Auntie Lil. "Remember where you are, please. You're in the presence of potential childbirth, and I'd be thankful if you'd both behave accordingly. Particularly you, Mort, being as how you've got such a big stake in the issue."

"I should think so, too," said Mrs. Brandon, glaring angrily at Uncle Mort.

"Now then, are we all ready?" said Auntie Lil.

"No," said Uncle Stavely. "What about Corporal Parkinson? Doesn't he get nothing?"

"Yes, what about Corporal Parkinson?" said Uncle Mort.

Auntie Lil smiled and said:

"Poor old warrior, he's fast asleep. I'll leave it to you to fill his sheet in for him."

"I'll do it," said Uncle Mort.

"I'll do it. Pardon?" said Uncle Stavely.

"Look, don't let's have no argy-bargy about it. Tear your papers in half both of you and do one each for him," said Mrs. Brandon.

This was done, and, when Uncle Mort completed his task before Uncle Stavely, he looked up and said:

"I finished mine before him, didn't I?"

Everyone looked at Auntie Lil. She wriggled her feet, sank back in her pillows and said softly:

"Now this is to be a democratic vote. My Bob was as keen as mustard on democracy, and that's why I'm doing things this road.

"I shall count up all the names, and the one what appears most on your lists shall be the one that is given to my child. Write your names on the tops of your sheets—block capitals, please. Ready, steady, go."

For a moment no one moved. Then Mrs. Brandon, shielding her paper from view with her arm, began to write.

"Come on, everyone, let's be having you," she said.

Mr. Brandon sucked his pencil and stared hard at the piece of paper on his knee. He looked at his wife, poised his pencil above the paper, and then used it to scratch the back of his neck.

Uncle Mort scribbled fiercely on his two sheets of paper, folded them neatly and said to Uncle Stavely:

"I've beat you again, you see."

Uncle Stavely snorted and continued his slow printing, pausing now and then to suck through his teeth.

The curtains of the bedroom billowed gently and fell back heavily so that the brass curtain rings rattled behind the pelmet.

"I told you there was a draught in this room," said Mrs. Brandon.

All that could be heard was the scratching of pencils on paper. Once Mr. Brandon let out a deep sigh.

Then Uncle Stavely said:

"How do you spell Vladimir?"

"Vladimir?" said Mrs. Brandon.

"Pardon?" said Uncle Stavely.

"You're never choosing Vladimir for a name?"

"He probably thinks the baby'll be born with snow on its boots," said Mr. Brandon.

"Don't be so vulgar, Les," said Mrs. Brandon.

"If it's his choice, let him write it down," said Auntie Lil, who was staring at the ceiling through one eye.

"It doesn't matter. I've thought of another one. Pardon?" said Uncle Stavely.

Mrs. Brandon waited for a few minutes, glanced round the room, hoisted up her bosom and said:

"We're all done now, Lil. You can collect the papers, Carter."

"Wait a minute," said Auntie Lil, rising from her pillows. "Don't rush. If anyone's got second thoughts, write now or forever hold your peace."

She paused and then said:

"Is everybody ready?"

"Half a mo," said Uncle Stavely. He unfolded one of the slips of paper, crossed out a name, slowly wrote in another and said: "He who laughs last laughs longest."

Carter Brandon collected the papers and handed them to Auntie Lil, who put on her glasses and picked up one of the slips.

"Now the first one I'm opening has 'Leslie Brandon' wrote on it in very neat block capitals," said Auntie Lil. "Well done, Leslie, they do you great credit."

"He always had a good hand, when he took the trouble," said Mrs. Brandon.

"The name Leslie has chosen for the girl is Celia."

"Celia? Wherever did you dredge that one up from?" said Mrs. Brandon.

"I like the name Celia," said Mr. Brandon slowly. "I think it's a grand name for a girl is Celia."

And he looked across the room and winked at Carter Brandon. Mrs. Brandon sniffed hard and said:

"Well, it's your own affair, but I would have thought you'd have done me the courtesy of choosing Anne. That's what we said we'd call our Carter, if he turned out to be a girl. I thought we'd decided on that long ago."

"And the name he's chosen for the boy is Gilbert," said Auntie Lil.

"Why Gilbert of all names?" said Mrs. Brandon. "Poor little mite. They'll call him Gil at school, and everyone'll think he's a goldfish."

"I like the name Gilbert. Pardon?" said Uncle Stavely.

"Do you, Stavely?" said Auntie Lil. "Would you like to tell us why?"

"No," said Uncle Stavely.

"Now the next one is compiled by Carter. And he's chosen for the little boy, Robert, and for the little girl, Lily. Ah, bless him, what a lovely thought, Carter."

Auntie Lil smiled at her nephew and mouthed a kiss. Then she picked up another slip of paper.

"Well, this one's got no name on top for a start off," she said.

"It's mine," said Uncle Stavely.

"Well, why didn't you put your bloody name on top?" said Mr. Brandon.

"Because I don't like my name, that's why. It's a daft name is Stavely," he said.

"Well, one man's meat is another man's poison, Stavely," said Auntie Lil, holding out the slip at arm's length. "And the name Stavely's chosen for the boy is Stavely."

"I thought you just said you didn't like the name Stavely, Stavely?" said Mrs. Brandon.

"I don't. Not on me. It doesn't suit me. I always wanted to be called Leslie."

"But that's my name," said Mr. Brandon.

"And it doesn't suit you either. Pardon?" said Uncle Stavely.

"Come on, please. Let's have a bit of hush," said Auntie

Lil. "You've not heard the name Stavely's chosen for the little girl."

She held out the slip again and inclined her head to the left. Then she said:

"And the name he's chosen for the little girl is Stavely."

"You can't call a girl Stavely, you daft bugger," said Mr. Brandon.

"I told you," said Uncle Mort. "He's going off his bloody beanpole."

"Are you sure you wouldn't like another go at the girl's name, Stavely?" said Mrs. Brandon.

"Hey, that's not fair," said Uncle Mort. "He should stick be the rules same as we've all had to."

"I think it's a very sweet name, Uncle Stavely," said Jessie Lewis.

"So does Corporal Parkinson," said Uncle Stavely.

Auntie Lil selected another slip of paper and discovered that it was none other than the one compiled on Corporal Parkinson's behalf by Uncle Stavely.

The name Corporal Parkinson had chosen for the little boy was Stavely. His choice of name for the little girl was also Stavely.

Uncle Stavely nodded gravely and said:

"He's got good taste when it comes to Christian names."

The door bell rang, and Carter Brandon went downstairs to let in Pat. He kissed her on the cheek, and led her into Auntie Lil's bedroom.

"Hello, Pat, luv," said Mrs. Brandon. "We're just choosing a name for Auntie Lil's baby. We'll not be a jiffy."

"The next slip has been wrote by Mort. And it's not in block capitals neither," said Auntie Lil.

"I'm sorry," said Uncle Mort.

"He's chosen Cyril for the boy's name."

"My mind just went a blank. I couldn't think of nothing else."

"And for the little girl he's plumped for Anne."

"Thank you, Mort. Thank you very much indeed," said Mrs. Brandon. "I'm glad to see someone in the family's got some thought for my feelings."

Jessie Lewis's was the next slip. Her names were Derrick and Linda.

"This one's our Annie's. Her selection for the little boy is Leslie," said Auntie Lil.

"I don't know why I bothered," said Mrs. Brandon.

"And her selection for the little girl is Elizabeth-Margaret with a hyphen."

"Well, I think it's only right to have a bit of royalty in the family, don't you, though, Lil?" said Mrs. Brandon.

The Uncle Mort version of Corporal Parkinson's choice was unfortunately disfigured by Auntie Lil, who spilled over it the contents of a glass of blackcurrant cordial.

Despite Uncle Mort's protestations his slip was declared null and void.

"And that's that," said Auntie Lil. "Now then, Leslie, would you like to count the votes."

Mr. Brandon picked up the papers, licked his thumb and began to flick through them. Presently he said after three recounts:

"Well, the winner for the boy is Stavely with two votes cast. And the winner for the girl is Stavely also with two votes cast."

"Stavely, eh?" said Auntie Lil. "Oh, we can't have that. We'll call the little girl Lucy, and the little boy Daniel after our old dog. Thank you very much for your help. Good night all."

Downstairs in the living room Mrs. Brandon said to Mr. Brandon:

"Have you noticed something funny about Corporal Parkinson, Les?"

"All that talk about democracy. It weren't worth the paper it were wrote on," said Uncle Mort, sitting by the fire with his head in his hands.

"What's funny about him?" said Mr. Brandon, who was reading his bi-monthly gardening journal.

"Well, he's been sound asleep for the past ten days," said Mrs. Brandon.

"He's just a bit tired, that's what it is," said Uncle Mort.

"I know, but sleeping continuous ten days non stop isn't the normal way of going about things, is it?"

"I slept for thirty-six hours solid after the Manchester United-Blackpool Cup Final," said Uncle Mort. "It drained me of all me energy."

"Aye well, it's probably draining Corporal Parkinson of all his energy, keeping hisself alive all this time," said Mr. Brandon. "I don't know why he bothers. He's flogging a bloody dead horse there."

"Les, I want you to go up and have a word with our Stavely about it, will you?" said Mrs. Brandon.

"I'll go," said Uncle Mort.

"You can stay where you are, Mort. I don't want no more

fisticuffs under this roof for many a long year, thank you very much," said Mrs. Brandon.

Mr. Brandon laid down his pipe slowly in the fireplace, folded up his gardening manual carefully, placed it on the seat of the fireside chair, stared at his wife and silently left the room.

"Well, how does it feel to be engaged again?" said Jessie Lewis.

"Smashing," said Pat, linking her hand into the crook of Carter Brandon's arm. "You don't know what you're missing."

"What do you like most about it?"

"How do you mean, Jessie?" said Pat, who had a small snag in her right stocking.

"What I say."

Pat looked at Carter Brandon and shrugged her shoulders.

"Well, it's difficult to explain really, isn't it?" she said. "I mean, it makes you feel dead nice inside. You know what I'm getting at?"

"No," said Jessie Lewis.

Mr. Brandon returned to the living room with the news that his elder brother was perfectly satisfied with the dormant condition of his aged companion.

"He says he often does it. It's some sort of hibernation, it seems," he said, resuming his place in the fireside chair, picking up his gardening journal and lighting his pipe.

"Is hibernation normal in a person of that age, Jessie?"

"It could mean that he's going to die very soon," said Jessie Lewis, and she stood up and left the room.

"Fancy that," said Mrs. Brandon. "Still, he led a very active life, didn't he?"

The roads were empty later in the evening on their way home from 'The Whipping Top', and Carter Brandon drove quickly. After a while he said:

"Do you think I ought to ask me mother to get rid of Jessie?"

"What for?"

"Well, you know."

"No, you can't do that, Carter," said Pat. "I mean, your mother will need her, when the baby comes along. What made you say that?"

"I don't know."

"Yes, you do," said Pat, placing her hand on his thigh. "I know what you mean."

"Do you?"

"Yes, and you'll just have to put up with space being

cramped for a bit. When you move into our new house, we'll
be able to share a room together. Are you looking forward
to that, luv?"

"Oh aye," said Carter Brandon.

A few minutes later they were drinking cocoa with Mrs.
Partington in her front room, and Pat recounted the substance of Carter Brandon's suggestion.

"Well, I've got the answer to that one," said Mrs. Partington. "There's no bother there. You can come and stay with
us. I'd be only too pleased to have you sleeping with me.
There's the box room lying idle, and it's got a lovely bed,
you ask your Uncle Mort. I mean to say, he stayed there
and there wasn't a murmur of complaint out of him. What
do you say to that then, Carter?"

"Aye. Well."

"You could bring your own alarm clock, so there'd be no
trouble about you getting off to work. And there's a cabinet
in the bathroom for your shaving gear so long as you remember not to throw your used blades in the dustbin. I
mean to say, it would be ideal, when all's said and done,
wouldn't it? You could say to your mother: 'Mammy, Mrs.
Partington has made the helpful suggestion that I move into
her house prior to me getting married,' you could say. 'She
says not to worry about the washing and ironing and to
rest assured that the food will be tip-top,' you could say."

"I'll see what she says," said Carter Brandon.

"And don't forget to bring your own flannel," said Mrs.
Partington as she went upstairs.

Carter Brandon kissed Pat and said:

"I think I'd rather stay at home."

Then he kissed her again and stroked her nipples until
they went hard.

When he got home, his mother was waiting up to tell him
that Auntie Lil had been rushed to hospital in an ambulance.

CHAPTER TWENTY-SEVEN

Only one thing marred the birth of Auntie Lil's baby, and
that was the death of Auntie Lil two days after that happy
event.

"I'm a bloody Jonah with wives me," said Uncle Mort.

"If only she'd have took those exercises I read about in me book," said Mrs. Brandon. "Poor Lil."

The funeral was a sad occasion as befitted the circumstances. Auntie Lil's remains were laid to rest in the Lark Hill cemetery alongside those of Auntie Edna and Cyril, and Uncle Mort said to Mr. Brandon:

"Well, if nothing else, we'll be able to have a few good hands of solo, when they drop the sods on me."

The three great aunts from Glossop came to the wake, for which outside caterers had been hired.

"I couldn't bring meself to bake. Not under the circumstances any road," said Mrs. Brandon.

The next few weeks were notable for the great gloom which descended on the Brandon household.

Auntie Lil's little boy which they called Daniel, in deference to her wishes, lay in an oxygen tent in the hospital.

They rang the hospital every morning and every evening and were told that the infant's condition was 'critical'.

"He's a right skinny little thing, too," said Carter Brandon to Pat. "He looks like a hot water bottle that's perished."

"They always do, if they're not your own," said Pat.

Corporal Parkinson's hibernation advanced a pace, and no one could rustle up the enthusiasm to tell the doctor.

"I suppose he needs all the rest he can get at his age," said Mrs. Brandon.

One evening Mr. and Mrs. Brandon and Uncle Mort were sitting in the living room. The tea things had been washed and stowed in the kitchen cabinet.

They had just received the good news that Daniel had taken a turn for the better, and that his life was no longer in danger.

"I'm sorry I got rid of our Cyril's clobber now," said Uncle Mort. "It would come in handy for thingie, when he grows a bit."

" 'Thingie'?" said Mrs. Brandon.

"Aye, whatshisname," said Uncle Mort.

"At least you could get his name right," said Mrs. Brandon. "Fancy forgetting the name of your own son and heir."

"I never could remember names," said Uncle Mort.

"Our Lil'd turn over in her grave, if she could hear you, God rest her soul," said Mrs. Brandon. "You ought to have more consideration for her."

"It's a pity you didn't have more consideration, isn't it?" said Mr. Brandon.

"And what do you mean by that?"

"You should have had more nous than bother Lil with all that talk about moving house."

"Are you suggesting that I was responsible for our Lil's death, Leslie Brandon?"

"Course he's not," said Uncle Mort.

"You keep out of it, Mort. It's got nothing to do with you," said Mrs. Brandon.

"That's right, go on, shout at me again," said Uncle Mort.

"If it's got nowt to do with him, who is it to do with?" said Mr. Brandon. "He's the one what sired the infant, in't he?"

"You're just twistin' me words," said Mrs. Brandon.

"You should have had more sense, that's all I've got to say on the subject," said Mr. Brandon, picking up the evening paper and putting it in front of his face.

Mrs. Brandon leaned across and snatched the paper away.

"Don't think you can get out of it like that," she said. "Talk about me having more sense. I suppose it was good sense gallivanting off home like that without telling a living soul where you was gone? I suppose that's the height of responsibility."

"That's got nowt to do with it."

"Fair's fair, Les," said Uncle Mort. "You didn't ought to have cleared off like that, you know."

"With another woman, too, I've no doubt," said Mrs. Brandon. "How do you think that affected our Lil?"

"She weren't even pregnant then."

"It's lucky for you she wasn't," said Mrs. Brandon. "It'd have been enough to make her give birth to a monster."

Mr. Brandon shook his head slowly and said to Uncle Mort:

"I'm going for a pint, are you coming with us?"

The dog accompanied them to the end of the street, and Uncle Mort said:

"Clear off. Home. Home."

The dog sank to its belly and yawned.

"Never mind bloody yawning. Clear off home," said Mr. Brandon.

The dog loped off down the street, looking at them over its shoulder.

Mr. Brandon steered Uncle Mort to the side of the bar. They rested their elbows on the counter and placed their beers next to the pile of pennies for the spastics.

"What the bloody hell am I going to do with the nipper, when it comes out of hospital?" said Uncle Mort.

"Aye, you're on a sticky wicket there all right," said Mr. Brandon.

"You see, I don't know one end of a bloody baby from the other. When we had our Cyril, I never bothered with changing his nappies or owt like that. The niff from him was enough let alone running round wiping his backside for him every five minutes."

"He were a long time getting house-trained, too, weren't he?"

"Too true," said Uncle Mort. "You're dead right there."

They ordered another round, and Mr. Brandon said:

"Course, you'll have Jessie to look after it, won't you?"

"Aye, that's true enough, Les, but I don't fancy the idea of a stranger tampering with him like that."

"How do you mean?"

"You know, a single woman like that, washing him and fiddling around with his little do-dah as she gives him a bath."

They had two more pints and left three quarters of an hour before closing time. They were just about to turn into the front gate, when Carter Brandon drew up in the car and opened the side window.

"Do you fancy a drink?" he said.

"Aye, go on," said Mr. Bradon, and he and Uncle Mort climbed into the back seat.

Pat was sitting in the front seat, and she turned and said:

"You naughty old stop-outs."

Carter Brandon made a three-point turn in the road that ran alongside the canal, and then he drove through the side streets into Derbyshire Road.

"Where are you taking us?" said Mr. Brandon.

"To the temperance bar," said Carter Brandon.

"Temperance bar?" said Uncle Mort. "Are you sickening for something?"

Carter Brandon jumped out of the car and said:

"Hurry up, they'll be closing in a minute."

He sprinted across the pavement and reached the door just as the owner was bending down to fasten the bottom bolts.

"Are we too late for a pint of sassy?" he said.

"At this time of night?"

"There are four of us."

"Come on then," said the owner. "I could do with the business, I suppose."

Carter Brandon waved his father, uncle and fiancee across and said to the owner:

"Four pints of sassy."

Mr. Brandon walked into the bar, peering from side to

side. Uncle Mort took off his cap and ran his fingers backwards and forwards along the peak. When the first drop of
sarsaparilla squirted into the glass, he jumped and began to
scratch his chest.

"What are you doing? Sobering up?" said the owner.

There were two gas mantles behind the bar, and they let
out a low, contented hissing.

"I haven't seen a gas mantle for donkey's years," said Mr.
Brandon.

"They're better for your eyes than electricity," said the
owner. "Careful where you drop your matches, I've just
swept that floor."

Mr. Brandon picked up his glass, winked at his son, took a
long drink and smacked his lips.

"By, that were good," he said. "By Christ and little fishes
it were bloody marvellous."

"Here, watch your language," said the owner. "We're
chapel here."

Mr. Brandon took another long drink and drained his
glass.

"Same again?" he said.

"Do you like it?" said Carter Brandon to Pat.

"I can't make up me mind," said Pat. "It's got a funny
taste, han't it?"

Uncle Mort had not moved from his original position a
few paces inside the door. He stood there, kneading his cap
and staring at his glass of sarsaparilla.

"Sup up," said Mr. Brandon.

Uncle Mort shuffled across the room slowly. They all
watched him silently.

He bent down, sniffed the glass and inclined his head to
one side. Then he lifted up the glass, extended it to the light,
peered at it intently and wrinkled his nose.

"Well, here goes," he said, and he took a sip from the
very edge of the glass.

"Well?" said Carter Brandon.

"It tastes like bloody boot polish," said Uncle Mort.

"I wouldn't know about that," said Pat. "I've never tasted
boot polish me."

"Auntie Lil liked it any road," said Carter Brandon.

Mr. Brandon stared hard at his son for quite a while. He
took out his pipe, and, as he was gazing into the bowl, he
said:

"Is that why you brought us, because of Auntie Lil?"

"Yes," said Carter Brandon.

The floor creaked, as Uncle Mort shifted his weight from

his left foot to his right. The owner opened the till and spread its contents on the counter. There wasn't much.

"I brought me Auntie Lil here on the way to her weddig," said Carter Brandon.

"I remember her," said the owner. "Was she getting married or something?"

"Yes," said Carter Brandon.

"To him," said Mr. Brandon, pointing to Uncle Mort.

"She's dead now," said Uncle Mort.

"Isn't it a shame?" said Pat.

"What the Almighty gives, so does He take," said the owner.

"Too true," said Uncle Mort glumly.

"She liked this place more than anything else anywhere," said Carter Brandon. "She used to sit just where Pat's sat, and she'd talk about all her old experiences and the things she did when she was a little girl.

"And she'd come out with some right sad things sometimes about what people had said to her and how she'd gone on a hike to Derbyshire. I thought they were sad any road, because of the way she remembered them in such detail.

"But she were always very happy. You could see her old peepers sparkling away, and when she was saying something she thought was right interesting she'd be tugging away at my sleeve and tapping her heels on the side of the stool.

"Then at other times she'd get dead serious. She'd talk about us all and say how she wanted us all to be happy and she didn't want to be no trouble to us and things like that. Aye, this was me Auntie Lil's favourite place, there's no getting away from that."

Carter Brandon finished off his drink in one gulp. No one said anything. They were all staring at him open-mouthed.

Mr. Brandon puffed hard at his pipe and said:

"I haven't heard you say so much in one breath since you was in short trousers."

"He's never talked that much before in all the time I've known him," said Pat.

"Mm," said Carter Brandon.

CHAPTER TWENTY-EIGHT

Sunday was a nice day, so after he had visited Daniel, Carter Brandon took Pat for a ride in the car.

"That's the tenth time you've visited the baby since he was born," said Pat as they were sitting in the car, smoking.

"Is it?" said Carter Brandon.

They were parked in a lay-by at the top of the road, which wound across the tops of the open moorland. Down in front of them was the dale. There were leaves on the trees that lined the river banks, and they were brown and golden and dirty yellow. The two great chimneys of the cement factory were in the distance, blurred by the haze.

A carrion crow landed on the dry stone wall near them, and they could see the iridescent blues and greens and purples in its plumage.

"You wouldn't think they'd got such lovely colours, when you only see them from a distance," said Carter Brandon.

They drove down into the dale and stopped in the main square of the market town. A party of hikers were leaning against the wall outside the mellow-stoned church. The light had a slatey-blue texture.

They had a pot of tea and toasted tea cakes in a cafe, whose garden ran down to the river. They couldn't see the water, because of the line of weepiing willows.

"You seem to have grown very fond of that baby," said Pat, spreading the blob of melting butter evenly on the surface of her tea cake.

"I've got to," said Carter Brandon.

"I know, luv," said Pat, patting him on the wrist.

"What do you know?"

"You're getting in practice for when we start having babies. That's right, isn't it?"

"Aye," said Carter Brandon. "Aye, that's right."

"I knew all along. I can read you like a book," said Pat. Then, after she had licked her fingers clean from the butter, she said: "Well, it's a relief to know you're starting to take our wedding seriously."

The waitress brought them a jug of hot water.

"Shall you be wanting any fancies?" she said. "We do a lovely Bakewell tart."

"No, ta," said Carter Brandon.

171

They lit cigarettes, and Pat settled herself comfortably in her chair. The willows made long violet shadows on the lawn and cutlery rattled in the kitchen.

"Carter," said Pat. "I hope you don't mind, but I'm going to ask you a personal question."

"All right."

"How much money have you got in the bank, if it isn't a personal question?"

Carter Brandon brushed a few specks of cigarette ash off his trousers, tightened the knot of his tie and pinched the end of his nose.

"About fifty quid I should think," he said.

"I didn't think you'd got that much. That's smashing," said Pat. "That's a right good start is that."

Carter Brandon paid the bill and their conversation was resumed on the way home.

Pat revealed that the sum of her personal savings was in the region of eighty-six pounds. Most of this was invested in national savings certificates, although a not insignificant proportion was deposited in the coffers of the trustees savings bank.

As they climbed out of the dale and commensed the drive over the moorland, Pat calculated that the sum total of their savings could be increased at the rate of five pounds per week.

If they were to be married the following April in order to claim a tax rebate in respect of Carter Brandon's marriage allowance, this would represent a grand total of approximately three hundred pounds.

When they reached the city boundary, Pat forwarded the proposition that they should seek a suitable house in a tasteful part of the city, in which to set up home.

Carter Brandon agreed at the precise moment they were halted by traffic lights outside the Nile Street Salvation Army Citadel.

By the time they reached the ropeworks of Flatman, Wrigley and Nutbrown it had been agreed that the money saved should be deposited with a building society in order to provide the substance of a mortgage deposit.

"You see, we'll have to wait years to get a council house, and I think we should think of the future and buy a house of our own straight away," said Pat.

"Mm," said Carter Brandon.

The Amy Carpenter Memorial horse trough was the scene of the decision to purchase a newly-built house.

"Because with a brand-new house, we should be able to get a ninety-nine per cent mortgage and then we'd have enough money to furnish the house from top to bottom without scrimping and scraping," said Pat.

No decision of note was reached outside the premises of Wally Singleton, 'premier crockery mart and fishing tackle specialists', but the roundabout outside the Town Hall provided the backcloth for Pat's comment:

"And, of course, it'll be a white wedding, won't it, Carter?"

"I suppose so," said Carter Brandon.

After coffee, biscuits and kissing in Pat's front parlour Pat said:

"I'll go and see the vicar early next week and fix things up with him."

"Good idea," said Carter Brandon, standing with his hand on the knocker of the front door.

"We'll have the full choir and organist, and you'd better see about who's going to be your best man."

"Right," said Carter Brandon.

They kissed, and Mrs. Partington shouted from upstairs:

"Ta ta, Carter. I'm right glad you and Pat have fixed all the details of the wedding."

Two days later Carter Brandon received a letter at his place of employ. He forgot about it until he got back home in the evening, and then he went upstairs, locked himself in the lavatory and began to read it.

It went as follows:

"Dear son of Mr. Brandon,

I have to address you in above fashion owing to the fact that I am temporarily indisposed of your Christian name. However, you can call me Celia.

I suppose your daddy will have told you all about me and the lovely days we spent together in dear old London town.

Therefore, with a view to clearing up these slanders I am putting pen to paper in the earnest hope that you will elicit the 'true story'.

First and foremost and lastly I had nothing to do with the shoehorn your daddy imputes I purloined.

I am not writing direct to your daddy owing to the simple fact that I appreciate it would cause certain domestic difficulties for same if I did so. Nonetheless I am writing to you in the hope that you will see your way to pass on the following information, i.e. that I crave for, hunger for, yes, yearn for, blandishments and embraces of same.

If you do not reply by return or at your earliest convenience, which ever is soonest, I shall be compelled to tackle your daddy personally at his place of residence.

Yours faithfully, Mrs. Otter (Celia)

PS. Your Daddy is conversant with my address."

Carter Brandon waited until the end of the evening meal before approaching his father. Then he said:

"Are you coming for a quick one?"

They went to the local, and Carter Brandon showed the letter from Mrs. Otter to his father.

Mr. Brandon took three long puffs from his pipe, blew the smoke at the ceiling and smiled.

"Well, lad, that's your pigeon, isn't it?" he said.

"What do you mean?"

"She wrote to you, so you'd better write to her."

Suddenly and without warning Carter Brandon thumped his fist on the table.

"It isn't bloody good enough," he said.

Mr. Brandon whipped the pipe out of his mouth, looked quickly over his shoulder and said:

"Hey up, calm down a bit, you'll have the whole pub listening."

"I don't give a tuppeny for the pub," said Carter Brandon. "They can all hear what I've got to say if they want to."

Mr. Brandon gripped his son's sleeve and said:

"Now calm down, lad, calm yourself down."

Carter Brandon shook his sleeve free from his father's grasp, and leaned across the table and said quietly through clenched teeth:

"You've got a right cheek you have. You sit back there puffing your pipe with a great grin like a Cheshire cat. You drag me into your problems and then you sit back and tell me to sort them out.

"Well, I'll tell you this straight, mate, I'm not doing your donkey work for you. You can sort it out yourself and bloody good luck to you.

"There's all of you think you can trample over me, and I'll not say a dicky bird. There's me mother always nagging me about me responsibilities. There's Pat always nagging me about the wedding and saving up. There's her mother always nagging me about buying curtains and bed settees.

There's Jessie Lewis always nagging me about taking her out. There's everyone just using me as a bloody dog's-body."

"Hey up, hey up," said Mr. Brandon. "Don't get your rag out with me."

"I'm just a bloody unpaid chauffeur for you lot. 'Drive me here, Carter, drive me there, Carter. Run your Uncle Mort to the chemist's. Run Jessie Lewis to the clinic. Take your Uncle Stavely and Corporal Parkinson for a drive.' Yak, yak, yak.

"All right then. I'm giving you notice here and now—all that's over and done with. There's a new regime starting now. And it's starting with you. You can sort yourself out with Mrs. rotten Otter. Do you own dirty work for a change."

And so saying, he put on his coat and left the pub.

"What was all that about?" said Teddy Ward. "Your Carter looked proper blazing."

"I don't know, Teddy," said Mr. Brandon, shaking his head sadly. "He's never talked so much since he were in short trousers."

Jessie Lewis was sitting in the front room reading when Carter Brandon arrived home five minutes later.

He flopped down in the arm chair, and she smiled at him and continued reading.

Carter Brandon ruffled his hair, sank deeper into the arm chair with his legs draped across the arm and stared at her.

Her hair was freshly brushed, and it glowed in the firelight. Her slippers had fallen to the floor, and he could see her toes.

They were nice toes, slim and shapely. Most women had rotten toes, he thought. Pat's toes were all red and fat and twisted over each other. Whenever he saw them bunched up in her shoes, they reminded him of little piglets in a sty.

"Little bloody piglets," he said out loud.

"What did you say?" said Jessie Lewis without looking up from her book.

Carter Brandon jumped and mumbled:

"I was just thinking to myself."

"You?" said Jessie Lewis, looking up from her book. "You, thinking to yourself. Good Lord, what's happened to you?"

"That's the whole trouble with the lot of you," said Carter Brandon. "I'm always thinking to myself, if anyone took the trouble to notice."

Jessie Lewis smiled at him slowly. She ran her tongue over her front teeth and said softly:

"I believe you, Carter."

Then she returned to her reading. Carter Brandon looked

at his watch. It was eight o'clock. His mother and Uncle Mort would be returning from hospital soon.

"Come on," he said, "I'll take you out for the evening."

They didn't speak in the car. Carter Brandon didn't drive quickly. He allowed his hand to rest on the lever, and he didn't move when Jessie Lewis pressed her hip into him and rested her arm on the seat behind him.

He pulled up outside the Luxor Club and backed into a space between a Hillman shooting brake and a Ford Popular.

"Super. A strip club. I've never seen strippers before," said Jessie Lewis.

"We can't go in there, it's stag night," said Carter Brandon. "We'll go into the gaming room."

"Super," said Jessie Lewis.

The bouncer opened the door for them and glanced at Jessie Lewis's ankles as they passed.

There were large multi-coloured glass dice lit up from the inside hanging from the ceilings, and the croupiers were dressed in the style of river boat gamblers.

"Ugh," said Jessie Lewis.

"Not 'super'?" said Carter Brandon.

Jessie Lewis grinned, linked his arm and said:

"Sarky."

They sat on stools at the bar, and Carter Brandon bought two double whiskies. After taking a sip of her drink Jessie Lewis said:

"So what it's all about, Carter?"

"What?"

"Come off it, sweetie, you know what I'm talking about. Had a row with Pat, have you?"

"No."

"Well?"

Carter Brandon rubbed his chin and tugged the lobe of his right ear. Then he said:

"Aye. Well."

And before he could stop himself he had shown her the letter from Mrs. Otter. She laughed loudly.

"And how did 'daddy' become involved with the old bat?" she said.

Carter Brandon told her. He started with the day his father failed to return home from work. He told her about eating a mixed grill with his mother in the Trocadero grill, about Mrs. Warrender ushering him out of the house, about the piece in *The News of the World*, about the postcard they had received from Stevenage.

Once he started he found it impossible to stop. Jessie

Lewis listened intently, smiling to herself from time to time, but always nodding sympathetically at the appropriate moments.

When he had finished, he said:

"I shouldn't have told you all that, you know."

"I know."

"You'd better promise you won't say anything about it."

Jessie Lewis whispered into his ear:

"Does Pat know?"

"No."

"Well, you know you can rely on me, Carter," she said, brushing his lobe lightly with her tongue.

They played roulette for half an hour, and Carter Brandon won eight shillings and sixpence.

On the way home Carter Brandon stopped the car outside the cemetery, where his Auntie Lil, his Auntie Edna and his cousin Cyril lay buried. He closed the windows, and there in the quietness and the dark he began to kiss Jessie Lewis.

She did not resist him. She lay back and allowed him to fondle her breasts for quite a while.

When they got home, Carter Brandon found a note for him from his mother, asking him to drive down to the daily for a carton of milk from the machine.

He scribbled on the bottom:

"No. I'm too tired."

CHAPTER TWENTY-NINE

Mrs. Brandon said nothing to her son about the note.

She looked at him rather strangely over breakfast, but Mr. Brandon shook his head and put his finger to his lips.

Later as he sat next to his son in the car on the way to work he said:

"There's a hell of a niff of scent in here, Carter."

"You know what you can do, if you don't like it," said Carter Brandon.

The sun was shining, and the frost on the rooftops glinted. There were needles of ice clinging to the outfall pipes on the side of the wireworks near the canal. Carter Brandon adjusted the sun visor, but he still had to screw up his eyes as he drove in the long stream of traffic.

"Who were you with last night then?" said Mr. Brandon.

"Jessie Lewis. Any objections?"

"You'd best not let Pat find out."

"That's my business, isn't it?"

Carter Brandon dropped his father off outside the factory gates.

"Ta ta then. I'll see you this evening," said Mr. Brandon.

"Mm," said Carter Brandon.

There was a union meeting in the canteen at lunchtime. One of the shop stewards, Ted Madely, had been dismissed for bad time-keeping, and his colleagues had assembled to discuss the matter. The district organiser was present.

"Now you're quite clear in your own mind what this means," he said. "Before you take any action whatsoever, brothers, I want you all to understand the full implications behind Brother Madely's dismissal."

"It's because he were always bloody late, that's why," said Sid Skelhorn.

"Wrong, Brother," said the district organiser. "You know as well as me that Brother Madely's dismissal is a clear case of victimisation. Victimisation, brothers."

"Bollocks," said Sid Skelhorn.

"Here here," said Eric Black.

"But, Brother," said the district organiser, who had a pink comb sticking out of the breast pocket of his jacket. "But, Brother, have you thought why Brother Madely was at times allegedly tardy in his time-keeping? Have you tried to fathom out the reasons?"

He paused and scanned the faces of his colleagues, sitting among the dirty plates and the remains of corned beef fritters and syrup pudding.

"Brother Madely's alleged failure to meet in full the clocking-on regulations—and the management has yet to convince me and you of the veracity of their case—was simply and solely, precisely for the very reason that he was engaged in union interests."

"Bollocks," said Sid Skelhorn.

"Here here," said Eric Black.

The meeting continued for three quarters of an hour, but long before then Carter Brandon had left to take a walk in the sunshine along the canal bank.

"Daniel's coming home from hospital tomorrow," he said.

There was no one to hear him. He sat on an iron bollard overgrown with weeds and began to scratch a name in the cinders on the path.

"Daniel," he wrote in block letters. He scrubbed it out

with his front foot and said to the swan, which had paddled
to the bank in search of food:

"Our Daniel'll be home tomorrow."

Mrs. Brandon had spent all the day putting the last minute
touches to her preparations for the reception of Daniel.

It had been decided that Uncle Mort should vacate the
room he had shared with Auntie Lil. This had been adapted
to fulfill the needs of a nursery. There was a cot, a wicker
linen basket, a Mickey Mouse frieze, a set of scales, a large
Teddy Bear and Carter Brandon's train set, among other
things.

Jessie Lewis would move into the nursery to keep constant
watch on the infant. Carter Brandon would return to his
own room, which he would share with his Uncle Mort. The
rest of the arrangements was a clear case of status quo.

"That's the best I can do, so I don't want no belly-aching,"
said Mrs. Brandon. "We've all got to knuckle down to make
the little feller feel at home."

After tea they settled down for the reading of Auntie Lil's
will.

"I just found it this morning at the bottom of her trunk,"
said Uncle Mort. "It's not a proper will in the accepted sense
of the word. It's more like a letter to tell us all how she'd
like her clobber distributed."

"Aye, but it'll not be legally binding, you know, Mort,"
said Mr. Brandon.

"If it's what she wanted, we've all got to stick by it," said
Carter Brandon.

Mrs. Brandon looked at her husband and raised her eyebrows. He shook his head and said gently:

"You're right there, Carter."

Uncle Mort took from his inside pocket a long manilla envelope. Out of this he pulled a large sheet of paper, on which
could be seen Auntie Lil's precise but spidery handwriting.

He took off his spectacles, blew on them, wiped them on
his handkerchief, replaced them and coughed.

"I'm not very good at this sort of thing," he said.

"I'll read it," said Carter Brandon.

"But you're not very good at this sort of thing either,"
said Mrs. Brandon. "I don't ever remember you reading out
a will before."

"I'll read it," said Carter Brandon firmly.

Pat, who had come round for the evening, looked at him
with surprise, and Jessie Lewis smiled to herself behind the
magazine she was reading.

Carter Brandon placed the paper flat on the coffee table and began to read:

" 'First and foremost to kick off with I won't begin that this is my last will and testament, because I think that's very formal and always casts a damper on proceedings.

" 'I have had some experience in dying intestate, because that is precisely what my Bob did under most tragic circumstances.

" 'However, enough of my woes and let's get down to brass tacks. I hereby bequeath all my belongings and possessions to my unborn child.

" 'I hope that my present husband, Mortimer Alfred James, will not 'do his nut' over this, but I am sure he will realise that my issue has prior claims on my worldly goods. I hope he will take it in spirit in which it was meant and look after everything until my child is old enough to know what's what.

" 'However, there are certain items which I am going to give as presents to the members of the family hoping that they will remind them of the happy days we spent together.' "

"She shouldn't have bothered," said Mrs. Brandon.

"Don't interrupt," said Carter Brandon, frowning. Then he continued reading the will.

" 'To my husband, Mortimer Alfred James, I give my late husband, Bob's, Rolls Razor, because I know he was always trying to get his hands on it, and he could do with a close shave any road.' "

Uncle Mort ran his hand over his chin and neck and said:

"It's the water round here. I'm buggered if you can get a good lather no matter how hard you try."

" 'However, I would ask him out of consideration to others not to strop it early in the morning for nothing is more annoying to others than my Bob stropping his razor while I was trying to get some sleep.

" 'To my sister-in-law, Annie Brandon, who has been such a tower of strength in my confinement, I leave the blue and cerise dress I wore for my going-away outfit in the hope and knowledge that she will be able to let out the bust.' "

"It's just what I wanted," said Mrs. Brandon. "Thank you."

" 'To my brother-in-law, Leslie Brandon, I couldn't really decide what to bequeath. However, I have finally plumped for my Bob's rubber overshoes and waterproof trousers so that, if he uses them in the winter, he'll stop getting the permanent snuffles. Also, if it's not too much trouble, I'd like him to use two pounds eighteen shillings from my insurance money to buy a tree for the back garden, so that it will come out a riot of colour in the spring and you'll think of me and the way I used to like sitting under the pear tree, knitting. Could he also string up some suet for the tomtits in my tree?' "

"Aye, but that's easier said than done," said Mr. Brandon. "You see, I'll not be able to plant nothing till March at the earliest, so she'd had her chips as far as the riot of colour's concerned next spring."

"Well, knowing our Lil, I'm sure waiting a year won't kill her," said Mrs. Brandon. "I mean, I'll think of her sat under the pear tree regardless, won't you, Les?"

"Course, I could always force something in the greenhouse," said Mr. Brandon.

"And there's no trouble about the suet," said Uncle Mort. "You can hang that up in the pear tree."

"Don't talk so bloody empty," said Mr. Brandon. "You stick suet in the pear tree, and you'd have your blossom gone before you could skin a cat."

"I didn't know that," said Uncle Mort, rubbing his chin again and fingering the stubble round his Adam's Apple.

Carter Brandon knocked on the table with his knuckles, and, when everyone fell silent, he resumed reading out the list of bequests.

Auntie Lil had forgotten no one. She left Uncle Bob's scout whistle to Jessie Lewis "with the desire that she will blow it hard three times, if she's followed home by strange me late at night."

To Pat she left a Wedgwood brooch and matching earrings. To Uncle Stavely she left her copy of the sheet music of "We're Riding Along On The Crest Of A Wave,' autographed by Ralph Reader.

Corporal Parkinson was the recipient of her woollen dressing gown "plus the camera my dear nephew, Carter, lost on his day trip to New Brighton, if it should turn up, because I think he should have a hobby at his time of life to keep his mind active."

" 'Finally,' " read Carter Brandon, " 'I come to my nephew Carter's dog, who was such a good housedog that I never had no fear of burglars nor footpads. I'd like Carter to use some of my insurance money (not more than fifteen shillings at the outside) to buy him a new collar. And will he also buy him a medallion for it and get inscribed his name, address and telephone number in case of accident, and on the other side could he have wrote 'A present from Auntie Lil'."

"Hey up, you're getting a new collar," said Mr. Brandon to the dog, poking him with the heel of his slipper.

The dog looked up at him out of the tops of its eyes and wagged its tail twice.

"I'd give him a Bob Martin's, if I was you, Les. Look at his nose, it's as dry as a bone," said Mrs. Brandon. Then she said to the dog: "Who's got a dry snibbie then?"

"There's more to come," said Carter Brandon sternly.

"Sorry," said his mother meekly.

" 'I should like to finish with some words of advice after expressing my thanks to you all for the way you received me in your house and went to all that trouble to keep me ever happy and cheerful.

" 'I'd like you all to keep your peckers up, regardless of what life has in store for you. My Bob, when he was alive, was of the firm opinion that every cloud has a silver lining, and could often be heard whistling the song of that name whenever he was down in the dumps, which was very rare, because he was a dear sanguine soul by nature. Follow this, and you'll none of you come to much harm.

" 'I hope Corporal Parkinson is feeling very much better now, and I hope that my husband, Mortimer Alfred James, will learn to control his temper better in future. I am very grateful to the way he made me a reasonably good husband, but I do wish that from henceforth he will cut down drastically on the swearing.' "

"That's what I've said all along," said Mrs. Brandon. "You never swore in front of mother, Mort. I don't know what's got into you all of a sudden."

"Annie," said Mr. Brandon. "Shut up."

Carter Brandon continued:

" 'I know what Annie's going to say now. She'll be thinking I've forgotten my dear, treasured nephew, Carter. Well, Annie, luv, I haven't. I have left to Carter something more precious than anything I've given to you others. He knows what it is, and I know he will always look after it and lavish on it the same love, tenderness and devotion he showed to me, and I hope he'll not tell no one what it is, because it's a secret between him and me.

" 'To conclude this last will and testament. Thank you all for the lovely time you gave me and I hope my funeral didn't put you to too much trouble.' "

Mrs. Brandon began to sob. Nothing her husband said could staunch the flow of tears.

Long after her son had left with his fiancee for a drink at 'The Whippet' the crying continued.

At length she blew her nose hard and stopped.

"I wonder what our Lil left him then?" she said.

"She probably left him the bloody knitting machine," said Uncle Mort.

"There you go again, Mort, swearing. Have you no respect for the departed?"

Uncle Mort hung his head and went out to the kitchen to wash the pots and brew another pot of tea.

"He could at least tell his own mother what our Lil left him," said Mrs. Brandon. "It's not considerate. I mean, it might be something that needs airing, mightn't it?"

"There's something funny about him altogether these days," said Mr. Brandon.

"I know," said Mrs. Brandon. "I've never seen him talk so much in his life before."

"He can't stop rabbitting, can he?" said Uncle Mort, coming in with the pot of tea.

"Aye, and I heard him talking to hisself in the back garden the other night," said Mr. Brandon.

"He seems to be thinking his own thoughts all the time," said Mrs. Brandon.

"Aye."

"It's very worrying."

CHAPTER THIRTY

"Carter," said Pat. "You never told me what your Auntie Lil left you in her will."

They were sitting in the car outside her home. Her mother was entertaining.

"I can't."

"Why not?"

"Because I can't. Now give over mithering."

"Charming," said Pat. "That's a right carry on, in't it? You won't even tell your own fiancee what your present was. That's a right good start to being married, if you're going to have secrets from me before we even get married, in't it?"

"Now listen to me," said Carter Brandon in a voice so loud and sharp that Pat put her hand to her face and knocked her knee on the botton of the dashboard.

She waited for him to speak, searching into every cranny of anger in his face, but there was no response.

Carter Brandon was thinking to himself, peacefully and

icily. He felt much better after that, and he said quite tenderly:

"I wouldn't ask me, if I was you, Pat."

"All right, Carter, luv, I'll not," said Pat in a faint little voice.

Next morning Carter Brandon rose early, shaved himself carefully, put on his best suit and said to his mother:

"Righto then, I'll drive you over to collect Daniel."

"There's no need to trouble yourself," said his mother coldly.

"It'll be no trouble," said Carter Brandon.

His mother placed the tea pot wearily on the chrome-plated stand.

"Have a bit of sense, Carter. We said we'd be there at eleven," she said.

"That's all right, I'm taking the day off work," said Carter Brandon.

Mrs. Brandon sat down at the table and rubbed her hand across her forehead.

"Honestly, Carter, I think sometimes you just go out of your way to be awkward," she said.

The sky was overcast, and it was cold. There were leaden grey clouds rolling in over the moorlands. Someone had written an article about bathing beauties in the morning paper.

Carter Brandon finished his breakfast and went out into the garage. He placed three rugs on the back seat of the car, and then he returned to the kitchen to boil the kettle for the hot water bottle.

"Right," he said. "I'm ready."

He was accompanied to the hospital by Mrs. Brandon, Jessie Lewis and Uncle Mort. He parked near the main entrance of the hospital and said:

"I'll wait for you here. Don't be too long or the hot water bottle will go cold."

Uncle Mort sat hunched up in the back seat. He had used his legacy for the first time that morning, and there were scores of little nicks on his neck. Some of them he had patched up with scraps of toilet paper. Others had run on to his collar, leaving it stained with blobs of red.

"I felt just like this when I were waiting for Johnny Carey to lead the lads out in '48," he said.

"Come on, Mort," said Mrs. Brandon. "Shift yourself before I lose me patience."

They were away for twenty minutes.

Then they reappeared with the baby. Jessie Lewis was

carrying him in the bottle green carricot, which they had purchased out of Auntie Lil's insurance money. Further souvenirs of Auntie Lil were provided by the hand-knitted blanket and Uncle Mort's Fair Isle mittens.

"How do, Daniel," said Carter Brandon. "You're going home now."

Jessie Lewis gave the child his first feed shortly after they arrived home, and they all gathered round to watch.

"Look at his little hands how he's grasping the titty bottle," said Mrs. Brandon.

"It's a bit of all right that, isn't it, Daniel?" said Carter Brandon.

"He's a rum-looking little bugger in't he?" said Uncle Mort.

"Who?" said Mrs. Brandon.

"Thingie," said Uncle Mort.

"Thingie? Thingie? How many more times have I to tell you his name's Daniel?" said Mrs. Brandon. "And what's rum about him any road?"

"Well, look at his head," said Uncle Mort.

"What's wrong with it?" said Mrs. Brandon, bending over the cot with alarm.

"There's nowt wrong with it in the medical sense," said Uncle Mort. "It's just the size of it. It's like a bloody globe."

"I won't tell you about swearing again, Mort," said Mrs. Brandon. "Honestly, I don't know. Fancy talking about your son and heir in that fashion. He's got a smashin' little head on him. You'd go a long way to find a better head on a baby than that."

"Agreed," said Uncle Mort. "All I'm saying is he's got such a lot of it."

The baby lay on his back in the cot. He had piercing, steel blue eyes and a cold distant smile on his face.

"You liked that, Daniel, didn't you?" said Carter Brandon. "She's a bit of a dab-hand with the titty bottle is Jessie, isn't she?"

He tickled the baby's ribs and made clucking noises with his tongue.

After lunch Mrs. Warrender, the neighbour from number thirty-six, came to inspect the new arrival.

"He's perfectly formed, in't he?" she said. "Look at his little elbows."

"Aye, but look at the dome on him," said Uncle Mort. "I'll bet you a straight ten bob my cap wouldn't fit on it."

"Mort," said Mrs. Brandon. "If you can't make any more sensible comments than that, kindly leave the room and clear the decks for us."

Uncle Mort shrugged his shoulders, put on his coat and said at the door:

"And he's just farted, too. Are you coming for a quick one, Carter?"

They drank their pints slowly. The fire hadn't been lit in the smoke room, and there was a draught whistling under the door. The calendar hadn't been turned over for two days.

"At times like this a man's utterly helpless," said Uncle Mort. "Completely and utterly bloody helpless."

"Aye," said Carter Brandon.

"The women take charge, and we might just as well clear off and scratch ourselves. It were the same when our Cyril was born. They put this message out for me over the public address. Well, it put the fear of God up me, I mean, they stopped the bloody match for it."

"Did they?"

"Course they did. 'Go to the bloody maternity hospital,' they said. In front of a fifty thousand gate, too. I don't know where to put meself."

"You wouldn't."

"Course I wouldn't. And to crown it all I had to wait half an hour for a tram. They didn't run the twenty-seven on match days, so I had to get the seventeen B and walk it from the cemetery."

"Did you?"

"Course I did. Then when I gets there, your mother's waiting outside the ward, and she plays merry hell up about me not bringing no flowers. Well, how can you get flowers at a football match, you tell me that? That's women all over, they don't think of things like that."

"No," said Carter Brandon. "Same again?"

"Aye, go on then," said Uncle Mort. "What it is, they don't want us to steal their thunder. You try to show an interest by remarking on the size of its dome, and, bang, they come down on you like a ton of bricks.

"If it were left to me, I'd go to the doctor and tell him I wasn't satisfied. I'd point out the size of its dome and ask him what he was going to do about it.

"But, no, women know better. Next thing they'll be wanting to circumcize the poor little bugger. They always do. They think they're getting their own back. Your Auntie Edna could hardly wait to get our Cyril done. I told her everyone would think he was a yid, but she couldn't listen. Off it came."

"Come on then, sup up," said Carter Brandon.

"What's all the rush for?" said Uncle Mort.

"I want to make sure Daniel gets his next feed on time," said Carter Brandon.

All through the afternoon Carter Brandon kept his attention firmly fixed on the welfare of the baby.

"Does he need feeding?" he asked Jessie Lewis.

"Shut up, Carter," she said. "He was only fed an hour ago."

"Should he be dribbling like that?" he said to his mother, when she discovered him, bending over the cot in the nursery.

"It's just sheer irresponsibility," she said. "You could easily have gone back to work this afternoon instead of idling your time away here."

"Does he need feeding?" he said to Jessie Lewis, as they sat in the front room, watching the racing on television.

"I'll belt you round the ear with his bottle, if you don't shut up," she said.

Shortly after six o'clock Mr. Brandon returned from work. He went up to the nursery, took off his hat, bent over the cot and said:

"How do, Daniel."

Then he went downstairs to the kitchen and had a good wash.

When Pat came round in the evening, Carter Brandon took her upstairs to see the baby. She linked his arm tightly.

"Can you imagine what it'll be like, when you and me have our own baby, Carter?" she said.

"Mm," said Carter Brandon. "He doesn't half twitch in his sleep, doesn't he? Should he be twitching like that?"

"I think we should wait a bit, though, before we start having babies, don't you, Carter? I think we should get the house right first, don't you?"

"Mm," said Carter Brandon. "Should he be sucking the sheet like that?"

The baby woke up and began to cry.

"What's he crying for? What's up with him?" said Carter Brandon.

He peered into the cot, and the baby screwed up its face and began to hiccup.

"He's going purple," said Carter Brandon.

Pat pushed him to one side and lifted the baby out of the cot. She held him in her arms, rocking backwards and forwards and crooning softly. After a while he stopped crying. She looked up at Carter Brandon, and she blushed.

"He must like you," said Carter Brandon.

"Shush, you'll wake him up again," said Pat, replacing the

baby in his cot, and smoothing down the sheet beneath him.

They crept out of the room, and on the landing Pat threw her arms round Carter Brandon and kissed him on the lips.

"I do love you, Carter," she said. "Honest, I do. Do you love me?"

"Oh aye," he said. "Won't he get a draught with the window open like that?"

* * *

They went to bed early that night. Uncle Mort stood at the bedroom window in his pyjamas, gazing out over the moon-lit garden.

"I haven't seen much of your owl recently, Carter," he said.

The clock struck eleven, and the dog began to scratch in the newspaper in its box.

"It's rum the way dogs bury bones, isn't it?" he said.

His pyjama jacket was buttoned up to the collar. He was still wearing his socks and suspenders.

Someone flushed the lavatory, and then the water began to judder and clank in the pipes. Then it stopped, and Uncle Mort said:

"Are you asleep, Carter?"

He drew the curtains and got into bed.

"I've been talking to me bloody self for the past half hour," he said to himself.

Then he switched off the light and after a few minutes took off his socks and dropped them at the side of the bed.

Frost began to form on the windows. Uncle Mort's snores were echoed by those of Mr. Brandon. Then at midnight the baby began to cry.

Carter Brandon was awake in a flash. He pulled back the bed clothes from his head and listened to the crying. It was soft and disjointed at first. In the intervals of silence he could hear his heart thumping.

What's up Daniel, he said to himself, what's up, mate?

After a short period of silence the baby began to cry again. This time its crying was shrill and prolonged, and after each gasp for breath its volume increased.

Carter Brandon sat bolt upright in bed.

"Uncle Mort," he whispered. "Uncle Mort."

He leaned across and shook his uncle by the shoulders. There was no response.

Hold on, Daniel, he said to himself. Hold on, mate, I'm coming.

He got out of bed, put on his dressing gown and went into

the nursery. Jessie Lewis was lying sound asleep in bed. She had one bare arm resting lightly on top of the eiderdown, and there was a smile on her face. He bent over her and squeezed her wrist.

"Jessie," he whispered. "Jessie."

The baby began to shriek. He hunched his head into his shoulders, and his skin turned a deep scarlet.

"Jessie," said Carter Brandon, shaking her wrist roughly. "For Christ's sake, wake up."

Jessie Lewis opened one eye and yawned. When she saw Carter Brandon, standing over the bed, she pulled the bed-clothes up to her chin and her eyes opened wide.

"What do you want?" she said.

"The baby's crying."

"For heaven's sake," she said angrily, sitting up in bed. "For heaven's sake, clear off. Are you mad or something? What do you think your parents would say, if they caught you in here?"

"The baby. It's crying," said Carter Brandon, holding her wrist more tightly.

She shook herself free and hissed at him:

"Get out. Go on. Get out."

He could see her breasts rising and falling inside her night-gown. Her hair had come asunder from the band that held it in place during the day, and it lay tossed and wild over her shoulders.

The baby stopped howling. He lay in his cot, sobbing softly to himself.

"He's stopped now," said Carter Brandon, but he could not keep his eyes off Jessie Lewis.

No one moved in the house. Mr. Brandon continued to snore. Slowly he knelt down on the bed beside Jessie Lewis.

"Jessie," he whispered. "Jessie."

"No, Carter," she said. "Please."

He put his arms round her shoulders and drew her into his chest.

"Carter. Oh, Carter," she said, and she began to shiver.

He pushed her away from him and began to take off his dressing gown. She watched him and then slowly drew back the bedclothes.

"Be quick," she said.

He began to slide into bed beside her, undoing the knot in his pyjama cord as he did so. He pulled up her nightgown round her neck and buried his head in her breasts. And the door opened.

Jessie Lewis's body froze, and Carter Brandon's heart began to pound in his chest. He could feel it hammering into the springs of the mattress.

"What are you crying for, Lil?" said Uncle Stavely. "Pardon?"

The cheeks on Carter Brandon's bottom tightened, and his toes began to tingle as Uncle Stavely shuffled across to the bed.

"Are you all right, Lil?"

Very softly and slowly Jessie Lewis rolled over on top of Carter Brandon.

"Lil?" said Uncle Stavely. "What are you crying for?"

He stood at the foot of the bed, peering into the darkness. Jessie Lewis lay across Carter Brandon, shielding his head with her arms.

"It's all right, Stavely," she said.

"Pardon?" said Uncle Stavely. "What did you say, Lil?"

"I said I'm as right as rain, thank you, Stavely," said Jessie Lewis.

Uncle Stavely moved round from the foot of the bed, and Jessie Lewis gripped Carter Brandon more tightly. He was halfway round, when he caught his hip on the cot. They heard him running his hand along the woodwork.

"What have you got in there, Lil?" he said.

"It's my baby, Stavely," said Jessie Lewis.

"Pardon?" said Uncle Stavely, stepping back heavily.

"He's called Daniel," said Jessie Lewis.

"Oh," said Uncle Stavely. "That must be what I heard crying."

"That's right, Stavely."

Uncle Stavely shuffled back to the door. Then he stopped and said:

"I thought you said he was going to be called Stavely. Pardon?"

Very silently Jessie Lewis got out of bed. She walked carefully to the door and took hold of Uncle Stavely by the shoulders, then she kissed him full on the lips, running her arms up and down his back and pressing her stomach into him.

"Good night, Stavely," she said softly.

"Pardon?"

She kissed him hard again and steered him through the door.

"Good night, darling Stavely," she said.

Uncle Stavely began to laugh.

"Wait till Mort learns about this," he said. "Pardon?"

CHAPTER THIRTY-ONE

The days following Daniel's arrival gave Carter Brandon much pleasure.

Before he went to work in the morning he would go into the nursery and say:

"Hello, Daniel, it's a grand day today."

Or, if the weather were inclement, because of the cold or the rain, he would say:

"Hello, Daniel, it's a miserable day today."

At lunchtime he would go to the phone outside the canteen, ring his mother and say:

"How's Daniel going on? Did you remember to feed him at the right time?"

And invariably his mother would say:

"I wish you'd stop bothering me like this, Carter. I've enough on me plate without having to break off to talk to you."

Each evening he would dash home and say to Daniel:

"Hello, Daniel, it's been a grand day today, hasn't it?"

If the weather had been bad, he would make the suitable adjustment to the comment.

He particularly enjoyed watching Jessie Lewis bath the baby. He would stand in the bathroom, carefully keeping out of the nurse's way, but prepared to respond to her every order.

"Fetch me the towel, Carter," she would say, and he would need no second bidding to comply with the request.

"Pass me the talcum powder," she would say, and, lo and behold, the tin of powder would be passed to her promptly.

Sometimes he would sit in the nursery after Daniel had been put to bed. He would sit there for hours in the darkness, listening to the infant breathing, waiting for him to begin to cry so that he could take him in his arms and soothe him back to sleep again.

His mother said to her husband one night, when her son was upstairs in the nursery, keeping his vigil:

"It's not natural, Les. I know I've always been on at him to take an outside interest, but I hardly think this is suitable for a lad of his age, is it?"

"It takes all sorts," said Mr. Brandon.

On one of the rare occasions when he took Pat out, Carter Brandon said:

"We've got an understanding between us have Daniel and me."

"Have you, luv?" said Pat. "Well, I think it's marvellous the way you take such an interest in him."

Later in the evening she said to her mother:

"It's the best thing that's happened to him for ages having that baby."

"I agree with you there, Pat, luv," said Mrs. Partington. "But don't you think it's a bit strange a lad of his age, taking such an interest in someone else's baby. I mean, if he wants to learn all that sort of thing, he could easy go to night school and get expert instruction free of charge."

At weekends Carter Brandon would wheel the baby in his pram to the park in the morning.

"You want your bloody head examined," said Derrick Warrender one Saturday morning when he caught Carter Brandon wheeling the pram out of the front gate.

"He needs all the fresh air he can get," said Carter Brandon.

"Course it does," said Derrick Warrender. "But it's not your bambino, is it? It's your old lady's responsibility is that. Stick it in the garage and come and have a pint with me."

"No ta, Dekker," said Carter Brandon. "I promised him I'd take him out. I can't let him down."

On Sundays Carter Brandon would get up early, call the dog and wheel the pram through the streets, whistling to himself.

The dog would trot at his heels, the baby would stare at the sky with cold, distant eyes, and Carter Brandon would feel very contented.

Sometimes Pat would join him on the walks, even though her mother warned her against the neighbours' gossip.

The rumours did not bother Carter Brandon. Linda Preston said to him one lunchtime in the canteen:

"You want to think of Pat's reputation, kid?"

"Why?"

"Well, it looks a bit funny, doesn't it? It looks a bit bloody odd you and Pat wheeling a pram about."

"Why?"

"Honest to God, kid, you're as thick as two planks sometimes," said Linda Preston. "People are saying the kid belongs to you and Pat."

Carter Brandon smiled and said:

"He does belong to me in a way, though."

"I've been looking in the house ads and I've found this new estate they're building," said Pat.

They were driving back from the cinema, and Carter Brandon was hoping that they would reach 'The Whippet' before closing time.

It was the first day of December. In the morning there had been torrential rain, which had turned to sleet in the afternoon. In the evening it had begun to freeze, and there were patches of ice on the roads.

"Me and me mother went up there last night to have a look. Honest, Carter, they're smashin' little houses. They're not big, you know, but they're in this contemporary style. They call them Danish ranch house, have you seen them advertised?"

"No," said Carter Brandon.

"Any road, this feller who showed us round said we'd only to put down £100 deposit."

The car skidded slightly as Carter Brandon turned into the car park of 'The Whippet'.

"How much does the whole house cost?" he said.

"Somewhere in the region of £2,750 without extras," said Pat.

Jessie Lewis was out with Derrick Warrender that evening, so Carter went into the nursery when he returned home and said:

"I'm buying a house, Daniel."

The baby woke and turned his head towards the direction of the noise. In the past few days it had learned to recognise Carter Brandon's voice. Whenever he spoke, the baby would smile to himself, and sometimes he would chuckle. Whenever Carter Brandon came into the room, the baby would turn to him and stretch out his arms falteringly.

"Well, I couldn't give a tuppeny meself, but Pat seems to think it's best, so I'm going along with that.

"The point is, Daniel, there's no point in me sticking me oar in. If that's what she wants, she might as well have it. She'd make me life a bloody misery otherwise."

The baby began to chuckle softly, and Carter Brandon lifted him out of the cot and rocked him backwards and forwards in his arms.

"Fancy me buying a house, Daniel," he said.

You must be off your bloody rocker, Carter, he said to himself.

"You're right there, Daniel," he said. "I must be going off me bloody beanpole."

What sort of a house is it, Carter?

"Danish ranch house, Daniel," he replied.

What's that like, Carter?

"I haven't a bloody clue, Daniel," he said.

The baby stared at him, and a wide smile spread over his face.

Are you looking forward to getting married, Carter, he said to himself.

"What do you think, Daniel?"

I'd say you hadn't thought about it too much, Carter.

"Well, I've thought about getting me end away and things like that, Daniel," he said.

Anything else?

"No," he said. "To be perfectly honest with you, Daniel, I haven't."

What about Pat, though?

"Aye. She's a funny lass is Pat, Daniel. I can't make it out really. She gives me a pain up the spout most of the time, but I can't help liking her, when it comes to the push," he said.

That's not much of a reason for getting married, is it, Carter?

"Aye. Well."

Aye. Well? Is that all you can say after you've poured your heart out to me, Carter? Is that the only comment you can offer on this vital subject?

"Aye. Well," said Carter Brandon, and he began to pat the baby tenderly on his back.

The clock struck midnight, and his mother shouted from her bedroom:

"Is that you, Carter?"

"Yes."

"What are you doing?"

"I'm just saying good night to Daniel."

Within seconds Mrs. Brandon had appeared at the door of the nursery.

"I'll not tell you again about disturbing the little feller, Carter," she said. "You're going to do him some damage, mauling him like that. Now put him back into bed and be off with you."

She took the baby from her son's arms. Immediately Daniel began to howl.

"See what you've done," she said. "You've woken him up. I'll not tell you again about tampering with him. He's not a plaything, you know."

"Good night, Daniel," said Carter Brandon. "See you in the morning."

Mrs. Brandon's reserves of tolerance and understanding were further depleted by the curious behaviour of Uncle Stavely.

"It's your duty to nail him on the subject, Les," she said.

"You'll never change him at his age," said Mr. Brandon.

"Let sleeping dogs lie, that's been your motto for as long as we've been married," said Mrs. Brandon. "Well, it's not good enough for me."

The earnestness of her mien compelled her husband to pay attention while she recounted some of the more outstanding examples of Uncle Stavely's strange behaviour.

His attitude to Corporal Parkinson's hibernation had been culpable enough, but, she felt his manner with Uncle Mort since the arrival of the baby had verged on the callous.

She pointed to the occasion when Uncle Stavely had entered the dining room in mid-morning and said:

"How do, Mort, it's done your Lil the world of good having that baby. Pardon?"

Mrs. Brandon, always a stickler for the truth, had replied:

"But Lil's passed on, Stavely."

"That's what you say, but I know different," Uncle Stavely had said. "And the fluences have started again."

Worse had come two evenings later, when Uncle Stavely had said during a lull in the conversation:

"You want to pay more attention to Lil, Mort."

"What are you on about, you daft chuff?" Uncle Mort had replied.

"Neglect a woman after she's dropped a baby, and you're asking for trouble. Pardon?"

They had tried to ignore him, but just before retiring he had said:

"Deprive them of love, and they start casting round for new attractions."

Then he had left the room and left them pondering over the significance of the remark.

Mr. Brandon listened patiently to his wife's expressive recital of woe. When she had finished, he said:

"I'll have a word with him, if he comes down tonight."

"If? If?" said Mrs. Brandon. "If you had any sense of responsibility, you'd be up there tackling him right now."

Before Mr. Brandon could act on this suggestion Uncle Stavely knocked on the door and shouted from the corridor:

"Is the baby in there?"

"No, of course he isn't. It's long past his bedtime," said Mrs. Brandon.

Uncle Stavely opened the door and came into the room.

"Pardon?" he said, glancing rapidly from side to side.

He was wearing his overcoat, and he had a long navy blue woollen muffler round his neck.

"Are you coming for a quick one, Les?" he said.

"In this weather?" said Mrs. Brandon. "At this time of night? At this time of year?"

"I wouldn't say no to a quick one, Stavely," said Mr. Brandon.

Mrs. Brandon sniffed hard as her husband left the room to fetch his walking-out clothes.

"Don't blame me if Stavely catches his death of cold, that's all I've got to say on the subject," she said.

"We'll not be long," said Mr. Brandon. "I'd put some slack on that fire if I was you, before it gets any lower."

The darts team was playing away at the 'Yew Tree' so the local was uncrowded.

"Now then, Stavely, what have you got to tell me?" said Mr. Brandon, when they had settled themselves in.

Uncle Stavely looked over his shoulder and then beckoned Mr. Brandon to move closer. His instructions were followed.

"It's about Mort," he said softly.

"Mort?" said Mr. Brandon, following the *sotto voce* example, of his brother.

"Pardon?" said Uncle Stavely. "It's him and Lil. I think their marriage is starting to bust up."

Mr. Brandon moved even closer and said even more softly:

"What makes you say that, Stavely?"

Uncle Stavely looked over his shoulder again and placed his mouth very close to Mr. Brandon's ear.

"She's started making eyes at me. Pardon?"

Mr. Brandon rocked back on his chair and stared hard at Uncle Stavely. The old man nodded gravely.

"I see," said Mr. Brandon.

"She's out to seduce me," said Uncle Stavely. "She's doing to me what she did to Corporal Parkinson before she had the baby."

"What's she done to you then, Stavely?"

Uncle Stavely was almost whispering when he said:

"Dragged me into bed with her and kissed me on the chest. Pardon?"

CHAPTER THIRTY-TWO

On the following evening the doctor came to examine Uncle Stavely, for the brief encounter with his eldest brother had been enough to convince Mr. Brandon that medical attention was both desirable and imperative.

The doctor was a locum, standing in for their regular adviser on medical matters. He was Irish.

"What part of the Emerald Isle are you from then?" said Uncle Mort.

"I'm from Cork," said the doctor. "Now shall we see the patient?"

"I've always fancied a holiday in Ireland me," said Mrs. Brandon. "The only thing that puts me off is the long sea crossing."

"I'll say this about your lot," said Mr. Brandon. "I'd rather have one on my side in a scrap than against me."

"Aye, they're handy with their mitts are the Paddies," said Uncle Mort.

"Honestly, you two, what will doctor think of us?" said Mrs. Brandon.

"Sure and begorrah, he's not after worrying at all at all at all, are you?" said Uncle Mort.

"I'm not," said the doctor, smiling. "Now shall we go and see the patient?"

"I'll tell you another thing that puts me off from going to Ireland," said Mrs. Brandon. "Is your food the same as ours? I mean, would it be suitable?"

"Spuds in their jackets. That's what your lot eat, isn't it?" said Uncle Mort.

"And buttermilk," said Mr. Brandon.

"Oh aye, and buttermilk," said Uncle Mort.

The doctor picked up his bag and pointed to the stairs.

"Now I'm thinking he'll be upstairs, Mrs. Brandon?" he said.

"In't it funny the way they say 'tinking'?" said Mrs. Brandon, and she led the way up to the attic.

They stopped outside the door, and Mr. Brandon knocked hard on it with his knuckles.

"Come on, Stavely, open the door. We've brought the doctor to see you," he shouted.

"Pardon?" said Uncle Stavely.

"Well, at least we know he's in the land of the living," said Uncle Mort.

"Clear off," shouted Uncle Stavely. "I don't want to see no doctors. Clear off."

Mrs. Brandon looked at her husband, but, receiving from him a look that could only be interpreted as hopeless resignation, she said to the doctor:

"Perhaps it would be a good idea if you was to have a word with him, doctor?"

"I will so," said the doctor, and he bent down and shouted through the keyhole: "Hullo there, this is your doctor speaking."

There was no reply, but a series of thuds and scrapings from behind the door suggested that some sort of barricade was being erected to prevent an unauthorised entry being forced.

"I'll tell you what to do," said Mr. Brandon. "Why not write him a note and shove it under the door?"

"What a good idea, Les," said Mrs. Brandon, and the doctor concurred.

He ripped out a sheet of paper from his notebook, took out a ball point pen and wrote:

"Now then, old chap, what seems to be the matter with us today?"

He slid the note under the door, and they waited for a response. Nothing happened.

"He'll not answer you," said Uncle Mort. "You're wasting your bloody ink on him."

His pessimism, however, was proved incorrect almost immediately by the appearance of a note thrust under the door. On it was written:

"I'm being chased by our Lil."

The doctor read the note, handed it to Mrs. Brandon, and said:

"Who's Lil?"

"She's dead, doctor," said Mrs. Brandon.

The doctor scratched his head. Then he ripped another piece of paper from his notebook and wrote:

"Look, old chap, stand with your chest against the door and say 'Arrrgh'."

He slipped the note into the room and placed his stethoscope against the door.

"Arrrgh," said Uncle Stavely very faintly. "Pardon?"

"He sounds a bit chesty to me," said Mrs. Brandon. "Stavely, open that door at once and let doctor have a look at your ankles."

There was no reply, and after ten minutes the doctor shook his head and said to Mrs. Brandon:

"I think 'twill be better if I come round again in the morning, when he'll be in a better frame of mind, please God."

"Thank you, doctor," said Mrs. Brandon, and she escorted him off the premises with warm courtesy.

"If there should be any signs of disimprovement, ring me at once," said the doctor. "Good luck, Mrs. Brandon."

Sure enough the doctor did return the following morning.

To Mrs. Brandon's surprise her aged brother-in-law made no objection, when he was summoned to descend the stairs from the attic and present himself for medical examination.

He said nothing as the doctor applied the stethoscope. Throughout the examination he gazed silently and patiently into space.

Even more surprisingly he made no attempt to prevent the doctor and Mrs. Brandon from making their way to the attic to inspect Corporal Parkinson.

The old soldier lay in his hammock, his withered body slightly crooked to the left, his eyes closed and his lips dry and cracked.

Jessie Lewis stood at his side and removed the bedclothes. Corporal Parkinson did not stir. There was scarcely a sign of breathing from the bony hollows of his chest. His hand hung down limply when the doctor raised his arm to take his pulse.

They went downstairs and joined Uncle Stavely in the front room.

"Well, old chap, I think you should be climbing into bed for a few days," said the doctor to Uncle Stavely. "I think it would be best for all concerned."

Uncle Stavely nodded and allowed himself to be helped to his feet and escorted to the attic by Jessie Lewis.

When Mr. Brandon returned from work in the evening, he was told by his wife that Corporal Parkinson was fading away peacefully and painlessly and that Uncle Stavely, tired and worn, might shortly follow his example.

"Poor old sods," said Mr. Brandon.

"Poor old buggers," said Uncle Mort.

"There must be a jinx on this house as regards death," said Mrs. Brandon.

"It makes you think, doesn't it?" said Carter Brandon to Daniel.

He was sitting in the nursery. The nightlight flickered

softly in the saucer on the bedside table. The house was silent, for the hearts of its inhabitants were heavy with grief.

"Poor old devils," said Carter Brandon. "Fancy snuffing it that way. I mean, they've seen life, haven't they? They've been all over the world, and they've had some right exciting adventures."

Too bloody true, Carter, he said to himself.

"The funny thing is you can't imagine it happening to them, can you? When they tell me things what they've done in the past, I always picture them looking like what they do now.

"I'm always the same with old codgers me. Take your mam, Daniel. When she was telling me about the days she spent with Uncle Bob, I could see it all, but I could never think of her being all young and pretty and bothering about her hair and her legs and how she looked."

That's right interesting is that, Carter, he said to himself.

"Uncle Stavely's the same. There was this night he told me about his adventures at sea. There was this here brothel he went to in South America. Well, it were like a bloody great palace.

"There was crystal chandeliers and red velvet seats and this sort of balcony that went round the hall.

"They was sat at these little tables, drinking wine and stuff like that, you see, Daniel. Any road, this woman what owns the place comes up to their table and asks them if they're ready.

" 'Aye, righto,' says Uncle Stavely. So she claps her hands and these women come down this great marble curving staircase.

"There must have been about a dozen of them. There were negresses and Jewesses and blondes and dark-haired gypsy types and this little chinky piece with long dark hair falling down her back.

"Well, they was all immaculately dressed in silks and laces and brooches. But the funny thing was they'd all got their bosoms with nothing on.

"Any road, this woman what owns the place tells them to pick the one they want. So me Uncle Stavely says he'll have the little chinky piece with the long dark hair."

The nightlight spluttered as a sudden sharp draught came through the half-open windows. It lit up the baby's face so that his big round eyes, fixed hard on Carter Brandon, glowed and then smouldered in the falling darkness.

Carry on Carter, this is right interesting, he said to himself.

"Righto, Daniel," he said. "Well, she were a little darlin'

was this chinky piece. She'd right big almond eyes and her
skin was a sort of smoky brown colour, all smooth and silky
with moles on her shoulders.

"She took hold of Uncle Stavely's hand and she led him up
the staircase and along the balcony till they came to this
white door with dragons and peacocks and pheasants painted
all over it.

"Any road, she opens the door with this gold key she's
got strung round her waist with a silk cord and there in the
middle of the room was this gynormous bed with a canopy
of white net spread above it.

"It had precious jewels encrusted all over the woodwork
and the ceiling was painted with little fat babies blowing
through horns and floating on clouds, and there were tiger
skin rugs all over the floor.

"Any road, this little chinky piece takes hold of me Uncle
Stavely's hand and leads him across to the bed.

"His old ticker's going thump, thump, thump and his knees
was like jelly. And she kept tickling the palm of his hand
with her fingers so all the little hairs on the back of his neck
stood up.

"Any road, she gives him a push in the chest, when they
gets to the bed. It wasn't a hard push. It was more like a
playful push, and he just flopped back on the bed. It was a
feather mattress, there must have been a good two ton of
feathers in it, and he just sank back in it.

"Well, the funny thing was she didn't do owt for a bit. She
stood there at the side of the bed, smiling at him."

Smiling at him, Carter? Is that all?

"Aye, and there was this funny smell in the room, too. It
was like the inside of a cogger church. It made him feel a
bit dizzy like, Daniel, but it weren't unpleasant or anything
like that. In fact, it was all right really.

"Any road, she suddenly fiddles with a cord at her waist,
and the next minute all her clothes fall away from her body,
and she's stood there in the nude.

"He could hear the silk rustle on her ankles as she stepped
out of the clothes. Christ, it had got a lovely body on it,
Daniel. She were right tiny really, but she were perfectly
proportioned not like them midgets you see at the circus
with big heads.

"Her breasts weren't big. They weren't all big and floppy
like the ones you see in *Health and Efficiency*. They were
like little rosebuds, and she'd a lovely little rounded belly
on her and a tight little bum.

"But the thing he couldn't take his eyes off was this great

jewel she'd got in her navel. It were a red ruby, and it lit up the whole room. It were like a fire burning deep inside her, Daniel.

"Any road, she kneels down on the bed beside him. He's not looking at owt bar this bloody great ruby. It sort of mesmerized him. He felt he were being put in a deep trance, and the smell got stronger and made him dizzier.

"Then she bends over him and takes the ruby out of her navel, and do you know what she did, Daniel? She starts to rub it slowly over his forehead and down the side of his cheek and round and round the smooth part behind his ears.

"Well, he'd never felt owt like it in his life before. Nobody had ever rubbed a ruby over him before, Daniel. It were funny really, because sometimes this ruby felt as cold as ice on him and other times it were all tingling and hot as though it were alive.

"She must have been at that for a good half hour and then she starts to take off his clothes. He didn't want to kiss her or owt like that. He just lay there, staring up at the ceiling while she took off his clothes one by one very slowly like and tenderly.

"And then he noticed these mirrors all round the room. They were sort of tinted a rose colour, but the funny thing was that each one seemed to reflect a different picture of him. In one of them he was big and bold and brave. In another he was all weak and defenceless. In another he was a big handsome bastard, in another he was skinny and ugly.

"And each one seemed to reflect him at a different age in his life. In one he was a little baby like you, Daniel. In another he were all acky and spotty, and in another he'd got his hair parted in the middle with long sideboards. And in the one farthest away from him he could see himself all old and white-haired with a hollow chest and great thick purple veins twined all round his legs.

"And the rum thing was, Daniel, that he felt like each one of the reflections in the mirror. They were all inside him, but each one was separate, if you know what I mean."

I think I do, Carter, he said to himself.

"Any road, when he's lying there with nowt on, this little chinky piece takes hold of this sash on the top of the bed and gives it a bloody good tug. Well, there's a great gonging noise, and it fills the whole room, and his head starts to spin.

"Before he knows what's what the door opens, and these two huge buck niggers come in wheeling a trolley. By God, they were right fearsome-looking, Daniel. Their teeth was painted orange and sharpened into little points like daggers, and they'd got muscles like bloody Hackenschmidt.

"They were right down to the canvas bar these thick gold belts they'd got round them like loincloths. Solid gold they was, Daniel, and they were kept in place by these great iron padlocks, which clanked as they walked.

"They pushed the trolley to the side of the bed, and they bowed so low that their noses rubbed on the marble tiles of the floor. And then they crawled out of the room backwards, bowing and scraping and licking their lips.

"It were a fantastic sight was this trolley, Daniel. It were covered in bottles of every shape and size and colour. There were fat bottles and thin bottles, and bottles with twisted necks and bottles with necks like serpents. And they all shimmered and glinted in the light.

"And then in addition there was hundreds of little pots. They were all the same colour, a deep dull red with little veins of silver and copper running all over them, and they was shaped like hearts.

"Any road, Uncle Stavely's little piece gets off the bed and starts taking the stoppers off the bottles. Straight away there was this overpowering scent filling the room. There was a sort of vapour coming out of some of the bottles, and in others the liquid turned milky white, and in others it clouded and started to twist and writhe in on itself."

You're describing it very well, Carter.

"Thanks, Daniel," he said. "And there was this tremendous scent from the pots, too, when she took off the lids. Old Uncle Stavely leaned across to have a dekko and he could see they was all full of ointments.

"There was thick black stuff like treacle, and yellow stuff, and blue stuff and stuff so clear you could look straight through it and see the bottom of the pots. And there was one ointment that was an amber colour, and it had little striped insects in it with their wings spread out perfectly as though they was resting.

"Any road, she starts to pour some of the stuff from the bottles on her hands, and the next thing he knows is she's rubbing it all over his body.

"At first it stung something chronic. It seemed to be burning his skin right off. Then she put some more stuff on him, and all the stinging went and every little nerve under his skin relaxed, and his muscles seemed to spread open and close all lazily like, and he could feel it working its way into his pores and going deeper and deeper inside him.

"She'd got a fantastic touch. Her hands was so delicate. All he could feel was the soft little pads under the ends of her fingers.

"She ran them right into his armpits and then followed his body down to the soles of his feet. Up and down, up and down they went.

"She ran them round and round over his chest and over his belly, and she massaged the insides of his thighs with her fingers all slow and tender like."

Go on, Carter, go on. What happened next?

"The funny thing is, Daniel, when he was telling me all this, I could picture it dead vividly. I could smell them ointments, and I could feel this little chinky piece's hands running all over me.

"But it wasn't Uncle Stavely as a young man I saw. It was him as he is now. I could see him lying there with this woman kneeling beside him, saying 'Pardon?' every five seconds.

"I could see that great wiry hair he's got on his chest all coiled up like a spring, and his leathery belly. I could see the segs on the soles of his feet, and his toenails, which wanted cutting, and, above all, I could see that bloody great dewdrop he's always got hanging on the end of his beak."

Carter Brandon laughed and lifted the baby out of the cot and rocked him gently in his arms.

"And look at him now, Daniel. He's up there in the attic, slowly snuffing it. He's got a bottle of red medicine for his chest and box of blue tablets for his heart and a jar of yellow ointment for his bed sores.

"He's covered in a pair of sheets me mother got with her ciggy coupons, and the only person who appears when he bangs on the floor is me mother or me Uncle Mort.

"Poor old sod. Fancy dying in a house like this."

He put the baby back in the cot. Daniel's eyes were closed, his breathing was steady, and there was a deep, contented smile on his face.

"I'll take you into them soon, Daniel," he said. "I think you should say 'How do' before they go and snuff it."

Ta, I'd like to do that, Carter. Ta very much. Aye.

CHAPTER THIRTY-THREE

Upstairs in the attic the two old men were drawing peacefully to the end of life's journey. They lay in bed silently side by side.

Corporal Parkinson, who had been transferred to a bed, did not open his eyes. Uncle Stavely did not open his lips.

The clocks ticked, soot fell from the chimney from time to time, the posters on the walls curled at the corners and the smell of Jessie Lewis's perfume lingered and dawdled among the smell of ointments and liniments.

Voices were hushed in the house. Sadness reigned supreme, and the dog's nose grew drier and hotter, and its hairs fell out on the rugs and the carpets.

"Poor old fellers," said Pat.

"Aye," said Carter Brandon.

"Any road, I've fixed the date for the last Saturday in March, and we're going to see the vicar next Tuesday so's he can get to know you."

"Mm."

They were sitting in Pat's front parlour, and the coke on the fire was spitting and crackling.

"I'm not going to go into all the details of guests and arrangements, Carter, because I know that sort of thing doesn't interest you. What me mum and me think is that all that should be sorted out between us and your mam. So you'll not have to bother yourself about that at all. Am I doing right?"

"Yes," said Carter Brandon.

Pat snuggled her head into Carter Brandon's chest and ran her hands up and down his thigh.

"I knew you'd be pleased, Carter," she said. "You see, I really know you inside out now."

"Mm," said Carter Brandon.

Then he said to himself, she really knows me, does she, Daniel?

"I don't know, Les," said Mrs. Brandon. "I'm just losing interest in life."

"Mm," said Mr. Brandon.

"What's to become of us all? This past year or so's been one long chapter of incidents. It started with our Edna dying,

205

then we lost our Cyril, our Bob, our Lil, and now there's them two poor old souls upstairs."

"Mm," said Mr. Brandon.

"Who's going to be next, that's what I can't help thinking, Les. Which one of us is the next to be took?"

"Mm," said Mr. Brandon.

"Then there's our Carter. What's happening to him? First he starts talking our socks off. Now he spends all his time with Daniel, and we can't get a peep out of him.

"It's as though he's been took over by those fluences that used to pester our Lil," said Mrs. Brandon. She sighed and rolled up her knitting. "Who's fault is it? Am I to blame? Are you to blame? Are we being punished for something we know nothing about? It seems that happiness is snatched from our grasp at the last moment every time."

"Mm."

"Someone up there doesn't like us, Les."

Upstairs in the darkness of the nursery Carter Brandon said softly to the baby:

"She thinks she knows me, Daniel, but she doesn't. She thinks I don't say much, because I've not much to say. But she's wrong, in't she, Daniel?"

I've not made up me mind yet, Carter, he said to himself.

"Haven't you, Daniel?"

Jessie Lewis opened the door and looked inside.

"Oh, it's you again, is it?" she said, and closed the door and continued on her way to the attic.

"Pat thinks I don't know why she's not consulting me about the arrangements, but I do, Daniel. She just doesn't want to share it with me. She'd be happy spending the rest of her life, making wedding arrangements.

"Saving money, buying curtains, ordering sausage rolls, making dresses for the bridesmaids, measuring up curtains —that's her life, Daniel. She's happy doing that, because that's the only thing she's good at.

"I tell you this, though. When it comes to the push, she'll be scared out of her pants. Our wedding day will be the high-spot of her life, past, present and future.

"I bet really deep down, if I was to say we'd postpone it for another year, she'd jump at the chance. It'd be another year's grace, another smashing year of choosing carpets, buying material in the market, ordering paper cups for the trifles, seeing her Auntie Louie about baking the wedding cake.

"She thinks she knows me, Daniel, but she doesn't know the half. There's only you and me Auntie Lil knows me proper, Daniel."

Pat had decided that they should only go out once a week. If this were rigorously adhered to, she maintained, the savings campaign would reach a successful conclusion.

Adhered to it was, on Pat's part, although she was very pleased to welcome Carter Brandon into her home on evenings which did not coincide with their duty night out.

"I've been thinking, Carter," she said on such an evening. "I've been thinking, don't you think we ought to get one of them little books."

"Which little books?"

"Them little books, which tell you all about it."

"All about what?"

"It."

" 'It'?"

"Oh, Carter, you do make things difficult," said Pat. "Them little books, which tell you how to go on on your wedding night and things like that."

"Oh."

"I mean, it's no good leaving it to chance, is it? We want to know all the ins and outs of it, don't we?"

"I suppose we do."

"You see, luv," said Pat, placing her arm round her fiance and drawing him down beside her on the sofa. "You see, luv, there's so many marriages break down because of what goes on on the honeymoon night. I mean, I think we owe it to ourselves to be prepared for any eventuality, don't you?"

"I suppose we do," said Carter Brandon.

Mrs. Partington returned from her whist drive and joined her daughter and future son-in-law for cocoa and eccles cake.

"Well, I never thought I'd live to see the day when a Co-op whist drive didn't give a booby prize," she said. "I says to Mrs. Eglington, I says: 'Mrs. Eglington, I never thought I'd live to see the day, when a Co-op whist drive didn't give a booby prize,' I says."

"And didn't they?" said Pat.

"No, they most certainly did not," said Mrs. Partington. "And you should have seen the lady's first prize. A headscarf, that's what they give as the lady's prize.

"Well, as I says to Mrs. Eglington, Carter, I says: 'I remember the days, Mrs. Eglington, and they're not too far distant, when the first prize used to be a full bedroom suite with maple veneer,' I says."

After Mrs. Partington had retired to bed, Carter Brandon kissed Pat several times.

"Carter?" she said, as he lay on top of her on the sofa.

"What?"

"Have you had experience?"

"What sort of experience?"

"You know, with a woman or owt like that."

Carter Brandon pressed his lips firmly over her mouth and rubbed his chest up and down over her breasts.

"I believe you," she said. "Thousands wouldn't."

Carter Brandon took Daniel for a walk in his pram on the Saturday morning.

It was too cold to stop in the park, so he wheeled the pram along the tow path of the canal, talking to Daniel as he went and ignoring the puzzled glances of the anglers, huddled up on their camp stools.

"I had a right bloody day yesterday, Daniel," he said.

Did you, Carter, he said to himself.

"Aye. First of all I got this bollocking from the shop steward for not going to the union meetings. I'd have laid him one on only he comes from Glasgow.

"I told him I didn't give a tuppeny shag either road whether we went on strike or stayed at work. I told him it were all right by me whatever they did.

"But you know what these shop stewards are like, Daniel? That's not good enough for him. He's got to have his numbers there, you see, so he can make a good show with the district organiser.

"I know that as well as you. But he goes on about the men thinking I'm a boss's man, if I don't turn up for the meeting. About me not caring for the welfare of me mates, about me being the first one to complain if they make a decision I don't like.

"I told him I couldn't care less, but he didn't believe me. No one believes me when I tell them that Daniel."

Poor Carter. No one understands you, lad.

"They bloody don't an' all, Daniel. Everyone seems to think you've got to have a point of view on everything. If you haven't got a point of view, they think there's something up with you. It makes me bloody sick does that, Daniel."

On the same evening Uncle Mort said to Mr. Brandon in the local:

"Life's not worth bloody living, is it?"

"What's up with you then?"

"Look at it through my eyes, Les. I've got a baby, and I'm not allowed to go nowhere near it. Every time I set foot in the nursery, I'm shooed out as though I'm going to give it the plague or something.

"If I go near it, when it's downstairs, your Annie jumps up and clutches it to her bosom as though I was a bloody vampire."

"I thought you said you'd no interest in babies," said Mr. Brandon.

"I haven't, and that's what infuriates me. All I want to do is to go up and give it a dig in the ribs and say 'How do'. After all, I am its bloody father."

They walked home slowly. There was a clear sky, and the stars shone brightly. They stopped and looked up at them glistening through the frosty air.

"Do you believe in heaven, Les?" said Uncle Mort.

"Why?"

"I was just wondering if I'd go there, when I snuff it."

Mr. Brandon patted Uncle Mort on the shoulder and pushed him homewards.

"Don't mither, Mort, you'll end up somewhere, when your time comes."

"That's just what's bothering me," said Uncle Mort.

They were running the new turbines in the testing bay.

Crouched behind the steel protective barrier, Carter Brandon looked up at the engineers in the glass-panelled control room.

He knew them all by sight. The bald one with the fuzzy ginger moustache often drank in 'The Pack Horse' on Sunday evenings.

He must be prematurely bald, Daniel, said Carter Brandon to himself. I mean, he's with a different bird each time you see him.

Once he had seen him with the secretary, who now sat at the side of the control room, her head bent over the notebook on her lap.

Her white coat had fallen apart, and, if he inclined his head to the right, Carter Brandon could see the tops of her stockings.

Sid Skelhorn was looking at them, too. He glanced at Carter Brandon, licked his lips and rolled his eyes.

They couldn't hear each other speak, for the whine of the turbines hammered at their ear drums, boring through the protective wads of cotton wool.

In his pocket Carter Brandon had a letter. It was from

Mrs. Otter, and it had been waiting for him in the foreman's office, when he arrived at work that morning.

He hadn't opened it, but the envelope was already tattered at the edges and smeared with his fingerprints. He felt in his pocket and rubbed the corner of the envelope with his thumb and forefinger.

Are you like this with letters you don't want, Daniel, he said to himself.

I don't know, Carter. I'm not old enough to get letters, am I?

That's true, Daniel, he replied to himself. Well, when you get old enough, don't keep them in your pocket for hours before you open them like I do. It's balmy, when you come to think about it. I mean, it makes no difference to what's in them when you open them, so you might as well open them as soon as you get them.

I'll bear that in mind, Carter.

Sid Skelhorn tapped him on the shoulder and pointed up at the control room. The secretary's skirt had rucked up a little further, and they could see the flesh of her thighs above her stockings.

Sid Skelhorn hung out his tongue, waggled his hand in front of his flies and began to pant vigorously. Carter Brandon nodded.

Do I look like that, Daniel, when I'm talking about women? Do I look so bloody stupid?

Look at him. You wouldn't get a woman under fifty-five who'd look at him, and then she'd have to be short-sighted.

Blokes like him are all the same. They spend all their time with their mates, talking about birds, and when they get home, they're right under the thumb of some great acky boiler with a face like the back end of a tram.

Have you seen Sid's wife, Daniel? God save us, what a woman. Fancy laying in bed with a woman like that. Fancy seeing her getting undressed with all the elastic marks from her knickers on her backside. Fancy having to sit on the same lavatory seat.

I wonder if that'll happen to Pat and me, Daniel? I wonder if we're all old and acky underneath?

I mean, you look like an old feller sometimes, because you've got no teeth and you're as bald as a badger. You look like you'll look when you're as old as Corporal Parkinson.

I bet there's an old bloke like Uncle Stavely inside me at this very moment, wheezing and panting to keep up with me and making up the lies he's going to tell you, when you get to my age.

The turbines were switched off, and the engineers came down on to the floor of the bay. Sid Skelhorn stood behind the secretary, making faces at Carter Brandon and thrusting his stomach backwards and forwards.

The secretary turned and caught him in the middle of the act.

"Don't let me catch you doing that again," she said. "If there's any more of that, I shall report you to Mr. Lancaster, and then you'll be for it."

"No harm meant," said Sid Skelhorn. "I didn't mean owt."

After he had washed the grease from his face and hands, Carter Brandon went into the lavatory and opened the letter from Mrs. Otter.

It said:

"Dear Carter,

With ref. to mine of 13th ult., still no news from daddy.

Accordingly I should be most grateful if you would set the wheels in motion to remedy this unfortunate situation, otherwise I shall be compelled to take action under the terms specifically laid down in mine of 13th ult.

I have also in my possession a certain article, which might prove of interest to daddy. 'Nuff said.

I remain your daddy's ardent admirer and trust that tidings to this effect will be passed on to person in question.

Yours faithfully,
Mrs. Otter (Celia) XXXXXX

PS. I am now residing in your town and can be contacted through the agency of the Poste Restante services of the GPO head office."

When Carter Brandon showed the letter to his father, he said:

"I knew all along she'd drag me shoehorn into it."

"Never mind the shoehorn," said Carter Brandon. "What about her coming to live in town?"

Mr. Brandon shrugged his shoulders and rubbed the stubble on his chin.

"I'll tell you what," he said. "Why don't you toddle over and have a word with her?"

"Like bloody hell I will," said Carter Brandon.

"All right, all right, there's no need to talk like that to your own father," said Mr. Brandon.

"I could say more," said Carter Brandon.

After the evening meal he went into the garage to clean the plugs on his car. The electric light had failed so he had to fix up the storm lamp.

I'll tell you, Daniel, he said to himself, he can sort himself out of the mess. He's not dragging me into it.

Good for you, Carter. You stand up for your rights.

I've a good mind to land him right in it, though.

How would you do that, Carter?

Easy, Daniel. I'd write to her and tell her the old feller's madly in love with her and wants to divorce the old lady, but he's too shy to tell her himself.

Diabolical cunning, Carter.

Too bloody true, mate. And then I could tell her to come round one night, because me mother was going to be out, and she could see the old feller on his own.

And your mother would be in all the time, Carter?

Precisely, Daniel. By God, the old feller would swallow his pipe red hot and smoke would come streaming out of his ears and belly button.

You wouldn't do that, though, would you, Carter?

"You're right, Daniel," he said. "I couldn't do that."

"Talking to yourself again, Carter?"

It was Jessie Lewis, standing at the door, smiling at him.

He shook his right shoulder, coughed and said:

"I always do, when I get brassed off."

She came into the garage, opened the front door of the car and sat in the driving seat.

"What's troubling you then?"

"This," said Carter Brandon, throwing Mrs. Otter's letter into her lap.

She glanced through it quickly and said:

"Same response?"

"He wants me to go round and see her."

Jessie Lewis picked up the muffler, lying on the seat beside her and wrapped it round her neck. It was cold in the garage.

"Would you like me to go round and see her?"

"You?"

"As an impartial observer. As a peace-keeping mission. I could wear a light blue beret with a white cap badge, couldn't I?"

Carter Brandon blew on his hands and wrapped up his

tools in the oilskin pouch, thoughtfully provided by the makers for such a purpose.

"No," he said. "I don't want you getting involved in it. Christ knows what you'd get up to."

He stowed the tools in the boot and got into the front seat beside Jessie Lewis, and they lit cigarettes.

He put his arm round her neck, but she shifted away from him.

"No, you don't," she said. "I've read too much about what goes on in parked cars at this time of night."

Carter Brandon switched on the radio, and they listened to the music and smoked two more cigarettes.

"Wedding getting you down, is it?" said Jessie Lewis.

"Mm."

"I don't know why you're going to all the bother. Why don't you just go down to the registry office and get it over with there and then?"

"That'd be popular, wouldn't it?" he said, and she laughed.

"You're not going out much these nights."

"Neither are you."

"Do you fancy coming out with me tomorrow night?"

"No."

"The night after?"

"No."

"Why?"

She turned to him and said:

"Because I don't know whether or not I like you, Carter."

Bloody charming, Daniel, he said to himself. Sorry I bloody spoke.

CHAPTER THIRTY-FOUR

It was the weekend before Christmas Day. To be more precise, it was Sunday evening, and the state of the weather was rain with wind from the east.

There had been discussions about Christmas presents, and it had been decided by Mrs. Brandon that gifts should be bought for Uncle Stavely and Corporal Parkinson.

"It seems a waste of money to me," said Uncle Mort. "Why can't we hang on to it and put it towards the funeral expenses?"

"What a mercenary mind you've got, Mort," said Mrs. Brandon. "Where's your Christian charity? Where's your love and mercy and forgiveness at this festive season?"

"I don't know," said Uncle Mort.

It was decided to buy an umbrella for Uncle Stavely and a book token for Corporal Parkinson.

"It'll cheer them up no end," said Mrs. Brandon.

Before this statement could be disputed Jessie Lewis looked in to say that she intended to take a short rest, but would be available for service, if required.

After she had gone Uncle Mort said:

"Aye, she's a grand lass is Jessie. I can't understand it."

"Understand what?" said Mrs. Brandon.

"Why she hasn't got herself fixed up with a regular feller."

"It is a bit of a mystery," said Mrs. Brandon. "Les, pass the dates round, will you?"

"She's a good-looking lass, no one can deny that," said Uncle Mort. "She's a good worker, she's got qualifications, she's a lovely temperament, she's well-trained round the house. What more could a man want?"

Mr. Brandon munched slowly on his creamy whirl caramel, staring hard at Uncle Mort.

"Getting interested yourself, are you, Mort?"

"Hey up," said Uncle Mort. "Give over."

Mr. Brandon chuckled to himself and took out his pipe. "No, you'd make a bloody good match you two," he said. "Beauty and the bloody Beast ride again."

"That's enough of that, Les. Don't start putting ideas in his head for heaven's sake," said Mrs. Brandon.

The disinterested silence which greeted this remark was in marked contrast to the angry scene taking place between Miss Patricia Enid Baines Partington, spinster, and Mr. Carter Brandon, bachelor.

Its setting was the interior of the latter's car, homeward bound from the former's home, where tea had been taken and discussions on wedding arrangements advanced.

"Why can't you come?" said Carter Brandon.

"Because we're saving," said Pat.

"It's only the firm's Christmas Social. It's not a bloody state banquet."

"I'm quite well aware of that, but I'll still need a new dress," said Pat. "And mind where you're going. You'll have that cyclist off, if you're not careful."

Carter Brandon swung out away from the cyclist, and an oncoming van flashed its headlights rapidly at him.

"Get a new frock then," said Carter Brandon, after he had placed the car on the correct side of the white line.

"How can I get myself a new dress, when we're supposed to be saving up?"

Carter Brandon pounded on his horn as a car began to edge its way out of a side road in front of them.

"We never go anywhere these days," he said. "Where's the fun in that?"

"Saving up to get married isn't supposed to be fun," said Pat. "Any road, I've told you I don't mind you going on your own."

"I can't go on me own, talk sense," said Carter Brandon. "You can't go to a Christmas Social on your own, when you're engaged. Where's the fun in that?"

Pat's response was delayed by the grinding of gears, which resulted from her fiancé's inept performance in turning into Crumpsall Street.

When it came, however, its effect was considerable.

"I know," she said. "You can take Jessie Lewis."

"Jessie Lewis?" said Carter Brandon. "Are you mad?"

"I can trust you to behave yourself with her, luv," said Pat. "And it would give her a lovely break from all that nursing and such."

"You must be mad," said Carter Brandon.

"I think it would be a lovely unselfish gesture. It would show her just how much we appreciated all the fine work she's put in looking after your relatives."

"You mention that, and there'll be bloody ructions," said Carter Brandon, stamping hard on the brakes, as he swung the car into the garage.

His threats were in vain. When Pat saw Jessie Lewis in the front room she said immediately without bothering to greet her fiancé's parents and uncle:

"Carter was wondering if you'd like to go to the firm's Christmas Social with him, Jessie."

"Thank you, Carter, I'd love to go," said Jessie Lewis. "Lovely of you to ask me."

Mrs. Brandon's puzzled glance was not picked up by her husband, and Uncle Mort's raised eyebrows made not the slightest impact. For the rest of the evening conversation was formal and a little strained.

In the car on the way back to Pat's house Carter Brandon said the following words to himself:

She must be going mad, Daniel. It's affecting her head all these wedding plans.

Put yourself in her place. If you were going to be married

in March, would you allow your fiance to go off to a social with another woman?

I certainly bloody wouldn't, Carter.

"You see, I don't believe in being jealous, Carter," said Pat. "I don't believe in being possessive. I learned my lesson, when I nearly lost you through being too suspicious."

And what's behind Jessie accepting the invitation so swiftly, Daniel?

A plot, Carter?

Mm.

"But I don't want to go with Jessie Lewis," said Carter Brandon. "I'd rather go with you."

I would and all, Daniel. That's what a fiancee's for, to go to socials and functions with.

"I know, luv, but you've got to think of other people's feelings," said Pat. "Jessie's got no people of her own and going out to that social will make a lovely Christmas for her."

"Mm," said Carter Brandon.

Pat kissed him full on the lips and nibbled his ear. When she got out of the car, she said:

"Have a lovely time at the social, Carter. And remember, I trust you, luv."

As Carter Brandon climbed into bed that night Uncle Mort said:

"Are you really going to the social with Jessie?"

"So it seems," said Carter Brandon. "Why?"

"Nothing," said Uncle Mort. "Fetch us a drink of water, there's a good lad."

"Jessie Lewis?" said Linda Preston in the canteen the next day. "You must be bloody mad. What if Pat finds out?"

"She suggested it," said Carter Brandon.

"Well, it can't be the sun, can it?" said Linda Preston. "She must be sickening for something."

Carter Brandon finished off his rice pudding and said: "It's all these chuffin' wedding arrangements."

"Getting brassed off with it, are you, kid?"

"Course I am."

"You want to chuck it in, kid. Get yourself a special licence from the registry office and go and do the dirty deed on the sly."

There was a message from Pat waiting for Carter Brandon, when he came home in the evening, telling him to ring her immediately.

This he did, although, in fact, the instructions were not

obeyed to the letter for he first removed his coat, washed his hands, glanced at the sports page of the evening paper and smoked a cigarette.

"Hello, luv," said Pat.

"What do you want then?" said Carter Brandon.

"I just wanted to tell you to have a good time tonight."

"Thank you."

Carter Brandon waited for her to reply, but all he could hear was her steady breathing.

"Ta ta, then," he said.

"Wait a minute, hold on," said Pat.

"What now?"

"Have a nice time then," said Pat.

"Thank you."

"Carter?" said Pat.

"Yes?"

"What's Jessie wearing for the social?"

"I don't know. I've just got back from work, haven't I?"

"I suppose you have," said Pat. "All right, I'll let you get your tea then. Have a nice time at the social. I hope you enjoy yourself and you know I can trust you."

Before he went into the bathroom to wash and shave Carter Brandon visited Daniel in the nursery.

"How do, Daniel," he said. "Are you asleep yet?"

The baby stirred, opened his eyes, and, when he saw Carter Brandon, he began to chuckle and gurgle.

"I'm going to the bloody social in a few minutes," said Carter Brandon. "I'm not looking forward to it, though."

You should have been firmer, Carter. You should have said there and then when Pat invited her that you wasn't going.

"True, Daniel, but it would have caused a scene, and I can't stand scenes. I can't stand seeing people showing their feelings. It makes me feel right uncomfortable when people start going off the handle, or sobbing or telling each other how much they love each other. Do you feel that way, Daniel?"

I'm not old enough to yet, am I, Carter, you daft bugger?

"True, Daniel. True."

He did his washing and shaving with some care. His mother had starched and ironed a light blue shirt for him, and Uncle Mort had cleaned his brown calf shoes.

He went downstairs to the front room and his father poured a glass of sherry for him while he waited for Jessie Lewis.

They were joined by Uncle Mort, who declined the offer of a sherry, but accepted the alternative offer of a glass of whisky.

"It's a bit rum, is this, isn't it?" he said.

"Is it?" said Carter Brandon.

"Aye, you'd think Jessie Lewis would get a feller of her own to take her to the social, wouldn't you? I don't know what's wrong with you youngsters these days. If I was your age, Carter, I'd be falling over backwards to take Jessie out."

"That's just what he's doing, you daft chuff," said Mr. Brandon.

"I know that, Les. I don't mean Carter himself personally. I mean other blokes. I don't mean Derrick whatshisname neither. I mean other blokes more suitable."

Mr. Brandon poured him another whisky and said with a twinkle in his eye:

"I'm surprised you haven't asked her yourself, Mort. You're the bloody Romeo round here, aren't you?"

"Less of that talk," said Uncle Mort.

Mrs. Brandon was the next to enter the front room.

"I've just left them sleeping peaceful in the attic. Poor souls, I said a little prayer for them."

She took a sip from her glass of raspberry cordial and, turning to her son, said:

"It's a bit rum is this, isn't it?"

"Is it?" said Carter Brandon.

"Don't be so silly. Of course it is. I've never heard anything like it before in my life."

"That's what I told him," said Uncle Mort.

"You ought to be ashamed of yourself, taking another girl out, while your fiancee's at home sat in front of the fire like Cinderella. You want to take a grip on yourself, young man, before you lose that girl for good and all. And then where would you be? What would you do with all your curtain material and underfelt, tell me that?"

When Jessie Lewis entered the room, there was not the slightest doubt that her appearance met with the unqualified approval of everyone present.

She had swept her hair up at the back and combed it in a fringe across her forehead.

"You're a little belter, Jessie," said Uncle Mort, gulping down his whisky.

She was wearing a black dress with black net over the arms and low-cut bosom. The net was gathered into a ruff round her neck and wrists, and the hemline was an inch above her knees.

"Have a sherry," said Mr. Brandon. "Aye, have a sherry."

Round her waist she had a black cord with tassels, to which she had attached Auntie Lil's whistle.

"What an unusual touch, Jessie," said Mrs. Brandon. "It's right original is that luv."

"Can I have a blow at it, Jessie?" said Uncle Mort.

"Don't be so vulgar, Mort," said Mrs. Brandon. "Well, you two, have a smashin' time at the social."

When they had left, she said to her husband:
"I do hope this doesn't lead to anything, Les. She knows her onions does Jessie, you know."

"Do you think so?" said Uncle Mort.

"Get off with you," said Mr. Brandon. "Our Carter wouldn't know what it was, if he fell arse over tip over it."

"I think I better have another sherry," said Mrs. Brandon.

CHAPTER THIRTY-FIVE

The Welfare Club Christmas Social and Dance, single tickets seven and six, double tickets fourteen shillings, was held in the Azalia Ballrooms, Tunnicliffe Road (buses twelve, thirteen, and ninety-six from city centre).

They called in at the neighbouring public house, 'The Drover's Arms' before venturing into the ballroom.

The french chalk was still covering the dance floor, and the people, sitting at the tables along the side of the room, were grave in face and silent in manner.

The bar was in the balcony above the stage and most of the drinkers had their backs to the hall, which was decorated with multi-coloured paper streamers with red crepe paper over the globe lampshades.

"Ugh," said Jessie Lewis, when she joined Carter Brandon after depositing her coat in the cloakroom. "Let's have a drink."

Carter Brandon kept a few paces behind her as she walked straight across the middle of the dance floor. She left a trail of footprints in the french chalk, and her walk was fluent and graceful.

They sat at a table at the edge of the balcony, overlooking the dance floor. Linda Preston, Connie Watkinson and their companions were shouting and laughing at the bar counter, but around Carter Brandon and Jessie Lewis there was silence.

"Are you enjoying it?" said Carter Brandon.

"No. Are you?" said Jessie Lewis.

"No," said Carter Brandon. "Let's have another drink."

Presently they were joined by Sid Skelhorn and his wife.

"Do you mind if we join you?" said Sid Skelhorn. "It's a bit too boisterous for me by the bar."

"I hope we're not going to be sat here all night," said Mrs. Skelhorn. "I didn't come out just to sit here, watching you sup all night."

"No," said Sid Skelhorn.

"I didn't put me dancing frock on just to sit like a wall-flower all night."

"Yes," said Sid Skelhorn.

"I expect to spend most of me time dancing."

"That's right."

"And I hope they've got a decent buffet on. I'm starving."

See what I mean, Daniel, said Carter Brandon to himself.

Mrs. Topping and her Yuletide Rhumba Ensemble struck up with 'I'm Dreaming Of A White Christmas', and a couple emerged from the gloom by one of the illuminated 'Exit' signs and began to dance.

"You always get these bloody show-offs at dances," said Sid Skelhorn.

His reflections on dance hall behaviour patterns were interrupted by Linda Preston, who jumped on his knee, kissed him on the forehead and said:

"Here he is, lads, old Casanova himself."

"Hey up," said Sid Skelhorn, glancing at his wife. "Give over."

Connie Watkinson pinched his right ear and said:

"Come on, Sidney, give us a kiss like the one you gave us on the outing. A real, juicy, smoochy smackeroo."

"I'd like to dance," said Mrs. Skelhorn, moving from her chair with surprising speed for a woman of her bulk.

Sid Skelhorn pushed Linda Preston off his knee and rushed after his wife.

"Go it, Sidney, cha cha cha," shouted Linda Preston, as Sid Skelhorn pushed his wife round the dance floor, his left arm extended rigid sideways, his bottom sticking out woodenly and his legs stiff to the knees. He heaved his wife round a corner and glared darkly up at them.

"Should we dance, Carter?" said Jessie Lewis.

"Right," said Carter Brandon, and he led her by the hand downstairs to the dance floor.

Mrs. Topping and her aged companions were playing a slow fox trot, and Jessie Lewis pressed herself into Carter Brandon as they began to dance.

Their cheeks touched, and her breasts and thighs rubbed against him. He glanced up at the balcony and saw Linda Preston staring down thoughtfully at him.

She pouted her lower lip, cocked an eyebrow and then shook her head slowly.

When the music stopped, Herbert Lowfield came on to the stage and took the microphone in his hands. He blew down it vigorously and said:

"Testing, one, two, three, four."

Then there was a roll of drums, and he began to speak.

"Right, listen this way, ladies and gentlemen, lads and lasses. Now then, the purpose of this function is enjoyment, and I want to see everyone enjoying theirselves and joining in with the games and Paul Joneses and progressive barn dances.

"Now then, in order to engender the festive spirit, funny hats will be provided for everyone in the hall. Much fun can be derived from this, the comic possibilities of inappropriate headgear being legion.

"And finally, there's a phone call for Mr. Carter Brandon in the manager's office."

"What's up now?" said Carter Brandon.

"Go and find out. That's what I'd do under the circumstances," said Jessie Lewis. "I'll see you in the bar."

The manager's office had a tannoy in the corner of the room to keep him in touch with events in the ballroom. His dinner jacket hung over the back of his chair, and he was eating fish and chips from a newspaper on his desk.

"Over there," he said, pointing to the telephone, which stood on a green filing cabinet by the door.

Carter Brandon picked up the receiver and said:

"Hello."

"Carter? Is that you?" said Pat.

"Yes."

"I just thought I'd ring to ask if you was enjoying yourself."

"Mm."

"Are you?"

"Not bad."

"What's Jessie wearing?"

"A sort of black thing."

"Oh," said Pat. "Is she enjoying herself?"

"Not bad."

"Well, have a good time. And, Carter."

"Yes?"

"You know I can trust you. Ta ta."

"Ta ta," said Carter Brandon, and he put down the receiver and nodded his thanks to the manager.

He found Jessie Lewis at the bar, surrounded by a group of apprentices from the engineering shop. When she saw him, she came straight across and handed him a drink.

"For you," she said. "Who was it? Pat?"

Carter Brandon nodded, and Jessie Lewis laughed. They went over to a corner of the balcony, and resting their arms on the ledge looked down on the hall.

She moved closer to him, and he put his arm round her shoulders and ran his hand up and down her net-clad arms.

"That's nice," said Jessie Lewis. "We might as well give Pat a good run for her money, I suppose."

They stood like that for some time until there was a tap on Carter Brandon's shoulder. He turned to see Eric Black frowning at him.

"There's a phone call for you, Carter," he said. "They've put it through to the foyer. I'll show you where it is."

He led Carter Brandon across the dance floor, through the swing doors and pointed to one of the hardboard shields, which acted as a telephone booth.

"You want to be careful, you know," he said. "People are watching you. It could get back to your bird, you know."

"She knows."

"You're a rum bugger you," said Eric Black.

Carter Brandon smiled and picked up the phone.

"Hello, Pat," he said.

"How did you know it was me?" said Pat.

Because I'm a bloody genius, eh, Daniel?

Bloody spot on, Carter.

"I just made a guess," he said.

"Are you glad it's me?"

"Yes."

"I forgot to tell you. There's no need to ring me when you get home."

Who says you were going to, Carter?

Bloody spot on, Daniel.

"Righto," he said.

"Are you enjoying yourself?"

"Oh aye."

"A lot?"

"So so."

"Is Jessie enjoying herself?"

"I think so."

"Well, enjoy yourself, Carter. Ta ta."

"Ta ta," said Carter Brandon.

There was a sickly sweet smell of perfume and perspiration and cigarette smoke coming from the hall, so he sat down on one of the old cinema tip-up seats in the foyer and lit a cigarette.

"What are you doing here all on your jack?"

It was Sid Skelhorn, standing in front of him. He was wearing his raincoat and holding his wife's red umbrella.

"Resting me feet," said Carter Brandon. "Are you off?"

"It's her," said Sid Skelhorn, pointing to the ladies' cloakroom. "What a bloody night. She played hell up about Linda Preston and Connie Watkinson."

"Did she?"

"What? She never stopped. 'Who's this? Who's that? What does she do? Do you work with her? Was she on the outing?' It was like the Spanish bloody Inquisition."

"It's the same every year. We always leave at this time. I've not seen the balloons come down from the ceiling yet. I think she only comes because it makes a change to have a row somewhere different from our back kitchen."

He kicked a cigarette butt glumly with his foot, and sank his hands deep into the pockets of his raincoat. He looked back over his shoulder at the door of the ladies' cloakroom. A young girl from the packing department came out. Her stockings were wrinkled at the ankles, and there was a beer stain on the seat of her skirt.

"These birds are all the bloody same," said Sid Skelhorn. "It's all a big illusion. They look all right now, when they're all dolled up, but think what they look like on t' po early doors."

Carter Brandon stubbed his cigarette on the floor and stood up.

"Aye well, I'll see you," he said.

"Aye," said Sid Skelhorn. Then he clutched hold of Carter Brandon's sleeve and said with a grin: "Hey up, though, that one you're with tonight's a bit of all right, in't she? What? Does she give you a bit of leg over?"

"Ta ta, Sid," said Carter Brandon, and he went back into the hall in search of Jessie Lewis.

She was sitting in the bar with the engineer with the fuzzy ginger moustache.

"Pat again?" she said.

"Aye."

"It's all rather amusing really," said Jessie Lewis to the engineer. "His fiancee keeps ringing him up every five minutes to see if he's enjoying himself."

"Are you dancing?" said Carter Brandon.

"Yes," said Jessie Lewis, and they walked hand in hand to the dance floor.

They danced close together again, and Jessie Lewi rested her head on Carter Brandon's shoulder. Her hair was coming loose from the clip, which held it in place at the back, and it brushed against his cheek. He took hold of a strand in his teeth and gave it a sharp tug.

"Lovely," said Jessie Lewis, pressing him into her.

At half past nine they served the buffet. Jessie Lewis said she was not hungry, so they went to the bar for more drinks. They were joined by the engineer.

"Weren't you one of the gang in the testing bay the other day?" he said to Carter Brandon.

"That's right."

"I'm developing these new turbines for the Royal Navy," he said to Jessie Lewis.

"Are you indeed?" said Jessie Lewis. Her eyes were sparkling, and her hair had loosened even more.

"It's quite hush hush, of course," said the engineer.

"Of course," said Jessie Lewis. "Would you mind excusing me a minute while I fix up my hair?"

The engineer stood as she left and said to Carter Brandon: "Classy."

"You think so?" said Carter Brandon.

"I don't think I've met her before. Jessie what is it?"

Here's your chance, Carter. Step in, mate.

Right, Daniel.

"Skelhorn," he said.

"Jessie Skelhorn, eh?" said the engineer, tugging the ends of his moustache. "Interesting."

Should I go all the way, Daniel?

Course you bloody should.

"Do you want her address?"

"Okay," said the engineer, smirking.

Carter Brandon gave him Sid Skelhorn's address and telephone number, and the engineer seemed well satisfied.

There was a roll of drums from the stage below, and Herbert Lowfield blew into the microphone and announced that party games would commence.

The fun was intense as the revellers threw themselves wholeheartedly into the games.

That was a good joke, Carter.

A TOUCH OF DANIEL

Not bad, was it, Daniel?

Not bad? It were a bloody cracker.

Do you think so?

You know the trouble with you, Carter, is you're too bloody modest.

Mm.

"Looks as though your bird's left you," said the engineer, for it was half an hour since Jessie Lewis had gone to fix her hair.

"Maybe," said Carter Brandon, and he went to the bar to get himself another gin and tonic.

He had taken two sips from his drink, when Herbert Lowfield announced that there was another telephone call for him in the foyer.

He forced his way through the crush on the dance floor, went into the foyer, picked up the phone and said:

"What is it this time, Pat?"

"Are you enjoying yourself, Carter?"

It was Jessie Lewis.

"Where are you ringing from?" he said.

"I just thought I'd let you know that I met this old friend of mine. He's taken me out to supper."

"I see."

"Well, we're neither of us enjoying ourselves, so it seemed to be the best thing."

"Mm."

Someone spoke softly to Jessie Lewis, and she giggled.

"See you then," she said, and she put down the phone.

Carter Brandon shrugged his shoulders. See what I mean, Daniel, he said to himself.

I'd go and get stonko, if I was you, Carter.

That's just what I'm going to do, Daniel.

He drank steadily with Louis St. John, the West Indian fitter. They didn't say much to each other.

Someone upset a tray full of drinks on the dance floor, and everyone applauded. There was a slight scuffle on the steps to the bar, and Eric Black took off his coat and punched one of the apprentices in the eye.

At midnight coloured balloons descended from the ceiling. Eric Black stuck one down the front of his shirt, and Cyril Chadwick punched him in the stomach. The balloon burst, and Eric Black fell back into a row of chairs and bumped his head on a corner of the table.

"You can't help laughing, man, can you?" said Louis St. John, peering intently into the dregs at the bottom of his glass.

Carter Brandon wandered off to sit on his own. He unloosened his tie and rested his feet on the ledge of the balcony.

I first met Pat at a do like this, Daniel, he said to himself.

Did you, Carter? Why don't you tell me all about it?

Shall I?

Don't be so bloody stupid, Carter. I know you're bursting to tell me.

Aye well, it were Christmas, you see, Daniel, and me and Tommy Coghill was having a few jars in this pub. We'd got nothing lined up, so we were just going to have a bit of a pub crawl and take a carry-out to Tommy's place.

Any road, this group of birds comes in all togged up in their best frocks, and one of them was a bit tight, and she kept making remarks. A right gunje-pot she was.

Any road, Tommy Coghill starts chatting one of her mates up, and she says they're going to the firm's do and would we like to come.

Well, Tommy was all for it, but me I'd have preferred to stay in the pub supping. They'd got some good turns on later, you see.

Any road, I sees this bird, who's not opened her mouth since they've come into the pub, and she's sort of sizing me up in a quiet sort of way. So I thinks to meself, well, you never know, I might click, so I decide to go.

I didn't take no notice of her, of course. We go into the ballroom place, and Tommy starts dancing straight away with this bird he's been chatting up, so I goes to the bar.

I thought to meself, if this little bird is interested, she'll come up after me. I don't see why I should bother chasing it.

Any road, I'm in the bar for bloody hours and there's no sign of it, so I thought I'd go home and see if there's owt good on the telly.

I'm just about to sup up, when I sees this little bird standing at the door. She's pretending she's talking to one of her mates, but I could see she wasn't, because her mate starts giggling something chronic, when she sees me looking.

Any road, I sort of saunters over and asks it if it wants to dance. I wasn't bothered either road really, Daniel.

I mean, if I really fancy something on a dance, I goes and stands by it at the ladies' invitation and waits for it to ask me.

Any road, I asks this one, and we gets on the dance floor, and it doesn't want to know. It's pushing me away all the time telling me to behave meself.

Bloody rotate I thinks to meself. There's two more quick steps to go and I'm stuck with it. Any road, I'm thinking how I can make me escape, when she says she knows me cousin, Cyril.

I thought, hello, she must be interested. So I thinks, I might as well ask it if it wants to be taken home. Yes, she says. So I does.

And that's how you started with Pat is it, Carter?

Yes. Dead romantic, in't it, Daniel?

"Hey up, dreamy gob."

He jumped, and the unlit cigarette fell from his mouth and spilled tobacco down the front of his shirt. Linda Preston laughed.

"Are you driving us home?" she said.

"Righto," said Carter Brandon.

They got into the car, and Linda Preston said:

"Open the windows, kid, I feel like throwing up."

She began to sing very loudly, and then she slumped to her right on to Carter Brandon. He tried to move her away, but she would not budge, and he had to drive in second gear all the way to her house.

The lamps were out in the street, and his headlights picked up a dog with a bandaged paw, hobbling across the pavement into an alley.

He shook Linda Preston by the shoulders. She grunted and began to sing again very softly and out of tune.

"Come on, you're here," he said.

She threw her arms round his neck, and tried to find his lips with her mouth. She was unsuccessful.

"I knew I'd had too much," she said, and she began to giggle.

Carter Brandon opened the door of the car, backed out and began to pull her towards him. By the time he had manoeuvred her out of the car, her skirt had ridden up round her thighs and she had lost her shoes.

He held her upright, but her legs collapsed under her, and she clung to the lapels of his coat.

He put his arm under her armpits and dragged her across the pavement across the front door of her house.

"Where's your key?" he said.

"Unlocked."

He opened the door and helped her inside. Then he went back to the car to fetch her shoes and handbag. When he came back, he found she had fallen to the floor, so he picked her up, carried her into the back kitchen, and placed her on the sofa.

Her make-up had run from he eyelids and left watery

black smears on her cheeks. Her face was pale, except for a cluster of pimples, which made a red blotch on her chin.

"Coffee," she said.

"What?"

She licked her lips again and pointed to the cupboard over the draining board.

"In there," she said.

The shelves of the cupboard were sticky with grease. A loaf, covered in grey-green mould, lay among a bag of sprouts, and there was a comb with grey hairs matted in its broken teeth.

Carter Brandon put the kettle on the stove, washed a cup in cold water and filled it with three spoonfuls of coffee.

"Give is us black," said Linda Preston, and when he handed her the cup, she grasped it with both hands and began to shiver.

"Are you all right?"

"Did she back-heel you then?" said Linda Preston.

"If you're okay, I'll be getting off home."

Linda Preston pulled up her skirt and began to fiddle with her suspenders.

Both her stockings were laddered. She had a graze on her right knee, and the blood had stained black the edges of the hole in the stocking.

"Give us a hand with these bloody things," she said, and then she hiccuped, and the cup of coffee slid from her hand and smashed on the tiles. The coffee streamed and ran in a cindery rivulet to the fireplace.

"What's up with you then, kid?" said Linda Preston, pulling off her stockings and throwing them over the back of the sofa.

Carter Brandon stood at the end of the sofa, lit a cigarette and watched her begin to tug at the zip of her skirt.

"What's up with you then?" she said again, and the skirt fell open at the waist. She tried to wriggle out of it, but it caught on the backs of her knees and she began to slide off the sofa.

"Back-heeled you, did she?" she said.

Upstairs a woman was coughing. They were deep rattling coughs, and the springs of the bed creaked.

Linda Preston had pulled off her blouse. She was sitting on the floor, her back resting against the sofa, her legs wide apart in front of her. She twisted her brassiere round and tried to unfasten the hook.

"Jessie bloody Lewis," she said, as the hook snapped and the brassiere fell to her waist.

"Just take a look at that, Daniel," said Carter Brandon.

"What?" said Linda Preston.

"Have you ever seen anything so bloody awful in your life?" he said.

"What are you on about?" said Linda Preston, and she put her hand under her left breast and stared glassily at the nipple.

He threw his cigarette into the fireplace, took Linda Preston roughly by the arm and dragged her up on to the sofa.

She clung hold of his neck and tried to drag him down on top of her.

"Come on, kid," she said. "Let's be having it."

He put his hand under her jaw and thrust her away from him. She slumped backwards on to the sofa, her head dropped forward on to her chest, and a dribble of urine appeared on the inside of her thigh.

"Take a long look at that, Daniel," said Carter Brandon. "That's a sight to remember for the rest of your life. Let that be a warning to you."

There was a note waiting for him, when he returned home. He rang Pat, and she said sleepily:

"Did you enjoy yourself?"

"Not bad."

He slept well that night and was half an hour late for work.

CHAPTER THIRTY-SIX

"I'm not the least bit surprised, luv," said Pat, when Carter Brandon told her about Jessie Lewis's behaviour at the social. "And that's why I did it."

"Did what?" said Carter Brandon.

It was their duty night out, and they were sitting in the newly-opened Wimpy Bar opposite the Town Hall.

The remains of two cream cakes lay on their plates, and Pat's mug of Horlicks had a wrinkled layer of skin on top of it.

"I sent you off to that social with Jessie to teach you a lesson."

"Oh aye?"

"To show you just what sort of a woman Jessie Lewis really is," said Pat, removing the skin with her tea spoon.

Carter Brandon had a headache, the result of the previous

evening's drinking, and the smell of frying onions made his stomach knot and gurgle.

"I knew what was going on all along, you know, Carter," said Pat. "I knew you was secretly fancying Jessie and wondering what she'd be like and all that. I knew you was trying to pluck up courage to ask her out, so I thought I'd step in first and arrange it for you."

"Thank you," said Carter Brandon.

"Any road, you're so disgusted with her behaviour, you're so annoyed by the way she treated you and made you look such a fool in front of everybody, that you've worked her right out of your system, right, Carter?"

"Right," said Carter Brandon.

"What did you do after she'd gone off without you?"

Carter Brandon coughed and, licking his forefinger, began to use it to pick up the cake crumbs from his plate.

"Aye well," he said. "I took Linda Preston home because she weren't feeling too good."

"Linda Preston," said Pat. "Now there's someone who'd make two of Jessie Lewis. I know she's a bit coarse in her manners but underneath she's got a heart of gold."

"Mm," said Carter Brandon, and his stomach rumbled. "Do you fancy a drink?"

"No, luv, we can't really afford it, can we? Let's go home and have a kiss and a cuddle."

The kissing and cuddling duly took place, and Pat said, as they lay side by side on the sofa:

"Do you remember when we first met, Carter?"

"Aye."

"It was dead romantic, wasn't it?"

"Oh aye."

"I'll never forget the way you was looking at me. You'd got a right dreamy far-away look in your eye, and you was ever so polite and nice to me. You bought me a Babycham in the pub, and you went back for a cherry, because I dropped the first one on the floor. Do you remember that?"

"Mm," said Carter Brandon.

Cherry? What's she on about, Daniel?

"And when we got in the dance, you stuck close to me all night. I was bursting for you to ask me to dance, but you was too shy, you big softie. I thought I'll wait while the ladies' invitation and then I'll ask meself, but when it come, I was in the lavvy."

"So was I."

"Snap," said Pat, and she laughed and ruffled his hair. The

fairylights on the Christmas tree flickered, the fire spat and a piece of cake clattered into the mesh fire guard and dropped smouldering into the fireplace.

"And then, when you asked me to dance, we just seemed to sink into each other," said Pat. "It was like floating round on a cloud, and your arms felt so strong, wrapped round me, Carter. And you whispered such nice things into me ear. It was dead romantic, wan't it?"

Well, someone's got something wrong somewhere, Carter. Pardon?

Christmas was celebrated in a quiet fashion. The two old men in the attic were constantly in their thoughts, and, before they started their Christmas dinner, Mrs. Brandon said a little prayer.

"Oh Lord," she said. "For what we are about to receive may the Lord make us truly thankful."

"Amen," said Uncle Mort. "Pass us the bread sauce, Les."

"I haven't finished yet, Mort," said Mrs. Brandon. "Now close your eyes and put your hands together."

Uncle Mort obliged, although he kept one eye open, which he used to respond to Mr. Brandon's wink.

"Oh Lord," said Mrs. Brandon. "Well, all I want to say, Lord, is as how I hope Thou willst look over our Stavely and Corporal Parkinson and give them the benefit of your love and mercy. I know, Lord, that they have sinned, but then again, Lord, be fair, when all's said and done, we are all poor sinners, when it comes down to brass tacks, and I hope as Thou willst not come down too hard on them. Amen."

She paused, looked up at the attic, and a little tear forced itself out of her tightly-shut eyelid and trickled down her cheek.

"Come on, Les, start carving," she said.

Their plates were filled with turkey and sausage meat stuffing and roast pork.

"Would you like some of my crackling, Jessie?" said Uncle Mort.

"Thank you, Uncle Mort," said Jessie Lewis.

Mrs. Brandon handed round sprouts, carrots, peas and mashed potatoes.

"Give Jessie some more of them sprouts, Annie," said Uncle Mort.

"Thank you, Uncle Mort," said Jessie Lewis.

Then came the Christmas pudding. Mrs. Brandon poured brandy on it, and Carter Brandon set it alight.

Uncle Mort helped Jessie Lewis to the white sauce, and he personally supervised the cutting of a second slice of pudding for her.

"Jessie and me'll wash up for you," he said after they had finished their meal. "It's only right being as how we're guests."

The washing up was completed, nuts were consumed, cigars were lit, tangerines were peeled, whisky was drunk, the Queen's speech was heard, commented upon and digested in drowsy silence.

Then Mrs. Brandon said:

"I think we ought to introduce our Daniel to the two old men before it's too late."

"He won't catch anything, will he?" said Carter Brandon.

"Honest to God, Carter, you're worse than an old woman with that child," said Mrs. Brandon.

They all trooped upstairs, and Carter Brandon took the baby from Jessie Lewis and led the way into the attic.

The two old men had their eyes closed. The sheets were drawn up to their chins, and only their faint breathing disturbed the peace of the sick room.

"Stavely," said Mrs. Brandon softly. "Stavely."

Uncle Stavely's eyelids fluttered, but his eyes did not open. The old men's presents lay unopened on the bedside table.

Mrs. Brandon leaned over Uncle Stavely and tapped him gently on the shoulder. The old man opened his eyes wearily and stared up at her.

"Happy Christmas, Stavely," said Mrs. Brandon.

"Aye, and many of them," said Mr. Brandon.

"Look what we've brought you, Uncle Stavel," said Carter Brandon, holding up the baby in front of his eyes.

"What is it?" said Uncle Stavely.

"It's a baby, Stavely," said Mrs. Brandon.

"It's Daniel," said Carter Brandon.

Uncle Stavely tried to lift himself up, but the effort was too much for him, and he sank back in the bed and began to shiver.

"Take it away," he said. "Take it away."

Carter Brandon held the baby over him and said:

"That's your Uncle Stavely, Daniel, give him a kiss."

Uncle Stavely tried to turn his head away from the baby, but he could not prevent his forehead being touched by Daniel's mouth.

"He likes you, Stavely," said Mrs. Brandon. "He's just given you a kiss."

Uncle Stavely's eyes opened wide in panic, when Carter

Brandon held the baby over Corporal Parkinson. He clawed at the sheet round his neck, and, when he saw the baby touching Corporal Parkinson, he screamed:

"Take it away. It's an evil fluence."

Jessie Lewis calmed him down. She smoothed the sheets, tucked them into the side of the bed and wiped the old man's cheek and forehead with a damp face cloth. His eyes were filled with fear, and they did not close until Carter Brandon took Daniel back to the nursery.

"Don't upset yourself, Stavely," said Mrs. Brandon. "It's only a baby. It'll not harm you."

Uncle Stavely's mouth twitched at the corners, and then he let out a deep sigh.

"Evil, evil, evil," he said softly to himself.

"That was your Uncle Stavely and Corporal Parkinson, Daniel," said Carter Brandon in the nursery.

The baby stared at him and smiled. He bounced him up and down on his knee, and the baby began to chuckle.

"You'll be like that one of these days, Daniel," he said. "You'll be a right old codger like them."

Christ almighty, will I, Carter? Honest?

Pat came into the room and stood by his side.

"You'll be holding your own baby like that one of these days, Carter," she said. "Are you looking forward to it?"

"Will you be jealous, Daniel?" said Carter Brandon.

"Course, he won't, will you, Daniel?" said Pat. "You'll be right good chums with our baby, and you'll play together, but you mustn't be too rough, because you'll be bigger than our little one."

"You'll be able to knock about together," said Carter Brandon. "You'll go on long walks in the countryside with a packet of sarnies and a bottle of Tizer. And you'll pick flowers and dam streams and climb over stiles and roll down hills in the grass and throw sheet shit at each other."

"Carter!" said Pat. "They'll do no such thing. They'll learn to have some respect for their clothes. I mean to say, luv, dry cleaning costs a fortune these days."

On Boxing Day there was a severe frost, and the match was postponed.

"That's what I've got against rugby," said Uncle Mort. "You spend half your bloody time having it cancelled, because the ground's too hard. Have another whipped cream walnut, Jessie."

"Thank you, Uncle Mort," said Jessie Lewis, and she winked at Carter Brandon, who turned his head away from her.

Mrs. Partington came round for tea, and afterwards was taken up to the attic to pay her respects to Uncle Stavely and Corporal Parkinson.

When she came down, she said:

"Well, I must say they neither of them look as badly as I expected, Mrs. Brandon. From what Pat told me, I expected the pair of them to be looking as though they was at death's door. I says to Pat, I says: 'Don't be surprised, luv, if I come down looking all upset, when I've seen them, because the sight of death always reminds me of your father,' I says.

"Well, that's far from the case, Mrs. Brandon. There's neither of them looks as though they could run the hundred yards dash, but they don't look as though they're at death's door by a long chalk."

"Don't you think so?" said Mrs. Brandon.

"I don't. I do not, Mrs. Brandon. I had quite a long chat with Uncle Stavely, and I told him straight, I says: 'Hello, Uncle Stavely, I'm right glad to see you.' And he says: 'Hello Mrs. Partington, compliments of the season,' he says. 'Same to you, luv,' I says. 'Same to you. How are you keeping?' 'Mustn't grumble Mrs. P.,' he says. Well, that's not the sort of conversation you expect from someone who's supposed to be at death's door, is it?"

"You never know, it might be a temporary rally," said Mrs. Brandon.

"Well, I hope so for their sakes, bless them," said Mrs. Partington.

At eight o'clock it was decided that an excursion to the local public house would make the perfect ending to the perfect day.

Jessie Lewis said she was quite willing to stay behind to look after the baby and the two old men, and, as she was to leave for Bristol the following day to spend a few days with a friend, the objections were not too prolonged.

"I'll stay with you, Jessie, and keep your company," said Uncle Mort.

"That's very nice of you, Uncle Mort," said Jessie Lewis.

A most convivial time was had in the public house, and after supper had been taken at the Brandon residence, Carter Brandon drove Pat and her mother to their home.

"Do you like babies, Carter?" said Mrs. Partington, when they were in the kitchen drinking cocoa.

"Not bad."

"Well, I think it's marvellous the way you treat that little lad of your Uncle Mort's. I think it does you great credit. I do. I really do. Pat, would you go upstairs a minute and fetch me the aspros?"

Mrs. Partington got up when Pat left the room and stood with her back against the door.

"Shssh," she said, putting her finger to her lips. "I want to get this in quick before Pat comes back. Don't get too fond of babies, Carter. Do you follow me?"

"No," said Carter Brandon.

"What I'm trying to say is, well, I mean, well, don't get too fond of babies too soon. Do you follow my meaning?"

"No," said Carter Brandon.

"How shall I put it? Well, if you're fond of having babies, there are ways you can stop yourself having them. Do you follow what I mean, Carter?"

"Not really."

"What I'm trying to tell you is to go to the doctor and say to him: 'Doctor, I'm about to get married to Pat Partington and we're both very fond of babies, but we don't want to have them until we've settled some of the bills on our new house in Tunstall Avenue, so could you make some suggestions in regard to the sort of action we should take?' Do you follow me now, Carter?"

"Oh aye," said Carter Brandon.

The next day was Saturday, the day Jessie Lewis was to leave for Bristol. Uncle Mort rose early and crept quietly out of the bedroom so that he would not disturb his nephew, who was sleeping soundly.

He went into the kitchen and put the kettle on the cooker. Then he went into the dining room and set two places on the table.

After this had been done, he returned to the kitchen, placed a lump of dripping into the frying pan and proceeded to fry six rashers of bacon, two eggs, two tomatoes and a slice of fried bread.

He crept quietly upstairs, knocked on the door of the nursery and whispered through the keyhole:

"I've cooked your breakfast, Jessie."

"Thank you, Uncle Mort," said Jessie Lewis.

Mrs. Brandon was most surprised to discover that her brother and Jessie Lewis had breakfasted together, but she was not entirely displeased.

"It's good to see you making yourself useful round the house for a change, Mort," she said.

"All part of the service, Annie," said Uncle Mort gaily, and he went up to the bedroom and said to Carter Brandon: "I tell you what, though, Carter, people in this house are making a right convenience out of you with that car of yours."

"You can say that again, Uncle Mort," said Carter Brandon.

"I don't want to interfere or owt like that, but, if I was you, I'd put me foot down. I'd tell them straight you wasn't going to be imposed on like that in the future."

"I've already done that more or less," said Carter Brandon.

"Good for you," said Uncle Mort. Then he went into the kitchen and said to Mrs. Brandon. "Is Carter taking Jessie in his car to the station?"

"That's an idea, Mort. It'll not take him a minute, will it?" said Mrs. Brandon.

Uncle Mort nodded to himself and went upstairs to the bathroom where Carter Brandon was shaving.

"What did I tell you?" he said. "Your mother wants you to run Jessie Lewis down to the station."

"Oh aye?" said Carter Brandon, swilling the soap from his cheeks.

"Now I don't want to interfere or owt like that, but you've made your decision, haven't you?"

"Yes," said Carter Brandon, carefully patting the shaving rash under his chin with the towel.

"Well, you bloody stick to it," said Uncle Mort. "That's the soundest advice I can give you on the subject."

Carter Brandon completed his toilet activities and, by-passing the kitchen, the front room and the dining room, went into the garage.

He opened the bonnet of the car, removed the distributor head, took it to his work bench, put on his overalls, switched on the transistor radio and lit a cigarette.

Soon he heard his mother walking down the path, so he took out a pair of pliers and began to probe at the distributor head.

His mother came into the garage and said:

"Carter, be a good lad and run Jessie to the station, will you?"

"I can't."

"And why not?"

"Because I'm working on the distributor head."

"Well, can't you leave it there for a moment and do it when you come back?"

"The car won't go without the distributor head," he said slowly and carefully.

You lying sod, Carter. There's nowt wrong with it.

True, Daniel, but she doesn't know that, does she?

"You don't need to make excuses to me, you know, Carter," said Mrs. Brandon. "It's quite obvious to me what's behind all this."

"Mm."

She's not as thick as you think, Carter.

Mm.

"You're just sulking because Jessie left you at the Christmas Social," said Mrs. Brandon.

"Am I?"

Course you are, Carter.

I'm bloody not, you know, Daniel.

"You know perfectly well you are," said Mrs. Brandon.

Carter Brandon pushed past his mother and went to the cabinet, where he kept his tools. He took out a screwdriver and turned to make his way back to the bench. His mother blocked his way.

"What about Pat?" she said. "How do you think she feels about it, seeing you moping about Jessie like this?

"Poor lass, she doesn't know whether she's coming or going. I almost dropped through the floor with shame that night she come home and asked Jessie if she'd go to the social with you. You didn't see the look in her eyes. It was tearing her apart. I could see that without looking.

"I've never seen anything like the way Jessie looked neither. She were proper mortified. She just didn't know where to put herself.

"And then when she does the decent thing and clears off and leaves you on your own, you turn all sulky and mopey about it, all spiteful and vindicative. And that's why you've got the distribution head off."

"Distributor," said Carter Brandon.

"I'll tell you this for nothing, if you don't snap out of it soon, you'll have Pat going off with someone else and Jessie leaving here for good and all. And then you'll have fallen between two stools and serve you right.

"Well, I've had my say, and I hope you'll give it serious consideration and act on it. And for a start off, you can stop this silly pre-occupation with Daniel. It's not natural for a lad of your age to pal around with a baby. Look at the age difference. What you've got in common with each other is beyond me."

She doesn't know, does she, Daniel?

She hasn't a bloody clue, Carter.

"The more you talk, the longer it'll take to put this distributor head back on," he said.

His mother turned on her heel angrily and went back into the kitchen. She saw that Jessie Lewis was wearing her coat and that Uncle Mort was standing by her side, clad in overcoat, cap and Fair Isle mittens.

"It's all right, Uncle Mort, I can manage quite well myself. It's only a small case," said Jessie Lewis.

"No, Jessie, Uncle Mort will go with you," said Mrs. Brandon. "There's at least one male in this house what's got some manners—and he's on my side of the family, I'm glad to say."

Lunch was eaten in silence. Mr. Brandon was in bad odour, owing to the fact that he had allowed the dog to roll in a patch of manure in the allotment. Carter Brandon's disgrace was more deep-seated, and his mother scarcely glanced at him during the meal.

"Eat up, or we'll be late for the match," said Mr. Brandon.

"Right," said Carter Brandon.

"Match!" said Mrs. Brandon scornfully. "It's a pity you can't find any thing more useful to do than go to a match."

"Such as?" said Mr. Brandon, taking a second helping of marmalade sponge pudding.

"Well, for a start off, Carter could get himself off to his new house to give Pat a hand."

"The builders haven't finished yet, woman. They're still putting the bloody roof on," said Mr. Brandon.

"He should be there to see they're doing it proper," said Mrs. Brandon. "And don't call me 'woman'."

Mr. Brandon and his son were due to leave the house at five minutes past two in order to catch the special bus which stopped at the top of the street at eight minutes past two.

At one minute past two Uncle Mort returned. He came straight into the dining room without taking off his overcoat and cap and said:

"I've proposed to Jessie."

CHAPTER THIRTY-SEVEN

"You've what?" said Mrs. Brandon.

"You've what?" repeated her husband.

Uncle Mort stuck out his chin, fingered the lapels of his

overcoat, rocked on the balls of his feet and said with dignity:

"I have asked Jessie to do me the great honour of accepting the offer of my hand in marriage."

"You've what?" said Mrs. Brandon.

"You've what?" repeated her husband.

"So put that in your bloody pipes and smoke it," said Uncle Mort.

And with those words he left them and was not seen again until supper time, when he entered the dining room, took a bite from his cream cracker and Cheshire cheese sandwich and said:

"This cheese is going off, Annie."

Mrs. Brandon's lips curled, and she placed her cup carefully on the saucer on the table in front of her.

"Oh, it's going off, is it, Mort?"

"Aye. If I was you, I'd try Lancashire. It's got a better flavour for one thing."

"Oh, it's got a better flavour, has it, Mort?" said Mrs. Brandon.

"When me and Jessie set up home, you'll not get no Cheshire cheese when you come round for supper, I'll tell you that," said Uncle Mort.

"Oh, we'll not get no Cheshire cheese, shan't we, Mort?" said Mrs. Brandon.

"Both Jessie and me are of one mind as regards cheese," said Uncle Mort.

"Oh, you're of one mind as regards cheese, are you, Mort?" said Mrs. Brandon.

The minutes passed without any addition being made to the duologue between Mrs. Brandon and Uncle Mort. Hot water was poured into the kettle, crumbs were eaten from the rug by the dog and a telephone call was received from Carter Brandon to say that he was stranded in his car with a faulty distributor head.

Then Uncle Mort said:

"Well, aren't you going to ask me for details?"

"Details about what, Mort?" said Mrs. Brandon.

"Tell her, Les," said Uncle Mort.

"Tell her what, Mort?" said Mr. Brandon.

Uncle Mort nodded to himself, tapped his feet, coughed and said:

"Right then, if you don't want to know, I'll not bloody tell you."

"Right then," said Mrs. Brandon.

Carter Brandon's return home did not take place until

three in the morning. He looked into his parents' bedroom to inform them of his arrival.

"It was your distributing head, was it?" said his mother sleepily.

"Distributor," said Carter Brandon, and he bent over Daniel's cot, which had been transferred from the nursery, and said very softly so that his parents would not hear:

"It would be the distributor head, wouldn't it?"

"Sssh, not too loud, Carter, you'll wake me up and I'll start bawling.

Uncle Mort watched his nephew get undressed. Then, when he had climbed into bed, he said:

"I'm sorry it's worked out this way, Carter."

"Oh?"

"Still, all's fair in love and war, eh?"

"What are you on about, Uncle Mort?" said Carter Brandon, pulling the eiderdown over his ears and shuffling his feet to get warm.

"I don't want you to take it too hard, Carter. I don't want you to let it come between us," said Uncle Mort.

"Mm," said Carter Brandon, feeling the warmth creeping slowly into the cold hollows of the bed. Then he tentatively extended his right leg into the icy lower reaches of the bed.

"All right, you've lost, I've won. But you've more battles ahead of you, Carter. And one day you'll win one of them, and, when you do, it's up to you to be as generous in victory to your opponent as I am to you."

"Mm," said Carter Brandon, and his eyelids closed softly and drowsiness seeped through his body.

"You see, Carter, where women is concerned, life's full of disappointments," said Uncle Mort, turning over on to his back and resting his head on his hands. "I've had me fair wack of them, God knows. There was your Auntie Edna passed on, there was Dolly Wignall what kept getting gum boils, there was Ella whatshername what ran off with Ernie Thingie, there was Iris Booth what decided to be a bloody nun. Oh aye, I almost forgot, there was your Auntie Lil, of course. She goes and dies on me only this year."

"Mm."

"Look at it this road, Carter. You and me was rivals. Right? Now then, I beat you. Right? But you and me's also mates. Right? We was mates long before either of us met Jessie. Right? So there's no reason why we shouldn't go on being mates. Right?"

There was no reply from Carter Brandon's bed. Uncle

Mort sat up and peered into the gloom. Then he sank back in bed and said loudly:

"He's bloody fallen asleep on me again."

There was no opportunity the next day for Uncle Mort to enlarge on the details of his proposal of marriage to Jessie Lewis, for the Brandon family was wholly occupied with the startling transformation in the health of Uncle Stavely and Corporal Parkinson.

It was discovered by Mrs. Brandon, who had gone into their bedroom the first thing in the morning to give them their medicine.

She called to her husband, summoning him up to the attic.

"What do you think to that then?" she said, pointing to Uncle Stavely, who was sitting up in bed, trying to put on his spectacles.

"Morning, Les," said Uncle Stavely. "Pardon?"

His complexion was still pallid, his movements were still weak and his body was still frail, but there was not the slightest doubt that a substantial improvement had taken place in his condition.

"How are you feeling, Stavely?" said Mr. Brandon.

"Champion," said Uncle Stavely. "Could I have some potted meat on toast with the crusts cut off?"

"Certainly, Stavely," said Mrs. Brandon. "And you can have a cup of Bovril, too."

They inspected Corporal Parkinson, prodding him with their fingers and pulling back his eyelids.

"He's still out cold," said Mr. Brandon.

"I know, but he seems to be coming nearer to the surface, doesn't he?" said Mrs. Brandon.

"Aye, he's giving the odd twitch now and again," said Mr. Brandon.

"He says he's feeling very much better and he'll shortly be waking up to play his full part once more in the activities of the household. Pardon?" said Uncle Stavely.

The little speech left him breathless, and Mrs. Brandon helped him to a more comfortable position in bed.

The doctor confirmed their assessment of the situation, when he said:

"Amazing, amazing. Still, don't hope for too much, Mrs. Brandon. They sometimes make a temporary rally like this before relapsing into the final decline."

Uncle Mort took no part in the discussions. He just sat in a corner of the front room, cleaning his boots and sulking.

"Aren't you pleased?" said Mrs. Brandon.

"It'll be more trouble for Jessie," said Uncle Mort.

"For who?" said Mrs. Brandon, leaving the room before her brother could answer.

Midway through the afternoon Uncle Stavely said to Mrs. Brandon:

"Can I hear a baby crying, Annie?"

"Yes," said Mrs. Brandon. "It's Daniel."

"Pardon?" said Uncle Stavely. "Who's he?"

"It's our Lil's baby. You met him when he came to say 'How do' on Christmas day."

"Is our Lil keeping well?" said Uncle Stavely.

Over tea there was only one topic of conversation, which was, of course, the state of health of Uncle Stavely and his companion.

"I think it's marvellous," said Pat.

"And so do I, luv," said Mrs. Brandon. "And do you know what caused it?"

"No," said Pat.

Mrs. Brandon pointed up at the ceiling and said:

"Him up there."

"Our Carter?" said Uncle Mort.

"No, you silly devil," said Mrs. Brandon. "Him."

"Who?" said Uncle Mort.

"Him. The Almighty. God. Our Lord," said Mrs. Brandon.

"Oh," said Uncle Mort. "Him."

"I've been saying a little prayer to Him regular, and now He's answered me. It makes you want to believe in God, when things like this happen, doesn't it?"

They took Pat upstairs to see with her own eyes the result of His intervention in the affairs of Uncle Stavely.

"This is Pat, Carter's fiancée, Stavely," said Mrs. Brandon.

"Hello, Uncle Stavely," said Pat. "You do look well."

"Pardon? Does it look like Lil?"

"What?" said Mrs. Brandon.

"The baby."

"I'll bring him in to show you," said Carter Brandon.

When Uncle Stavely saw the baby, he cringed and put his arms in front of his face.

"What's to do, Stavely?" said Mrs. Brandon. "It's only a baby. It'll not do you no harm."

Carter Brandon took Daniel across to the bed, and Uncle Stavely began to whimper.

"Take him away, take him away," he cried. But when Carter Brandon made to do as he was bid, he cried: "No, bring him back, bring him back."

Carter Brandon held Daniel tightly as he took him back to Uncle Stavely. The old man's eyes were wide with fear, and his limbs were shivering, but, when Carter Brandon showed signs of hesitating, he beckoned him on impatiently.

"Let him touch me," he said.

Carter Brandon lowered Daniel to the old man's face. Their cheeks touched, and Uncle Stavely screwed up his eyes tightly and clenched his fists.

Then, when Carter Brandon withdrew the baby, he relaxed his tense body, let out a deep sigh of contentment and said: "That's better, that's better. Now do it to Corporal Parkinson."

Not a word was spoken as Carter Brandon placed Daniel's lips on Corporal Parkinson's forehead. They all held their breath and waited to see how Uncle Stavely would react.

"That's better, that's better," he said, letting out another deep sigh. "He says he feels much better for that. Pardon?"

"What do you make to that, Les?" said Mrs. Brandon in the corridor outside.

"Aye, it's a bit rum, when you come to think about it," said Mr. Brandon.

Further food for thought was provided later in the evening. Mr. and Mrs. Brandon had been to the attic to pay their respects to the two old men, when they heard Uncle Mort's voice coming from their bedroom.

They peered round the door and saw him, sitting at the side of the cot, talking to the baby.

"You see, thingie, when all's said and done, you need a mother," he said. "That has been the guiding light in everything I've done. Your interests have been paramount, mate.

"I sized it all up, looked at the pros and cons, both for and against, and thought to meself—all right, Mort, find yourself a bloody missus.

"Now then, who do I know, who could fall into that category? Simple. There was just two candidates—Jessie Lewis and Mrs. Partington."

"Mrs. Partington? Her?" said Mrs. Brandon in a soft hiss. Her husband put his finger in front of her lips and took hold of her arm firmly to stop her entering the bedroom.

"Now Mrs. Partington's all right, if she's living on the other side of town. But on top of you—no. Talk? She must have been vaccinated with a bloody gramophone needle."

"Just listen to his language in front of that baby," said Mrs. Brandon.

"So the only alternative, as you might say, was Jessie. You see, you seem to get along all right with her, don't you?

There's no embarrassment on your part when she's supervising your ablutions, is there?"

Mr. and Mrs. Brandon hastily stepped back out of sight as Uncle Mort stood up and walked to the window.

"So I thought to meself, I'll have a bash. I mean, as regards good looks and such like I'm not out of the top drawer. I've seen better. But as regards maturity and common bloody sense, I'm a bloody catch for any girl, no matter what her age.

"So I takes her bags to the station. I takes her for a cup of tea and an individual fruit pie in the buffet, and I asks her to do me the great honour of accepting my hand in marriage. You should have seen her face, mate."

"I can just imagine it," whispered Mrs. Brandon.

"Delight wasn't in it, mate. Sheer bloody unadulterated joy was nearer the mark. 'Give me time to think, Uncle Mort,' she says. 'Righto, Jessie,' I says. So we'll be breaking the news of our impending wedlock official like when she gets back from Bristol. I'll tell you this, it's given me a new lease of life, thingie."

He stood over the baby, scratching his head.

"I wish I could remember your bloody name," he said.

The health of Uncle Stavely and Corporal Parkinson improved day by day. And day by day the silence of Jessie Lewis continued.

She was to have returned on the second day of January. She did not, and there was no communication from her to explain her absence.

No one in the house had her address in Bristol. When pressed on this point by Mr. Brandon, Uncle Mort replied glumly:

"I never thought to ask her, did I?"

The doctor brought his Irish locum to visit the two old men each day. And each day they issued expressions of amazement at the recovery shown by their patients.

Uncle Stavely's mobility had increased to such an extent that he could now pay visits to the lavatory unescorted.

Corporal Parkinson was still preoccupied with his slumbers, but there were distinct signs that he might shortly find a new interest in life.

When a light was passed to and fro in front of his eyes, his head moved weakly, and, when the doctor examined his chest with his stethoscope, muted clicking noises came from the old soldier's throat.

"He says he's feeling grand, and he'll soon be waking up,

because the rest has done him all the good in the world. Pardon?" said Uncle Stavely.

"The funny thing is that they seem to perk up every time I take Daniel to see them," said Carter Brandon to Pat one evening in the first week of January.

"What's so funny about that?" said Pat. "I mean to say, the sight of a bonny bouncing baby always acts as a tonic to old folk, doesn't it?"

"Aye, but it's something more than that."

"What?"

"When Daniel touches them, you can see a sort of red glow come over their faces."

"That's happiness."

"Is it?"

"Like the red glow that comes over me when you kiss me, luv," said Pat, wrapping her arms round his neck and kissing him on the lips.

Carter Brandon responded with the appropriate enthusiasm to her caresses, and then he drove home. The telephone was ringing.

"Is that you, Carter?" shouted his mother.

"Yes."

"Answer the phone, will you? We're all in bed be now."

Carter Brandon picked up the receiver and said:

"Hello."

"Hello," said Jessie Lewis.

"Who is it?" shouted his mother from the top of the stairs. She was dressed in her red dressing gown, and her hair was in curlers.

Carter Brandon shook his head and motioned her to be silent.

"Sorry I didn't ring before, but I've just got back from Austria."

"Austria?" said Carter Brandon.

"Who is it for heaven's sake?" said Mrs. Brandon. "It's not bad news, is it?"

"What were you doing there?" said Carter Brandon.

"I'll tell you when I see you," said Jessie Lewis. "I'll be arriving on the two-thirty-five tomorrow afternoon. See you."

"Don't you want to speak to Uncle Mort?" said Carter Brandon.

"Why should I? See you," said Jessie Lewis, and she rang off.

"Who was it?" said Uncle Mort, leaning over the banisters. "Was it a death?"

"It's all right, Uncle Mort. Just a friend of mine," said Carter Brandon, and he took his mother into the living room and explained the situation to her.

"What in the name of God was she doing in Austria?" said Mrs. Brandon to her husband after she had returned to the warmth of her bed.

"Bloody yodelling, I expect," said Mr. Brandon. "Now go to sleep."

"Austria?" said Uncle Mort. "Austria?"

"That's right," said Carter Brandon, who, on the instructions of his mother, had informed his uncle of the details of the telephone call.

"That's the other bloody side of the world."

"No, that's Australia," said Carter Brandon. "Austria's in Europe."

"Aye, you're right there, Carter," said Uncle Mort. "I always get the two mixed up this time of night."

Carter Brandon fell asleep almost immediately, but Uncle Mort lay awake, tossing and turning and listening to the chiming of the clock and the creaking of the floorboards.

Upstairs in the attic Uncle Stavely slowly peeled back the bedclothes and placed one bare foot on the floor beside the bed. He rested in that position for several minutes, and then removed his other foot from the bed and placed it by the side of its colleague on the floor.

Then he stood up and shuffled slowly over to Corporal Parkinson's bed.

"It's only me," he said. "Pardon?"

He bent down and withdrew a small black box from beneath the bed. He had to pause again for a few minutes to regain his breath.

When he had done so, he opened the box and took out a limp object. It was covered in feathers, and its neck had been wrung so tightly that its head was almost severed from its body. It was Bentley, and it smelled.

Uncle Stavely carried it across to the fire, which was smouldering contentedly under a mound of damp slack. He prodded it with the poker, and a hole appeared in the crust of slack, and flames shot out.

"Good-bye, Bentley," said Uncle Stavely, and he dropped the corpse into the flames. "Ke-wick, ke-wick, ke-wick."

CHAPTER THIRTY-EIGHT

"You're late," said Uncle Stavely crossly to Carter Brandon the following evening when he brought Daniel in to see them.

"I'm sorry. We had a union meeting," said Carter Brandon.

"Don't let it happen again. Corporal Parkinson's been expecting you for the past hour. Pardon?"

"I'm sorry."

"Come on then. Give us our dose," said Uncle Stavely.

Carter Brandon took Daniel across to his uncle and lowered his lips to the old man's forehead.

Uncle Stavely closed his eyes and sighed contentedly.

"More," he said. "More."

The effect on the old man was remarkable to behold. His skin glowed, moisture appeared on his lips, his neck tautened so that the folds and wrinkles disappeared, his hair took on a fresh, virile lustre and his body quivered with energy.

When Carter Brandon withdrew the child from his forehead, he let out four deep sighs and grunted with contentment.

His neck relaxed, but there did not seem to be so many wrinkles as before. His hair lost its lustre, but it was not so lank and lifeless as before. The red glow left his skin, but all the waxy paleness had disappeared.

"Are you all right, Uncle Stavely?" said Carter Brandon.

"Pardon?" said Uncle Stavely. "Now take him to Corporal Parkinson."

Carter Brandon repeated the routine with the old soldier, and Uncle Stavely propped himself up on one elbow to watch.

On previous occasions Corporal Parkinson had merely twitched in his sleep when the baby's lips touched his forehead. This time, however, his eyes opened, and the pupils began to focus on Carter Brandon and Daniel. The once lifeless body stirred. He opened his mouth, and very softly he began to cackle.

"He says he enjoyed his sleep and can he have something to eat preferably cheese and biscuits. Pardon?" said Uncle Stavely.

Carter Brandon dashed downstairs to inform his mother of the termination of Corporal Parkinson's slumbers, and

in next to no time everyone had gathered round the old
warrior's bed.

"It's true," said Mrs. Brandon.

"Aye," said Mr. Brandon.

"He says he's feeling very much better now, and could he
be moved away from Stavely," said Uncle Mort.

"Pardon?" said Uncle Stavely. "He says where's his cheese
and biscuits?"

Cheese and biscuits were provided for Corporal Parkinson,
and then the family retired to the front room to discuss the
situation.

Jessie Lewis's unauthorised absence, her skiing holiday
with friends in Austria were banished from their thoughts.

In each one of their minds was one subject—the spectacu-
lar transformation in the health of the two old men.

"I can hardly believe it," said Jessie Lewis. "They were at
death's door when I left."

"Aye, and I carried your bags to the station, too," said
Uncle Mort.

"It defies credence," said Mrs. Brandon.

"It's Daniel who's doing it," said Carter Brandon.

"Pardon?" said Mr. Brandon.

"Ever since Daniel kissed them they've been getting better," said Carter Brandon. "It's Daniel who's doing it."

"Don't be so silly, Carter," said Mrs. Brandon. "I've never
heard anything so foolish in me life."

"Aye, don't drag thingie into it," said Uncle Mort.

"Thingie? Thingie?" said Mrs. Brandon to Uncle Mort.
"How many more times have I got to tell you his name?"

Carter Brandon left the room and went upstairs to the
nursery, where Daniel had now been reinstated. He lifted
him out of the cot and held him in his arms. The baby
chuckled and tried to grasp his nose.

"It's you, though, in't it, Daniel?" said Carter Brandon.
"You're the one what's doing it all."

Hey up, Carter, don't drag me into it.

"No, fair's fair, Daniel. Credit where credit's due," said
Carter Brandon. "Don't be so bashful."

Aye. Well. You know how it is, don't you, Carter?

"You don't want to take any notice of what they say
downstairs, Daniel. They don't understand anything out of
the ordinary. Look at all the things I do that they don't
understand."

Such as?

"Well."

Well, what? What do you do that's out of the ordinary, Carter?

"I can't rightly think of anything off hand at the moment. But you know, don't you, Daniel?"

I'm sorry, Carter, but I don't. I can't think of a single thing.

"Bloody hell, don't you start on me, mate," said Carter Brandon, and placed the baby in the cot and shut the door quietly behind him.

Later that night Uncle Mort said:

"Carter? Are you asleep, Carter?"

"No," said Carter Brandon. "What do you want?"

"Jessie hasn't said anything to me, Carter."

"Hasn't she?"

"I went to meet her at the station, but I hadn't got no change for a platform ticket."

"Hadn't you?"

"No, and by the time I'd got some the train had come in, and there was no sign of her. You'd have thought she'd have waited, wouldn't you?"

"Mm."

"So I gets a taxi back—seven and bloody six it cost me—and she just says: 'Hello, Uncle Mort,' and goes on talking to your mother."

"Does she?"

"Course she does. And when your mother asks what she were doing in Austria, she just says: 'Oh that. I went with some old friends.' Do you think I've got a rival, Carter?"

"I don't know, Uncle Mort. Have you asked her if she's made her mind up?"

"I daren't in case she says 'no'."

The clock chimed the quarter hour, and a bin lid crashed to the ground in the next door garden.

"Carter," said Uncle Mort.

"Yes."

"Are you still awake?"

"Yes."

"Carter. Would you do us a favour?"

"What sort of a favour?"

"Well, tomorrow's Saturday, isn't it?"

"Yes."

"And you'll be seeing Jessie, won't you?"

"I suppose so."

"Well, would you do us a favour?"

"Yes."

"Would you find out from her if she's made her mind up?"

"All right."

"You're a grand lad, Carter," said Uncle Mort.

The next day was indeed Saturday. It was a clear morning. There had been a sharp frost during the night. The lawn in the back garden was white, the bark on the pear trees was pinched and cracked, and the birds made short work of the scraps thrown to them by Mrs. Brandon.

The milk had frozen in the bottles, and over breakfast Carter Brandon and Jessie Lewis ate it in lumps like ice cream.

"It'll not do your stomachs no good, eating it like that," said Mrs. Brandon.

"No, be careful, Jessie," said Uncle Mort.

"Oh, I'll be careful, Uncle Mort," said Jessie Lewis.

All morning Uncle Mort followed in Jessie Lewis's footsteps. He stood on the landing whilst she used the lavatory, he stood outside the bathroom whilst she washed herself, and he went upstairs to the attic with her and watched her tend to the two aged patients.

"Pass me the bowl, Uncle Mort," said Jessie Lewis.

"Certainly, Jessie," said Uncle Mort.

"Run down and fetch me some more warm water, will you, Uncle Mort?" said Jessie Lewis.

"Certainly, Jessie," said Uncle Mort.

"Shake the medicine bottle for me, Uncle Mort," said Jessie Lewis.

"Certainly, Jessie," said Uncle Mort.

"Kiss me backside, Uncle Mort," said Uncle Stavely.

"I'll punch his bloody teeth in," said Uncle Mort.

"Pardon?" said Uncle Stavely. "You should be looking after Lil instead of hanging round here."

"He's started. The only reason he's got better is so he can start tormenting me again," said Uncle Mort, and he advanced towards Uncle Stavely's bed.

"Don't let him hit me," cried Uncle Stavely, shielding his face with his hands.

Jessie Lewis took him gently by the shoulders and laid him down in the bed.

"Don't disturb yourself," she said. "He won't hit you, will you, Uncle Mort?"

"No, Jessie." said Uncle Mort.

He followed her downstairs to the nursery and watched her change Daniel's nappy.

"He likes you, doesn't he, Jessie?" he said.

"They like anyone who feeds them at this age, Uncle Mort," said Jessie Lewis.

"Little bloody gluttons," said Uncle Mort, cautiously prodding Daniel's stomach with his forefinger.

Carter Brandon called round for Pat, and they drove to their new house in Tunstall Avenue. The builders had left the previous day, and Pat had been to the estate agent's to collect the keys.

They drove slowly over the avenue, which was still rutted with the wheels of the builder's trucks and stopped the car some distance from the house.

Carter Brandon walked a few paces behind Pat, as she picked her way across the pre-nascent front gardens, which were littered with broken bricks, mounds of mortar, broken glass and other impedimenta of the builder's trade.

There used to be open fields here once, Daniel. We used to come and play here, when we were lads.

Oh aye.

Aye. And we used to build dens in the fields out of milk crates and branches and dried grass. One day we built this right big den with a sort of thatched roof over it and a hole so the smoke from the fire could get out. We baked spuds in the fire, and after we'd eaten, we smoked grass stems all afternoon, and when we got home, Derrick Warrender's old feller gave him a right good tanning, because he'd been sick all down his new khaki trousers.

Fascinating, Carter. Right fascinating.

It was a smashing den was that, Daniel. I lay on me back in it and pretended I was an explorer in the Congo and I was sick in a native hut, and they'd sent Doctor Livingstone out to find me.

And then I pretended I was an insect and if I wasn't careful some bloody big boot would come along and trample me to death underfoot.

What a fantastic imagination you'd got, Carter. Right fantastic.

What's up with you then, Daniel? What are you sarky about?

I'm sulking.

What for, Daniel?

The way you spoke to me last night. I've never been spoken to like that before—never ever.

"Come on, Carter, stop dawdling," said Pat.

"Sorry," said Carter. "I got a stone in me shoe."

She handed him the keys and said:

"Home sweet home, eh, Carter?"

"Mm," said Carter Brandon, opening the door and allowing his fiancee to enter the house.

They sat together half way up the stairs and Pat said:

"Now I think cerise should be the dominant colour for the master bedroom."

"The what bedroom?" said Carter Brandon.

"The master bedroom. That's what they call the main bedroom. Haven't you been reading the paint colour charts?"

"No," said Carter Brandon.

"And I think we should have fitted bookshelves in the living room. Do you think you'd be able to make them, Carter?"

"Oh aye," said Carter Brandon.

"Well, you can just take the measurements and get cracking. And what feelings have you got with regards to draught excluder?"

"What?" said Carter Brandon.

"Just like a man," said Pat. "Head in the clouds and not a thought for the basic essentials. Now what I think is this. I think we should go down to Rathbones, get a good lot of that rubber draught excluder and fit it to all the doors."

"But we're not living here yet," said Carter Brandon.

"Precisely," said Pat. "If we put in draught excluders before we move in, we'll have the house nice and cosy for us. How about that for a good idea?"

"Mm," said Carter Brandon.

"Me mam thought of that."

Dusk was falling, and they went out into the back garden. It was fenced off from the neighbouring plots by a line of wooden palings, and in the night air it smelled damply of rotten roots and sour earth.

Carter Brandon dug his heel into the ground, but the soil, hardened by the frost and the putty and the cement and the brick dust, did not yield.

There used to be flowers growing here, Daniel. One day I came here on my own and I picked some for me mother. I stuck them in me saddle bag so's the lads wouldn't see them, and when I gave them to her, she told me off for being a pansy.

I'm not bloody surprised, Carter.

"Come on, Carter, we'll be late for tea," said Pat.

Just before they went into the dining room they were stopped by Jessie Lewis, who said to Pat:

"Are you doing anything special tonight?"

"No," said Pat.

"Good," said Jessie Lewis.

"Why?"

"Because you won't mind me coming out with you, will you?"

When tea was over, and the young ones announced that they were about to leave in order to embark on the evening's entertainment, Uncle Mort said:

"Can I come, Jessie?"

"No," said Jessie Lewis. "We're going dancing, and you wouldn't like that at all, would you, Uncle Mort?"

Outside in the car Pat said to Jessie Lewis:

"That wasn't a very nice thing to say to him, was it?" Jessie Lewis laughed. She was sitting in the back seat, and through the driving mirror Carter Brandon could see the deep tan on her face and neck.

"I don't suppose it was, but then I'm not noted for my 'niceness' round here, am I, Carter?" she said.

"Tell me something," said Pat.

"What would you like me to tell you, Pat?" said Jessie Lewis.

"Are you serious about Uncle Mort's proposal?"

"I think that's a matter for me and Uncle Mort, don't you, Carter?" said Jessie Lewis.

"I see," said Pat, and she straightened her back and sniffed hard.

They decided to drive to a small market town in the dales several miles outside the city. Carter Brandon said there was a pub there, which sometimes had a jazz band on Saturday evenings. On this particular evening there was no jazz band, so they went into the back room and played darts.

In the first game Carter Brandon beat Jessie Lewis. In the second game he beat Pat Partington. In the third game Jessie Lewis did likewise.

"I think it's a most uninteresting game is darts," said Pat.

"That's because you play it so badly," said Jessie Lewis. "Are we allowed another drink, Carter?"

They were. And after it was drunk Pat decided that it was time to return home.

"You were very fond of your Auntie Lil, weren't you, Carter?" said Jessie Lewis.

"Yes, he was," said Pat. "Very fond indeed."

"Well, if I become his Auntie Jessie, I hope he'll become equally fond of me," said Jessie Lewis.

Uncle Mort was sitting up in bed, waiting for the return of his nephew.

"Well?" he said. "Did you ask her?"

"Sort of," said Carter Brandon.

"What did she say?"

"She were talking about what would happen if she became my Auntie Jessie."

"That means it's all settled then," said Uncle Mort, sinking back into bed, a great grin of contentment on his face.

Carter Brandon switched off the light and settled into bed.

I'm sorry, Daniel. I didn't mean to speak to you like that? Am I forgiven?

"Auntie Jessie, eh?" said Uncle Mort, and he began to cackle softly to himself. "Auntie bloody Jessie."

Come on, Daniel, pack up sulking like this.

Go to sleep, Carter. Stop feeling sorry for yourself.

CHAPTER THIRTY-NINE

Monday was an eventful day. In the morning a letter was delivered to Mr. Brandon. In the car on the way to work he said to Carter Brandon.

"She's started writing to me at our house now."

"Mrs. Otter?"

"Aye, read that," he said, throwing the letter on to his son's lap. At the next set of traffic lights Carter Brandon had time to read the letter, which said:

"Dear planet about who my whole being orbits,

Nothing of yours to hand as yet. I have, therefore, to inform you that this most unsatisfactory state of affairs cannot be allowed to continue.

It is thus with heavy heart that I advise you that unless I receive communication from you within seven days of above date, I shall be compelled to bring to the notice of your good lady consort the 'true story' re Stevenage.

Flower, why no news? Oh, please put pen to paper and put an end to my torment.

　　　　Yours faithfully,
　　　　　Mrs. Otter (Celia) XXXXXXXX RSVP."

"What the bloody hell am I going to do now?" said Mr. Brandon.

"Put pen to paper," said Carter Brandon.

"Aye, but what will I say?"

"Search me."

"Will you write it for me?"

"No," said Carter Brandon.

They had only been at work for half an hour, when the shop steward came round to say that there was to be an emergency union meeting in the canteen. Attendance was compulsory.

"Still, it's better than 'Workers' Playtime', isn't it?' said Sid Skelhorn to Carter Brandon.

The meeting was addressed by the district organiser, who had with him on the platform an official from head office in London.

"Brothers," said the district organiser, "first and foremost I'd like to introduce you to Arnold Duffy, who has flown down here special from HQ to give us the benefit of his vast experience in matters of this nature. Brothers, Arnold Duffy."

"He looks like he's wearing his truss too tight," said Sid Skelhorn to Carter Brandon.

"Now then, brothers," said the district organiser, "the purpose of this emergency meeting is to acquaint you with the latest developments regarding the dismissal of Brother Madely and the subsequent attempts made on your behalf to effect his reinstatement.

"Yesterday evening in company with your branch treasurer and senior shop steward I had a meeting with the management. The news I bring you is, I'm afraid, grave. The management refuse categorically and unilaterally to meet us on any one of the points raised by us at our last meeting with them.

"The position is thus one of deadlock, iyee, they won't budge. They've dug their heels in. Now, I'm sure Arnold here will explain to you the official union view of the situation and the procedure we should follow. But I should just like, if you will bear with me, to expound on the general implications of the management's attitude to the case presented to them by me on your behalf."

The meeting lasted for a further half hour, and Mr. Arnold Duffy concluded his speech with these words:

"And so, brothers, if this branch, this branch, should decide to take strike action, strike action, in defence of the right of one of its members, one of its members, your union, your union, will give you official backing. It's up to you to make the decision. Up to you. I am in your hands. Thank you."

As they filed out of the canteen Eric Black said:

"Sure as eggs are eggs it's a strike."

"Struth, I'll get bloody murdered at home if we come out on strike again," said Sid Skelhorn.

Over the evening meal Mr. Brandon appeared to be not the slightest bit worried about the letter from Mrs. Otter. He also appeared to be eager to talk to his son.

Half an hour after the meal, when Carter Brandon had taken Daniel to the attic to bid the old men good night, he was approached by his father in the garage, where he was hard at work on the bookshelves for the new house.

"Well, it's settled," said Mr. Brandon.

"What is?" said Carter Brandon.

"The letter," said Mr. Brandon. "I showed it to Jessie."

"Jessie?" said Carter Brandon, and the chisel dropped from his hand and upset a tobacco tin full of tacks on the work bench.

"It was the obvious thing to do. I don't know why I didn't think of it before," said Mr. Brandon, settling himself in the old leather arm chair and lighting his pipe. "She's the only one in this house with a sensible head on her shoulders. It's part of her job, dealing with the personal problems of patients."

"But you're not a patient."

"She took it all in her stride. She read it. I explained the background. She'd said she'd fix something up, and Bob's your uncle, Fanny's your aunt."

"You must be bloody mad, letting a woman like that into your secrets."

"Hey, hey," said Mr. Brandon with a grin. "That's no way to talk about someone who might be your new auntie."

Well, what do you think to that, Daniel? He's bloody mad, in't he?

Don't drag me into it, Carter. I'm saying nothing.

Uncle Mort's confidence in the outcome of his proposition of marriage showed no signs of abating during the course of the week.

On Tuesday morning he said to Mrs. Brandon:

"It's a good job I put all me furniture in storage, when I moved in with you. It'll be right handy now."

On Tuesday afternoon he said to Uncle Stavely:

"I'll tell you what, Stavely, I might even let you be a usher at the wedding."

"Who's getting married?" said Uncle Stavely.

"Me and Jessie."

"You'd better not tell our Lil. Pardon?" said Uncle Stavely, who was now allowed downstairs for half an hour each afternoon.

On Tuesday evening he said to Mr. Brandon:

"She'll make a marvellous mother will Jessie. She's got real good child-bearing hips on her."

"You big soft pillock," said Mr. Brandon.

On Wednesday morning Carter Brandon cut this thumb on a lathe at work. His injury was treated in the ambulance room, and he had sausage, onions and chips for his lunch in the canteen.

On the afternoon of the same day Pat took her mother and Mrs. Brandon on a tour of inspection of the new house.

"In't it marvellous to see these youngsters making a go of things, Mrs. Brandon?" said Mrs. Partington.

"It is that, Mrs. Partington," said Mrs. Brandon.

"I mean to say, there's nothing in this world like owning your own house, is there? Nothing at all. I says to our Pat, I says: 'Pat, luv, you're very lucky. There's nothing in this world like owning your own house, luv. Nothing.'"

"That's right, Mrs. Partington," said Mrs. Brandon. "There's nothing like it, is there, when all's said and done?"

"Nothing, Mrs. Brandon," said Mrs. Partington. "Nothing."

On Wednesday evening Carter Brandon returned from work, and his thumb was throbbing. He took Daniel to the attic to see the two old men, and Uncle Stavely said:

"Can't you make it twice a day, Carter?"

"You'd better ask me mother," said Carter Brandon.

He took Daniel across to his uncle. The old man still showed signs of fear when the baby came near him. He still cringed slightly, although he did not attempt to cover his face with his arms, as he had done in the past.

"Thank you, thank you," he said, grunting with pleasure, when Carter Brandon removed the baby's lips from his forehead.

"Thank you, thank you," he said, when Carter Brandon had finished the treatment with Corporal Parkinson. "He says thank you very much, and could Daniel visit us twice a day. Pardon?"

"He'd better ask Daniel," said Carter Brandon. "What do you think, Daniel?"

The baby wriggled his legs and began to chuckle to himself.

"He says he'd be delighted to, because he thinks Corporal Parkinson is looking like a new man, Pardon?" said Uncle Stavely.

For the sake of accuracy, it must be recorded that Corporal Parkinson did indeed look like a 'new man'.

He was now able to sit up in bed unaided, his movements were confident, and on occasions co-ordinated to a degree that had never been attained during his stay in the Brandon household.

There were signs of impending hirsuteness on a pate that had previously been unsullied in this respect.

And there was a definite increase of volume in the raspings, wheezings and grunts produced by his vocal cords.

Carter Brandon nodded and took Daniel back to the nursery. He stared at him silently and said:

"Well, I don't care if you're not speaking to me. I still say you're doing a grand job."

The baby looked at him with his piercing eyes, and then he lowered his huge head and fell into a doze.

When he went downstairs, Carter Brandon noticed that his thumb had stopped throbbing.

On Thursday morning it rained, and a bus skidded into a shelter outside the Town Hall, injuring three passengers and a passing pedestrian. Two of the injured were taken to hospital and treated for shock. One was detained.

On Thursday afternoon Uncle Mort and Jessie Lewis went into the front room and had not reappeared by the time the evening meal was ready to be served.

Carter Brandon was dispatched to summon them to the table. He knocked on the door and said:

"Tea's ready."

"You'd better go ahead without us," said Jessie Lewis.

"And give over disturbing us," said Uncle Mort.

"What do you think they're up to, Les?" said Mrs. Brandon, when she had been informed of her son's conversation with her brother and the object of his affections.

"I shudder to think," said Mr. Brandon. "Pass us another slice of bread, Carter."

A quarter of an hour after the end of the evening meal Uncle Mort appeared in the doorway of the dining room and said:

"You can expect a decision within the next half hour."

"It must be the proposal," said Mrs. Brandon after Uncle Mort had returned to the front room.

"Aye," said Mr. Brandon.

"Mm," said Carter Brandon.

For half an hour they waited. Mr. Brandon took out his pipe and began to fill it. Then he put down his pipe, stood up and began to pace up and down the room.

Mrs. Brandon took out her knitting and began to knit rapidly. Then she put down her knitting, took out her work basket and began to darn socks rapidly. Then she put down the socks and stared into space.

Carter Brandon crossed his legs and said to himself, am I forgiven, Daniel?

Aye go on then, Carter. But you and me must have some words later.

Righto, Daniel.

Then the door opened, and they all three jumped to their feet. Uncle Mort entered. He had a wide grin on his face, his eyes were sparkling and his tread was light and springy.

"Well?" said Mrs. Brandon.

"Well?" said Mr. Brandon.

Uncle Mort puffed out his chest, and, smiling broadly, said:

"My proposal of marriage to Jessie Lewis has been . . ."

"Accepted?" said Mrs. Brandon, turning white in the face.

"Rejected," said Uncle Mort.

"What?" said Mrs. Brandon.

"What?" said Mr. Brandon.

"You heard," said Uncle Mort cheerfully. And then he added: "But I've got other bloody strings to me bow, haven't I?"

CHAPTER FORTY

What were the other strings to his bow? On this subject Uncle Mort's lips were sealed.

His manner, however, seemed to provide conclusive evidence that the strings were strong indeed.

In the mornings he could be heard whistling in the bathroom. His appetite was enormous. His sources of energy were limitless.

Two or three evenings each week he would leave the house at seven o'clock, his shoes brightly polished, his shirt collars stiff and starched, his cheeks smelling sweetly of the aftershave lotion he had filched from Carter Brandon.

He seemed to bear no animosity towards Jessie Lewis. On the contrary, their relationship was cordial in the extreme, and he often accompanied her in the afternoon when she took Daniel out in his pram.

Jessie Lewis was equally reticent on the subject of the bow strings.

One morning Mrs. Brandon said to her:

"Do you know where Uncle Mort goes to in the evenings, Jessie?"

And she replied:

"Oh, he goes out in the evenings, does he?"

One evening Mr. Brandon said to her:

"Has he got another woman, Jessie?"

And she replied:

"Has who got another woman, Mr. Brandon?"

"Uncle Mort."

"What makes you think that?" said Jessie Lewis, and she went upstairs to feed Daniel.

And so the weeks slipped by. Arrangements for the wedding were set in motion. Carter Brandon and Pat spent most of their weekends decorating their new home, and the home team at long last hit a winning streak.

Time, the great healer, certainly lived up to its reputation as far as Uncle Stavely and Corporal Parkinson were concerned, for these two gentlemen were positively blooming with good health.

With Corporal Parkinson the blooming took the shape of a light downy fuzz on the top of his head, and the appearance of three teeth in gums which had hitherto been completely toothless.

"I think he's cutting a new set of teeth," said Mrs. Brandon one day after she had been upstairs to inspect the old soldier.

"Do you?" said Mr. Brandon.

"Well, he's dribbling a lot, and they normally do that when they're cutting their teeth, don't they?" said Mrs. Brandon.

With Uncle Stavely the blooming took the shape of increased and almost uncontrollable activity. He had resumed cooking operations in the attic, he rose early in the morning to wake up the household with his marching and drumming and it was only with the greatest difficulty that Jessie Lewis could force him to retire to bed in the afternoon for his two hour nap.

He, too, was the recipient of a new growth of hair, and his limbs had become firm enough to enable him to carry Corporal Parkinson downstairs for tea one afternoon.

"Well, it's a real tonic to see the two of you looking so well," said Mrs. Brandon.

"You look very well yourself, too," said Uncle Stavely.

"Thank you, Stavely," said Mrs. Brandon. "Well all of us do. We all feel marvellous. There's none of us had a cold so far this winter, and Les hadn't had a moment's trouble with his piles."

It was quite true. Never before had there been such an abundance of good health in the Brandon family. Each one of them felt its tingle in the morning. Their lungs were clear, their eyes glinted, their tongues were uncoated and they slept deeply and soundly at night.

Pat was quick to notice it. She said to Carter Brandon one Sunday morning when they were painting the banisters of their new home:

"I've never seen you look so fit, Carter."

"I've never felt so fit," said Carter Brandon.

"It's funny, but every time I go to your house I seem to feel better meself," said Pat. "You know, if I call round in the evening. I often feel tired after a day's work, but as soon as I set foot in your door I feel right bucked up. It's a strange feeling."

Mr. Brandon noticed it, too, but he had more important things on his mind. One evening he said to his wife:

"You remember that time we overheard Mort talking to Daniel in the bedroom?"

"Yes?" said Mrs. Brandon.

"Well, you remember what he said about choosing a wife? He said there was two alternatives. One was Jessie and the other was . . ."

"Mrs. Partington!" said Mrs. Brandon.

"Right."

"Good God. I must have a word with Carter about it."

This she did, and her son confirmed that Mrs. Partington was wont to spend two or three evenings each week away from home. However, he refused point-blank to approach her on the subject although he agreed to make a note of the days when she was absent from home.

Sure enough, that week her evenings spent away from home coincided with those spent away by Uncle Mort.

"It must be. It must be," said Mrs. Brandon to her husband.

"It certainly looks like it," said Mr. Brandon.

"Well, there's only one thing for it, Les," said Mrs. Brandon. "I'll have to bring it out in the open with Mrs. Partington. There's no point in tackling our Mort. I'll get it straight from the horse's mouth."

And so Mrs. Brandon invited Mrs. Partington to take afternoon tea with her at her home. At a quarter to three on the afternoon in question Mrs. Partington knocked on the front door, and was led into the front parlour by her hostess.

Remarks on the weather were exchanged by the two women, and then Mrs. Brandon coughed and said:

"Well, what I've got to say now, Mrs. Partington, is, how shall I put it, well, it's rather a delicate subject."

"Now you're not to worry yourself on that account, Mrs. Brandon," said Mrs. Partington. "I know why you've asked me round here, and I don't mind you mentioning it in the slightest. Is it fresh cream in them eclairs?"

"Yes," said Mrs. Brandon.

There was a silence, and Mrs. Brandon coughed nervously and licked her lips. Then Mrs. Partington spoke.

"Look, luv, I'll tell you what I'll do," she said. "I'll raise the subject meself."

"Thank you," said Mrs. Brandon.

"Well, you're not to bother yourself. We're both very happy the way things are going, and we're certain it's going to turn out a huge success."

"A huge success?" said Mrs. Brandon weakly.

"We've talked it all over, and we've decided we can manage ourself without any assistance from you."

"Without any assistance from us?"

"I've got a nice little bit of money put away, and I says to our Pat only the other day, I says; 'It's me what's spending, luv. It's my money and I always said when Mr. Right came along, I'd not hesitate in spending every farthing of it,' I says."

"Mr. Right?" said Mrs. Brandon, and once more her face turned pale.

"And your Carter is certainly Mr. Right as far as I'm concerned," said Mrs. Partington.

"Our Carter?" said Mrs. Brandon.

"Well, don't look so surprised, luv. Who did you think I meant?"

"Our Carter," said Mrs. Brandon, and her face returned to its normal colour.

"So we're very grateful for your offer of help, very grateful indeed, but there's no need for you to worry. We can manage everything ourselves perfect so long as Mr. Brandon will give us a hand arranging the benches and tables in the church hall on the morning of the wedding."

"Benches? Les? Yes, I'm sure he will," said Mrs. Brandon.

"And how's Uncle Mort going on these days, Mrs. Brandon? Has he recovered from the shock of his wife dying like that, Mrs. Brandon? Wasn't it tragic? Poor soul, he seemed so lost without her at Christmas. I hope he's bucked up since then."

"Oh yes, he's bucked up since then," said Mrs. Brandon. "Have another eclair."

"Well, who the hell is he knocking round with?" said Mr. Brandon, when his wife told him what had happened between her and Mrs. Partington.

"Search me," said Mrs. Brandon.

"He's your brother. You're the one who should be tackling him on the subject."

"And you're a man. You're the one who should be discussing matters like that with him. Not me, I'm a woman."

These words stung Mr. Brandon into action, and he invited Uncle Mort to partake of a pint or two with him that evening.

"Who's the bird then?" he said, when they were established in the pub.

"Bird?" said Uncle Mort.

"Who's the woman you're tailing?"

"Woman?" said Uncle Mort.

"I don't know. I can't keep up with you and your romances," said Mr. Brandon. "You're like something out of the Arabian bloody nights."

"There's no need to be personal," said Uncle Mort.

"A bloke of your age, chasing women. You're worse than a bloody tom cat."

"Do you really want to know what I'm doing, Les?" said Uncle Mort placidly.

"That's why I'm pinting you up, isn't it?"

"Are you really sure, absolutely certain?"

"Course I am."

"Right I'll tell you then," said Uncle Mort. "I'm minding me own bloody business."

No one could deny the justice inherent in that remark. Natural and health curiosity about Uncle Mort's activities remained, but positive attempts to elicit more information from him were abandoned.

It was Jessie Lewis who brought another topic of conversation into the domestic forum when she said:

"I think you should get the doctor in to look at Uncle Stavely and Corporal Parkinson."

"Why, Jessie?" said Mrs. Brandon with some alarm. "They've not been took badly again, have they?"

"Far from it, but there's something very peculiar happening to them."

A further inspection of Uncle Stavely and Corporal Parkinson took place there and then, and Mrs. Brandon was forced to agree that there had been a substantial change in their appearance.

Uncle Stavely's skin had lost a good fifty-five per cent of its wrinkles, the curve had disappeared from his spine, and the tight knot of veins on the backs of his hands was no longer to be seen.

Corporal Parkinson's appearance was even more remarkable. He now had seven teeth and his head was covered with a splendid growth of auburn ringlets.

Jessie Lewis beckoned to Mr. and Mrs. Brandon and their son and pulled back the bedclothes from the old soldier.

"Look at this," she said. "It started last week."

They looked, and what they saw caused them to gasp with astonishment. Where once there had been two withered stumps, there were now distinct signs of growth.

"He's growing a new pair of bloody legs," said Mr. Brandon.

"Precisely," said Jessie Lewis.

"It's our Lil's baby what's done that," said Uncle Stavely.

"Auntie Lil's dead, Uncle Stavely," said Jessie Lewis.

"He's the one what's making us better," said Uncle Stavely. "I think he should be allowed to visit us twice a day, and then we'll be completely cured. Pardon?"

"And so do I," said a strange, high-pitched voice behind them.

They turned and stared. There wasn't the slightest shadow of doubt. The voice had come from Corporal Parkinson.

Downstairs in the dining room Mrs. Brandon said:

"We can't call the doctor, that's out of the question."

"Not a soul outside these four walls must know of this," said Mr. Brandon.

"The scandal of it," said Mrs. Brandon. "We've never had anything like this in the family before."

They were interrupted by a knock at the door. Carter Brandon went to answer it, and, when he opened the door, he saw a man standing there with the dog in his arms.

"I didn't stand a chance," he said. "He ran out right in front of me."

"Is he dead?" said Carter Brandon.

"No," said the man. "He's still breathing. I think you ought to call the vet."

They carried the dog into the house and placed it on the rug in front of the fire. It lay there quite still. Its eyes were shut, it had a deep cut on its muzzle, and its flanks were plastered with mud.

The vet came round within a quarter of an hour and examined the dog thoroughly.

"Well, doctor, tell us the worst," said Mrs. Brandon. Her cheeks were lined with tear stains, and there was a tremble in her voice.

"I'm afraid there's not much hope," said the vet.

"What's to be done then?" said Mr. Brandon.

"That's up to you," said the vet. "He's not suffering. You could take a chance and see if he pulls through by the morning. Personally I'd doubt it. It's probably better to put him down."

"But there is a hope for him?" said Carter Brandon.

"A slight one, yes," said the vet.

"Right. We'll keep him till morning," said Carter Brandon firmly.

As soon as the vet and the man who had run over the dog had disappeared, Mrs. Brandon burst into tears.

"Bless him, bless him," she said, bending over the dog. "Poor little feller. Why didn't you look where you was going, you bad dog?"

"It would be kinder to destroy him," said Jessie Lewis.

"No, it wouldn't," said Carter Brandon, and he left the room. A minute later he returned, carrying Daniel in his arms.

"What are you doing, Carter?" said Mrs. Brandon.

"I'll show you," said Carter Brandon, and, before anyone could stop him, he bent down and pressed Daniel's lips to the dog's head.

"Oh my God, no," said Mrs. Brandon, burying her face in her hands.

All that evening they stayed by the dog's side. They covered it with blankets and put a hot water bottle next to its back. Mr. Brandon rubbed some brandy on its nose, but it had no effect. The dog did not stir.

They bathed the cut with warm water, and Carter Brandon cleaned the dirt from its side with a soapy sponge.

At midnight they went to bed heavy of heart and sad of mind.

Do your stuff, Daniel, do your stuff, said Carter Brandon to himself over and over again, as he lay in bed. Please do your stuff, he said, and then he fell asleep.

At half past two Uncle Mort said:

"Carter? Carter? Are you asleep?"

Carter Brandon groaned and clutched at his pillow.

"Carter. I think I can hear the dog," said Uncle Mort loudly.

Carter Brandon threw back the eiderdown from his ear and listened. There were noises of movement from downstairs.

He jumped out of bed and ran down the stairs three at a time. He switched on the light in the dining room.

The dog looked up, wagged it tail and walked groggily across to him.

"Good dog, good dog," said Carter Brandon, kneeling down and burying his face in its fur.

When he stood up and turned round, he saw his mother, his father, Uncle Mort and Jessie Lewis, standing in the doorway.

"I told you it was Daniel," he said.

"Dear Lord have mercy on us," said Mrs. Brandon, and then she swooned into Mr. Brandon's arms.

CHAPTER FORTY-ONE

Carter Brandon had been at work for half an hour when he received a telephone call from his mother.

"Daniel's missing," she said. "Come home quick."

It took him twenty minutes to drive home. There was a police car outside the front gate, and a small group of people standing outside the house of Mrs. Warrender, the neighbour from number thirty-six.

His mother was waiting for him, red-rimmed of eye and distressed.

"I put him out in his pram in the front garden just after you'd gone," she sobbed. "He was only out of me sight for ten minutes at the most, and when I went out to pay the milkman, I saw he'd gone. Oh, Carter, Carter, who can have done such a thing?"

Mr. Brandon came in with two more policemen. He comforted his wife whilst she explained to the detectives the circumstances of Daniel's disappearance.

They wrote in their notebooks, and one of them went outside to radio a message to his headquarters from the police car.

"Mort's gone out with Jessie to look for him round the

back," said Mrs. Brandon. "Oh, Les, what an awful thing to happen, and he were only out of me sight for five minutes. It couldn't have been a second more."

"Come on, come on," said Mr. Brandon. "Turning on the water taps isn't going to find him, is it?"

The detective returned from the police car.

"Well, we've got every man on the beat keeping a look-out for the child," he said.

"Now will you and Mrs. Brandon come with us in the car, and we'll make a tour of the streets immediately round here," said his colleague.

"No sign of him out the back," said Uncle Mort, coming in through the back door. His shirt was unbuttoned, his hair was awry, and he was panting. "Jessie's still searching, but I thought I'd be more use here."

"Aye, we'll need someone to stay in so we can keep up contact," said the detective. "Have you got a car, lad?"

"Yes," said Carter Brandon.

"Well, don't just sit there. Get out looking for him."

"That's just what I'm bloody well going to do," said Carter Brandon.

He passed Uncle Stavely at the foot of the stairs.

"What's all the commotion?" said Uncle Stavely.

"Daniel's missing," said Carter Brandon.

"Pardon?" said Uncle Stavely.

Carter Brandon jumped in his car and pipped his horn sharply five times to clear a way through the crowd of people, who had gathered in the street.

Two policemen were working their way up the street, questioning the people in their houses.

"All right, Daniel, I'm coming," he said. "Hold on, lad, Carter's coming."

He drove to the end of the street, turned right into the main road and then turned right again at the next side road.

There was a bakery van parked half way down on the righthand side. On the other side the houses stood shoulder to shoulder, their front windows a mute riot of pottery Alsatians, indoor geraniums, budgerigar cages, mirror backs, teddy bears, seven day clocks, nymphs and shepherds, cactus plants, brass gongs and cut-glass vases.

He turned into another street and a few yards in front of him saw a young woman pushing a pram. She wore a red coat and fur boots, and there was a length of dirty sisal wound round the brake lever of the pram. He halted the car beside her and jumped out on to the pavement.

Without speaking he grasped hold of her arm and looked

into the pram. It contained a pale, thin baby with ginger hair, sucking a dummy.

Before the woman could cry out with alarm, he had raced back into the car and driven off.

"I'm coming, Daniel," he said. "I'm coming."

He drove down each one of the side streets. He saw three women with prams, and each time he left his car, looked into the prams and drove off without speaking.

"I'm panicking, Daniel," he said. "I should never have left you with them. I'm sorry, Auntie Lil. I haven't done my duty. I'm coming, Daniel. Don't worry, lad.

"It's my fault, Auntie Lil. I'm the one who's to blame. They don't understand him, you see. They're frightened of him, because he's, well, he's a bit unusual.

"I'm not frightened of you, though, am I, Daniel? You and me understand each other. We chat to each other. We tell each other secrets.

"We tell each other secrets, Auntie Lil, do Daniel and me. I've told him all about you and Uncle Bob and going dancing and hiking round Hayfield and knitting Fair Isle jumpers and keeping all your treasures in the trunk and making Uncle Mort take his vest off in bed.

"Don't worry, Daniel, I'm on me way. They'll not keep us apart for long."

Someone waved to him from the pavement. It was Jessie Lewis. He stopped the car, and she got in the front seat alongside him.

"Nothing?" he said.

She shook her head and panted for breath.

"We'd better go back and report," she said, when she had regained her composure.

"Right," said Carter Brandon.

They didn't speak to each other as they drove back. Jessie Lewis stared out of the side window, and Carter Brandon looked straight ahead, gritting his teeth.

Most of the crowd outside the house had dispersed. The police car had left, but there were two vans there. A policeman with a dog was standing in the front garden, talking to one of the detectives. The dog was straining at the leash, its front legs scrabbling in the lawn.

"Any news?" said Carter Brandon.

"Who are you?" said the dog handler.

"He's the son," said the detective. "Are you Nurse Lewis?"

"Yes," said Jessie Lewis.

"Right. Well, I shall want a statement from you. Shall we go inside?"

Mrs. Brandon was in the front room, holding a bottle of smelling salts to her nose.

"No news, Carter?" she said.

"No," said Carter Brandon.

She began to sob and sniffle, and Mrs. Warrender, the neighbour from number thirty-six, said:

"There, there, luv, don't upset yourself. It'll all come out in the wash."

"He was only out of me sight for two minutes at the most. It couldn't have been a second longer," said Mrs. Brandon.

"Stop your crying, Annie, and I'll tell you a story," said Uncle Stavely.

The detective took Jessie Lewis into the back room, and Uncle Stavely said:

"Once upon a time there was Corporal Parkinson."

"Give over, Uncle Stavely," said Carter Brandon. "We don't want to hear your bloody stories now."

"I was only trying to help. Pardon?"

"Poor little mite," said Mrs. Brandon. "She wants whipping whoever's done it. Whipping, that's what she wants."

Jessie Lewis came into the room with the detective, who said:

"I think you'd best put her to bed and call the doctor."

"Right," said Jessie Lewis, and she and Mrs. Warrender took hold of Mrs. Brandon by the elbows and led her upstairs.

Carter Brandon went out again with the police car in the afternoon. The driver told him dirty stories about his army days in Egypt, but there was no sign of Daniel.

At eight o'clock they were visited by the detective superintendent who took Uncle Mort into the kitchen and talked earnestly with him for a quarter of an hour. Then he said to the gathering in the front room:

"All we can hope now is that whoever's got him knows how to look after him."

"Aye," said Mr. Brandon.

"They usually do, you know," said the superintendent. "Don't worry, we'll find him before long."

Carter Brandon put on his coat, and went out into the back garden. There was a bitter east wind. It scoured the streets and rattled the slates on the houses.

He crouched down in the lee behind the greenhouse and lit a cigarette. It was quite warm there, so he sat on his haunches, resting his back against his father's wheelbarrow.

What a bloody mess, Daniel.

You can say that again, Carter.

Where the bloody hell are you, any road?

Aye well, Carter, this is where all this conversation between you and me falls down, in't it? It's no bloody use in a situation like this, is it?

Aye, you're right there, Daniel.

He went inside. Uncle Mort, Mr. and Mrs. Brandon and Jessie Lewis were sitting in the front room. They did not look up when he entered the room.

"One minute. That's all. One minute. It couldn't have been a second longer than that," said Mrs. Brandon.

"No one's blaming you, Annie," said Uncle Mort.

Carter Brandon suddenly felt the dog pressing its nose into his knee. He looked down and the dog wagged its tail and made its way unsteadily to the door, looking back at him.

"He wants to go out," said Mr. Brandon.

Carter Brandon opened the door, but instead of making for the kitchen, the dog hobbled to the foot of the stairs, looking back over its shoulder.

It wagged its tail again, and, when Carter Brandon moved over to it, it began to mount the stairs slowly.

"What's up?" said Carter Brandon.

The dog whimpered. It was panting with the effort of climbing the stairs, but it was obvious that it intended to lead Carter Brandon on.

It climbed to the first floor and then turned towards the attic stairs, still looking back over its shoulder.

"What do you want?" said Carter Brandon.

Slowly and painfully the dog limped up the stairs, and, when it reached the attic door, it lay down and began to whine and scratch at the carpet.

The door opened, and Uncle Stavely looked out. The dog brushed past him, and, when Carter Brandon followed it into the room, he saw it pawing at the bed now vacated by Corporal Parkinson in favour of the hammock.

"Keep it away, keep it away," said Uncle Stavely, tugging at Carter Brandon's arm.

He brushed the old man aside and went over to the bed. He looked down.

"Come on. Up here in the attic. Quick," he shouted at the top of his voice.

Feet clattered on the stairs. First into the room was Mr. Brandon closely followed by Uncle Mort.

Carter Brandon pointed to the bed, and Uncle Mort said: "Bloody hell, it's thingie."

CHAPTER FORTY-TWO

They had rung the police. Daniel had been taken downstairs, fed, bathed and put to bed.

Mrs. Brandon had been restored to her bedroom and placed under sedation, Uncle Mort had been restrained from punching Uncle Stavely on the nose.

Now it was time for the explanations.

"We just wanted to make a protest. Pardon?" said Uncle Stavely.

"Protest? What the bloody hell are you talking about?" said Uncle Mort.

"About Daniel," came the high-pitched, cracked voice of Corporal Parkinson.

"We think he should be held on a rota system," said Uncle Stavely.

"Rota system? What are you talking about?" said Mr. Brandon.

"About Daniel," came Corporal Parkinson's voice once more.

"We think we should take turns in holding him," said Uncle Stavely. "We should work out a time-table so's everyone gets his fair share of having him. Pardon?"

Jessie Lewis settled the two old men down for the night, and Mr. Brandon locked them in the attic. Then they went downstairs to the dining room to discuss the situation, and Carter Brandon made them cups of cocoa.

"I said we ought to call in the doctor," said Jessie Lewis.

"We can't do that," said Mr. Brandon. "No one outside the family must know of it."

"They ought to have their noses punched, and then we should send them packing back to their bloody home," said Uncle Mort.

Neither of these suggestions found favour with Mrs. Brandon, who said over breakfast next morning:

"It would be sheer cruelty, sending them back to that home. Besides, they wouldn't understand about Corporal Parkinson's legs, would they?"

"I suppose not," said Mr. Brandon.

In the evening Carter Brandon prepared to take Daniel up to the attic, but his mother said:

"Not tonight, Carter."

271

"Why not?" said Carter Brandon.

"Because he's never going up there again no more," said Uncle Mort. "I'm its father, and I say he's not to have anything to do with them two upstairs."

"Well, it's your prerogative, Mort," said Mr. Brandon.

And so a decision was reached. Daniel would be kept well away from the two old men. Never again would they be allowed to touch him.

"It's him or them," said Mrs. Brandon. "He's only starting out in life. They've had their fair share. They must take second place, when it comes to looking after Daniel's interests."

"Then they might as well go back to the old folks' home," said Uncle Mort.

"No," said Mrs. Brandon. "They must be allowed to die surrounded by people they love and trust. It's only being kind."

For a short while the two old men held their own. Each morning and each evening they complained about the absence of Daniel.

"Where is he?" said Corporal Parkinson.

"You're signing our death warrant," said Uncle Stavely.

But then slowly and surely the decline set in. Corporal Parkinson lost two of his teeth, and his power of speech disappeared.

Uncle Stavely's hair began to fall out, the wrinkles came back to his neck and the veins stood out on the backs of his hands.

Sometimes Carter Brandon was able to crack the tight security mesh and smuggle Daniel upstairs to them.

"More, more," Uncle Stavely would say, when the baby's lips touched his forehead.

"Sorry, I can't keep him here any longer," said Carter Brandon. "They'll go mad, if they find out what I'm doing."

Mrs. Brandon fretted and moped throughout March. Grey hairs appeared at her temples, and her eyes were constantly watery.

"It's awful, it's awful," she would say. "Fancy having to sentence your own brother-in-law to death. I've never done that before."

"We've done right, Annie," Mr. Brandon would say, patting her on the shoulder. "At least, you have. It was your decision."

Uncle Mort had no regrets. There was no curtailment of his evenings out, and his jauntiness increased daily.

"We've done the right thing, Annie," he would say. "At least you have. It was your decision."

"So you're going out on strike, are you, kid?" said Linda Preston one lunchtime in the canteen.

"Tomorrow," said Carter Brandon.

"That'll put the mockers on the wedding, won't it?"

"Why?"

"Well, you'll look a bit of a silly nelly, getting married when you're out of work."

"Mm."

"Still, you'll be able to have an extended honeymoon. Bloody rotate, eh?"

"I don't see why you don't ignore it," said Pat that evening. "You don't agree with the strike, do you?"

"No," said Carter Brandon.

"You want to keep on working, don't you?"

"Yes," said Carter Brandon.

"Well, why don't you just go to work tomorrow as though nothing's happened?"

"I can't," said Carter Brandon. "It's against the rules."

"You've just no thought for my feelings," said Pat, and she began to sob.

Mrs. Brandon showed little interest in the strike. When Carter Brandon told her of the latest developments, she said:

"Oh, I suppose you'll be in for your dinner every day, will you?"

On the first morning of the strike Carter Brandon was on picket duty outside the main gates. He arrived there at eight o'clock and was given a large banner by the district organiser.

"If the television people come, make sure you stick it up in front of the cameras," said Arnold Duffy. "And all of you, all of you, look angry, sullen and discontented, eh?"

"I know where I'd like to stick it up," said Sid Skelhorn.

It was cold, and Carter Brandon's fingers turned white. Sid Skelhorn stamped his feet, and Eric Black's teeth chattered all through the meeting addressed by the district organiser.

At opening time they went into 'The Magnet,' which was opposite the factory gates. The pub was dark, and the edges of the bar were splintered. It smelled of coke dust. The landlady said to them:

"It's hard work being on strike, in't it?"

"You're right there, missus," said Sid Skelhorn. "Can we have this one on the slate?"

"Like hell you can," said her husband, passing through the bar on his way out of the pub.

"He's off to see his fancy woman," said the landlady. "He must think I'm gormless or something. He must think I'm not all there. Go on then, you can have these on me, luv."

They sat next to the coke fire and sipped their pints slowly.

"I think I'm getting a cold," said Sid Skelhorn.

"You must have been drinking out of a damp glass, luv," said the landlady.

"Aye," said Sid Skelhorn, wiping his nose on his cuff. "You know what, I've a bloody good mind to go back into work tomorrow."

"There'd be ructions, if you did," said Eric Black.

"They couldn't be worse than what they are in our house," said Sid Skelhorn. "I had to get me own breakfast this morning. Can you fry eggs, Carter?"

Mrs. Brandon was in the attic when her son returned for his midday meal.

He found her standing a few inches inside the door, dabbing her eyes with the corner of her pinny.

"Just look at them, Carter," she said.

Corporal Parkinson was lying in bed motionless. His eyes were closed, and there were bald patches on his head, where the auburn ringlets had dropped out.

Uncle Stavely was propped up with two pillows and a bolster. His skin was pale, and his eyes were sunken into his head.

"Daniel," he said weakly. "Where's Daniel?"

"It's sheer cruelty, in't it?" said Mrs. Brandon. "It's terrible to behold. Poor Uncle Stavely, poor Corporal Parkinson."

In the afternoon Carter Brandon took Daniel for a walk.

"Now don't keep him out long," said his mother. "It's bitterly cold out there."

Carter Brandon walked to the park. He wheeled the pram along the paths beside the bowling green and stopped in a shelter for a smoke.

"I'm on strike, Daniel," he said after he had lit his cigarette with the sixth match. "What a bloody caper, eh?"

The baby stirred at him and wriggled his feet under the blanket.

"We went on strike once before at the other place I was

at. It was lovely weather, too, so when I wasn't on picket duty, I used to go out in the car and sit up on the moors.

"You get a wonderful view from up there. You can look down on the city and see all the chimneys. I used to wonder about all the people living in the houses there."

And what conclusion did you reach, Carter?

"I've forgotten now."

Typical.

"Pardon?"

In't that typical of you, Carter? In't that bloody typical?

"Aye. Well."

I've held me peace till now, Carter, but it's time you had a good talking to.

"Don't you start, Daniel."

This silly preoccupation with me. It's not natural for a lad of your age to pal around with a baby. Look at the age difference. What we've got in common with each other is beyond me.

"We've got a lot in common, Daniel."

What, for example?

"Our secret, Daniel."

Everyone knows that now, Carter. That's common bloody knowledge.

"Aye, you're right there, Daniel. But what can I do?"

Take a bloody grip on yourself, mate. Do something bloody positive for a change.

"But what? I can't think of anything positive to do, Daniel. That's my whole bloody trouble."

The baby looked at him and began to bounce up and down in his pram.

"All right, we'll take you home, Daniel," said Carter Brandon. "I know when it's feeding time."

His mother just nibbled at the evening meal, and Uncle Mort said:

"Can I have your corned beef, if you don't want it, Annie?"

"You want to have more respect, Mort," said Mrs. Brandon.

"What's up now?"

"There's two old men upstairs dying, that's what's up," said Mrs. Brandon. "I think you might at least have the decency to go up and keep them company once in a while."

"I can't tonight," said Uncle Mort. "I'm going out."

"Do you know how to boil eggs, Carter?" said Sid Skelhorn the following morning.

Once more they were sitting by the coke fire in the pub

opposite the factory gates. Earlier in the morning they had been addressed by the district organiser, who had assured them that their brothers in other unions in the factory were in full support of the stand they were taking against the management and could be expected in the near future to give practical demonstration of this support by joining them in their strike action.

"Were you serious yesterday about going in to work?" said Carter Brandon.

"If I could find someone to go in with me, I'd be back like a shot," said Sid Skelhorn.

"Right, let's go," said Carter Brandon.

"You're not serious, are you?" said Sid Skelhorn.

"You must be bloody mad," said Eric Black.

"Are you coming, or aren't you?" said Carter Brandon.

"I better not," said Sid Skelhorn. "She'd bloody murder me, if I lost me union card."

"I'll see you then," said Carter Brandon, and he got up and walked out of the pub.

The pickets had disappeared, and he crossed the road quickly and passed through the factory gates.

The long bay, where he worked, was deserted. The machinery was silent, and the black cat that lived in the storeroom lay curled up in a patch of sunlight on a wooden flat.

He went to his bench, took off his jacket and lit a cigarette. He had taken three puffs, when someone said from the other end of the shop:

"What the hell are you doing here?"

It was the foreman. He was not wearing his overalls.

"I'm reporting for work," said Carter Brandon.

"God help you, lad," said the foreman.

When he went into the canteen at lunchtime, people looked at him from the corners of their eyes and began to mutter. After his meal he went for a walk with Linda Preston.

"Well, you've had it now, kid," she said.

"I know."

"No one'll speak to you. They'll probably take your card from you, and then you'll never get work again."

"Aye."

They sat down under the railway arch that ran over the canal and lit cigarettes.

"Why have you done it then?" said Linda Preston.

Carter Brandon shrugged his shoulders.

"I don't know really," he said.

"You're a funny devil," said Linda Preston.

"I'm right proud of you, Carter," said Pat, when he told her what he had done. "At last you've had the courage to stand up for yourself. Well done."

"Are you sure you've done the right thing, Carter?" said Mrs. Brandon, when he told her of being jostled by the pickets when he left work in the evening.

"I don't know," said Carter Brandon.

"It doesn't do to stick your neck out, you know," said Mr. Brandon, when he was told of the threats made by the district organiser to his son.

"I know," said Carter Brandon, and he went upstairs to the nursery and said to Daniel:

"Well, I've done something positive, Daniel."

Oh aye?

"What's up? You don't sound very interested."

Pardon?

"I said you don't sound very interested, Daniel?"

I'm just thinking, Carter.

"What about, Daniel?"

Well, are you sure you've done the right thing, Carter? I mean, you've had it now. They'll probably take your card from you, and then you'll never get work again. It doesn't do to stick your neck out, you know.

Carter Brandon had to have a police escort on the following morning. The pickets shouted at him and waved their banners in his face.

At lunchtime no one spoke to him in the canteen, and all afternoon he sat alone at his bench.

It's all right Daniel, he said as he made patterns in the dust on the bench with his calipers. I don't care, mate.

It's not too bad really. I've never seen it so peaceful in here. Don't things look different, when you see them in a different way?

They do that, Carter.

They look like something else when you come to size it up. This place looks like a torture chamber in a great dungeon underneath a castle.

Does it, Carter?

Aye. They bring the prisoners in here and they strap them down, and they torture them until they reveal all their secrets.

What sort of secrets, Carter?

Do you fart in the bath? Do you stick your bogeys to the bottom of the tablecloth when no one's looking? Have you ever fancied a chinky woman? Would you like to creep into Jessie Lewis's room at the dead of night and throttle her? Are you pleased you're killing Uncle Stavely and Corporal Parkinson? Would you like to jack it all up and get married in a registry office?

Hey up, Carter, less of that talk. You're making me feel right uncomfortable.

The police escorted him through the picket lines in the evening, and he arrived home half an hour late, because someone had let the air out of the tyres of his car.

His father was waiting for him at the front door.

"Thank God, you're back," he said.

"What's up?" said Carter Brandon.

"It's your mother," said Mr. Brandon. "She's had a letter from Mrs. Otter."

"I told you something like this would happen," said Carter Brandon.

"Aye," said Mr. Brandon. "But Mrs. Otter doesn't exist."

"What?"

"I made her up. It was me what was writing all of them letters."

CHAPTER FORTY-THREE

At the end of the evening meal Mrs. Brandon took a letter from her handbag and passed it across the table. It was type-written. It said:

"Dear Mrs. Brandon,
    You won't know me, but I know, through the agency of your dear husband and your precious son, you. I have something urgent to impart to you and would urge you to contact me in company with hubby and son at above address this very evening.

                                    Yours faithfully,
                                    C. Otter. (Mrs.)"

Carter Brandon folded the letter in its well-worn creases and handed it back to his mother.

"Well?" she said.

"Well what?" said Carter Brandon.

"What's it all about?"

"You'd better ask him," said Carter Brandon, pointing to his father.

Mrs. Brandon looked at her husband. He began to turn up the corners of a table mat and said:

"Mm."

"Right then," said Mrs. Brandon. "Right then, we'll go and see this Mrs. Otter right away and find out what's behind it all."

And she got up from the table and went upstairs to wash and change.

"That's Jessie's address at the top of the letter," said Carter Brandon.

"I know," said Mr. Brandon. "What's she bloody playing at?"

"I told you you was asking for trouble bringing her into it."

"Aye."

"Does she know Mrs. Otter doesn't exist?"

"Aye."

"I don't know," said Carter Brandon. "What the hell did you invent her for in the first place?"

Mr. Brandon puffed at his pipe slowly and said:

"I just wanted to get a bit of attention."

Half an hour later they set off to meet Mrs. Otter. Mrs. Brandon sat next to her son in the car, and Mr. Brandon sat hunched up in the back seat.

There was not a drop of colour in his face. The stem of his pipe rattled against his teeth, and, when he dropped his box of Swan Vestas on the floor, Mrs. Brandon said:

"For heaven's sake, Les, sit still. Stop fidgeting."

Carter Brandon pulled up outside the old sandstone Victorian mansion, where Jessie Lewis had her flat. There were buds on the copper beech tree in the front garden, and there was a bowl of daffodils in the entrance hall.

They walked up the two flights of stairs to Jessie Lewis's flat and saw, pinned to the door, a note which read:

'Mrs. Otter (Celia) Please Knock Before Entering Same.'

Mrs. Brandon knocked sharply on the door, and a man's voice said softly:

"Come in."

Mrs. Brandon paused. Then she turned to her husband and said:

"I think you ought to go in first. After all, you'll be the one what's making the introductions."

Mr. Brandon wiped the palms of his hands on his handkerchief. There were cold beads of perspiration on his forehead, and his hands were shaking.

He pushed open the door, and they went inside.

"Hello," said Uncle Mort, rising from a leather sofa by the window. "Make yourselves at home then."

"Mort!" said Mrs. Brandon.

"What the hell?" said Mr. Brandon.

"I'm afraid Celia's been called out on business," said Uncle Mort. "So it's me who'll have to break the news."

"News?" said Mrs. Brandon.

"In the next month I am to be married to Mrs. Celia Otter, and I hope we'll both be very happy," said Uncle Mort.

"So do I," said Mr. Brandon.

It was almost midnight when they returned home. Jessie Lewis did not appear at her flat, so Uncle Mort had ample time to explain the circumstances behind his proposal.

"It was Jessie what introduced me to her," he said. "Celia was a friend of someone who'd been a patient of hers. It were love at first sight."

"What's his bloody game?" whispered Mr. Brandon to his son.

"We're made for each other are Celia and me. She's mature. I'll not say she isn't. But she's a lovely nature, and she bakes smashing rock buns. They just melt in your mouth," said Uncle Mort.

"Mort, Mort. Oh, Mort," said Mrs. Brandon, shaking her head.

"The bloody liar," whispered Mr. Brandon.

"It's a pity we can't arrange for me and Carter to have a double wedding," said Uncle Mort. "But with Celia having been divorced three times it would make things a bit awkward with the vicar, wouldn't it?"

"The bastard," said Mr. Brandon to his son. "He's stolen my bloody thunder."

Just before they got into bed Mrs. Brandon said to her husband:

"But how is it this woman knows you and Carter?"

"Aye, well," said Mr. Brandon. "That must have been Jessie telling her all about us."

Mrs. Brandon began to sob. She blew her nose violently into a tissue, and then she said:

"If only our Edna had looked where she was going when she got off that bus, none of this would have happened."

Next morning Carter Brandon got up early and went into the nursery. He shook Jessie Lewis by the shoulder to wake her up and said:

"What the hell are you playing at?"

"What?" she said, yawning and rubbing her eyes.

"What have you done to Uncle Mort?" he said.

"Oh that?" she said. "It's a bit of a giggle, isn't it?"

"What's going to happen, when me mother finds out about Mrs. Otter?"

"I couldn't care less," said Jessie Lewis.

Carter Brandon sat down on the bed beside her and said: "You know what you said about not knowing whether you liked me or not?"

"I think so."

"Well, I'll tell you this."

"What?"

"I bloody detest you."

Later in the morning the personnel manager scratched his head, took off his spectacles and laid them on top of the file of papers on his desk.

"So you see how we're placed, Mr. Brandon," he said.

"Yes," said Carter Brandon.

The office had Venetian blinds. The personnel manager had a wart on his left thumb. His secretary had thick ankles.

"I'm sorry, but that's how it is."

"All right," said Carter Brandon.

Half an hour later he was in the dining room of his home. The house was empty, so he picked up Daniel in his arms and took him upstairs to the attic.

"Just a few minutes, Uncle Stavely," he said, and he lowered the baby to his uncle's forehead.

The old man opened his eyes and smiled weakly.

"Thank you, Carter," he said. "I'll not forget you, when I go."

Carter Brandon took the baby over to the withered, emaciated Corporal Parkinson, and Uncle Stavely said:

"And neither will he."

It was raining slightly when Carter Brandon got outside, so he put up the hood of the pram. He set off in the direction of the city centre.

"So I've been fired after all that, Daniel," he said, and two women at the bus stop stopped their conversation and stared at him.

"They calls me in and tells me they've sorted things out with the union over Ted Madely. Fine. They're taking him on again, but the union won't go back unless I'm dismissed. They won't work with a black leg."

The rain began to fall quite heavily. Carter Brandon was

not wearing a raincoat, and the knees of his trousers were soon sodden.

"So I'm fired. I'm given fifty quid compensation on the quiet, and here I am, out of work, Daniel. That's what comes, when you do something positive.

"Still fifty quid's not bad, is it? We could get out of this bloody place and be free. We could buy a horse and caravan with it and you and me could set off and go trotting round the lanes.

"We could make a fortune out of it, if we set about it right. 'Daniel, the Wonder Healer.' That's it. We'd stick up a sign saying that on the side of the caravan, and we'd go around these markets in these country towns.

"And I'd stand at the door of the caravan, and I'd thump this bloody great drum, and I'd shout at the top of my voice: 'Roll up, roll up, come and be cured by Daniel the Wonder Healer.'

"Christ, we'd be laughing, Daniel. We'd make a bloody fortune out of it. People would come flocking to us to be cured.

"There'd be hunch-backs and cripples. There'd be lunatics and people with only one lung. There'd be old people coming on crutches or holding white sticks in front of them, and I'd shout at the top of my voice: 'Come and see Daniel, the Wonder Healer, the only known cure for being brassed off with life.' "

The rain was beating down. There were little pools of water on top of the baby's blanket, and, before he got home, Carter Brandon had to bale out the pram with his cupped hands.

"Just look at that baby. He's soaked to the skin," said Mrs. Brandon.

"You must be mad," said Jessie Lewis.

Carter Brandon sneezed and went upstairs for a mustard bath.

"You did right, luv," said Pat later in the evening. "You're best out of that place."

"Aye," said Carter Brandon.

"I never have liked the idea of you working with your hands like that in all that muck and filth. And, as for the people you work with, well, least said about them the better."

"Aye, but I'm not of a job now," said Carter Brandon.

"That's just where you're wrong, luv," said Pat, snuggling closer into his chest. "You know Mrs. Garside, what runs the salon?"

"No."

"Well, you know her husband?"

"No."

"Well, he has this business selling ladies underwear."

"Oh aye."

"Well, what he does is go round the markets, selling it cut price. Any road, he's lost his driving licence and he needs someone to drive his van for him."

"Mm."

"So I was telling Mrs. Garside about you, and she spoke to her husband about it, and he said he'd be willing to take you on."

"Did he?"

"But there'd be prospects, Carter. It wouldn't be just driving him around. There'd be opportunities for advancement. He's looking for a partner, you see, and if he likes the look of you, he might be prepared to take you into the business."

"Mm."

"Carter?"

"Yes."

"I said you'd go round to see him tomorrow afternoon. Will you?"

"I suppose so."

Pat took him in her arms and kissed him on the lips.

"Oh, Carter, I knew it would turn out for the best in the end," she said. "We're going to be so happy, aren't we?"

"Mm."

"Let's hope Mr. Garside likes the look of you."

Mr. Garside did indeed like the look of Carter Brandon. The job was his, and he could have a week off for his honeymoon, provided he returned in time for the market on Saturday afternoon.

The doctor, however, did not like the look of Daniel. He diagnosed pneumonia.

The baby's life hung in the balance for four days. At the end of that period he died, and they had a funeral.

Carter Brandon stood in the back garden and smoked a cigarette whilst the family was eating the funeral tea in the front room.

"I'm sorry, Daniel," he said. "I just didn't think."

Uncle Mort placed his hand on his shoulder and handed him a cup of tea. They stood together, resting their backs against the greenhouse.

"I heard you say that," said Uncle Mort. "I heard you say that to Daniel."

"Did you?" said Carter Brandon.

Uncle Mort put his arm round his nephew's shoulder and said:

"Don't talk like that, lad. It were all for the best really. He'd only have proved an embarrassment to Celia and me. And it wasn't your fault at all. I always said his dome was too bloody big for his body."

Carter Brandon went upstairs to the attic. The two old men were hovering peacefully on the brink of death. He stood there for some time, looking down at their wasted bodies, listening to their faint breathing, inhaling deeply the scent of old age, which clung to every cranny in the room.

I'll have to do something positive now, Daniel.

You will and all, Carter. Fancy taking me out in the rain like that so's I catch me death of cold.

I'm sorry, Daniel.

You big soft ta ta.

CHAPTER FORTY-FOUR

Everyone was most distressed by the sudden marriage of Mr. Carter Brandon to Miss Patricia Enid Baines Partington.

"Fancy getting married in a registry office on the sly," said Mrs. Brandon. "He's just no thought for my feelings, Les. I were really looking forward to that wedding after all them funerals. I'd bought meself a new suit special. I mean to say, it's not every day of the week your only son gets married in a church with an organ, is it?"

"Fancy getting married in a registry office on the sly," said Mrs. Partington. "I just don't know where their senses was Mrs. Brandon. I do not. I says to our Pat, I says: 'Pat, luv, what about your wedding frock? You didn't think of that, did you?' You see, Mrs. Brandon, that frock's got five yards of taffeta in it, and it's not as if it'll come in handy any other time. I says to our Pat: 'It's not as if it'll come in handy any other time, Pat, luv. It's the sort of thing that's useless out of context, in't it?' Honest, these young people, I just can't fathom them out. I can not."

"Young bugger did right," said Uncle Mort. "Celia and me heartily approve of what he done. A registry office wedding is the best of the bloody lot."

"Mm," said Mr. Brandon.

However, there was no doubting the happiness of the young couple, who found the state of wedlock eminently suitable to their mood of the moment, which was a desire to cherish, love and honour each other in sickness and in health until the time when death would release them from these obligations.

After a brief honeymoon in Scarborough, which included a day trip to Robin Hood's Bay, they returned to their new house in Tunstall Avenue, where Carter Brandon had heard the pony whinny.

It had been furnished most tastefully by Mrs. Carter Brandon (nee Partington).

There was a mock stone fireplace in the front room, flanked by bookshelves Carter Brandon had built from a design in an old *Hobbies* fretwork manual.

The living room was the Danish-style dining suite, the present of Mr. and Mrs. Leslie Brandon (groom's parents), and the sideboard and display cabinet, the present of Mrs. Nelson Partington (bride's parent).

Uncle Mort had saved up his cigarette coupons to buy the stereophonic record player that rested on the coffee table, presented by Mrs. Myra Garside (sole prop. Maison Enid's salon de coiffure).

"Are you happy, darling?" said Pat, as they lay in bed one Friday evening.

"Mm," said Carter Brandon.

"Are you glad you married me?"

"Course I am."

She stroked the back of his calves with her foot, and snuggled her head into his chest.

"Wasn't I a balmy chuff to be so jealous, though?" she said, running her hands down his thighs inside his pyjama trousers.

"Jealous? What about?"

"About Jessie Lewis."

The clock struck nine, and the puppy in the kitchen began to whimper.

Carter Brandon went downstairs, picked it up in his arms, and carried it up to the bedroom.

"You used to carry Daniel like that, darling," said Pat, sitting up in bed. Her right breast hung out of her nightgown.

He put the puppy on the Lloyd Loom chair by the glass-topped linen basket and threw himself on the bed beside her.

He kissed her, and she groaned softly and slowly pulled off his pyjama trousers.

Pat awoke early the next morning and noted with pleasure that the sun was shining, for it was to be the day of the young newly-weds' house-warming party.

She washed, dressed and went to the kitchen to make breakfast.

"Carter! Carter! Darling!" she called from the foot of the stairs. "Come on, lazy bones, show a leg, breakfast's all ready."

Carter Brandon appeared in the breakfast room, yawning and scratching his arm pits. He picked up the morning paper, but Pat snatched it out of his hands, saying:

"Now come on, Carter, shift yourself. There's no time for reading. Get yourself washed and shaved and changed. You've a lot to do before the party you know."

Carter Brandon's activities in the bathroom did not take long, and, when he came downstairs, Pat said:

"Now you can get yourself down to Tommy Coghill's and collect his tape recorder, Carter, luv."

"Aye," said Carter Brandon.

"And then you can call at Mrs. Casey's and pick up them French loaves and Danish pastries."

"Aye."

"And when you've done that, you can call in at the beer-off and ask if you can lend twelve wine glasses and enough beer glasses for them as wants them."

"Aye."

The day went quickly and just before the guests were due to arrive Pat said to Carter Brandon:

"Let's just have a few moments to ourselves, darling, before everyone starts arriving."

"Aye, let's have a quick sup from the barrel."

"I'll have a sweet sherry, if you don't mind."

Carter Brandon took the drinks into the front room, where Pat was sitting on the goat hair pouff. He had put coloured paper over the lampshades, and the room was bathed in a dull red glow.

Pat was wearing a purple cocktail dress with simulated mink on the hem and three-quarter length sleeves.

"We could have invited Jessie Lewis, if you'd wanted to," said Pat. "I wouldn't have minded, honest."

"No, I don't want her to come. She's best off at home, looking after Corporal Parkinson and Uncle Stavely."

He drank his beer slowly, smacking his lips loudly.

"Well, the barrel's settled all right," he said.

Pat came to sit at his feet on the uoor. He began to stroke her hair, and she said:

"Hey, give over, you'll have me hair looking like I don't know what."

Her stockings rasped as she turned to rest her chin on Carter Brandon's knee.

"Would you rather it was Jessie Lewis sitting like this instead of me?" she said.

"Stuff Jessie Lewis," said Carter Brandon. "Give us a feel."

"Ugh, Carter, you are crude at times, honest."

The guests were received in the hall by Pat and served with drinks by Carter Brandon.

Mrs. Partington said to Mrs. Brandon:

"Don't it bring tears to your eyes, though, Mrs. Brandon? It seems like only yesterday since our Pat was a little girl in her party frock and ankle socks. I used to do her hair in pigtails in them days, Mrs. Brandon. She were ever so proud of her pigtails. I used to say: 'I know pigtails are a bit old-fashioned, but at least they have the virtue of keeping her looking neat and tidy.' Don't you agree, Mr. Brandon?"

Uncle Mort and Mr. Brandon stood by the barrel, drinking beer with their host.

"By bloody hell, it's a good drop of lotion is that, Carter," said Uncle Mort. "What a pity Celia couldn't be here."

"I've a bloody good mind to blow the gaff," whispered Mr. Brandon to his son.

As the evening progressed and the young people danced to the music provided by Tommy Coghill's tape recorder, the old people became more and more preoccupied with their memories.

They congregated in the kitchen and discussed to their hearts' content days gone by. Suddenly, however, their nostalgia was interrupted most rudely by a telephone call from the police.

"Hey up, your house is on fire," shouted Carter Brandon to his parents.

In the ensuing panic Mrs. Brandon was left behind, but Carter Brandon managed to accommodate his wife, his father and his uncle Mort in his car, which he drove rapidly to the home of his parents.

They could see the glow as they turned out of Derbyshire Road, and, when they came to the street where the house was, they could smell the acrid fumes from the fire.

A policeman stopped them at a barrier and said:

"Sorry, there's no through road at the moment."

But when the circumstances were explained, he nodded and allowed them to pass.

There were two fire engines outside the house, and an ambulance with its siren whining.

They jumped out of the car and pushed their way through the crowd of firemen and policemen. Smoke was billowing out of the downstairs windows and flames could be seen in the attic.

Two ambulance men brushed past them, carrying a stretcher on which was a body completely covered by a sheet of tarpaulin.

"It's Jessie Lewis," said Mrs. Warrender, the neighbour from number thirty-six. "She jumped out of the attic window and impaled herself on the railings."

"Is she dead?" said Uncle Mort.

Mrs. Warrender nodded, and turned to be sick in the gutter.

What do I do now, Daniel?

Do something positive, Carter.

"Do you see that fireman with the big nose?" said Carter Brandon to Pat. "He's the one I was telling you about what got bitten by a monkey on me Auntie Lil's wedding day."